AF223874

Humble
and
On My Knees

A CHURCH LOVE STORY

ADRIENNE SEALY

TO MY PARENTS THOMAS AND RUBY SEALY:

The Best Role Models for a Love Story I've Ever Seen.

To My Son Shomari Hardesty Because I Love You.

The Black Memorial Baptist Church shines bright like the brightest lights in the historic community downtown. Paving the way to new frontiers the Black Memorial Baptist Church is well-organized with smart Christians. They represent a whole gamut of occupations including teachers, architects, contractors, daycare center owners and professional athletes, with one soccer and one baseball player. Much ground has been broken for the completion of the church, especially the center of the church. Engineers, medical staff including nurses and doctors also play a role in the renovation and the new ground breaking of the church.

The Supreme Being didn't pick you because you're perfect but because you have purpose. Painted brick with sandstone borders makes up the foundation of Black Memorial Baptist Church. The church shines in the community. It has a purpose. There have been major renovations to the Sanctuary where everyone comes together to kneel on bended knees and to be humble before God. The dining hall was completed due to determined and dedicated Christians. There have been unique stained glass window projects and Athletic program. The church is still working on an athletic program for the young people of the church and their friends. A nursery and summer Vacation Bible School and a real estate Community Development Corporation are at Black Memorial Baptist Church. A church Credit Union has also been formed. This church, a traditional church, with Romanesque Architectural structure has air conditioning in the summer. There is a jet propelled heat system in the cold weather months. The church is located in the Historic District of the City. It has the thickest walls and is well-built. Sadaya Ruby Day is proud of her church. She is proud to be a member of the Black Memorial Baptist Church. As the pastor stated to the congregation: "May the Lord bless us as we march ahead, doing justly, loving mercy and walking humbly with our God." Stay close to Jesus Christ was the pastor's recommendation. Ask any pastor and he or she will tell you the best conclusion to come to is the church is the best place to be. When you've got nothing to do and when you have nothing but something to do, do it in church. Serve God, always.

The Church took up a whole neighborhood block. This particular church is known nationwide for seminary students to come and to learn and to see how to serve their God and His people.

Sadaya Ruby Day sat with one leg crossed over the other while she waited for choir practice to begin. Sadaya loves clothes and shopping. You look any where about town where there is a clothing store and Sadaya has spent her money there almost going broke in the process. Tonight, which is choir rehearsal night she wore a black leather dress with a peek-a-boo appliquéd turtleneck blouse and leather boots.

"The sister looked good", two choir members turned their heads and said as she walked down the hallway to get a drink of water. Her face was fully made up and she carried a black leather shoulder bag with thick shoulder straps. Sadaya looked down at her clothes and how she was dressed, and she thought, "I look good," heh hehheh, she laughed. Sadaya is a professional woman. When she graduated from college she promised both God and herself that she would never forget Him. Sadaya is a born – again Christian woman determined to lead an obedient and "Godly" life. She is significantly dedicated. She goes to choir practice and Bible Study during the week and church services on Sundays. She is also a teacher of 6th grade mathematics and a part time Social Studies teacher.

Sadaya had a beautiful, welcoming smile. Everywhere she looked she smiled. People complimented her about her smiles and people genuinely loved being around her for long periods of time, because of her winning personality.

"Help somebody . . . help me. I need your help somebody . . . help me please," the young man said. He looked to be about 33 years old. When he asked for help, the Sexton of the church asked what the problem was. The young man introduced himself as Cobb Jackson. The Sexton looked at Cobb Jackson and he started laughing as if someone had just handed him a one thousand dollar bill. "You. There's no doubt that I know who you are. You're that great basketball player with the NY Boxers Basketball Team," said the Sexton Mr. Williams, who shook hands vociferously with Cobb. Cobb explained that he had been having car trouble and his cell phone battery was dead. Cobb wasn't happy with the inconveniences he was now suffering. The Sexton volunteered to assist him in his misery. "I'm so happy this church is here", Cobb said.

Sadaya looked outside the door of the choir room. She walked outside into the hallway. Choir practice hadn't begun. There the Sexton stood there speaking with Cobb Jackson. Sadaya recognized Cobb right away as a basketball superstar with the N.Y. Boxers Basketball Team. Sadaya almost purred when she saw Cobb Jackson. Ooh la lalalala;a! WowsaWowsa. What a catch!

Cynthia Persons called Sadaya on a Saturday night. Sadaya was invited to her Saints Divine Prayer Church by Cynthia. Sadaya told Cynthia Persons "yes" she'd love to attend her church one Sunday. When a loved one leaves or when sickness or disease happens, it causes us to become humble and to bend our knees to the Lord more often. Sometimes all we can do is bend our head and our knees and moan. Cynthia when speaking to Sadaya began to cry tears of joy and thank God for how He brought her out of what seemed like the fire of Hades when her boyfriend died. I was crying and on my knees so much that I began to go outside like my pastor said, Look outside and look up at the sky. No man could put that sky up there. We are covered. We are covered under the warmth of the sky when the sun shines and when it rains. "I needed to look up at the sky and to remember to be humble and on my knees.

I thought I saw Jimmy Coleman. You thought so, I thought so too, Cobb was wondering and remembering his school days. He had seen his greater enemy Jimmy Coleman from his school days past. Jimmy gave Cobb so much trouble and he spoke nasty to Cobb. Cobb asked Jimmy Coleman if he was his punishment from God. Whatever could be done to make Cobb's life miserable was accomplished that day. Bills went up. Prices went up Nobody showed up for scheduled meetings with him. His barber got sick and he couldn't get his hair cut. The Sexton witnessed Cobb's woes. He spoke sullenly to Jimmy. Jimmy wasn't' friendly either. "Do you feel lucky, punk? Keep messing with me. When you mess with him, you mess with me. God gave me faith and sense with it," the Sexton said. My God said I'm forgiven no matter what I do. If I punch you in the nose and you land on your behind I'm forgiven. It's like trying to put a size 16 body into a size 10 tee-shirt. Jimmy Coleman and Mr. Williams don't fit. Keep them a distance from themselves.

Before sitting down again Sadaya was curious about the jet propelled heat system of the church. She walked over to the thermostat panel and she pushed the 'on' button. "That was easier than I thought," she reported to another choir member. This time Sadaya Ruby Day went back into the choir room. She realized the hour was still early. She picked up her newspaper she sat back down and she read. On the back of the newspaper was the picture of a very handsome man. Cobb Jackson, of course. Dot matrixed photographs are fabulous when in color and shot with camera Technicolor resets. Sadaya looked at the basketball player and sighed. Why couldn't I meet somebody like him and we fall in love with each other?! She sighed again. The article pointed out that the ball player Cobb Jackson had his way with "the ladies," the majority of the time. He was always lucky with women and his girlfriend of 3 years was especially miserable. She cried and she cried. The article said he was from the Blue Mountains region, Virginia. He always said he was a "Country Boy," the ladies flocked to him. He cheated on his girlfriend frequently. The newspaper said his girlfriend was "unlucky."

When Cobb Jackson asked Sadaya if she wanted to attend the basketball game, she had no idea she'd take it so seriously. She began to think of the ways she would prepare for it. She took a bath and ended up staying in the tub for almost two hours. She found herself practicing skin science. After all, there were moisturizers and skin lotions to be put on for radiant shine and sheen. She took a considerable amount of time trying to decide if she was going to the beauty salon or if she would do her own hair. Finally, she decided. She went to the beauty salon and she treated herself. The beautician gave her the perfect look she needed to impress the basketball player. "Since it's rumored that he has so many women," Sadaya thought, I'd better be somewhat tempting. I want his eyes to be refreshed when he looks at me. I want looking at me to be a downright blessing.

Cobb played a fantastic game that day but his priority was Sadaya. When the game ended, he walked over to her seat and offered to have dinner with her. Sadaya said she was rushing because she had to get to choir rehearsal.

Sadaya was not in choir practice yet. Mr. Austere the Choir Director said he would be ½ hour to 45 minutes late. Still waiting, Sadaya thought about the Book of Matthew in which God tells his people not to worry about clothing or meals.

Matthew 6:28-31, 38 Kings James Version

"Why take thought about clothing? Consider the lilies of the field, how they grow: They neither work nor do they spin. Yes, I say to you that even Solomon in all his glory was not dressed like one of these. Therefore if God so clothes the grass of the field which today is here and tomorrow is thrown into the oven, will He not much more clothe you? Therefore take no thought, saying O you of little faith? Therefore, take no thought saying what shall we eat or what shall we drink or what shall we wear? I seek first the Kingdom of God and His righteousness and all things are added unto me."

Sadaya did like she was taught in the church. She bowed her head and she quickly said a prayer of thanks for her beautiful clothing. Sadaya set an example for everyone in her church to follow as it pertained to clothes. They were always beautiful on her. Mr. Austere was no joke and he wasn't joking. He was very fast wrestling his body from catastrophe's grip. With a bold smirk on his face he laughed . . . and then he left feeling victorious and triumphant. A married woman had tried to hug and kiss him today; but he was able to withstand the temptation. How victorious he felt. His prayers which he uttered each day helped him. Mr. Austere and Sadaya, servants of the Lord in the church.

The argument started in the back of the sanctuary. What wears on us as human beings daily are the mental health psychological stressor of poverty, police harassment, police brutality and domestic unrest as well as domestic distress. "I would be very concerned about the stigma associated in poor mental health," Sadaya confided in Cobh. Won't feel so bad about it if you would go with me to the sessions. The counselor estimates it should take only about 6 months of therapy for us. For many people mental illness is a secret shame, honey but I would be honored if you would go with me; Sadaya asked I understand this is common for many people who would like to change their lives. "Also, taking medication is a position of strength not an act of weakness," she said. "It is a part of the solution. One of the most powerful solutions we have nowadays," she said, "OK, you talked me into giving a donation," he said. I don't mind giving about $10,000.00. Will that be enough? Cobb asked, "But what about going to the therapy together" she asked. Please come and go with me darling, Sadaya pleaded. Cobb was quite uncomfortable. He did not agree with Sadaya at all. He didn't feel he needed any kind of therapy, couples therapy or otherwise. He knew if he stayed around Sadaya he would catch twice the trouble for not considering her request; to go to therapy. I've got to go. I'll call you later, he told Sadaya he left. Cobb felt strongly about Sadaya but it was a relief to exit the church building that day. We only known each other 7 months and she wants to do couples therapy. "Oh wow," Cobb thought. I put my hands in my pockets like I was shielding them from the cold but I was actually so angry, I had clenched fists.

Cobb confessed to his mother on his cell phone. His mother told him to come to her house to visit with her so they could discuss this further. "I've always got a wink and a smile for you. See you in about an hour, mom," Cobb said. After hanging up the telephone Cobb's mother frowned to herself. All of his life she had been Cobb's mother and his mentor and his private coach. "I'm starting not to like Sadaya, even if she does go to church." Cobb's mother confessed to God.

The night was right. The moon peaked out from behind the dark place in the sky. The clouds signified only the clearest weather by far: The white clouds looked pink and sometimes black at eight.

Cobb looked masculine and pharaoh-like at night. His eyes were circular inside like raw coals. The brightly lit lights of the city were friendly tonight with anticipation of love and expectation and cheerfulness. It was almost 12 midnight; getting late, Cobb exclaimed; ready to go.

I always find it interesting when I see woman throwing themselves at men. The men seem to find it comical, Sadaya mused inwardly. I surely threw myself at him enough, she thought. I finally got him to notice me too, She quipped. Let's snuggle, wuggle and cuddle up, baby, she said to him. Cobb was very interested. He began to call Sadaya and have a dating relationship with her. She also thought about some of her lessons in Bible Study some of which she memorized. Softly to herself she whispered the woman who said "Awake O north wind and come O south wind! Blow upon my garden that its spices may flow out. Let my beloved come to his garden and eat its choicest fruits," she remembered from the Book of Solomon. I charge you O daughters of Jerusalem if you find my beloved that you tell him I am faint with love. "Open to my beloved but my beloved has turned and was gone. I called him but he gave no answer."

Sadaya looked at the empty chair in front of her and she quietly muttered, After all, God's people get lonely too.

"Bye mom, see you later. I'm in a hurry, said Sadaya. Remember I'll be at the church in the choir room," she repeated. "Ok honey, bye" Millicent said. By the way, mom, I'm very proud of you for working on your Master's degree. Soon you'll graduate and get your degree and I won't have to answer those kinds of questions that you've been asking lately. Right? Sadaya said. "Right," said her mother. "See ya," said Sadaya. "See ya," said her mom. When you get home, your dinner will be in the microwave. Sadaya waved goodbye and went outside to her two door couped car. Sadaya loved driving and the feelings of being in control that driving gave to her. The idea of getting into your car and being able to go somewhere or anywhere almost gave her a feeling of superiority really. She was thinking she would say, Get out of my way, World. I'm in control and I'm taking over, she thought to herself again.

Sadaya loved to shop mostly for clothes and shoes and boots. She felt good about how she looked. She thought about this while she drove to the Black Memorial Baptist Church; where she had choir practice. She looked cozy and chic in her skirt suit which was made of the best wool. Her all leather satchel bag was a nice accessory as it matched her all leather boots. Her face was fully made up and she wore a gold necklace with hoop earrings. She liked to dress up for the people at the church at school and of course, for God first, as a role made for Him. She purchased new shoes from the D'acy's Dept. Store. They were high heels, mind-boggling in height. Sadaya found herself quoting the Scriptures after she put them on. "I can do all things through Christ who strengthens me."

He's fine and he's all mine, I hope.

You always smell so good; especially during a nice long warm embrace! I was looking for someone nice, warm and cuddly to kiss. What do you do when the man you love has an unlimited appetite for other women besides you? For some women, if their husband was guilty of the above he'd be dead. Dead as a doorknob and dead as those heroes I learned about in my history class. He said to his wife "I'd rather die first before I see you bring another hat and shoes into my house," her husband said. Leave my hats alone the wife shouted. "You know, I shall never forget them or ever give them up. Oh yes you will," he said. Oh NO! No! No! I won't. Yes you will. Oh no I won't, she stubbornly said.

The proceeding story was a very quick exchange between the parents of one of the children in Sadaya's 6th grade class. They met briefly with Ms. Day as Sadaya was called and known as. She helped them with conflict resolution and with their communications skills and things started to get better for the Whole family.

The father figure was revealed as kind of gruff: "Father is like a bull in a China closet. He doesn't know how to phrase his words where they won't hurt people," his daughter said. She gave him a copy of the poem. The Guest which teaches about respect for the host of the places you visit as a guest. Many parents should educate their children about respecting the houses and the places they visit.

<u>The Guest</u>

When you are invited to someone's home
act as though you are in your own
Don't shout and get too excited Because
remember you were invited Just relax
and be cool
There's no need to act the fool I
don't have to say the rest you know
how to act your best
and remember you're the guest

George Waters

"Cobb Jackson had nothing but a great big smile for me every day I saw him. How nice," Sadaya smiled to herself. He didn't see her sister Pamchera prancing and dancing up and down the staircase to get a better peep at him.

Her father and Sadaya Ruby Day's mother lived with their daughter: They didn't worry about Sadaya driving back and forth to church because she was a safe driver. "I've got two questions to ask you from my favorite game show. What's the name of the Game Show?" Sadaya asked. "You ready for this? O.K. It's called My Favorite Game Show," her mother Millicent Day said. "What's the first question?" Sadaya said laughingly. Name something people do at a bachelor party that they also do at a bachelorette party. Sadaya liked this question but she felt almost ashamed of answering it in front of her mother. My answers would be male strippers, eat, dance, said Sadaya. Her mother Millicent said, "All right! My daughter Sadaya got game! Try the next question: Name someplace a cheating man goes to meet his mistress," Millicent smiled at her daughter. Sadaya laughed, "This one's easy. I think the answers are in the car, in a motel or hotel at a restaurant, in a bar, at the movies. How many answers you need?" she asked her mother. "There are no set amount of answers you should give. Thank you. I have enough from you for my purposes," her mother said.

The talking and the listening crowd. The pastor of Black Memorial Baptist was a wise man. The talking portion was 25% and the listening portion was 75%. Use those statistics as your goal when you're in a conversation. Use this as a goal when you're in a conversation with relatives and friends. Most importantly use those statistics when you're in a conversation with your enemies. "Do not spread or engage in talk that is idle talk," the pastor emphasized. Idle talks are details that are not confirmed as being true; usually reports about other people. He used James 1:26 Kings James Version as his reference point: "if anyone considers himself religious and yet does not keep a tight rein, on his tongue he deceives himself and his religion is worthless NIV."

Sadaya heard the commotion outside and she looked out of the door of the choir room. Choir rehearsal hadn't begun yet so she walked out into the hallway. Besides that, Sadaya was thinking, we have to go to the Sanctuary tonight to meet for choir rehearsal. There in the hallway, was the Sexton Mr. Williams who takes care of the church grounds speaking to Cobb Jackson. Are my eyes deceiving me or is that good looking man the great basketball hot shot player Cobb Jackson? Sadaya thought. Cobb Jackson was very upset because he had just bought his car brand new and the car stopped on him, and it was smoking. For what reason it caught on fire, he did not know. He didn't know whether the mechanic should be called at the new car dealership or the Fire Department. Mr. Williams, made a suggestion to call both. Sadaya has no expertise when it comes to cars but she overhear the conversation between Mr. Williams and Cobb Jackson. She went over and stood by the two gentlemen and waited for the right time to introduce herself again. Hello Mr. Williams I haven't seen you in a long time. How are you? Fine, I hope. Please meet Mr. Cobb Jackson superstar athlete for The Boxers Basketball Team. This is one of our outstanding members of the church. She's very active in the church. She is Sadaya Ruby Day. Cobb liked Sadaya Ruby Day.

He liked how her clothes looked on her and he liked her pretty–looking eyes. Her hairdo was nice too. Interestingly, Sadaya was checking Cobb out too. He was well-dressed with a white shirt French collar and cuff links. His hair was neatly cut into an S-curve on his head. "Wow, he's good looking," she thought. "The man was so beautiful to me; he became by instant temptation," Sadaya thought. "He made me hot in the seat," I sensuously thought, "he's what makes my thing complete. Hallelujah. The Bible says when you thank God it makes Him happy. I was privately thanking God for meeting Cobb, and I know God was happy. I was thanking God repeatedly," said Sadaya. Sadaya's friend Sheila Godfrey said, gladly to Sadaya, "I'm a woman who knows how to get and to keep her man I'm ready for service so that I can trust God and sing like a champ in my church's choir. Would you like to come to church services on Sundays and hear my choir sing sometimes," Sadaya asked. "Yes, I'd love to" Cobb Jackson said. "Good; here's my telephone number," Sadaya said. "Can I have yours? Of course you can," he answered. It is because God loves us that we have the gift from Him called the Choir. Please pray for me that I might sing his songs beautifully, Sadaya said to the Choral group. Some of the members came out of the room. My heart is happy because the money we have provided will give much to the people in need; to the less fortunate. The Church Choir will bring us God's Good Luck too, the Choir Director said. Cobb didn't leave before giving $10,000.00 that night to Sadaya for the less fortunate. "Thank God and thank you," our pastor will be ecstatic and excited she said.

Sadaya was close friends with a sportscaster friend whose name was Larry J. Johnson. She was going to introduce him to Sheila her friend. He was on the TV show called "Was Not Injured" as the host. This year there were many fights in sports, especially in the area of basketball. There was violence in both men and ladies' sports. Also there were 5 Christians on one team that complained about the violence. The NLBT, Inc. which stands for National Ladies Basketball Teams, Inc. are usually very friendly, cooperative and they move together as a team. Some, however, are becoming more violent, hitting, kicking and slapping their opponents unprovoked, event pulling hair. The Christians held a press / interview session which said they abhor violence. They said they'd rather not fight at all which makes them at least civilized. They said seasoned Christians "and there are many of who abhor violence. Lights, cameras, action and smiles one member of the team The Listeners and the team The Starrettes chimed in with many smiles and kisses to you. While the topic of the hour was violence in sports, one player's ex-wife held up a sign.

"And with what he's done to me he can forget he ever knew me."

An Ex-Wife

She said, I'd rather see a team member go and to carry a large pot to help to feed the less fortunate than to see that team member scratching the eyes out of a fellow teammate like he or she doesn't have good sense. I have a great son. If he should decide someday to play sports, I wouldn't want him hurt on the court or out on the field because someone couldn't control himself. When he goes to parties I say remember if you don't do anything I would not do, you'll never have any fun. I'd rather have the violent ones in football and traded to other teams. It's called relocation.

Matthew 20: Kings James Version

"So the last will be first, and the first last. For many are called, but few chosen". The Dialogue Coach for Peaches Films Corporation, a cartoon filming company says the NLBT Inc. is starting to relocate athletes to other states all over the USA to separate those who might be overly violent. It's not how much you score but how you play the game. When the Great Scorer comes, he will not ask how many points you've scored but how you played the game.

Basketball Player, Cobb and Sadaya. He was asked if he was ready to get married by a reporter from Sports Gazette. "I am most likely capable of changing my mind about this question at any time. Right now, inwardly I guess I'm looking for a wife but I'm in no rush. Three days ago I went to a wedding. It was a beautiful wedding with orchids spread around the altar and everywhere. When it came time for the bride to throw the bouquet every one of the single girls and women shouted with glee to try and to catch the bouquet. Then, of course, it was time for the groom to throw the garter band to the single men. Ha haha, it was the funniest thing I ever saw. When the groom threw the garter all of the single guys or men ran away from the direction of the garter as if someone was throwing a bucket of hot water and they didn't want to get scald," laughed Cobb.

There are so many beautiful women in the world that I think they've spoiled me actually; the beautiful women I've met. Would you believe one woman called me a self-serving ego-maniac who has a chip on his shoulder. She said these things to me because I refused to take her to dinner. She slammed the door in my face, but she's the only woman that's ever been that drastic with me besides Sadaya, say if I was marrying someone right now I'd say what bold, revolutionary undertaking this is; to marry. I can tell you one thing she'll be fearfully and wonderfully made; a lot like me. I'd have pure respect for her and her body, no matter what size you are, I'd say. I'd tell her I have allowed myself to get to know you and your body. Now I wouldn't trade an inch of you; you're my Queen of Sheba. This is why I'm so irresistible to women. I know how to treat them. Until I meet Miss Right I will be on delay. I'll be delaying putting myself into just one woman's heart. "See ya fellas," Cobb said while he smiled at a lady crossing the street.

The winds blew briskly and hurried through the trees in the back of the house where Sadaya and her parents lived. In the back yard the squirrels gathered to eat their nuts behind the Day house and household. They hid themselves and their nuts inside the bark of many trees. Here, they found great solace, while the sun draped its glamorous rays around the tops of the trees. The squirrels bowed.

Don't bother me now. Can't you see I'm reading my infant books? I'm doing research so that maybe someday I can write a book too. My school books taught me that the longest journey begins with the first step. Research is my journey right now. After I finish with the Infant Books, I'll go onto elementary and junior high /middle school books. Then lastly, adult age books. I will then take a representative sample of all of them from Infant Books to Adult Books. I'll decide what level books I want to write and I'll take my time. I'll probably write a few books within the next couple of years. When I was tapped on the shoulder by you I was reading about different materials that infants like such as terrycloth, cotton, and how they respond to touch. Please talk to me much later or tomorrow during lunch time. I was even fully awake not sleep which I get sometimes during this 1:00 p.m. hour. The principal said, "Ok well I see you're very busy so I'll meet you tomorrow same time same location." "yes maam," Sadaya said.

Sadaya took her job very seriously. She never wanted the students in her class to be bored. Fun and thrills are what the children experienced with her. On their class trips they had museum filled trips to interesting places. There was Logoland, which was only a block from Bricks 'R Us for discovery. While the other children in the school were going to typically boring places, Sadaya's class went skydiving for children and other non-boring trips. Her class was able to build, learn, try indoor skydiving and discover new things in sports and the arts. Sadaya won many awards for her community involvement and her work with the children. The children in her class enjoyed role playing; movement and music while she incorporated math and social studies. There were messages sent around the community about what a great teacher she is from the children. The children went home excited and they'd ask their parents and/or guardians, "guess where we went." They even went to sports centers. Each child became a mover and shaker in the community. They also participated in Double Dutch contests. Sadaya's tutelage helped them to win every year, every contest. They also participated in ice skating and they were tough to beat every time. There was a free African American and Latino Love Program for young music students to learn many instruments. Sadaya or Miss Day which the children called her loved to spoil her class. She certainly asked basketball player Cobb Jackson to be a special guest on Media Day. When Cobb showed up at the Media Day event the kids gave a shout like some of their fathers do. They also made a gingerbread house in the school cafeteria. Cobb was thrilled.

Sadaya was a great success at her job; she was truthfully excited; somebody had the gift of gab. "So he's got the gift of gab. The man could unapologetically talk my skirt off of my body and my blouse too. Heh heh. I love the guy to tell you the truth," she said. About Cobb Jackson, of course. Sadaya went outside to catch a fellow member Brother Leon to tell him something but she stumbled down the steps and bruised her knees. By then Brother

Leon was gone. Sadaya limped back into the church. This felt like violence. Since when is violence as well-liked as love? Sadaya was going to confide in Brother Leon the following: The minute I laid eyes on him I loved him. Maybe God didn't want her to share this love with Brother Leon. "Whatever I was thinking I had to switch my mind and think about something else after bruising up my knees," Sadaya said.

He wet his tongue river-like. He then put his finger on his wet tongue in pathways of his apple- shaped eyes. "Aah! You bring me great release," he said to Sadaya. She was his pride. His name was Cobb. Cobb Jackson. In the next few weeks. "He's fine and he's all mine".

He' Fine And He's All Mine.

I don't get drunk on whiskey and wine I
like him very much. I love it when
I feel his touch.
He says he's taking me to dinner
Because I'm a winner.
He's fine and he's all mine,
Hallelujah!
He's fine and he's all mine

© Adrienne Sealy

Sadaya thought while she sat waiting for choir practice. Sadaya arrived early. She rushed to read her newspaper before choir rehearsal started. She dreamed of Cobb Jackson and how fine he was to her but she didn't waste any more time. Mr. Austere the Choir Director said jokingly, "All right all of you "heathens," Good God Good grief lets all go eat I'm hungry. I feel really blessed I'm especially proud of you. I'm also ready to read some part of the Word of God everyday to help me to understand God wants good things for me. This is the way the lord is moving and leading me to speak to you tonight. This is for any black woman who has had a significant problem with a man; call me she said: my friend Sheila would like to say a few words. "I'm a woman who knows how to get and keep her man, Sheila said, call me," if I can help. It is because God loves us that we have the gift called the choir. Please pray for me that I might sing his song beautifully Sadaya said and after Sheila finished speaking. My heart is happy because the money we have provided will give much to the people in need. The church choir will bring us God's good Luck too, the Choir Director said. We have raised money for the needy and we will be blessed a hundred fold.

In 1894 the US Golf Association was founded. I could be playing golf right now but... It's a Saturday afternoon... I'll just rest. Every closed eye is not sleeping and every open eye is not seeing Kenny thought to himself. Kenny T. Pretended to be asleep while looking and narrowing his eyelids so he could see if Cobb was coming. Finally after 3 weeks of this investigating Kenny saw Cobb's white Bentley drive- up to the driveway across the street from the stadium.

Kenny T. had visions and fantasies of himself choking and punching and physically throwing Cobb up against the cars and bicycles on the street. With tears running down his cheeks, Kenny T. wasted no time yelling, "Grown men don't cry. Get out of the car so I can wring your neck. I'm too angry at you not to wring your neck," said Kenny T., holding his tears back." Kenny said, "My daughter told me what you're up to and how you've been cheating on her. Come over here and take it like a man you no good cheater. Come over here so I can knock you senseless and dead too." Cobb said, "Sir, I know you love your daughter but you must understand I love her too."

It's amazing what loves drives people to do.

With the unsturdiest of steps Kenny T. yelled at the top of his larynx. You say you love my daughter. Well if that's the case why do you date other women? Kenny reasoned. I'm trying to follow the rules with your daughter, Sir. She's just very sensitive and she figures if she calls me and I don't call her right back that I must be fooling around on her, Cobb said. "And furthermore I'm not getting out of this car because you're too angry with me. I don't want to fight you. I'll wait here until you calm down," Cobb said.

Thinking of the glass as half full is the best way to look and feel when you think your mate is fooling around on you. Be optimistic and please encourage your husband or wife to be optimistic, "is the best advice Sadaya could get, "Sadaya said coyly.

By the way, Sadaya's church The Black Memorial Baptist Church put out a special announcement which said, 'please join Voices from the Sky HIE/ADS Ministry for the World ADS dinner Family and Friends Day on Sunday. Come and celebrate with us and you'll be further blessed. We are asking all members to wear red and gold. You could win a $500 gift card. Church member should have at least 10 people in attendance to qualify. HIE /ADS testing will be implemented. Just see the church secretary." When Sadaya read the church bulletin, she found herself giving advice to a couple of parents who admitted they have the diseases HIE/ADS. She began to tell them about being optimistic and keeping hope in their lives. She wasn't just matter of factly in her approach to these parents of one of her students. She really cared about them and she came across as caring and unafraid to discuss a very difficult subject: Disease and how not to lose hope in the face of it. She explained that it didn't make sense to stay angry about their diseases because anger acts like poison to the body.

It is often easy to surrender to negative feeling and thoughts when diagnosed with disease but its best to "find the positive not to dwell on the negative," was Sadaya's advice. "Life has a way of interviewing and causing us to learn this lesson again and again until we learn it well," said Sadaya.

Sometimes she doubts herself. The doubting person is like a wave of the sea blown and tossed by the wind. – She must have more faith. The Universe was formed — at God's command not Cobb's nor anyone else's.

Sadaya thought of some verses she had memorized a long time ago that she tucked into her heart that she might not sing against God: I will bless the lord at all times. His praise shall continually be in my mouth. My soul shall make her boast in the Lord: the humble shall hear thereof and be glad. O magnify the Lord with me and let us exalt his name together. I sought the Lord, and he heard me and delivered me from all my fears. They looked unto Him and were lightened: and their faces were not ashamed. This poor man cried, and the lord heard him, and saved him out of all his troubles. The angel of the Lord encampeth round about them that fear him, and delivereth them. O taste and see that the Lord is good: blessed is the man that trusteth in him. O fear the lord, ye his saints: for there is no want to them that fear him. The young lions do lack and suffer hunger: but they that seek the Lord shall not want any good thing. The righteous cry, and the Lord heareth, and delivereth them out of all their troubles.

Sadaya used the verses Psalms 34:1-10 Kings James Version to give peace and comfort to those parents because they were diseased and they needed to be reassured. They needed to be told that God is alive and he does hear them when they cry out to Him and that He will respond. He's worked it out and soon they'll hear from Him", was how Sadaya phrased it. It has been said that we process about 10,000 thoughts a day. The heart is the deepest part of man, the seat of the mind. Proverbs 4:23 Kings James Version says, "Guard your heart," and Philippians 4;8 Kings James Version says, Sadaya continued to tell the parents, "Finally, brothers, whatever things are true, whatever things are honest, whatever things are just, whatever things are pure, whatever things are lovely, whatever things are of good report, if there is any virtue, and if there is any praise, think on these things. She convinced the parents to rid themselves of all of the things that were holding them back and hindering their life advancement. She would have made a great school psychologist. "I'm giving you a positive out look at life. I'm also giving you forgiveness. Forgiveness is the way to heal anger. Never forget what I've just told you," she told them. The parents promised they would never forget.

Thinking of Cobb; He's fine and he's all mine Sadaya thought while she sat in her seat waiting for choir practice to begin "Oh no," Sadaya a thought. "I forgot. I'm supposed to be in the Sanctuary for practice to night. I hope they haven't started already. I'm glad I came early." This is like a gift from God to meet Cobb and to have him take my, "heh heh" she said. The choir director had called ahead and said he was going to be late. Mr. Austere is the choir director's name.

I am so anxious to use this phone number that's Cobb Jackson. I'll probably get the voicemail, Sadaya thought. She sat for another 10 minutes, then she ran across the hall to where the choir was meeting. She had gotten the voice mail. She couldn't speak to Cobb, but she still did the Lord's work.

I guess I'm pointing out what you already know said Cobb. You know I think you're pretty smart girl and you're sensible. "He's fine and he's all mine. Cobb is the he and he's my consultant on many issues whenever I write my book. I give myself a couple of years. I'm in no rush," Sadaya said. "I might even write a book about how it feels to wait for sex until after my marriage. I would like to give the Holy Scriptures and what the Holy Bible says about celibacy, how being celibate can increase our relationship to God" Sadaya said to Cobb. When Sadaya revealed her true feelings about sex to Cobb, some of it he thought was nonsense such as the part about writing a book. He did not like the subject matter. He felt like he would have to reveal intimate moments that he was not ready to reveal. Some of his friends that he would ordinarily recommend to Sadaya for interviewing would hear details about themselves too, that might not be too flattering. He wanted to say, Sadaya pick another hobby besides writing a book.

Sadaya and Cobb made an agreement that heavy petting was something that would be appropriate, but no sex yet. Other than that their passion had no boundaries. Since Cobb and Sadaya only saw each other every 2 ½ weeks; it was difficult. Since both of them were pretty and handsome there were other love interests all of the time. Cobb liked having different women around him. "It made him feel smarter and it boosted his self-esteem," he said. If I had to just depend on Sadaya I'd be mighty frustrated in the sex area. My mother keeps telling me that Sadaya is a great woman and that I should settle down and give my mother some grandchildren. She knew that Sadaya was holding out and waiting to have children after she was married; whenever that would be, she didn't know but she but she said she was "waiting on God." Sadaya's natural body reactions and secretions got stronger. The more she waited, the stronger her sexual urges and desires. Since seeing Cobb was her mainframe, she found herself calling out his name in bed at night.

With Cobb, it was different. He was always around women. Sadaya was sweatin it through and phewin it too.

Maybe I'll not call her and I'll wait until she calls me. Then I won't let her come back to me so easily. We're supposed to pick up right where we left off. I believe I have to respect the relationship I have with Sadaya, that's what I believe. I feel so mixed up and confused about the fight we'll have one over my other women. I don't know whether to get rid of the other women or not. Sadaya's not like Maxine and some other women I know. With Maxine all I have to do is text her and honestly, she comes a runnin. With Sadaya I wonder if I'll ever see her again. I've also discovered that Sadaya can be mouthy sometimes. I guess my dates with other women really got to her sensibilities like she said. The interesting thing about it is I love those women that I date too. I have been finding out I just love Sadaya a little more. I like the way we look together, "said Cobb. Plus, I'm honoring my grandfather's wishes to marry a school teacher. "Marriage".

Marriage? Shouldn't you make sure she'll speak to you first?" said his best friend Stanley Jensen, "honestly if you keep fooling around, I want you to know you could lose her. Be nice to her. Be very nice to Sadaya all of the time. "Please," said Stanley. Cobb wanted to tell Stanley that he didn't want to take his advice, to tell Stanley to butt out of his business but inwardly, Cobb knew that Stanley was right and he's always given good advice to Cobb. So Cobb was quiet after awhile and he listened to his friend. From what my friend Stanley says I need to take some time and reflect about my future and then figure out what I'm going to do with my girl Sadaya Ruby Day.

This time she was shining in a smile and a liquid knit turtleneck tunic, which is called non-floppy turtleneck. She was dressed in a very sophisticated and modern way of dressing. She always dressed with nice fabrics and she looked like a professional model or a clothes buyer for a department store. Her chiffon ruffle blouse was exquisite. She looked well-groomed in the most modern fashions although she was overweight. She looked foxy because sexy isn't a size. She looked nicest in cashmere and wool usually skirt suits. Sadaya had the nicest poshest suede boots with coyote fur reaching from the ankle to just below the knee caps .The coyote fur was a mixture of white gray and brown fur.

She had on coyote fur but she looked foxy.

Sadaya was thinking about Cobb for the past 2 weeks. In a couple of days she will meet him somewhere, or she'll just tell him to come over to her house. Her parents' Sadaya lives with her parents. She was privately trying to decide if she should tell Cobb that she yearns for him in the bed in the middle of the night and she has sexual urges and that she cries out his name in her bed; usually on lonely nights. It was not a quiet event because Sadaya suffered from sinus congestion and allergies and she had to take medicine to help her to breathe better and safer. Sadaya decided to tell Cobb what she had been going through. She thought he'd be happy to hear about how she wants to write one or two books and how she yearns for him at night, sexually. Cobb did respond in a cold fashion, he said, "I'd better get a new and improved Sadaya then," he said. He said if he were someone just observing he'd described them as a couple. He said they'd say, "They seem like a nice handsome couple who most times are trying to follow the, rules that would make their marriage work but they're not married yet. They are seeming to have a few disagreements. The best solution is communication. They must communicate and if their communication skills improve, their relationship can come together. They can make a most powerful comeback with a good counselor like myself," Jaime a friend of Cobb's said. You mean so much to each other's hearts. You should try a good counselor like me, he repeated himself. Cobb was less than excited. He was thinking about the pastor of Black Memorial Baptist Church. He does pastoral counseling. "I'll try him" Cobb replied.

"Thanks for all of your good advice. The most important thing is that I love her," said Cobb to his best friend Stanley Jensen. I'd better be first at making up to and with her. I want to go and wrap my arms around her after I call her. If she's not talking to me I'll just have to wait until she is", Cobb said. I'll visit her and say "Come here. Let's play catch up. I've missed you and then I'll give her a big kiss," Cobb said. "Of course I'd play it cool but I'm not sure of what I should do. If I play it cool I'd hardly say anything to her and visit. I guess I could take her to the movies man, I guess maybe to get some latte coffee, or take her for a ride somewhere, I love her Cobb said. "I tell ya I'm a nervous wreck. Even my palms in my hands are sweaty. I think I'm going to play it cool. I might end up taking her to the movies man, I guess, maybe to get some latte coffee," Cobb said. Stanley Jensen was very supportive of Cobb and he helped Cobb to reason through what moods Sadaya might be in, how to handle those moods. For instance if she was fearful over the potential breakup of the two of them Cobb was advised to carefully watch what he said. "Be careful not to insult her any further. Choose your words wisely. It's better not to say anything at all rather than to insult her," Stanley said. Pride leads to destruction.

"Sometimes the women that volley for my affections and attention are annoying" Cobb told Stanley. They want to get right into the sex thing but life is not only about having sex. Life is about appreciating God and putting God first and foremost in my life. To the women I've dated, some of them, as a matter of fact most of them I must say a hearty goodbye to. Some of the women I've met from various churches have been so wild that they reminded me of women of the world or inner-city streets. They don't dress up for God or anyone including me. They don't present themselves like they have the Authority of Christ and our Amazing Authority of God through Jesus Christ. If my girl Sadaya was here, she be jumpin and she'd say, "And neither do the men I've met, dance, for God unless they were a pastor or someone of high rank in the church. She'd put a lot of people to shame in a nice way", Cobb said.

Cobb took more time to think about what he'd do about the fight he had with Sadaya. He prayed to God to lead him and to guide him about her. After praying, he thought of the following approach to use with her. "I'm so happy that the two of us could get together and do some love talk. I'm sorry we argued. You're more than just a pretty face to me and I want us to communicate better," he said as a phantasmic fantasy.

"Vibrant, uplifting, inspirational, football, motivational too. This is a self-appraisal, of course.

I give myself an A" Cobb said.

After an argument and a fight: Who you gonna call? My ex-boyfriend Sadaya thought of her ex-boyfriend Thaddeus and she called him. She called and left a voicemail message. I hated him because he was always so sexy for me and about 5 others, if you can imagine. Yes he cheated on me, she said.

Dead battery car overheated and helped me to meet Sadaya Ruby Day. All things work together or good for those who love the Lord. I think I love her. I had hoped to write the greatest love story about two people looking for God and they find each other in church.

Sadaya was frustrated. The weather was cold and she wanted to speak to Cobb but each time she called him the voicemail came on. Sadaya, being "naturally spoiled," according to her mother, was very upset that Cobb didn't pick up the phone and speak to her. "Unbelievable. Still the voicemail. Maybe he's on the telephone doing business. I'm going to make myself a nice hot cup of cappuccino and warm myself up," she thought. Sadaya sat down in her reclining chair and enjoyed her hot cup of cappuccino. "Ok. I'm going to call just one more time. If he doesn't answer this time I'm going to get fatter by drinking more cappuccino", she thought. She picked up the phone and dialed slowly and deliberately. Dialing Cobb's number caused her to feel cautious. "Again the voicemail. I can't win for losing," she later told a friend. Sadaya's hand hit the side of her recliner and she hung up before she intended to.

Sadaya Ruby Day is a highly qualified certified teacher. She also tutors in her spare time. She writes the column, Your Child's Smile and she writes the column Happy Endings for the newspaper called the Experts. Sadaya Day teaches 6th grade mathematics and social studies. She is also very active in her church where she serves in the choir, Bible Study and church services Sundays.

O.k. do a quick self-examination. How are you holding your body right now. Is your body slouched on the couch? Are you hunched at your work desk honestly, I don't see why I have to go through the trouble. What's the purpose? I'll just let my flab-borgastic body be limp. Michael said. "I'll just move forward fat like I am." Ha Ha ha, case closed, he said.

"Well Michael, you're just joking with me. Please tell me you're joking with me. Even if you really did slouch at your desk every day I'd have to admit I slouch too on my couch. My figure is not what it used to be but honey, I love you." Sheila said. Opening her arms enthusiastically and lovingly. Michael danced at her and said, "we've got to have faith in each other. I'll give you a hug for now but there's got to be a promise from you that more is forth coming;" he said laughing and pulling her closer to him requiring an embrace.

After kissing and embracing each other Sheila showed Michael a poem written by Minola Taylor entitled:

"Count Yourself In On The Goodness Of Life" Michael said. He memorized it for edification of God first and then himself, because God wants good things for us. He doesn't want there to be anti-fat bigotry and pro-diet propaganda which Cobb Jackson my friend pays attention to all of the time. Besides that, I have sense. I know how to dress for my body type," he said.

† † †

<u>"Count Yourself In On The Goodness Of Life"</u>

Count yourself in on the goodness of life
Each and every day.
Count yourself in on the success of life,
This is the better way.
The way to have what you want to have,
To be what you want to be.
Repeat this affirmation to yourself,
Control your destiny.

© Minola Taylor, Hollywood, California

Poem II Untitled

Whatever you have within your mind
Or give your attention to,
You magnetize yourself for this thing
And it must come to you.

© M.T.

The time has come to set aside childish things. Sheila has a brother who is catching twice the trouble he had before. He and a friend were both sent to "Helleview".

Catching twice the Hades they were both sent to 'Helleview' for mental problems after smoking weed in front of the police station. They're lucky they didn't send them to the undertaker. They were only sent to Helleview for observation. (Cobb's little cousins at the funeral home). Sadaya began to feel sorry for herself. Sadaya she ran up to him and yelled at him. I am my beloved's, and my beloved is mine. Solomon 6:3 Kings James Version

Michael and Sheila Godfrey were devout members of the Black Memorial Baptist Church and close friends of Sadaya's. The pastor remembered Michael in his prayers with specific emphasis on his weight status. Michael was the type to joke around whenever someone hinted at the fact that he was obese. Don't hold it against me just because I slouch on my couch or No fun for the rotund, were often characteristic of his comments. It made him feel good to know that he had a wife Sheila and that Sheila loved him regardless of his body size. She often called him "sexy' in and out of the bedroom. Michael and Sheila were making plans to go away and they invited Sadaya, telling her to invite Cobb and they could make it a double date. They would go 2 hours away to a first class resort, go swimming in the swimming pool and relax to meditate. Cobb spoke to Michael and told him he was exercising and he had to go away with his team to exercise more. Although he couldn't go away with Michael and his wife, Cobb offered to pay their way. Michael was grateful to Cobb for the offer but he declined it. "I'm happy. I know you Cobb. You're a rare man and I won't forget you and your hospitable personality," Michael said. In the back of his mind Cobb really wanted to invite Michael to a special obesity camp that Cobb's team sponsors. Great timing. Michael said, "I guess I'd better stick my head in at the gym and try to melt some of this flesh off of me. Although my wife tells me she loves me just the way I am. "Sadaya is always talking about being adorned and dressed by the Holy Spirit. I like how she talks because a lot of women today don't think of being molded and shaped by God. After I lose weight, I want to be like Cobb. I want to be good to my wife and count her in on the goodness of life. I want to buy her a new car and myself lots of new clothes to fit my new figure. I want to hear her call me sexy and mean it, because being sexy isn't a size," Michael said.

Although choir practice was being held, Sadaya slipped away from the sanctuary. She saw Cobb Jackson and she recognized him from television and the newspapers. She was looking especially pretty. She admired his handsome looks too. She said she was herself Sadaya, explaining that she had been a member of Black Memorial Baptist Church since she was a little girl. "I am so happy to be a member of this church. It's a place that gives me a warm fuzzy feeling ever time I'm here. Of course there's more to church than it just being a pretty building. In this church I see where my hard-earned money is being spent and where it's going. I am also excited about the new construction projects. I love it. Are you visiting or have or have you joined our church?"

Sadaya asked Cobb. Now that Cobb was able to get in touch with his mechanic he was free to talk to Sadaya. "I really hadn't planned to join the church although I like the people. I was asked to do volunteer work and I'll see if I can fit it in my schedule. I figure I'd better help God. He certainly is helping me," Cobb said. "I told the Sexton I'd try to help out every 2 to 2 ½ weeks. They are trying to get new shoes for senior citizens. They also need a person to help with security," Cobb said.

Cobb, being the single man felt magnetism between himself and Sadaya. He asked for her phone number and he got it. They promised to talk before the week. "I love her already, I think." "That beautiful hunk of a black man," Sadaya thought of Cobb while she stood in the church's Freedom Hall where workshops are held. "Cobb Jackson you light up my heart." Just my type, she thought, clean-cut. He flashed his Cheshire cat-like smile at Sadaya and she felt herself wilting like a daffodil flower. Sadaya loves Cobb. She studies his every movement and maneuver. She fantasized freely. She imagined that she was asked the most important question of a couple's life: 'Will you marry me?' She imagined she studied Cobb's face before answering this all–important question. When Cobb is volunteering at the church Sadaya notices how many other women are noticing him. She starts speaking fast when she's upset nervous or anxious. "You don't know that what you're doing. You sure you know what you're doing?" he asked her. "Yes Cobb I'm just a little concerned," she said. "The question is do all of these women know what they're doing with you?" she said. You need another woman like a hole in the head. Need I say more? You need them like a fish needs a bicycle.

Sometimes Lord, Cobb can be so nice to me. Like the time he gave me a new tub for my birthday. I was so surprised. This was the highest quality tub complete with the hydro massage jets for my sore muscles and joints. I really hadn't known him for a long time; only about 8 months. The same day I received the beautiful tub, I met a female pastor. She said, "You will get everything that you want Sadaya Ruby Day. God loves you very much. Don't panic and don't stop talking to God no matter how it feels. I believe God intends to reward you," the pastor exhorted.

In her prayers Sadaya asked God to have Cobb Jackson, present himself with a lifetime guarantee. Well, you know what she means, "marriage;" the pastor asked for it interceding in Sadaya behalf, to God to The Almighty God of the Universe. With both Sadaya praying and pastor interceding for her, Sadaya felt more confident and she figured, "I can't lose with the stuff I use." Ha ha ha Ha ha ha Ha ha ha. Praise the Lord with such positive thoughts on her mind, Sadaya got into her bed. She sank down deep down in under her platinum down comforter and prayed herself to sleep.

† † †

Count Yourself In On The Goodness Of Life

"I am happy that I was given luggage from Cobb Jackson," Sadaya said. Cobb bought the expensive set of luggage. Sadaya loved the luggage because it was expandable and efficient and it had many features. It was also gender friendly meaning men could use the luggage with pleasure. Cobb laughed and put 2 tickets to go on a cruise inside of the smallest luggage bag. Of the luggage set, Sadaya opened the smallest luggage piece. She screamed and shouted when she found the tickets. "Wow," she said and then she dropped everything to kiss him on his neck and all-around his face. Another feature she thanked Cobb for getting was the feature actively blocking people from stealing her identity, meaning all of her credit cards are blocked and protected. It's called force field blocking protection. People such as thieves can no longer use their computer signals to steal from her credit cards. "Yay," Sadaya was very comfortable with the features given to her from Cobb. She didn't want her information to get into the wrong hands. This man Cobb is such a winner. He gave me radio frequency identification. Hallelujah for a man like him. I could really fall for this guy Cobb.

Cobb was on his usual traveling schedule with the NY Boxers Basketball Team. "Oh Dear Sweet God I never thought I'd admit it but I miss Cobb. I miss the way he winks at me, I miss his laughter. I miss him escorting me to the stadium and pointing out all of the players to me. I miss him giving me friendly texts and picking me up from work at night after school. I truly miss him. Oh boy does he have me worried about him. Most of all I miss his beautiful smile," Sadaya quipped. Thank God for praying people; ones that know how to bless.

Yes, Cynthia said. "As you know I am a born again Christian determined to lead an obedient Godly life. I go to choir practice every week, Bible Study every week and church service every Sunday. Sadaya told Cynthia, your boyfriend was a pretty boy and he was the love of your life. When I think about the two of you I think about King Solomon and the Queen of Sheba. Every time he smiled at you Cynthia, my heart went a flutter. I felt his love for you." Cynthia told Sadaya, "I'm so lonely now. Don't God's people men and women get lonely too? Yes, they do. God's people, men and women get lonely too and sometimes children," said Sadaya.

The pizza hot dog party was held before Bible Study began. The pizza was in the shape of a heart, the bottles of wine were ribbonized with each ribbon holding strings of hearts.

Cobb stood up and Sadaya stood up at the same time and facing each other. When the two stood, he was eating a frankfurter which he put the other end in her mouth too. They both ate opposite ends of the frankfurter. It was fun to watch the two of them having fun with their hotdogs. They did this twice with the frankfurter hot dogs, which most kids call the frankfurter balanced between both sets of lips. When Cobb and Sadaya came together, a good time was had by all. One of the most wonderful feelings Sadaya was happy about is that Cobb never stood her up. He said he'd come to pick her up or he said he'd meet her in the subway at said street and he was always there. "That gives me a fabulous feeling of security," Sadaya said. Well, Cobb has finally told me he loves me. Although he told me he loved me it was said so low I hardly heard it I think there are real issues around him telling that he loves me. I doubt he even realizes he said it, honestly. Sadaya told her pastor. Oh that's great, the pastor said. I was planning to call him into the church to do more volunteer work. You're here often, so that should work out well. I'm in prayer about it. The pastor said and I'm sure you must be too. Keep preying and I'm praying too that God will make a special plan and work it out especially for you and him.

"That frankfurter hotdog day was full of fun and enjoyment except for one situation. The more I think about it the hotter I get about it, pastor," Sadaya said. When we were making plans about how to entertain everyone with the food, I asked Cobb to pass me a frank. He hesitated. I repeated myself and I asked him to pass me the frank. He said, "OK chubby," Sadaya reported. I felt hurt and I looked at him and I said are you calling me fat, Cobb. One of the members of the church said, "Oh oh. Those are fighting words." "Well, you wouldn't want me to call you 'rotund' would you?" Cobb said to Sadaya. "Plus, if you had an hourglass figure you'd probably be too hard to get along with."Sadaya was her usual confident and outspoken self. She told Cobb if he didn't like her figure he could get out of the relationship right away. You are so egotistical Cobb. You irritate me now. "I can't' help it because I like women with hour glass figures," Cobb said laughing but Sadaya didn't see anything funny or comical. She told him off and left for 15 minutes before coming back to the pizza hotdog party. She kept her distance from Cobb that whole day after that.

In the meantime, somehow Cobb had to get the main message to Sadaya that he was worried too. He had doubts in his mind about visiting her ever again, as time, went on and he was able to think things through. With how she shouted on him trying to cramp his style, she made him think about never speaking to her and cheating on her too. But Cobb spent too much time in church to pursue the tactics of the world on his best girl, Sadaya even though he was lonely. Cobb began to expose himself to more sports venues and extra basketball practices. He was already excellent at all-around teamwork; passing the ball and getting it to the right teammate but he wanted to practice more at scoring. Sadaya never called Cobb after this fight. He went home and cried out to God and confessed that he loved her and he didn't mean to argue with her and he asked if God could fix this problem between he and Sadaya.

Some women can be oh so charming but the evil that lurks inside of her can reveal her heart to be oh so cold; oh so soul deep in its coldness. Cobb was pensive and he thought about someone he dated. Her name was Katrina Fava King. She, being of great wisdom, knelt down near the altar inside of the sanctuary at the Black Memorial Baptist Church. "I want to wash away all of the allergens and irritants I'll call sins but that's God's job." Katrina Fava King knew one of her best friends Sadaya was in love with Cobb Jackson but Katrina Fava moved in on Cobb, quicker than a bee on hives of honey. "You can rest your hand on my shoulders honey. All of the time I was away I dreamed about those warm kisses of yours," Katrina Fava King said. "I missed you so much. Visiting the care of the nativity in Bethlehem was a beautiful trip baby. I wish you had been there," Katrina said. "I know I'm amazingly thin and you'd like to see me gain more weight. I'm doing my best honey. Cobb said; "Again?" he said. Now noticing her thinness. "My life is so empty without you," she said. Cobb never could resist Katrina physically, sexually. "Too much lust for me," he thought. "Come here and erase these lonely moments from me, honey." My polished eyelet can't seem to catch up with you baby," he said, winking his eye at Katrina. "My little trip increased the intensity of my love for you, honey. Be with me," she said. And he was with her.

"Every closed eye is not sleeping and every open eye is not seeing. She kept telling me how she loves me but it felt like there was a boot on my neck. He felt negative sometimes about Katrina and then he loved her. Cobb was looking but he could not see the evil eyes of Katrina. She really wanted to defeat Sadaya. Sadaya was too wise. She stayed far away from both of them. And so in the shadow of the hills she drove trying to forget Cobb, the love of her life. She would have had a fight over him if she had let it get that far. There would have been chairs thrown to and fro chairs falling and bumping into table had Sadaya spoke to Katrina. It would have been big time fight time. 'I would have pulled her hair out and spat her guts out on the street' was a part of a fantasy that was improbable. It was Sadaya fantasy.

There was one situation that occurred when Sadaya took the children to Pancake Farm. The children were bragging about stacking pancakes. One of the parents became very disagreeable and jealous of Sadaya but Sadaya told her since she was dissatisfied she would change the child's class away from Sadaya's class. The child became disagreeable and hard to get along with too because the student wanted to stay in Sadaya's class. The principal settled the area of conflict by putting the child back into Sadaya's class and telling the parent the school would not take the child on trips that include pancakes. Sadaya was intelligent, smart and hardworking. The parent fought for her child to be back in Sadaya's class again and as stated earlier her wish was granted.

Cobb called Sadaya and he received the voicemail because Sadaya was at work and very busy. Sadaya was a very happy woman when she glanced at her cell phone and she saw Cobb number. She had been having uncomfortable feelings about the friction in their relationship stemming from the therapy conflict. Cobb still didn't want to have counseling with Sadaya. I miss you was the message on the voice mail. Do you still love me too? I surely love you, said Cobb with laughter in his voice. He let her know that he's looking to get to her soon and make up. Yes, yes, yes Sadaya replied.

Bizness life goes on. Cynthia tries to sell life insurance to Cobb for 'cheap', Cynthia says: "it's been so hard to get in touch with you. I need to talk to you about life insurance and I want to sell it to you. Like I said, for 'cheap." I promise you. I like you. I wouldn't try to pull the wool over your eyes. Where have you been? I sent you an on line exclusive." The Insurance Collective, Inc. is the name of our company. "We're here to help you," said Cynthia.

Simplified Term Life Benefit Summary Prepared for Cobb Jackson: This was prepared for Cobb Jackson to give to his family as a Christmas Gift Cynthia was the insurance agent who is currently trying to sell Cobb Jackson insurance for 4 or 5 people which is not cheap, even to Cobb Jackson. Cynthia tries to sell the insurance for "cheap," according to Cynthia Persons at the Insurance Collective, Inc.

Dear Cobb Jackson,

We're here to help you. This insurance package has everything you want for a Simple Life Plan Portfolio. It is easy to get the life coverage you want. Our application process lets you apply for up to $200,000 life benefits. The rest of the terms you will read about in the enclosed package your insurance agent, Cynthia Pearsons will fill you in

and answer any questions you have. Save on every
plan we have.

Yours truly, Victoria Eglottia

There is nothing funnier than watching Cynthia Persons
trying to sell life insurance to Cobb Jackson. When she was on the
telephone with her boss Cynthia said, "one of the biggest prospects
is Cobb Jackson, a great Athlete who makes plenty money. She
ended the call quickly so she could meet with the Cobb. She had
rushed to the stadium to meet with Cobb. She caught up with
Cobb and asked him if we could meet quickly.

"Where can we quickly meet?" she asked Cobb again. Cobb
Jackson walked in a hurried pace Sadaya had come along with
Cynthia to keep her company." I came along to help Cynthia to sell
Cobb Jackson insurance but I see she sells well and has a nice sales
pitch. I'll wait in the car," Sadaya said. As Sadaya turned to walk
to the car, Cobb said he wanted Sadaya to sit in on the meeting,
"if you don't mind." Sadaya smiled with delight. "O.k.," Sadaya
said. Cynthia was thinking, "I don't like the look on Cobb's face.
I hope he doesn't turn me down. Dear Lord, please don't let Cobb
Jackson turn me down. In the Name of Jesus Christ, Amend.
'Ah, maybe she was just going for the bait the Devil has to offer
when he wants us to defeat ourselves in our minds by thinking
negative emotions. Emotions such as "I'm scared" or "nothing
good is going to happen to me" or I'm going to be dishonest right
now;' these were all the emotions I had before when I didn't sell
anything. I must remember to think more positive and to trust
God's move, Cynthia Persons said to herself while walking to the
room to meet with Cobb Jackson. In the meeting : I've drawn up
a beautiful insurance benefits package for you Cobb. I know you
usually help the people at my church. I'm hoping you'll help me.
Cobb was trained well. He knew better than to sign any copy of ay

papers without reading it first. To his credit Cobb read the papers through and through then she shoved them aside.

To Cynthia, Cobb looked like he was ready to leave the premises. In an effort to keep him from leaving, Cynthia said, 'I only need you to sign something. I need your signed authorization now. Don't you want to get the prepared insurance package? "Cynthia asked Cobb said, "no, not really." He stood up and turned his head to walk out of the door. Cynthia screamed at him, "Cobb."He turned his head nonchalantly saying, 'what."

"Well, how am I supposed to process your application for insurance? For a Billionaire he was awfully cheap Cynthia thought. Cynthia let out a great big SIGH. I don't understand," she said further. "Don't you want the insurance now? Does a bear read a Reader's Digest in the woods? No. Right now, that's how I feel about this insurance situation. "No," said Cobb with lowered volume. All I need is a check and for you to sign your name. I also need for you to answer some health questions. I included your additional person's coverage in the package. You can buy with confidence from me. I represent one of the strongest and most financially secure institutions in the country. Although I seen bowel movements I've thought more of – Cobb, Cynthia thought. Stick with me Cobb don't leave me. Shall I get on my knees and beg you, Cobb? "with you, I'm humble and on my knees again. Sadaya had been quiet up until now. She had sat in on these types of meetings before but she'd never seen her friend Cynthia Persons so despaired. Sadaya interrupted the silence.

As the meetings coup de resistance had come to a resounding silence, Sadaya said, "I would like to everyone except for Cobb Jackson to leave the room. Cobb honey, I want to speak to you." Everyone left the room except for Cobb. "Cobb hone, I never get involved in your business affairs bit I feel this is necessary. You know Cynthia and I have been friends since we were little girls. I love her like a sister. 'When her mother and her boyfriend died, I was there for her. Honey, I think you should buy this insurance from her. She was getting on her knees to you. She must need the money awfully badly," Sadaya said. Cobb said, "give me a few minutes to think about it and then I'll give you my decision." Cobb sat for another 9 minutes and thought about whether he should buy the insurance from Cynthia or not. He finally decided to meet Cynthia at the church which is Black Memorial Baptist Church in one weeks time because he has to check on his finances. When Cynthia was called back into the room she was told he would meet her at the church on Sunday after service. 'Oh, you need more time to decide I see. O.K. I'll see you Sunday. Cynthia then left and she left Sadaya with Cobb to be dropped off to her home by him. This was a potentially promising day. We'll see what this Sunday brings," Cynthia thought, as catching a sigh of relief.

"There is an African Compound which I am pondering opening. It will have 24 hour staff. The area where I'm thinking about having the African Compound is known for their restaurants," he said. I'm predicting that people will want to visit my African Compound again and again. Cobb has colors in mind for his stay overnight restaurant similar to a bed and breakfast inn. "I am concerned about security" he was thinking. I wanted people to feel they're having a good time but to feel safe too. Cobb thought he have a patrolling 4x4 SUV to roll around the grounds of the African Compound. They will be known for their, seafood particularly lobster and shrimp. This is why I have to take so long to make up my mind about insurance and whether to spend more money or not,' said Cobb. What does the future hold? We'll see what happens this coming Sunday after I check with my accountants. When Cynthia returned to the room she was told about Cobb's new plans for an African Compound and that she would have to wait until Sunday. To see if she'd sold Cobb the insurance or not. Cynthia said, "I'm ready. I'm excited and I'm thinking very positively. I'll see you guys on Sunday with a smile regardless of what happens. See you Sunday. May you have blessing not stressing. God bless you, she said in a loud voice.

The day is a beautiful day, a lovely day. The sun is shining and the winds are low. I'll be letting Sadaya and depression have their release soon enough," Sadaya said. Bye bye sadness bye bye depression, she said.

† † †

Sadaya took another glance at Cobb. She saw his posterior. It was shaped like half of a cantaloupe.

"That beautiful hunk of a black man," Sadaya was thinking of Cobb again. She was thinking of Cobb while she stood in the church's Freedom Hall where workshops are held. "Cobb Jackson, you light up my heart. He's just my type, she thought, clean-cut. He flashed his Cheshire cat-like smile at Sadaya and she first swallowed then she found herself again wilting like a daffodil flower plant.

Sadaya loves Cobb. She studies his every movement and maneuver. She fantasized freely. Sadaya thought to herself an all-important important question of a couple's life: 'Will you marry me?' Sadaya could imagine herself studying Cobb's face before answering this all–important question. Fantasy as usual.

When Cobb is volunteering at the Black Memorial Baptists Church Sadaya notices how many other women are noticing him. She started talking fast which she does when she's nervous, anxious or upset. Talking too much, she was. "You don't know what you're doing. Are you sure you know what you're doing?" "Yes" Cobb said. "Yes Cobb I'm just a little concerned. Can you handle all of those women, Cobb and keep our relationship in intact?" she said. Sadaya was thinking about Cobb; 'I bet he has a million women that want to meet him. I guess I'd have to make me like one of all of those many women because he surely is fine and a basketball player. What a catch. This is more serious than I would like to think. I'll go for Cobb; interceding for him. I'm staying on bended knee for this one. We are covered under the warmth of the sky

40

when the sun shines and when it doesn't I can see it. Now. I'll be crying and on my knees but let me a least enjoy this.

Meanwhile Cobb was being criticized for not calming people. Did you notice people caught attitudes when they saw Cobb hadn't called them back?' Live and let live, I always say,' Sadaya said. My feelings run deep for Cobb," Sadaya was thinking. Cobb was hard to catch up with. Sadaya thought about going to God's church people.com to mingle. Well, if I went to a relationship agency I'd only be trying to meet someone like Cobb so I might as well stick with him. Cobb's the one I want God. Please help me to get him maybe I'll marry him, Lord God. Help me, please, lord God Almighty. Help us to get closer. I thank you for this opportunity of prayer. In the Name of Jesus Christ. I love you Lord and I put you first in my life. Amen. Sadaya.

That's Why I Love You

That's why I love you. You're so full of excitement.
That's why I love you. You're so family-friendly
That's why I love you. You're so nice
That's why I love you. You're so intelligent
That's why I love you. You're so successful
That's why I love you. You're the Best!

© A. Sealy

Sadaya said "Oh Lord, Cobb is sweeping me off of my feet. I'm afraid I'm falling in love with him. I love the nice treatment he's shown to me and given to me thus far. I'm starting to feel like this is the man for me. Sometimes the quickest way to the heart is through a hole in the head. Help me Lord. Give me inner strength to be able to handle any kind of situation be it from Cobb or any other type of situations. Keep my mind strong and capable. Thank you Lord, in the Name of Jesus Christ Amen," Sadaya said. "There we have it. Sadaya got up off of her knees and sat on her living room couch. A large smile came to her face. She could always count on God to make her feel better after talking to him. She breathed in and out and said, "this is great. I feel like I just had a refreshing drink, like a cold soda after being in the desert for 3 days. Aahaahaah Sadaya laughed to herself. "I feel good."

"The church is not just a bureaucracy but a love story with arms wide open Cobb remembered. He wanted to attend pastoral counseling alone. To help with the healing process, Cobb Jackson called and made an appointment with the pastor for pastorial counseling. He wants to find out why he's too shy to tell Sadaya how he feels about her. The pastor said he'd be taping the sessions. He was asked if he Cobb minds being taped. Cobb said no. Cobb was required to explain his tactics used with Sadaya to the pastor and to go under hypnosis. This modification of behavior by suggestion helped Cobb. The pastor knew how to get Cobb better faster and how to heal deep wounds, especially from childhood. How Cobb loved his Sadaya. He explained how he usually feels comfortable and how she usually says something that impresses him. Sometimes they argued about his women. Whenever Cobb wants to tell Sadaya just how much she means to him he clams up. He's even thought about the subject of marriage and as long as they're joking he can talk but as soon as he tries to get serious, he can't speak. The pastor had him to do jaw exercise, put him under hypnosis gave him scriptures to read and watched his progress. Cobb is a tough fighter but sometimes he felt like he was climbing up a mountain of broken glass without shoes on. He told the pastor Sadaya said she is not like other women. She said she had a self-discipline they couldn't understand. Cobb makes basketball seem effortless but when the pastor asked "did you tell her how much she means to you?', No, I couldn't yet' he said: the most celebrated Athlete of our time stuck without words.

The weather outside had been frightful. The meteorologist had been predicting 14-16 inches of snow accumulation with the wind chill factor being 15 degrees or so. The weather by temperature was 22 degrees Cobb, who was scoring high, left with his basketball team. The last game which he played, he scored 44 points. I'm kind of proud of myself for sure. Thank you, God. As Cobb looked up and smiled he felt stronger than ever. God sir, I love you. One day this week I'm going to the Black Memorial Baptist Church and help with whatever they want me to help them with. I promise you, sir.

In Jesus Name, Amen,' Cobb said this prayer.

Cobb thought about Maxine and how he had treated her. His conscience was bothering him. He called her and the voicemail came on. "Hi Maxi, called to see how you're doing and how you're feeling. Call me. Cobb, he said. When he hung up from Maxi's number, the other line rang and it was Sadaya, his favorite. Technically even though he'd just called Maxine, he really didn't feel like talking to anyone. He let the system go straight to voicemail.

Oh Ms. Candy how wonderful to see you. Today is Media Day and my class wanted to meet you. You being a great writer, the school principal bought a copy of each of your last books for each of our students. What a beautiful surprise. Let me erase the blackboard. The students will have no homework tonight; they're going to love you. I'm going to put you in the ante-room. You'll have about a ½ hour layover wait. We have a guest Bank president speaking to the children later on. We want you to stay and have dinner with the children in my class, Ms. Sadaya Day said. Also the Basketball Team will be sitting in on the next two sessions.

See you in ½ hour, Ms. Candy. "O.k." see you and the children later.

Library Media day was long and tiresome but well worth it for the students. They asked lots of questions and took lots of notes about their guests. The principal Ms. Osgood also took notes and gave Ms. Day a glowing evaluation. Ms. Day as Sadaya was known as made 2 cakes and shared them with the students and their guests. What a successful day at school.

Sadaya writes a column. You've gotta admit it. Children do weird things sometimes. They can't explain why they do them but they do. Kids usually out grow these in their arsenal. There is also information about people who specialize in preparing students for state wide tests. And admission test. There are newspapers that the children at Sadaya's school put out called Sunshine. The Expert headed and editorialized by her. Sadaya lets the kids do movie review every week. They love this feature Sadaya and her 6th grade class also feature ballets specials. Right now Sadaya's students are too young to join the teenagers. You must be 16 years old. Most of them are anxious about joining and they have predicted they will do well when their time comes. There are dancers that have graduated from the ballet company and have come back to watch. They say the each cry a little during some of the scenes because they are so touching. Sadaya had a great column for adults and for their children. They even had winter break activities for the children and their parents. Hint hint; skiing is affordable.

When Cobb Jackson saw her Sadaya's column he sent her the most beautiful flowers with the following notes attached; That's why I love you. You're so talented. That's why I love you. You're so wonderful. That's why I love you. You're so excellent. That's why I love you. You're so loveable.

Sadaya liked hearing from Cobb Jackson. It feels lovely to feel like and to be told that you are loved," she thought. Secretly, Sadaya felt that Cobb could make a better husband in good times, bad times and all times. He'd make a better father, when the time comes. Sadaya told her mother, Cobb Jackson's investment fortune comes from multiple investments which she'd like to get a closer look at. He has private investments and independent ones. Either way, I'd love to take a peak. Sadaya confided in her mother.

I also hear and see the Cobb Jackson is generous with his wealth.

Sadaya shared this information with a few of her girlfriends at her place of employment. Later in the daytime Cobb surprised her and visited her elementary school.

Sadaya who quickly said, "If I eloped I doubt my mother would ever speak to me again, my father wouldn't speak to me either. I'd be in hot water. My backsides would be raw hot; cooked like souse meat and hamburger. Man oh-man would I be in big troubles," Sadaya said. My mother would have killed me almost. Cobb laughed and agreed.

By the way, the police officer that you didn't agree with: I remember him now he came over to the church book fair and arts and crafts fair last week. He smiled at us and he spoke to all of the ladies. He was so very polite. I can appreciate a man like him who respects God and the church said Sadaya. "Oh yes, well I'm glad he fit in because my cousin like him" Cobb said. As a matter of fact my cousin so stuck on him she wants to marry him. She said so. Even though she doesn't know him well. We were hoping someone like him with a job and a pleasing personality will come along. He being single of course would sweep her off her feet. I'll let you know if anything happens between now and the next 6 months. In the meantime he'll continue to be a police officer, with no girlfriend. I did manage to find out he doesn't have one. Before the week is over I plan to visit him at the precinct and tell him about my cousin. Vivvie Jackson. Oh good Cobb, I could kiss you thinking of your cousin and looking out for her. Then again, I could kiss you for any reason anyway, Sadaya said. She kissed him on the cheek. Sadaya kissed him again proudly and she said, "My man Cobb loves only me as his lady."

Cobb almost choked on his chewing gum.

Cobb Jackson's future ex girlfriend Maxine showed up to his basketball practice to take Cobb to lunch like she used to, but Cobb's reaction to her was negative. He didn't smile instead he frowned. He said, "Whatever you're doing here, you're supposed to call me first and not just show up unannounced." Maxine, who worked as a bank teller and part time bank executive explained. She had been thinking about him and she showed up because she loved him and she wanted to see him. She took half a day off from her job to come to see him. A flurry of circumstances caused her to think with her heart and not with her head. "What a mess I'm in," she thought. Finding romance with him isn't easy now.

Maxine said, "I was addicted to nasal sprays for a long time. I'm awfully tempted again. Finding romance with Cobb is hard nowadays. I think this is why I'm tempted by nasal sprays again. My mother once said the most wonderful way to the heart is through a hole in the head."

"I think its mean of him. Pure meanness to treat me like this," she thought further. Maxine called Cobb 3 day later hoping to find out if he was over his cranky mood. Cobb again wasn't ready to tolerate much from Maxine or Maxi as her friends called her. When Cobb picked up the telephone, he was still distancing himself and still thinking negative about her. He accused her of nagging. He said she was a nag and that she wanted to argue most of the time. "I want to fly away like an eagle every time she does call me to accuse me," Cobb said. "Sometimes she makes me angry enough to hang up on her but I've just rushed her off the phone so far," Cobb was thinking. In Maxine's point of view Cobb is conceited and sometimes hard to work with but he's famous and he's got a lot of money. He's lucky he travels a lot. It gives the people he's offended a chance to get over his quirky personality. He got a monster load of energy, and he's nice when he wants to be. For instance, Sadaya, thus hasn't had many, any problems with him. As a matter of fact Cobb told Sadaya he wanted her to come to different states and be in the audience. After the games were over, the plan was to take her to dinner for respite and refreshments. Also to introduce her to some of his friends in different cities. "Cobb Jackson, you old goat you. I know you're probably cheating on Maxine; as nicely as she has treated you," a Slick Rick Magazine reporter said.

Sadaya knows about Maxine and Maxine knows about Sadaya the way I understand it. To cheer up Sadaya and to have Sadaya not to worry about the fact that there's a girlfriend Maxine, Sadaya bought clothes. After shopping she realized that she had clothes in handbags which she hadn't opened yet. The Lord is so good. He wants us to adorn ourselves with the peace and quiet of the Holy Spirit too, along with the clothes we wear. Be assured. I will adorn myself with what the Holy Bible says He wants me to," Sadaya said. That coupled with going to church suits me fine she said. It is not just a bureaucracy but church represents a love story with arms wide open.

Church. Church: one of the most loved places in the world. It was not just a bureaucracy but church represents a love story with arms wide open. Church is a building used for Christian worship. They came to church with me. Noun: the church. House of God two churched people Sadaya Ruby Day and Cobb Jackson, both heroes in their chosen occupations. Cobb Jackson phrased it best: the church is interesting and vital. There's food on my table and shoes on my feet. Chances are, with research, you'll find that the church had something to do with that," Cobb said, smiling. Church at Black Memorial Baptist Church was a gathering place for two people in love. They found each other and met at the Black Memorial Baptist Church. "There were the best of times and good times. Only a few scrapes did we have when I thought Cobb went out with Maxine. All around the crevices of my mind the sorrows grew deep. "He must be with her Cobb and Maxine I heard was his girlfriend's name. I never met her and I didn't intend to. Maxine tried to manipulate him into not attending church on Sunday mornings. If Cobb missed church 2 weeks in a row, he'd miss Sadaya something fierce. Sadaya drew Cobb closer in prayer, and she looked for him in church. They do not sit next to each other, most times. Sadaya sits upstairs with the mass choir and she's satisfied being there.

"Are you always this shy or are you just dangerously ignorant? I want you to look into the mirror tonight and I want you to say 'I was a bore today.' This is how Cobb Jackson spoke to Maxine his girlfriend of 3 years. She did not say much to him because she thought he was cheating on her again. According to Cobb, Maxine should have worked harder to keep him as her boyfriend.

Our heart is like an unfinished puzzle that is why
we search for the perfect piece to complete it.

Author Anonymous

Cobb Jackson sowed little patience for Maxine. When Maxine went into the ladies' room he called Sadaya and made a date for that night. He took Maxine home and he left her there. "When am I going to see you again?" Maxine asked. "I don't' know Maxine honey. I'll be very busy the next couple of weeks but call me, or I'll call you. Just remember, actions have consequences my dear." Saying goodbye as he opened her door to let her out of his SUV.

Cobb still had about an hour and a half before he was to meet Sadaya at the church. He thought nervously about her and all of his blues went away. In an hour and a half (he was to meet her and he thought he'd take her to get dinner at a place not far from the Black Memorial Baptist Church. Sadaya this time was smiling in her double-breasted jacket dress again from Dacy's dept. store and almost flattering suede scrunch jacket. Her bag matched her outfit.

Amazing what one kiss can do. Actions have consequences my dear, Cobb said to Sadaya. Because you touched my hand and I got so turned on by you I'd have to have at least one kiss. His body writhed against her body as they held one another, and the two felt like one flesh even with their clothes on. It had been a long wicked day when Cobb's phone rang it startled Sadaya. Cobb just let the telephone ring. He found his lips pressing against Sadaya's.

Hi had were large and strong. They gently touched the nape of her neck. Cobb had given her persistent touches. He found his lips pressing against Sadaya's. His hands were large and strong. They gently touched the nape of her neck. Cobb had given her persistent glances all evening. The glances were reciprocated by Sadaya who was falling deeper and deeper in love with him. Years before, Sadaya had made up her mind that she wasn't going to "make love" before marriage. This was and still is because of her deep religious beliefs. Cobb was careful of where he placed his hands. He was respectful of Sadaya's morals. After all, Sadaya wanted to take it very slow. The surprise kiss was filled with pleasure but Sadaya was careful to remind Cobb that she was not sexually active because of her religious beliefs. Cobb continued to scale his fingers up and down only her neck. 'What a big beautiful handsome man this was touching me' she thought. He had tremendous eyes. They glared through their sockets with clear radiance and love. They exchanged nervous but sensuous gazes and laughed. Voices could be heard approaching outside of the stained glass wall. The two potential lovers Cobb and Sadaya remained decent. He was in his clothes and she remained in her. Amazing what a kiss will do.

He succeeded at everything he tried. He volunteered at the church but Cobb went to supermarkets and dining clubs convincing the owners of business that meals are needed for the less fortunate. He went to art exhibits and he convinced the artists to donate tie-dye outfits. The artists were clever and the fashions were stunning. One artist, Yoko, was a woman with doe-like eyes and keen features. She asked Cobb for his phone number and he gave it to her. She invited him to escort her to a wedding and he said he might go. "Love the earth and the sun and the land; stand up for the best causes. Make whichever lady you're dating comfortable and if she becomes the sunlight in your universe appreciate her. Love your family too. "This is my creed," said Cobb to a friend. It should be like loving yourself. "It should be a 24 hour thing, I always say," he said. "It's hard to do the right thing when you don't know what the right thing to do is. God, there are a lot of people outside of our church that need you," the pastor prayed. Some men and woman who are corrupt in their morals pervade the city streets seeking whom they can devour and destroy just like their God. We are the people of the light. Let's act like it. Don't forget to wine and dine your wives and husbands and boyfriends and girlfriends; especially when they're in a lousy mood. Don't forget to cook and clean for them and say, 'I love you, baby,' the pastor said.

> A happy heart doeth good like medicine but a broken spirit dryeth the bone.

> Proverbs

The chemistry and the magnetism between Cobb and Sadaya was unmistakable. She was happy for two reasons: she was happy to be a member of Black Memorial Baptist Church and she was happy to have met such a famous basketball player who was usually treating her so swell. While it was true that Cobb Jackson traveled a lot, he usually visited Sadaya about every 2-2 ½ weeks. Their chemistry and magnetism carried the relationship. They always found something to talk about and they always seem to talk, love talk such as what the future might hold for them possibly moving to another state or country if Cobb should get traded to an international team. Sadaya did most of the talking. Cobb even mentioned "eloping" to reply Sadaya but he only asked her if she knew what it meant and joked around.

Sadaya wore a cashmere turtleneck, a cashmere shawl and leather pants with a lace blouse.

She felt good in what she was wearing. A big smile on her face. Yes, she wore that too.

The kitchen silverware was left out the setting table in the kitchen. Cynthia spotted them first and put the whole 8 place setting back into the drawer. The whole 8 place setting was unusually large for silverware but it remained attractive. It matched the 8 place dishes and was set extremely well. Cynthia was happy to have a dishwasher. Thank God for modern conveniences. All I have to do is put the dishes into the dishwasher and press a button. This dishwasher matches the cabinets in the kitchen/ kitchen cabinets. I'm very proud of my nice kitchen appliances and cabinets. Soon Cynthia would have a nice big dinner for her sister Aretha. Aretha would be turning 44 years old in 2 weeks. Cynthia bought Aretha a new set of red leather trim luggage. It was stunning and so was Aretha who bought 4 new outfits from D'acy's dept. store. Being red, her clothing matched the luggage well. She favored the beautiful queen of Sheba and so did Sadaya Day her first cousin. "Cynthia is both my cousin and my best friend. I love her" said Sadaya.

The thrill of the night was Cynthia and her montage of comical statements and jokes. Sadaya had heard her many nights but tonight was the crème de la crème of nights. There would be no turning back when it came to her stage presence. Her physical on-stage demonstrations and her voice pitch and elegance were all par excellence. On stage Cynthia was such a suave personality. She was even known to wear black sequins outfits on stage in front of the audience that gave her standing ovations because of her wardrobe. She was in the Good Lord's Hands and he was treating her with tender loving care. Along with taking good care of Cynthia, he also gave her an exquisite singing voice and gift of gab. Cynthia was an all-around voice talent. She was seen on the Bear News Network doing broadcast news production and television reporting. She often talked about television network news jealousies among the employees. So much drama was going on in Cynthia's life that she had to call Sadaya and make an appointment to have dinner at the Trusting God Restaurant, to talk. Today was the day for the two of them to meet at the restaurant and Cynthia was anxious, excited to meet Sadaya after a long exciting exhaustive day of expensive shopping.

"You look sleep deprived and you haven't' eaten a thing all day. I've been with you shopping all day. Not eating I believe is a big sin. Cynthia, already your body aches and you're not feeling well because of all of the catastrophes and disasters going on at your job. Let's have some ice cream," Sadaya said.

"Ditto Sister ditto dear," Cynthia agreed. Her nervous stomach was weak and she had to sit down to have a cup of tea to settle her too; to settle her stomach.

I think you should know that you're the subject of a lot of rumors, a lot of dirty nasty rumors. And to all of the people that told me about the rumors, promised I would be loyal and I wouldn't tell. I've heard so much gossip, my ears are wiggling. Yes it is possible for a person to heat so much gossip and casual conversation their ears can start wiggling. "For they sow the wind and reap whirlwind. God is not mocked. Whatsoever a man sows that shall he also reap.

There's something special about Sadaya but she has a negative side too, Cobb thought. The clouds burst open with rain bragging of thunder and lightning. She shared her umbrella with Cobb as they walked in the rain. "My spirit takes to hers. Sadaya. I plan to go to church more often. I'm going to church to worship God first and then to find her. Cobb prayed "I still love her," he said. I still love her even though she flew mad with me twice and she and I almost got into a fight over me having other women, vivacious women in my life. Cobb Jackson and Sadaya Day considered themselves a happy couple. Mascara running down the front of her face from too many painful tears, Sadaya was angry still. She pushed him with all of her might and then she kneed him in the middle of his groin area. He had serious plans. "Get me outta here. You won't be putting me in jail for punching my girlfriend dead," Cobb shouted. Cobb grabbed his coat and ran away. She kicked him lowly in his ribs the second fight. He walked into the Jerked Leg Locksmith Co. with truly a jerked leg. Cobb was still angry with Sadaya, not calling or texting her or communicating with her in any way. At the end of the 3rd week, Sadaya called him. He told her he's an accomplished man, he's a smooth dresser, he's got plenty money but many people don't realize he's a man of faith. He was trying desperately to stay away from controversy and conflict. "I thought I knew you. I never thought you'd be less than a woman and strike me," he said. How dare you Cobb retorted. When I think of you now I have to fall on my knees. I'm still sore from you fighting me. I have to get humble and on my knees again and again. I have time to.

"The way I feel now I don't know 'I'll ever speak to you again," Cobb said to Sadaya. "This works against my Christian faith," he said. I don't like this one bit. One of the things that I like about you was that you didn't just sit around twiddling your thumbs. You were always busy with constructive projects and activities. As far as I was concerned, you were a champion in every way; but now, I don't know. I used to think you could soar. I used to think you could fly like an eagle under the wind. Sometimes you can sow the wind and reap the whirlwind. God is not mocked. Whatsoever a man sows that shall he also reap. When two eyes cry, one body bleeds,' Cobb told his girlfriend Sadaya Ruby Day. "My eyes cry sometimes,' Cobb said.

Sadaya did not hear from Cobb Jackson and she was upset. She accepted a date with her ex- boyfriend Thaddeus. Thaddeus shocked Sadaya by getting married. He broke the news to her over dinner. She'd left choir practice early just to meet him. Tears came into her eyes and rolled down her face. Seems like whenever I get or hear bad news choir practice has something to do with it. I got a call from him and I knew something was wrong. Whenever I get news about my family or my job or my friend's death that's come when I get a phone call during choir practice. I should have known something was wrong because you called me during choir practice. Here I was wearing my favorite burgundy blouse and I cried all over it. He really broke my heart and tried to come back to me after he was married. It took some time for me to realize that Thaddeus is just a man that zips his pants up like any other man. The skunk.

Although Cobb and Sadaya got along well, they began to argue about Maxine, Cobb's ex- girlfriend. He said something harsh to Sadaya and she figured she's finish up the whole tiff. Cobb was telling her be careful of who your friends are, even if it is in church. She said, "you make me feel I'm more of a banana girl, soft and lickety-split. I would honestly pick my friends from the church, I feel at least they're trying to live right. Pick my friends from the church is what I'll stick to. Sometimes it's just a Christian's job to plant a seed. I dropped hints to him," she said. Every time I see him I get hot. Every time I don't see him I get hot about him. Now you know that's love. Only someone living their lives not as a Christian but in darkness would say. Might as well call me a gardener because I surely planted a seed today. I was witnessing for God not really foolin' around or anything like that" crude words. Watch your way of communicating to the world, I said. People watch Christians to see if they're going to stumble sometimes, Sadaya said. "If you don't love the guy, barf yourself silly. If you do love him, make sure you don't give him everything he wants. You could lose him that way too, you know" Sheila her friend said. "Well, I love my guy. Every time I see him, which is mostly in church I get hot. Now you know that's love," Sadaya said.

Kenny is Sadaya's father: "My daughter Sadaya told me she cried over you the other day and this as not the first time she cried over you," Kenny said, still angry at Cobb. Cobb was honestly speaking, there were tears but there were also smiles occurring around those tears. The love I have in my heart for your daughter is not a simple superficiality. I think it was a pleasure to date your daughter. She is so pretty and so refined and full of manners. I'm totally turned on by her ways. "When she speaks to me, I feel like a king." I really love her, Cobb said to Kenny. Sadaya's father said, "she knows how to make a hard life easy." "She is going to be the subject of all of my unbridled passion whether she's alone or in a crowd. She makes my sprit soar," smiled Cobb.

Now Cobb Jackson was always considered to be quite the ladies'man but he realized that he had grown accustomed to the love of one special woman in his life and her name was Sadaya Ruby Day. Whatever he was doing, wherever he went he thought of her. Actually, he was in love and he would have never entertained any thought of replacing her. Sadaya however, was not so sure of this relationship between she and Cobb. She often bent her knees at church and at home, asking God to give her inner strength and wisdom and to show her how to deal with Cobb.

Cobb thanked God that his basketball game wasn't suffering. He was still scoring high points with NY Boxers basketball.

Basketball Team. He was a role model for many. His mother and father liked working with youth groups at the church and they asked him to serve as youth chairman.

There was a pair of brothers. They were twins and their names were Kaisy and Jaisy. Being twins they looked so much alike they could have been like cuff links on a shirt. They had straight black hair and they were very handsome. When Kaisy and Jaisy were around other young people came around because Kaisy and Jaisy were popular. Younger teens would ask questions of a personal nature. "Are you married? Do you have any children? Do you drive? Ooh could you take me somewhere?" Could you take me around the corner or anywhere? Cobb liked Kaisy and Jaisy. They were known for their great ability in swimming. Cobb was a great swimmer too although he was paid to play basketball. He complimented Kaisy and Jaisy for bringing scholarships to their school and he visited the school to be the guest speaker for the swimming team group. Each time Cobb appeared some where he gave God credit for keeping him strong.

Cobb used young people like Kaisy and Jaisy as examples for other young people to follow. They were his new friends. They were young, cunning and smart. He talked to them about the importance of not letting anyone pressure them into doing something that they don't want to do. He also referred Kaisy and Jaisy who were church attendees, to their pastor for support and assistance with any problems they might have. Being swimming sensations issues such as jealousy and too many admirers among the girls came up but Kaisy and Jaisy did listen to Cobb's advice.

Mark Twain said it best when he said – no man is a failure who has friends.

Sadaya went to a bakery called Valentine's Day Bakers. There was a deck of card sitting on the counter. She picked up a card and it said, win a free birthday cake. Go to the cashier and answer one question. If you answer correctly you can win a big birthday cake free of charge and a cup of cappuccino. Sadaya decided to enter the little contest and she won. She took her cake and she called Cobb to share it with him. I think I'll just spoil Cobb. Kaisy and Jaisy left Cobb to go swimming. He needs me to engage him, give him special attention. I want to give him VIP treatment. What Sadaya didn't know is that Cobb was thinking about her too. At that movement the phone rang and it was Cobb. "I was thinking about you fiercely," he said. Sadaya loved to hear his deep masculine voice. He could envision her beautiful smile. He had been talking to Kaisy and Jaisy about how he saw Sadaya. To him Sadaya was a knockout. "I was so knocked out by her that I had to stop myself from calling Maxine and Katrina Fava. Maxine had been my main girlfriend. I had to stop myself from seeing her because it just wasn't the same any more. I only know I foresee Sadaya holding me tight night after night. She just doesn't know it yet. I believe it was love at first sight with us," Cobb told Kaisy and Jaisy on the phone.

Sadaya and Cobb talked and decided to meet at church to share the big birthday cake she won. In the back of Sadaya's mind Cobb might call her chubby. I won't eat too much cake especially in front of him, she promised herself.

Church: people gather for many reasons but one of the most important reasons has to do with the passions of the heart. Cobb Jackson met Sadaya Ruby Day and he decidedly romances her within the 4 walls of the church mostly. The church is the key to love and adoring emotions. "Two people in love and lost, in church is not the worst thing I've ever heard of" pastor said. Cobb has a secret intent to marry her. Two people in love and dating and serving God can be quite "cute." As long as they're honoring God and serving God, I don't see a thing wrong with the couple hanging out on church property a little longer than most people, the church Cardinal said. As a matter of fact, I find it rather charming. A church love story monitored by God and his people. What a refreshing beautiful idea. On the other hand, there is an on-going argument between Cobb and Sadaya about him seeing other sexy, vivacious and luscious women. Cobb's parents were ok with it but Sadaya's father and mother said choice words for Cobb which almost made him cry. "My God, what kind of man are you anyway? You are like vomit to me. Sputum. You are like vomit to me, worse than a piece of dusty mud. End this inhumanity to Sadaya before it effects us all even more. This is terrible. I can't even muster up a smile," Sadaya's mother said sadly. Among my family can be found my friends.

All of my family and friends say when a man cheats on my daughter he should be dropped Sadaya's father said. Every closed eye is not asleep and every open eye is not seeing. Cobb had a severe cough and cold problem making a nuisance of itself like his cheating. Outside of the times that Cobb wasn't cheating on Sadaya, they bonded well.

The winter weather was frightful and the meteorologists were predicting snow that could pile up 14-16 inches high. Cobb had accepted an invitation to the Red Brigade Club Diner. Sadaya would be his guest. As Sadaya was thinking, she thought, "this man is so good-looking he could charm my pantyhose off."Sadaya remembered the Bible said to flee in the face of temptation. She was determined to keep this in mind.

Sadaya had been shopping all month for clothes and jewelry for the Red Brigade Club event. Cobb called her and she had finally finished shopping. He thought it comical and he laughed when she told him she had been shopping for a whole month.

As a famous evangelist pointed out, soul-winning may not be on the agenda of most of our churches. But the Bible says man, even with housing, money and power is in a bad fix. It says that in Adam all men fell and since Adam we have continued to fall. It says that Adam did not just receive a slight bruise, he fell flat! Listen to what it says about unsaved men: Isaac says that man's head is sick. Mark, that man's ears are evil; David, that man's mouth is deceitful; James, that man's tongue is unruly and full of deadly poison. Paul, that man's throat is an open sepulcher; Jeremiah, that man's neck is stiff. Matthew that man's ears are dull; Solomon, that man's feet are swift in running to mischief; Job, that man's bones are full of sin; David, that man's thoughts are vain from man's foot to his head according to Isaiah 1:6 Kings James Version there is no soundness.

The pastor of Black Memorial Baptist Church had done thorough research on the nature of man and on drugs. He led his congregation in prayer. Dope pushers should be punished as heavily as if they, were murderers, because they are in reality. They are responsible for every person who has died from dope, because the person who died got the dope from or through a pusher.

I picture drugs as I do a pitcher plant. Take notice to the pitcher plant. There is a beautiful plant called the pitcher plant (carnivorous plant). It is very attractive. The attractiveness of this plant is a real death-house or trap for all insects who go into it. The lower edges of, the leaves are folded together to form a pitcher or tube. Insects enter into the plant's mouth and Start to eat. The delicious-tasting fluid, which is at the edges of the plant. Wanting more and more of this fluid, they climb deeper and deeper into this plant, where there is more fluid. The little spike-like slippery fibers make the going down very easy, but on the way out, the insect is trapped by these spikes, and escape is impossible. Finally, the insect loses its strength, and falls into the pit of the plant.

Young generation, what a beautiful picture this is for drugs! The way they trap you and destroy you. Pushers will tempt you by saying it will make you feel good. It might make you feel good, but it puts an end to your life. The young ones are deceived by the reaction of the drug, and begin to want to get higher. But finally, they get hooked and find they cannot find the road back home. It takes away all they have, even their lives. Dope is a trap. To be trapped means simply to be fooled. You think you are getting something which is good, but then things change and you end up trapped instead. I hope you will take heed of the pitcher plant.

There are many cases that do not make the headlines of the newspaper. For instance, it was reported in one of the hospitals that a 6-year-old girl was given LSD by her 19-year-old brother. LSD is one of the most dangerous drugs a person can take. Here is what LSD stands for: Lysergic Acid Diethylamide. The "L" is taken from "Lysergic," "S" is taken from "Lysergi C," and "D" is taken from "Diethy". All together it is called LSD.

THE TYPES OF DRUGS

Stimulants; Amphetamines—They stimulate the body processes, working on the central nervous system and causing an alert, energetic feeling. Common nicknames or terms: "Speed" (Methedrine) "Uppers," "Pep Pills."

Depressants; Barbiturates— Relax the body processes, causing a calm feeling. Common terms or nicknames: "Downers," "Goofballs," "Reds," "Blues."

Hallucinogens—Drugs that produce a false sense of reality. Common terms: "LSD." Taking LSD means you are taking a trip out of this world! It reacts on the mind. You have no ability to distinguish between fact and fantasy!

A 5-year-old boy was trick-or-treating, and someone had put heroin in his candy. I think it is terrible that someone could do this to a 5-year-old. It is not the child's fault that he ate the candy, but the person's fault who gave it to him. The child did not know that there was heroin in the candy. He did not know how to be careful of wicked people. He thought that whoever gave him the candy, meant him well.

Dope is flying everywhere, gathering its victims! They found a prisoner dead from an overdose of drugs who had somehow gotten into the prison-house. He had been in jail ever since he was 17-years-old. His arrests included automobile thefts and burglary. I suppose he had to rob to keep up his habits. Dope has also reached the GI's. So far military drug smugglers are a problem. For dope smugglers, Germany is used as the natural route to America. Germany also has lenient drug laws. In Germany there are some Turkish people who come from the country where opium is grown legally. Heroin comes from legally-grown opium that has been diverted from legal channels. Most of the opium comes into Germany from Turkey, although some comes from Pakistan and Lebanon.

Narcotics is one of the biggest problems of our time. Scientists should be urged to study ways of fighting it. Drugs form one of the most serious and threatening evils of our generation. Scientists should be urged to seek techniques of at least weakening the effects of narcotics abuse. A thirteen-year-old boy was killed by a glue-sniffing ex-convict. This ex-convict said that after sniffing the glue he wanted to see how much fun it was to kill someone. Police said that the murder followed a midnight glue-sniffing by five or six persons, including the boy who was slain. Twenty-six teenagers were arrested for possession of dangerous drugs. All were charged with selling such drugs as heroin, marijuana, hashish, amphetamines, barbiturates, hallucinogens, and LSD. Between January 1 and August 20 tosii0, 2,400 persons were arrested in one county on drug charges. A suspended elementary teacher was arrested for selling heroin to children.

Police say they had found an estimate of about 50,000 dollars' worth of drugs stuffed in a vacuum cleaner. This was the narcotics-seizer in the city in the last three years; this was a big-league operation. Another teacher was also arrested for possession of narcotics. A 19-year-old youth apparently on LSD leaped to his death from the rooftop of a building. A 25-year-old man was found dead, the result of a four-day amphetamine binge. A girl of 15 had been sent to school to break her heroin habit, and she was found dead of an overdose of heroin. An 18-year-old was shot to death by a security officer when he resisted arrest for possession of a pocketbook he had snatched. A 34-year-old man and a 24-year-old woman were found dead with bullet holes in the back of the head. People seem to think their death came about because they "sold bad stuff or failed to pay the dope pushers for narcotics they received."

A woman was arrested on the street for having 300,000 dollars in a shopping-bag she was carrying. Detectives said they found 6,250 glassine bags containing heroin and a three-pound bag of uncut heroin in the shopping bag. A man who said he was a private eye was arrested for carrying 750,000 dollars' worth of cocaine on a freight train docked for repairs. Two top narcotics investigators were charged with selling heroin. The two were paid $11,500 a year by the Narcotics Bureau. These two investigators apparently turned to the very thing they were supposed to be fighting against. These men had been recommended by the Federal Narcotics Bureau. These two men had recovered a half-ton of marijuana, the largest amount ever seized in this country. They were hired as special narcotics investigators. One of them was used in almost every case.

A man was shot and killed, according to a witness. He was shot four times in the chest and back by an unknown male. The man died on his way to the hospital. He had on him a quantity of heroin or cocaine inside a dollar bill and inside his sock. There was no reason for the shooting of this man given.

Ten college students were arrested on the campus. The arrest was made by plainclothesmen, a unit of black and Puerto Rican officers who usually work in slum neighborhoods. They found out that the ten students had dope in student lounges, cafeteria, hallways, and other places on the campus. The suspects were ranging in ages from 19 to 23; they sold drugs to the undercover society.

A rooming house known throughout the metropolitan area was described as one of the worst places in the city for the trafficking and shooting (taking) of heroin. The building had been hit many times by policemen, who had arrested 485 persons on drug charges in 15 months. The police said they just couldn't seem to eliminate the pushers and the users from coming to the building. Heroin pushers in the building led to the death of at least six persons in the building. One of the members from the drug group said, "If someone takes an overdose in this building, they usually walk or drag them out of the building and leave them someplace to die."

An ex-diplomat was indicted on drug charges. A former vice-counsel in the Columbian Consulate General's office was indicted on charges of smuggling and transporting $5,000,000 worth of drugs. A boy met a girl in the park, and that was the beginning of this boy taking drugs. Later, he died of an overdose of heroin. The girl that had given him the heroin is now a pill addict. She had to become a prostitute to keep up her habits.

The female addicts who have records for prostitution are rising. From an estimate of 90% of the cities, more than 100,000 heroin addicts are not receiving any form of rehabilitation. The cities' heroin addict population is now 10 times higher than the reported 10,000 addicts in 1964. Also, drug death rates rose from 200 in 1960 to 320 in 1965 and to 900 in 1969. Teenage drug deaths went from 32 in 1965 to an estimated 224 in 1969.

A cop trainee was arrested on dope charges. They arrested him for disorderly conduct. In inspection of the car, they found narcotics. Narcotics are being sold all over the country. The use of amphetamines may result in psychological dependence. The abuser feels a strong need or desire to take the drug more frequently. As people increase their doses, they may eventually have to take up to 50 pep pills daily trying to obtain the sensation they first had from one or two tablets.

You can usually tell when a person is in danger from amphetamines. The abuser may exhibit loss of appetite, dryness of mouth, nervousness, heavy perspiration, trembling, strange behavior, inability to sleep, and be very restless. The results of swallowing, inhaling or injecting LSD starts to affect the body within 30 minutes. Trips generally last from 8 to 10 hours. LSD acts mostly on the central nervous system and may result in symptoms such as: lowered temperature and increased blood sugar, chills and goose pimples, increased pulse rates, rapid heartbeats, nausea, and loss of appetite. The person may have the experience of having illusions, such as seeing sounds and tasting colors. One trip may lead the user to a long term of hospitalization, or death. When death results from LSD, an indirect cause may be one of the following—natural attitudes begin to disappear, common sense and normal judgment are no longer present, ability to tell when there is no danger no longer exists. Users of LSD have been killed because they believed they could fly, and tried to fly from some high place, or they believed they were invisible, and safe from oncoming cars.

It is no accident that some dope pushers turn out to be narcotic agents of the U.S. Government. If the Government really wanted to put an end to drug traffic, it could be done in a very short time. If the small class of rulers that run this country is making drugs available and fashionable, there is a hook in it somewhere; and it would not be hard to find, once we identify our lives with those of the oppressed people all over the world.

It is heart-breaking to know the conditions of drug victims, their families, and society. Signs of narcotics on some people are shown as the following: (1) marks on the arms and legs, (2) the use of odd-looking cigarettes, (3) spending time alone locked in rooms, (4) sudden loss of appetite and weight, (5), disappearance of belongings; etc., etc.

In one city alone, there were 500 young people who died in one year from the use of narcotics. Some cities have spent V2 million dollars for their yearly narcotics program. This means that one city estimated 25,000 addicts must raise from 500,000 to 700,000 dollars per day to support their habits. To pay the price, many turn to crimes such as shoplifting, forgery, burglary, and robbery. The active addict is not a potential useful citizen. He can be dangerous, demanding, and uncontrollable. He is a disturbed person with personality malfunctions that cause strange behavior. The teenage addict may be a quiet person who is quick to please. He usually has few friends; once drawn into narcotics he withdraws himself from Society. His grades begin to drop, and his habit makes him restless. He is frequently absent, moody and sensitive. The life of an addict is very, very dull. He lives from one fix to another. Police records contain many incidents involved in accidents in which some people said it. seemed like they were going slow, but in reality, they were going from 80 to 90 miles an hour. So, you can see for yourself that smoking pot is dangerous.

The drug user has a special language. The fear of detection is the reason. To identify the user, it goes something like this:

> Cocaine—known as coke, "C" or snow (usually
> found as white powder);
> Marijuana—known as pot, weed or reefer;
> Heroin—known as horse, or "H";
> Amphetamines—known as pep pills, bennies and
> co-piolets;
> Barbiturates—known as a goof ball, sleeping
> pills, yellow-jackets;
> Morphine—known as stuff or "M".

There are many excuses a person can give for experimenting with drugs. Drug abuse puts your body into a nervous and abnormal state. An overdose can cause convulsions and death due to paralysis of the respiratory center. An assembly man struggled for two days to get treatment for a narcotics addict desperately in need of dope. Finally, after making 75 phone calls to city, state, and private agencies and officials, he won a promise that the addict would be admitted to one of the state hospitals. He said it was a shock and disbelief that he found what insurmountable obstacles seemed to stand in the way of an addict seeking help—even with someone of his status behind him.

This drug addict had been a user for twelve years, with a fifty to seventy-five dollar a day heroin habit. He told him his wife and children had left him. The assemblyman told him he could get him help within half an hour, but it took a considerable amount of time. By helping this man, he also offered help to his neighbors. He was told it would take a month for his application to be processed, and there was an 18-month waiting list. He was introduced to heroin at 17, while serving the army in Korea. Since getting back to the States, he said, he had lied, cheated, and stolen.

They are putting up a new 41,000,000-dollar tomb. It costs the state $15,000 a year to keep prisoners in maximum security and $12.75 cents a day for inmates of a detention center. What cost can you put on a human life? We must help people!

The first state grant for in-school drug abuse programs has been awarded to the establishment for treatments of education and prevention programs. The grant of $181,000 is being awarded through the State Narcotics Control Commission, which is part of a 65,000,000-dollar program aimed at reducing drug abuse among the young people of America. The program staff will consist of a full-time director and two part-time consulting psychologists. In addition, 120 specially trained students will participate in the administration of the program. The program, for youngsters from grades 9 to 12, will deal with teenagers who are taking soft drugs as well as those on hard drugs. A basic thesis in the development of the program is that the formidable peer-group pressure on young people to use drugs is not being counted by any comparable peer group against drugs. The program which will be directed to more than 38,000 students in the twelve schools.

They should put a box in every school for students to turn in names of pupils on dope. I am sure you would get a lot of them turning in their own names. There are some students on dope who need help but don't want their parents to know, read some want to get advice and be cured without shame and letting the others know.

I believe people use their car wheels for dope. There is a man who is always jacking up his car, and the wheel tires are never changed. He never has a flat. Something is wrong!

A drug-addiction problem exists, regardless of what method of political pressure is used to take the ultimate extreme to stop dope. I don't believe dope would come into the country if we had stricter laws. Narcotics in the United States could not survive if we had cooperation from the cops, politicians, and the efforts of the Federal Bureau of investigation (FBI). How can the FBI be so successful in espionage activities and so unsuccessful in keeping narcotics from being smuggled into the country? Many types of approaches have been taken in the attempt to stop drug abuse among the younger generation. But as each day goes by, we hear of more and more incidents involving young people who are victims of drugs. This means that these programs and techniques are not serving their purpose as they should, for one reason or another.

I have taken a concerned look at this and made a few observations. Drug abuse should be one of the main concerns if the government and not something brushed off. The government should be involved more than they are. The young generation should be taught a better system about drugs than they have been taught already. Some people feel the government is not doing its part. Drug films are outdated and unreal. They should be more meaningful to the young generation of today. 15,000 drug addicts out of an estimated 200,000 in the U.S. are now being treated. You can get all the grants you want to, but if you don't cut off the supply of drugs, what good is the grant? More pressure should be put in pushers and smugglers instead of harassing the users. In many classrooms, students are confronted with impromptu periods of discussion headed by instructors who are pushing dope themselves. At home the same things happen with parents because some of them are pushing dope. Some of the parents as well as children have to be taught that dope is young people something very deep and destructive. We as young people should stand up for our rights and be counted!

I feel that this problem of dope could have been solved years ago. Why keep saying you are putting money in different programs when you should be spending some of the money to persecute the pushers? When my father was in the hospital for a kidney operation, there was a policeman in the same room with him. The policeman told my father that when he (the policeman) would find a dope addict and bring him to the stationhouse, as soon as he got out of the stationhouse he would see that same dope addict he had just locked up. Each time the policeman would bring a dope addict in, they would let him out again. This is disrupting the policeman's time, because he would be spending all of his time locking up the same dope addict all day. Actually, they are encouraging him to get more dope, because when they let him out all he is going to do is go buy more dope. They should keep him in jail, find out where he is getting all this dope, and treat him for it. They should make sure they find out who the pusher is. Each and every addict that has been caught, has a pusher behind him. That's why it is just as important to go for the pusher as it is to treat the user.

To the young generation: Don't let the pushers use you to satisfy their wants. The only thing they want is that five-letter word: money! As it says in the Bible in 1st Timothy 6:10 Kings James Version —"For the love of money is the root of all evil: which while some coveted after, they have erred from the faith, and pierced themselves through with many sorrows." 1st Timothy 6:9 Kings James Version —"But they that will be rich fall into temptation and a snare, and into many foolish and hurtful lusts, which drown men in destruction and perdition." Ecc. 4:13 Kings James Version —"Better is a poor and a wise child, than an old and foolish king who will no more be admonished."

The man who seeks money, regardless of how he gets it or uses it, the Bible calls a fool. The way dope is spreading among the young people, it is destroying some of them before they reach maturity, and some are left in bad shape. Can't you see that drugs are your enemies and that drugs are against you? I beg of you, if you are not on drugs, don't get on them, and if you are on them get off! Please!

These pushers are breaking one of the rules of the Ten Commandments. They are involved in murder. Please, Mr. Dope Pusher, turn to God. Please do not participate in destroying our great generation. To the public: We all should be concerned! While we watch TV, deciding what is best, the pusher is sending our young and old people to their eternal rest. Pastor.

Lord, I bow my head and bend my knees out of total praises to you. "Maxine, one of the women does drugs but I'm praying," his mom said. This situation with Cobb seeing other women has messed me up but the mess can be turned into success.

"We don't want Maxine's phony ways. We don't want Maxine, his mother said. There's your vote of confidence from the family." Making Cobb to miss church 2 days in a row would only make his heart grow fonder for the woman he's not seen in a few Sundays, I would think, his mother said. Meanwhile, she took 2 hour baths every other day to impress him hoping she would be complimented about her perfume-like smell. She really loved that man. "Un-huh, and what did he think of her?" asked the beauty stylist Aretha while doing her hair." Not much now," his mother said.

His women Maxine and Busy Bozzy tried to get Cobb to do a lot of things. Some he honestly did participate in but most things he didn't. I think he might have liked her around sometimes but he was in love with Sadaya enough to let Max go. And of course he did let Max go. Every other sin a person commits is outside of the body but the person who commits sexual sins, sins against his own body. God did not give us a spirit of fear but of love, power and self-control. Cobb's mother received a phone call from Maxine. Maxine admitted to drug use and she was afraid to go somewhere for help. Mrs. Jackson assured her that she was not the only person with a drug problem. She encouraged Maxine to seek help right away despite her fears.

Surprisingly, Mr. Austere's situation was similar. Sometimes Mr. Austere was brilliant and sometimes he spoke gibberish. His head was smashed with the basic elements of get drunk alcohol and his exuberances for any kind of drink were noted and noticed by his friends. The exhilarating luxury of a two hour bath was more than he could take so he ran out of Mr. Tubbles Bubble Bath. If I knew and could know what I knew then I'd know. I'm trying to know that I knew but it'd be like swimming the ocean to catch up; to do so. So now, I know what I know.

Sadly, Mr. Austere said "it would be too much work for me. I like the Christian life better. I'd be barren. I wouldn't be able to produce or perform, if I drank all of the alcohol people have given to me. Mr. Austere's barrenness was like barrenness to a land that is overwhelmed and overdone with drought. Parched. Still mumbling vociferously under his voice, he looked pale and thirsty. Some people are very selfish. They will only do a good deed if there is something in it for themselves. Of course, this something is usually money. A child can clearly touch someone's heart and play their heartstrings. A child can touch someone's heart with a few humble words. A child can touch someone's heart without even knowing it. All around the crevices of my mind, my sorrows grew deep. I've seen children and adults hurt because of the harmful effects of alcohol and drugs. This is why I brought this information to you with wise ears" the pastor said.

Maxine was known to do alcohol and drugs; a bad scene, in my opinion and Mr. Austere wasn't far behind her. He was making excuses every gulp of whiskey. He became quite loose, a choir member observed. He had already hit a least 5 notes the wrong way on the piano. One time he stood up and he said the piano needed tuning. Sadaya was inwardly praying Mr. Austere and for Maxine to stop boozing. Mr. Austere was a great musician despite his consumption of alcohol problem. He'd had good productive times before and Sadaya was convinced he'd have productive and successful times again. This time though, he messed up. Well lord, they messed up my solo. They made a mess of it; but the mess can be made a success. While Sadaya was secretly praying, in walked Busy Bozzy Scoggers, the Rock 'n Roll music legend, looking for Cobb. She hadn't seen him but he was supposed to come to the church later and meet Bozzy. If he said he would, then he will, Sadaya thought. I like him because he usually honors God by sticking to his word.

Sadaya had not realized that she'd caught Maxine's attention. Maxine felt she would never be his best girlfriend and eventually his only girlfriend again unless she privately turned into an actress without anyone knowing about it. Her smiles became bigger and wider. She was earnestly attached to the idea that she should fake it all of the way. Maxine thought "nothing is gonna stop me from getting to Cobb and stealing him away from her any which way I can, she quietly smiled to herself. Even if it means I have to visit his church a few times. Maxine caught a glimpse of Sadaya and Sadaya saw her too. They acted like they didn't see each other. Sadaya thought seeing Maxine is a dose of reality that I really didn't want. Sadaya knows that God has a beauty prescription He wants us to adorn ourselves and reflect both our inner and outer beauty. He wants us to include a gentle and quiet spirit. When you have peace and love inside of yourself, the outside world will find you attractive. They'll notice your beauty and your outward appearance, Sadaya, rise and shine! To get from one side of the hallway to the next both women had to pass each other. Maxine walked near to Sadaya and she stuck her foot out trying to trip Sadaya. Sadaya recovered from it fast. Maxine asked Sadaya what's the matter; couldn't hunt him down like I see you're doing? "I hate you, "Maxine said to Sadaya. "I'm not going to get into a retaliatory war of words with you. Good-bye and good riddance," Sadaya said. Sadaya glanced towards the door and it opened. Cobb caught a glimpse of Sadaya and he began to smile. His smile was cut short cause about 5 seconds later he saw Maxine. After his smile quickly disappeared he left almost as quickly as he came in. What was Maxine thinking and how did she feel? She was thinking about Sadaya and how many ways she could hurt her. "Shall I break her fingers? What an entertaining thought Maxine pondered. I won't worry about Cobb. I believe I can get him to be with me again. He's my real live fantasy man. My bed linen has circles and polka dots on it. I'd like to get in bed with him and I could pretend to cry-first with little whimpers and then louder noises. I'd leap into the bathroom, Maxine thought and put my hands under the faucet on the sink. Splish splash," she thought "Oh boy am I going to be convincing. Sometimes a person can take action and cause silly reactions to happen in another person, be they friend or foe. I'll cause him to turn around and love me again. Maxine said, "I festered on my own lies and I have deceived Cobb before she imagines. His lips quivered during the first sentence where he would tell her he still loved her. He told Maxine that he would leave Sadaya alone and come back to her. In her fantasies alone this happened. In reality Cobb had grown tired of Maxine. He preferred Sadaya. Maybe you should take more time and spend more time in deeper reflection he said. I don't want to lose you, she called and told him on the phone. She was planning a Black History and Latino History Celebration but she couldn't concentrate well. Too much thinking about Cobb. I can't believe it. It's like Cobb got me climbing up a mountain of broken glasses, again with no shoes on.

Cobb was thinking about some of the women he knew including Maxine. Geez, as he climbed into the limousine, "I almost started liking her again," Cobb thought. I can't tell anyone that unless I apologize to her for the emotional turmoil I put her through. It's ok to be yourself, act like yourself, respect yourself think for yourself. If it's completely ignorant, keep it to yourself.

Meanwhile Sadaya heard a fantastic sermon but she didn't call to tell him about it because they were still in disagreement about whether to get counseling or not. It's understandable. We have more power with God. Sadaya admitted that right now, she is nauseated by Cobb's inhumanity towards her desire to have therapy with him. They've had 2 serious arguments. On one phone call Sadaya found herself almost cussing at Cobb. She had to put her hands over her mouth to stop herself. "Someday when I get married, I'm going to marry the right man in a restaurant called Trusting God Restaurant. My wedding will be in New York. My future husband is going to be frisky for me and jovial too. Of course he'll be in love with me. He'll say it and I'll know it because of how he says it," Sadaya said. Cobb was in 'one of his moods' and Sadaya felt that counseling would be good for him. Of course he wouldn't budge on the subject. The only thing he entertained was pastoral counseling.

Cobb and his friends visited neighborhood bar. In her thinking, Sheila was still negative. She didn't trust anyone around her, especially when it came to Michael, Cobb's friend. She loved him but she didn't like him. Cobb convinced him to get pastoral counseling soon.

Michael was jealous of Sheila. He picked up a bottle and he threatened her with it. He said if she didn't leave those men alone he would sue her but right now, this bottle will do 'against you,' Michael said. Then Michael turned to his left and he looked at his brother Sam and Michael's friend Eddie. "I don't' want no trouble, man. You get too angry too soon for me and . . . "before he could finish the sentence Eddie felt the bottle. It hit Eddie fast, opening Eddie's skull. Cobb turned to get his phone to call the emergency ambulance and a bottle hit him too but it only grazed him on the arm. He looked again and the bottle broke after being heavily thrown on the floor. Eddie looked seriously hurt. He was crying like a baby when the back of his head hit the floor. Then he became unconscious; after he fell; unconscious from the bottle and hitting the floor. "There's bound to be brain damage somewhere, as big as the bottle was. This has got to be a bad dream. This is torment." His Cousin Vivvie said, "Everybody quiet down. Did anyone call the hospital? Those of you with cell phones please call now. Right away. She glanced at Cobb. She was glad he wasn't' hurt." Cobb can fight too along with basketball. Don't mess with Cobb no no no! Vivvie said, Cobb punched Michael and he restrained Michael well.

I hated to punch him because Michael and I are friends but right is right and wrong is wrong. Cobb said a prayer and told God that he had taken up boxing as a course in school and "it did me some good today," he said. He thanked God for there not being a broken bone in his body. He thanked God for his success: "I live and breathe what I believe. If I see it I can achieve it, if I choose to. "This time Lord God, I chose to bop him before he bopped me. I believe you taught me to refuse to lose. Michael, the guy I hit got right up but he caught a right to the jaw and another jab to the jaw. He retained the championship of the I Gotcha in a Fight Movement but I finished what he started. "I knocked the black off of him," Cobb said. "Cobb's probably too fast for you on his feet and his jabs are oh so sweet", Vivvie said. All we need was a referee. Oh yeah, we gotta help Eddie, his friend too," Sheila said. "Help Eddie. I'll help him. I'll help him up from the floor. Thats the best I can do," Cobb said. After helping Eddie up Cobb left to avoid any more confrontation and to hide from the press. He thought about Maxi and he decided to visit her.

Maxine was convincing. Cobb, I think I'm starting to notice it. There is a change and the change is in you. A wonderful change has happened for sure. Maxine said "God has treated you well. I hear you've been going to church. "Me too, believe it or not. I believe God will bless me and save me. I'm humble and determined not to stumble any more Cobb. Everybody I know now are believers of God. They're so nice to me, my church members. They make me want to work for God no matter what happens to me. It's similar to feeling a stuffed animal. It gives you warm fuzzy feelings all over. I was looking in the church for someone new; Maxi said when I met a brother at the church. You know he didn't mind walking me home. Well, never mind about his name. I have to beat the next woman at trying to get to his affections, Maxine said. I'm tired of men that have unlimited appetites for women besides me. Well anyway, time was going by fast and Maxine didn't appear to be joking. She said she trained herself to block out all distractions and to relax. "I reassured myself that another compatible man would come along. He did and I like him a lot," Maxine said. "He's taking me out this Saturday. He's an airline pilot. Well, call me sometimes anyway," Cobb said. Let me give you a word of caution. Respect yourself enough to know what you want and to make realistic goals for yourself. Understand your woman. Treasure her. I've seen a lot of cases, heard about a lot of lovers and loves but this situation has affected me more than any other situation. I never thought I'd suffer so much. I almost bleed to the touch, that's how raw I feel, Maxi said sadly. Keep working at the church. It will continue to improve your attitude. My cab is here. "Goodbye." Cobb waved and they both left in different vehicles.

Sadaya went home. She felt emotionally burdened. She couldn't wait to get down on her knees and to talk to God. Her mother opened the door looked in and closed it again. "Where's Sadaya," her father asked. She's bending her knees again crying out to the lord. I've been to many places. I even walked 1,000 steps up the shrine of St. Joseph's. I now bend my knees in my living room on my rug. You bend your knees your way and I'll bend my knees my way, Sadaya told her mother. Tonight, this bedroom will do. I feel compelled to pray, she said.

Her mother whispered to her father: "There's something special about Sadaya although she does not always see this in herself. While she was still in her bedroom Sadaya admired her facial reflection in the mirror. I will pray for myself. Her two long braids were tribal and beautiful. Being sensuous matters to me, although I'd have to work hard to be motivated in front of Cobb. I recognize it is essential to keep myself in prayer, she was thinking. The Sexton told Cobb that praying every day wipes away the day's depressions and sometimes tears are wiped away too; after a while. I decided to slow down and become celibate. God tolerated me making many mistakes, now it's all about Him. Just making sure I'm protected by Him and benefitting from His plan for my life. Maybe I'll start calling Cobb but I must get over my anger at him. He who cease from anger is blessed.

Cobb said he was fed up with Sadaya and him arguing. He called his best friend Stan. He explained that Sadaya as a strong black woman met he as a strong black man in a place called church. The women, the men and the children are all usually so nice you can marvel at the place. There's no doubt in my mind that the Spirit of God led me to Black Memorial Baptist Church to begin my spiritual advancement there and to meet and love Sadaya. The deacons and deaconess, missionaries, the choirs and making donations all have a prominent role in this story. They believe in empowering people with necessary church tools to equip their sophisticated minds. They taught me to brighten my holiday, smile and shine. I've only recently rediscovered my smiles thanks to the church. Although Sadaya is an adult like me I find her harder to talk to than I originally thought, especially about therapy and mental health issues. I've fallen for her though and I know it. It won't take much time before we're talking again. We're actually talking now but it's kind of strained. "Brother, I'm putting these little arguments in prayer right now. I believe God and good old male / female magnetism will keep you two together and tight, you will be. Say you believe it, Cobb," his friend Stan said. I believe you Stan, Cobb said. I need to speak to you every day, man. Thanks a lot. What are you doing Saturday? I'm going to the fight. A boxing match. Zipper Memphis is fighting Buckner Johns. "I'm going too. I'll see you there," Cobb said.

I like boxing matches a lot but sometimes the audience is rough. Some men and women who are corrupt in their morals pervade the city streets seeking whom they can devour and destroy just like their God. It's hard to do the right thing when you don't know what the right thing to do is and you mix your inner consciousness with people who are evil. You've got to be strong in the face of evil people lest they confuse you and make you weak inside. By the way I called Sadaya and I invited her to sit down and talk. I haven't heard from her. I was taking you to the fight but you've got a ticket already. 'Let me talk to Sadaya for you. Give me her phone number. Please give her phone number to me right now. I'll call you and tell you everything. You know that man," Stan said.

Stan called Sadaya and he convinced her to go to the boxing match with Cobb Saturday. Cobb told Stan he'd like to take Sadaya to dinner before the boxing match starts. They did go and all went well. The boxing match was exciting and Sadaya's fighter won which made Cobb laugh. He admired how she looked. She looked like I imagine the Queen of Sheba looked: beautiful, lovely and elegant. She wore fashions by Heidi Jay. She was fabulously adorned in an ivory colored 3 piece georgette diamond – laden outfit that everyone wondered if the diamonds were real or not. People weren't sure but Sadaya was thankful that she had a limousine to go home in that night. It's amazing what one kiss can do. For a long time Cobb didn't tell her he really missed her during the month and a half they did not speak and were estranged. The weirdest things happened.

Cobb explained that he, in the back of his limousine missed her and he kissed her. His body writhed against her body and the two felt like one flesh even though their clothes were still on.

It had been a wicked day and worse than that, it was hot in the limousine. This made it feel like her skin was crawling. Cobb's phone rang and it startled Sadaya. "Things will be looking up soon for this couple, she told herself. I can't stay out too long tonight. I'm singing for the 11:00 am service tomorrow," she said. What happened to Stan Jensen? I thought I saw him but he never spoke. He kept walking and I didn't see where he went but he was what I call vanished for the whole fight. Sadaya said. "I want you," to Cobb while still in the back of the limousine. She blinked a bewildered look in her brown eyes. Oh he felt, have sex but he didn't dare. She looked up and remembered they were in the car. Her inner lust burning her up with a desire that would not make a low flame chill but rise. He moved and scaled her fingers up and down the nape of her neck and his. He took deep breaths as he massaged her. What a big beautiful handsome man this is I've been missing. His touching me feels good, she thought looking at his eyes again. They glared through their sockets with clear radiance and love. They exchanged sensuous gazes and laughed. She was and remained decently dressed.

Looking at Cobb again, smiling. A thump on the back door startled them. It was the police. They said they were checking all limousines in the area and they were sorry for the disturbance. The robber they were looking for was described as Caucasian but he was seen in a limousine with two African-American friends. The police officer asked for Cobb's autograph, which he did give to him. He then looked at Cobb and Sadaya and complimented them on what a handsome couple they made. After that, he left. No tickets issued to Cobb, Sadaya or the Chauffeur. The Chauffeur spoke to Cobb through the back seat microphones. He said, "Phew that was anxiety provoking. Thank God that's over." Cobb looked through the black glass and he rolled the glass window up. He knew they would be ok when the police officer asked him for an autograph which he happily gave the man. "I'm glad that's over, too" Cobb said. I was looking for someone warm and cuddly to kiss and the police showed up. Some men experience lust, not love. Which one was I experiencing? Cobb wondered. I guess I'll find out in time. Right now honestly it feels like love. I can't even tell her so I'll just keep it to myself. Thank God we had no trouble from the police or anybody else. I'm satisfied this was a night to remember, but is almost over. "Would you like to get something to eat?" Cobb asked Sadaya. No thanks you. Remember I have to sing for the Sunday morning service tomorrow. I have to get home early tonight, said Sadaya. Cobb massaged his moustache. "I want to be able to snuggle, wuggle and cuddle up is what I feel now but I'll entertain your wishes and take you home early tonight. Sadaya I enjoyed being with you tonight. Let's do it again sometime soon," he said. "You have such a unique way of saying my name," she observed. The sound of my name on his lips was like a lighting thunder strike. I'm starting to love him a lot, Sadaya thought, meditatively. Sadaya Ruby Day, teacher of 6th grade mathematics and social studies asked herself could I actually tell him what I'm really thinking and feeling? Cobb had to admit he was feeling strong magnetism for Sadaya. Sadaya is a born again Christian determined to lead an obedient and Godly life. She goes to choir practice and bible study during the week and church service on Sunday morning. When Cobb Jackson volunteers to work in the church in his heart he knows Sadaya is his pick for a wife but he does not dare to tell anyone. Sadaya thought of Cynthia's boyfriend and how handsome and intelligent he was. He, though deceased, was the love of her life. They as a couple reminded her of King Solomon and the Queen of Sheba. She would have liked to have attended a boxing match like this, Sadaya was thinking. Every time he smiled, my heart went a flutter. When Solomon saw Sheba he was taken aback. Sometimes God's people get lonely. Don't God's people get lonely too? The woman: I am my beloved's and his desire is for me. Come my beloved let us go forth in the fields and lodge in the villages . . ." Sadaya would like to have done this with Cobb.

The women blow me kisses all of the time. Some of them dare me to take my shirt off and go shirtless, Cobb said. Some are lonely. When the lights were low and the guys and dolls wanted intimacy they used to inspire people with honk tonk songs. "Honey, honey it's the money, if you want to get along with me." And a good time was had by all, and the announcer would turn the lights on and off as a hint that it was time to go home. Sadaya Ruby Day's grandmother and her mother used to joke about the fact that if a man didn't have any money to show her off what was he hanging around for? He got to have a little money to show a woman a good time and to maybe see her again sometime in the near future. Whether a woman was a Christian or not, if she knew her way around, she would save her money and she would spend his money until he didn't have any if he let her. Sadaya fellow church member was at the table in the church bragging about how she spent her man's money down to his last dime and he let her do it. What a world. What a world, Cobb Jackson made a significant amount of money; approximately 10 million dollars a year. He'd been with the League 7 years and he just renewed his contract for another 3 years. He had 3 homes which were investment properties in upstate, New York. He also had 3 car dealerships, 2 restaurant chains, 3 car wash business, 2 bookstore chains, 1 broadcast television center and a lot of cash. Cobb Jackson, world traveled man was in a joking mood: 'if you were married to me I'd poison your drink. If you were married to me I'd drink it, he said. Ha ha ha . . . I got you on that joke. One more joke, one more joke please. My fiancée asked me "what cha doing today?" Nothing. You did that yesterday and the day before that. "Well, I wasn't finished," he said. I was giving my husband the silent treatment is true we're getting along better. Let's extend this for the next 20 years he said. Heh heh heh. I was just checking to see where your guy's sense of humor is. I hope you like my jokes. See you later. My game arm is a little sore tonight. See you at the next year's event. Bye and I'll have some new jokes by then. Cobb Jackson came back to the table where Sadaya was waiting for him. She was still laughing at his jokes, though. "Boy were they funny." She thought. The Red Brigade Dinner was something to see. Sadaya thought to herself, this guy's so rich he picked me up in a limousine.

He was picked up in a separate limousine. I'm feeling like I'm Cinderella arriving in a stagecoach. Every time he looks at me I wilt almost. I can't wait until we dance together. Cobb looked at Sadaya and he tenderly reached; touching her hand he said, "May I have this dance?"She said, "Of course my darling," sporting a big smile as they walked to the dance floor. The slow music was sophisticated and smooth, from the 1950's jazz revival time, mixed with percussion.

Neo classicist, Cobb quickly took Sadaya by her waist and he glided across the floor. Sadaya was mesmerized by Cobb. She felt his muscles in his strong arms as he held her waist. He then changed his posture and pulled her close to him; very close to him. Sadaya felt warm. "Hot was more like it," she thought. Oh my gosh he smells good and his muscles make me feel o so strong. Cobb put his right leg between her two legs and he superbly danced. "Wow," she thought. There were 2 slow songs. Cobb and Sadaya stayed for both songs. They danced to both songs and he kissed Sadaya on the dance floor. His kiss was moist. The kiss was exquisite. She felt she was falling in love with Cobb.

What a handsome couple Sadaya and Cobb made. She shimmered and she shined with her all over sequins evening gown. The fit looked flawless and flattering on Sadaya. Her hairstyle was changed to straighter than straight, all American girl style. She looked heavenly and Cobb did too in his full length tuxedo with white tie. A wonderful time was had by Sadaya. When they got back to their table, the whole table was clapping. They were clapping at the dance floor kiss. Oh my gosh Cobb is sweeping me off of my feet and I love it. The couple looked so well polished totally comfortable taking love to a whole new level. Sadaya sat down next to Cobb and she then excused herself to go to the powder room. As she was on her way to the powder room, an older woman who looked like she was about 70 years old complimented Sadaya. She said, I love your dress and your face is so beautiful. How lovely you are my dear. Sadaya thanked the woman and continued her walk to the powder room. Perfumes, colognes and facial wipes and deodorants were for sale in the powder room but Sadaya didn't need any of those items. She came with her own arsenal and supply. After she powdered her face and relieved herself Sadaya returned to their table number 3. She decided to ask Cobb to go to the movies with her. Someone handed her literature on choking because she had been choking herself. Cobb leg touched hers under the table as she read abut how to help someone who is choking.

<u>Choking</u>

Ask are you choking?
Call 911 it person can't speak or breathe
Person Is Awake
Make a fist
Place it above the person's belly button,
Well below the rib cage.
Pull sharply inward and upward
Continue until the food comes out or the
Person can breathe
Persons stops responding
Open the mouth. If food is there,
Take it out. If food is not visible,
Tilt the person's head back.
Pinch the person's nose. Place your mouth
Over the person's mouth and give two
Breaths.
Push hard repeatedly in chest
Center for 20 seconds. Check breathing
Repeat from start.

Sadaya thought this literature would be useful on her job. She intends to give a copy of this choking advice to her principal.

Babe, I have somewhere I want you to take me. "Where that?" Cobb asked. I want us to go to the movies this Saturday coming up. "I don't have a problem with taking you to the movies Cobb said. I only have one condition! You must kiss me every 10 minutes we're at the movies on Saturday. Then you must come home with me and make dinner." Cobb said. "Agreed. You've got a date," Sadaya responded. Which one are we going to, the movies theater near the water.

O.k. that sounds romantic said Sadaya. It's very quiet in the one by the water it's so quiet you can hear a lung collapse and a heart miss a beat. That's what going to happen if you don't shut up. Nowadays movies are so expensive and so are the food treats that go along with the movie. Cobb said, 'I think I can handle it. Both Cobb and Sadaya laughed. As they sat next to each other, Cobb rubbed his leg against her leg under the table. Cobb was thinking, this could be it. "This could be love. God please let me know if Sadaya is going to be my wife," Cobb thought. "Oh my goodness, Cobb you are and feel fascinating and you're making me purr like a kitten with all of that under the table action. Not long after making the kitten comment, the M.C. called for Cobb to be introduced. While Cobb was speaking to the audience, Sadaya thought, Oh Lord. This man. He's going to want to make love to me. She felt the love rising up. She felt the love rise up within her as she entertained those secrets of her mind. Meanwhile, Cobb gave a powerful performance when he spoke to the audience. He came back to the table and the people gave him a standing ovation. What a rousing applause he received for his comments. His comments were attention getting and compassionate. The Governor of our State was the last speaker. "It was a beautiful dinner," Sadaya told Cobb as they drove back home. They drove 2 hours back to Sadaya's house. By then there was a drowsy Sadaya sitting in the limousine, tired and sleepy from the drive and the events of the day. "Tired from the drive," she said.

Sadaya's sleep was disturbed. Her friend Cynthia called to discuss drugs. I don't breathe or inhale that junk; that stuff. Whether it be marijuana or any other drugs that are street drugs. There's a junk dope ban that should go into effect now. The smart students are staying away from the junk. They're finding places for theirs and others entertainment. They're getting into their classrooms and earning their degrees with more than C's. We need to talk but we hate to talk, the policeman says. We've doing a little better because we were able to catch some of the criminals and to satisfy the public. That's what one policeman said but the other one said, "I don't get it. Why do we have to ruin it by talking?" drugs are more of a dangerous business than some people think. It causes many societal dangers too. For instance, there was a group of young men that smoke marijuana. They then broke into a man's house, yelled at him, tied him up, made him say things he didn't want to say, sign things he didn't want to sign, made him drink toilet water and wouldn't let him eat or use the toilet the right way. Not long thereafter the same group of young men went outside and blocks away made whistling and cat calls at Sadaya and the rest of the choir. Big sighs of relief were heard up and down the block when Mr. King the minibus driver drove up in front of the church with the mini bus. "Man oh man were those men fresh," he said. Phew. Glad those junkies, drug addicts and whatever they were on are gone. People ought to think. If a person gets mad with you try to avoid arguments because arguments can lead to fights. Change the subject or topic of conversation if you can. You are greater in God's eyesight. I think it is ashame what is happening in the world today. Instead of doing harm to someone people should stop and think.

If you were that person would you want that sort of thing done to you? Instead of doing wrong things to people, try to help someone. Jeremiah 11:29 Kings James Version tells us that God wants what is good for us. God wants what is good for you. Hugs, smiles, grins, more hugs. God wants us to have these positive feelings about ourselves and others. Smiles and grins, more hugs and love are Christian – like behaviors. Leaning one to another, holding each other sometimes, holding hands and spreading glee and tolerance are all a part of being friends. Spirits of forgiveness and joy are what it takes to have successful relationships. The choir refused to call the men that broke into the house losers. Why? Simply put, we hesitate to call someone a loser because at any time in their lifetime, God can come along and make that person an outstanding and dynamic believer. In this sense, there is no such thing as a loser as most people would want God to come along and touch their lives. God can find anyone at any time and take them from "losership" to His "sponsorship." Some of the previous paragraphs were prepared by the pastorals department of the Black Memorial Baptist Church, and friends.

Cobb Jackson, the superstar basketball player has 2 job openings. He's looking for an in-house cook and an on-the grounds chauffeur. Cobb believes in paying his staff every 2 weeks. She is pregnant and she can't wait any longer. She's in her 8th month of her pregnancy. The current cook will be moving to "down south" before Christmas. Her husband will be moving with her to "down south."

Cobb Jackson doesn't like too many people in his business but he did let them know about the job openings. He arranged with the press to take anybody who is interested phone number or text number and other numbers and to give their information directly to him, Cobb Jackson. By the way, Cobb Jackson was well-dressed when he went to one of the channels for the interview about the job opening. He wore a S. Henson suede suit with S. Henson hat for his medium sized head. He had on a black velvet overcoat with black leather travel all's and he had on tot's all leather belt. He also had on men's all man perfume. He looked and smelled spiffy.

Cobb's phone rang and it was Sadaya. "Hello there, you wonderful hunk of my man. How ya' doing. What's up? I'm calling to say I love you. There. I said it. Smooches smooches and more smooches to you."Cobb started laughing. she said, "but seriously, I want you to know that I prayed had for you last night and God let me know that He is going to answer every one of my prayers, and that I must learn to Wait on God. A watched pot never boils. God let me know that too. My belly ached because of nervous tension. Sometimes I have to have a cup of tea to settle my stomach in immense proportions." "I had to fight back. I told one woman your shoes are too narrow your breasts too high and too big you got too much on and you've had too much lip surgery. You're just too zany" I told her.

You can imagine my surprise when I found out she really wasn't a woman at all. You need to tell that story. Go tell it on the mountain, girl. I know a lot of men who felt vengeful about situations like that. One man said, if I didn't think I'd have to do time for it. I'd chop your head clean off with these 20 inch scissor shears.

Cobb said, "Anyhow, this is not an area of my expertise." I got love on my mind tonight, baby what time can I pick you up and take you for a rider? Cobb asked. "I have a big presentation tomorrow at my job so I have to be in by at least between midnight and twelve-thirty. O.k. I'll pick you up by about 4:00 p.m. today, at your mother and father's house," Cobb said. "Beautiful. See you then," Sadaya said.

Colossians 3:8 Kings James Version but now yourselves are to put off all these: anger, wrath, malice, blasphemy, filthy language out of your mouth. It has been said that we process about 10,000 thoughts a day. Sadaya had on warm fashions of the cozy and chic genre. She sported her black wool jacket with wool pants and her high heel boots. Red color. Red bag to match her boots. I can do all things through Christ who strengthens me. Sadaya wore her high high heels today.

Barkie, the new little puppy dog that Cobb bought recently just barked. The doorbell rang. Barkie who was a friendly little puppy at his age, ran to the door and growled, mixed with barking. There was a loud noise at the door where Cobb was trying to get inside of his own house and he couldn't find his keys to the house. After speaking to Sadaya on the telephone and picking her up by 4:00 p.m. Cobb had left his house keys in his bedroom on the bed. "Luckily I still have a cook and a chauffeur who can let us into the house," said Cobb. Sadaya said hello to everyone including Cobb's mother and father. Whatever the cook was cooking smelled up the whole kitchen. Sadaya said, "It smells delightful in here. I'm really hungry today. When is dinner served?" Sadaya asked. The cook said, "Dinner is served in about 15 minutes." "Oh great," she said. We'll be having fettuccini; shrimp fettuccini alfredo, au beaute de broccoli and champagne du blaise or champagne du Apple Cider.

Cobb mother was outside in the backyard picking flowers; especially roses. His father was yelling at her telling her it's time to eat dinner.

Cobb Jackson's parents genuinely liked his girl "friends" and they were careful to tell him who they didn't like. They didn't like his girlfriend Maxine but they told him if he chooses someone they'd abide by his decision. "He's the one who has to live with the person; not "us," his father said.

Mr. and Mrs. Jackson were happy to see Cobb and Sadaya; especially Sadaya. They hadn't seen her in about 7 months, they told her and they wondered what kept her away from them for so long. Sadaya didn't tell Cobb but she bought each of his parent's gifts. The elder-couple received male perfume for him and female perfume for her. They loved them because there was lotion and body wash for both parents. Barkie got a boily-wood collar with rhinestone diamonds in it and Cobb got a big kiss chocolate candy unit. "Oh my dear, I love you. I think you're good for our Cobbie our son," his mother said. "Mom, dad, later on I'm going to take Sadaya for a drive and show her the lights and decorations in town,"

Cobb said. Thank you very much Mr. and Mrs. Jackson. I enjoyed dinner tremendously tonight. I was so hungry; I could hardly wait tonight for some reason. I don't know why, said Sadaya. "Don't get fat," Cobb said. Sadaya said nothing, Cobb said, "Wait until you see the lights and Christmas decorations in town. You're going to scream because the display is so bright and lovely, watch," Cobb said. As they approached the little town all of the homes were lit up like Christmas trees and tinsel was thrown everywhere. Tinsel all over the Christmas and evergreen trees was beautiful in the tinsel colors red, green, silver and gold.

There were also tingle ropes wrapped around the gates and fences of every house for an as far as you can see radius. There were stuffed decorations of Rudolph the red-nosed reindeer, Santa Claus, Mr. Snowman and little children everywhere too. What a sight to feast my eyes to see. I love these displays.

"What would you say if I told you I want to bring my 6th graders out here on a field trip?" Sadaya asked Cobb. I think they would like walking from house to house and looking at the puppets, the waterfalls, the ballerinas dancing at various houses and so much more. At one house they were giving out free popcorn. My kids would love this. I have to call the principal and see if I can arrange it for next week or the week after next. This is so important for the children's social values and moral values. I notice some of the houses have sayings printed on plasterboard, wood, cardboard and pegboard. This is so important, Sadaya said pleasantly surprised by the hugeness and the beauty of the display. When I get to work tomorrow I'm going to get to work on this right away. The children in my class have been hustling and begging me for a trip. This will be it. They are going to be so happy, Sadaya said, smiling. After I bring them to see this, we'll go to see the movies, she said. "Glad I didn't have to talk you into in," said Cobb who had been quiet for about the last 10 minutes. "I think I'll make a big 5 gallon container of fruit punch so everyone can have some before getting off of the bus. My kids are usually pretty neat. They won't spill the fruit punch on the seats. If I'm in an extra good mood I'll bake some chocolate chip cookies for them to have on the bus too" said Miss. Day.

From now on, the chauffeur said "I'm smart I'm going straight, not crooked. I said straight." The money was locked into a special desk safe. The amount was $450,000 which Cobb was going to possibly invest in a school and for insurance expenditures. 'Flippy' nickname for the Chauffeur overheard Cobb talking to his parents about the money. Flippy Johns was tempted: After all, this was not just 10 or 20,000 dollars. This is hundreds of thousands of dollars; very little though, compared to Cobb Jackson's usual salary. That's a lot of money for me Flippy Johns thought. He stood by the special desk safe for about 10 minutes negotiating with himself. "Either I will or I won't steal that money, dadgummit. I knew he had a lot of money around because he kept subconsciously touching his pockets Cobb did," the Chauffeur noticed. There was the night we went to that $1000 a plate Red Baron Dinner. As it turned out, the chauffeur did the right thing. He left the money right where he knew Cobb Jackson had put it "I said straight," he said. He meant every word of it. Thanks to him, Cobb was able to have $450,000 to do business with and not call the police. Timothy 6:10: Kings James Version for the love at money is the rest of all evil. While coveting after money, some have strayed from the faith and pierced themselves through with many sorrows.

Sadaya is really a special kind of woman because she doesn't jump into bed with every man she meets. She was overweight but shapely. She loved one man deeply and that one man is the inimitable Cobb Jackson. Whether he knows it or not is of no concern to her. The most important thing is her heart goes a flutter whenever she sees him. The important point is that the love that Sadaya feels for Cobb is everlasting and overflowing. The evidence of her love reveals itself in the fact that she doesn't mind doing things for him. She has done many things for him such as typed up address books on his computer, typed up a manuscript on the computer, cooked for an in numerable amount of times, played secretary and gotten him out of appointments and ran interference for him when there were other women trying to get closer to him. She has bought him expensive gifts. Bought clothing. Don't miss the next thrill; impressed Cobb. The next thrill involves body massages. Packed into her creative package of gifts. Yes, Sadaya loves Cobb but how does Cobb feel about her? Someone once said, 'the only person that Cobb really loves is Cobb. This was true. Cobb used to be in competition with the women he dated. Now that he's been dating Sadaya, her name is in every conversation. Sadaya wants to do this and my girl Sadaya would love to see this. There are not many things she shouldn't see or partake in. Had it been some women, he would have been avoiding them but not Sadaya. Sadaya is special to him. She seeks his advice. She even sings to him sometimes. She writes songs for him and sometimes for her 6th grade class. They each knew about each other. Yes, Cobb knew about her 6th grade class and her 6th grade class knew about Cobb. During Library Media Day Cobb was a huge success because he was the superstar basketball player. He was nice and answered Sadaya's invitation to come to the school. Nothing too complicated. Sadaya knew that sometimes Cobb was temperamental but she overlooked this flaw and she just hurried herself and him off of the telephone, when he got to be too hard to handle. It was very rare for him to accomplish the ridiculous and yell at Sadaya. One time he slipped and he then ended up laughing at himself. So did she laugh at him.

When I see a woman throwing herself at a man I wonder where herself – esteem is. I blame the man too because there comes a point in the relationship when the man is suppose to take over the relationship. He's supposed to say ok on such and such a time I will. I will be at such and such a place. I want you to meet me there or I'd like to meet you and take you out. He's supposed to do little and big things to let her know and to give her hints that he is interested in her and wants to take the relationship further.

Other than that he's just whimsical. When he goes to work and he earns money he is supposed to save money to take the woman/women that he is dating out to show her a nice loving time. There are many women especially in America who feel that way. There is a minority of woman who feel that the woman should be the boss of the relationship and that they should tell the man everything he is to do. Suit yourself. Cobb's mother gets credit for the above comments and sentiments.

Sadaya Ruby Day never liked smoking. She always felt it was a very nasty habit. Whenever she attempted putting a cigarette into her mouth, she would gag also, the smoke would clog her windpipes and esophagus and she'd choke and lots of water would come out of her eyes. "It was never meant for me to smoke. That's all there is to it" she said. She never did like people smoking around her. She still gagged from the smoke. Cobb. Sadaya wondered if he smoked or not. "Being an Athlete I would imagine not. All of the exercises he is required to do would be for nothing, I would imagine." Plus, Cobb is a natural musician. He plays saxophone, trumpet, piano and some other instruments she couldn't remember. Some of the instruments required him to use a lot of wind and effected his breathing. "I doubt he would smoke," she thought. "I also doubted if he would tell me if he did smoke" she said. Sadaya laughed to herself and thought"he'd probably say that's none of your business, lady. Mind your own business. Now there's an original idea," she thought and then she smiled to herself. She wondered if she was bold enough to ask him if he smoked and have a discussion. It is a very nasty habit, she felt and often said so.

Today, Sadaya felt extra special. The weather was sunny and the temperature was about 40 degrees with little wind drifts. She put on a pretty floral skirt set with a squared circle neckline. She usually had been wearing her long hair up but today she chose to wear her beautiful hair long and flowing. The skirt set revealed her attractive legs in panty hose. Cobb had told Sadaya that he loved her pretty eyes. She felt especially frisky today. He liked touching her attractive and pretty hands. With Sadaya "Cobb wasn't commitment-phobic, being of sound mind," Sadaya thought. To bring packed stadiums to their feet and then to come home; to make arrangements to see me was such a wonderful feeling. Just thinking about it made Sadaya hot and she didn't mind dressing up for him. "Bring him back. Bring him back. Bring him back," the students in her 6th grade class shouted one day after they asked how he was doing and did she ever see him again. She confessed to her students that she had been dating him. Cobb told Sadaya he couldn't come back any time soon. He told her he'd call them and she thought that was just great. Three days later, he called Ms. Day's class and he put another ball player on along with himself. The class went wild. The other basketball player's name was Super Wild Wayne Rogers. Super Wild was one of Cobb's best friends too but they hardly saw one another. Super Wild Wayne had gotten married and he and his wife Sandra become homebodies, except for when he was required to travel with the team. He was rumored to be trying out for the U.S. Skiing Team as well. "Knowledge is power and the Bible says my people perish for lack of knowledge," Sadaya said. I think I'm going to have each member of my class do research on each member of the team The Boxers. Anything they can find out; I want them to do a book report format. "Reporting back for the class isn't a bad idea," Sadaya thought. "We'll all learn something and never perish from lack of knowledge," she told the 6th grade class. Get all the information you can get. Yes, even find out how much money they make, if you can. Also find out how they feel about their sport having more women. Asking intelligent questions is important. Tell your parents and/or your guardians who in the Sports World you will be interviewing and tell what their opinion is about your interviewee. Some of the interviews were rare as stated before, but the one who was more excited than anyone was Sadaya. She told the kids the day they do their oral reports, she was throwing them a party. A big party.

A party with fried chicken, lasagna, salad and green peas would be served. She asked for 4 people to volunteer to help her to serve the food too. The whole class raised their hands. Sadaya was delighted. They had to put their names on strips of paper and Ms. Day put the strips of paper into a hat. Shelton picked people to pull out 4 strips of paper one at a time. These people she explained would be called hosts. They would say good night everybody. I hope you had a great time. See you at the next party, whenever that's going to be. Ms. Sadaya Day also was planning to bring a big Good Luck cake for everyone. "It would be delicious," Ms. Day said, "I want everyone to be on their best behavior. I'm also planning to invite Cobb Jackson back to our class for the party and we'll see if he can bring any friends with him. This is my 6th grade class. What they want, they get from me. They've been excellent in terms of their department and they have respected me now for a long time. They deserve to have a party. A Good Luck party.

Sadaya's Cobb the one who she said "He's fine and he's all mine." Well, he did show up for the Good Luck Party.

Sadaya did as promised fried chicken, peas, lasagna, salad and more peas. The cake she said she'd bring was so big each child was able to bring a nice big slice home to their parents. She even had a disc jockey. They were able to give the principal of the school some food slices to take home too. There were people trying to get in to the party but Sadaya kept it only for her class and yes, the principal and Cobb were invited and whomever he invited. They were all on their best behavior. They were all laughing at Cobb doing basketball tricks. He was really excited. There was a live disc jockey which the children loved; who played rock 'n roll, soul music and hip hop and classical music all jazzed up. And a great time was had by all is true, and one of the 6th grade students in Ms. Day's class yelled it out during the d.j. time. Everybody laughed and danced with each other and everyone got along swell. Cobb Jackson looked like he needed to unwind and of course he had his chance to with doing basketball tricks. Sadaya was proud, oh yes, and her mother and father were there. Mom helped to do the cooking and so did father.

"There were no losers in the room where our Good Luck Party was held," Sadaya was saying to Cobb. Everyone liked it so much, Cobb said; "those students those 6th grade students were the smartest students I've ever seen or met. One of them told me she knew the first half of the dictionary and she recited the definitions with the lead word all the way up to the D words. I had to stop her at D because I saw you were getting ready to serve the food," Cobb said. "Phew that was the best party I've ever been to for children, and I've been to a lot of them. Thanks for bringing me back to the school, he said. Sadaya said, "Now when can I bring you back to me?" Cobb said he was very busy with the U.S. Office of Sports which was established for sports and young people as an avenue to get young people into sports careers. He explained that their convention was in session all week and he's registered and obligated to attend. Sadaya was just joking but Cobb took it seriously: "Can I come with you and keep you comfortable in the room, order room service and all of that good stuff." Cobb laughed but he said that could be arranged. "I could leave the convention and come to get you. Oh yes, there's a $5,000 a plate dinner Wednesday night. You'll need to dress for that." "Ok'" she said. I'll be there at 7:00 pm he said.

I am glad you're coming. Let me go to take care of some business and everything will be done for when you arrive, he said. "Oh, that's right. I have to be registered, right. Of course you have to be registered sexy lady. The fee for registering is $500." I have no problem with registering you, my girlfriend. That is who you are, isn't it? he said. She said, "You know it I'm a very happy lady. That's why I make all of those sexy replies when you say something sometimes because I don't want you to forget me. I sigh, I giggle,

I laugh I asked you how can you mend this broken heart please help me because I don't want you to leave this relationship because I love you," Sadaya said. Me too, Cobb said. "Well I'd better run. Oh yes, by the way I must tell you this before we hang up. I have special desk safe where I locked up $450,000 in a desk thinking it was safe. Do you know that somebody stole my $450,000? I am so shocked. I was telling Flippy Johns one of my best friends and chauffeur, that I was so hurt," Cobb said. It's got to be one of the staff that stole that money," Flippy John said. It could have been neither the security guard, the cook or the chauffeur. You know if either of my parents had taken anything they would have asked me first. I never told any of them about the safe desk, however. Only my mother and father knew where the emergency key was to my house.

"Any day now, I'll find out who took my money. I'll talk to you about it later when I pick you up or perhaps at another time. See you at your mother and father's house at 7 pm. Explain that you'll be gone for most to the week. Thank God the job is off all week for New Year's Eve, and Christmas though not necessarily in that order," Cobb said. "O.K. honey, Sadaya said. "See 'ya. Bye. I love you." Said Sadaya. Listen to this before you go.

I'll leave you with this: 1 timothy 6:10 Kings James Version for the love of money is the root of all evil. While coveting after money some have strayed from the faith and pierced themselves through with many sorrows. 'I'll hang that scripture up in my office," Cobb said.

"Whoever it is that stole your money honey, I don't believe they're going to accomplish what they think. We'll talk later like you've said. See 'ya." Sadaya said. "Bye," Cobb said, "See you at 7 pm," Cobb repeated.

It was not 2 pm and Sadaya started running around the house trying to find something to wear to a $5,000 a plate dinner Wednesday. Well at least its only Monday. If I have to I'll go shopping tomorrow but I really want to go and get my hair done and my feet and nails done. Sadaya sat her parents down and she explained where she would be for the week. They gave her their blessings and she went back to her bedroom to find a week's worth of clothes to wear especially on Wednesday.

When a person believes in themselves they accomplish much more. For instance there were still many Johnny Harson TV Show fans left. Many times Johnny Harson had animals as his special TV guests. When animals made special appearance on the show he'd keep his distance and be fighting with the animal from across the show's room. Then when he thought he was safe, he'd get closer and then the animal would pounce on him, scaring the living day lights out of him. The audience would holler laughing. It was one of the show's best highlights. His ratings always went up before and after he had animals on the show. Mr. Harson believed in himself long enough to move back across the room to where the animals were. He knew how to entertain an audience and he was delighted too. Many times Sadaya would watch him tell jokes and other guest." For instance, at a party a man was comfortably drinking a drink. A woman walked over to him and she says, "If you were my husband I'd poison your drink, she said. If you were my wife, I'd drink it," he said. Heh heh heh. Cobb was telling jokes as a celebrity.

I wasn't finished. Ha ha ha. Heh heh heh. Another joke Cobb told: I once gave my husband the silent treatment. He said were getting along swell and great were getting along fine. Let's extend all of this getting along fine stuff to / for the next 20 years. Heh heh heh.

† † †

The ballroom at the Caterer's was the most fabulous catering hall either Cobb or Sadaya had ever seen. Neither one of them could stop talking about how beautiful the place was. There were Austrian – Straus Crystals everywhere. Middle of the ceiling chandeliers, wall chandeliers, and a waterfall with crystals in them too. There were also gold and ivory elephant tusks near the bottom of the wall chandeliers. The catering hall was large and extremely well-lit. Floral bouquets were extremely strategically placed at the dais. 6 foot vases were placed were also strategically placed on the floor. This place was a delectable sight. A sight to feast their eyes on. The chandelier lights reflected nicely on the ladies' jewelry and caused the jewelry to sparkle and glamorized the ladies' fashions. The tables were decorated with tall round balloon-like bouquets. One on each table. There were 300 tables. On each table were small packets of cigarettes, tooth floss, a small sewing kit and a nail grooming kit for manicures. There were 3 writing pens which had printed on each, because we love you, you're part of the elite and peace and love to you. "The sports office really out did themselves this time," Cobb said. The place is so beautiful that I have to spend some considerable time to take pictures of it with my cell phone camera. Sadaya was taking pictures of it too. It was something to see. Sadaya said "thank you God that you have such talented people who can decorate like this. Smooches to all."

The place was surrounded by cocktails and other types of drinks. Sadaya was voted the one between the two of them that would go to get the drinks and to bring them back for her and for Cobb. Sadaya met everybody. She met the Sportscaster Mr. Umbel, the Rock 'n Roll Superstar Hick Wagger the media stars, the basketball stars and the tennis stars were all so nice to Sadaya most likely because of their fellow celebrity Cobb Jackson who served as the Master of Ceremonies for the evening. Sadaya was at the height of delight. She met so many people and exchanged so many cards, it was almost mind boggling. What energy, she expended. Luckily it wasn't snowing outside and the chauffeur had taken a nap in the hotel part of the catering hall. The dance floor was smack dab in the middle of the catering hall. Sadaya was asked to dance many times but she stuck with Cobb. He was on the dais as the Master of Ceremonies and she didn't want to upset him in any way. "What a good girlfriend I am," she thought to herself. Anyway, the sports stars and the music superstars and the media stars all said they'd come to Sadaya's school and speak to the children. How wonderful." All I had to do is open my mouth about the kids and what they're working on and they asked me questions about where the school is located. There are lots of special days those celebrities can speak at in the school like graduation day, Library Media Day, Martin Luther King Day, Party Days, and many others. Sadaya was overjoyed to meet so many special people, known all over the world who would inspire and motivate her 6th graders. They also offered the chance to get concert tickets, sports outings tickets including tennis tickets where the dynamo sisters were playing and will continue to play. What a wonderful night, she thought and Cobb introduced her to the large audience of about 2,000 people.

The trip to the gala dinner for the Sports Organization was 5 hours each way. Of course Cobb and Sadaya did have chauffeur service. He would be with them until Cobb dismissed him. Cobb gave Sadaya $4000 and told her to take the chauffeur and to buy something Hallelujah. Thank you Jesus Christ. "Let's go," she told the chauffeur and climbed in the back seat. He told her about 2 shopping centers in the area that he knew of. Sadaya was in shopping Dreamland. She spent every penny of the $4000 Cobb gave to her and she did have about $300 left with which she treated Cobb to steak dinner and sweet potato pie dinner. Cobb looked at Sadaya and he was happy she had on new clothes which he bought her. She also bought a white gabardine with rhinestones outfit long down to the ankles evening gown which looked beautiful. As a matter of fact she looked stunning in the white evening gown. It was worn in good taste where her breasts weren't exposed, and hanging so everyone could see them.

In the meantime, Cobb did a magnificent job as the Master of Ceremonies for the Evening. He had the audiences laughing and he told the corniest, corniest jokes ever heard." There's more jokes more" he said.

Sadaya laughed. She also remembers when the Black Memorial Baptist Church was sponsoring a trip to the beach. The weather was varied. Hot one day, cold the next day. The beach was on Long Island about a 2 hour drive from where Sadaya and her parents lived. The weather was warm and sunny, people were out at the beach skinny dipping; Sadaya heard that Cobb was coming but she hadn't seen him yet. The way some of those people were swimming it was like looking death in the eye. Sadaya was happy with the warmer weather. She said, warm weather is finally here. She was able to swim after 15 minutes. She sat down and leaned her back against the tree. She closed her eyes and fell asleep. Cobb spotted her leaning against the tree asleep. He sat down next to her and put his head on her shoulder. At first she continued to sleep then she quickly awakened and he put his head back on her shoulder. She could feel him back on her shoulder. She could feel him smiling. "Oh oh oh. It's my beautiful boyfriend. Welcome." She said as she woke up fully. I'm fully awake now she said.

"Good" let's have fun. Let's do something. Let's play volleyball. See the net set up over there in the sand? I bet I'll beat your pants off in the volleyball game in the sand," Cobb said. "Not now honey, I'm too tired," Sadaya said. She leaned against the tree again. "Ahh ahh my back feels so good leaning against this tree," she said. Cobb got back down where she was and he sat next to her laying his head on her shoulder again. "Can't make any rapid movements with her because of her religious beliefs" he said. He kissed her neck gently 3 times. She blushed and smiled. She smiled and pulled away. She smiled and hugged him. "I couldn't help myself, she thought. After all, this is a famous man and a rich one too, she giggled to herself. Cobb got up to get a frankfurter. Earlier he and Mr. Williams had been conversing. Cobb told him he didn't mind teasing Sadaya about 80 % less fat and chicken wings. "I love her," Cobb admitted to Mr. Williams, the Sexton.

"Oh yes I've had those feelings many times. If my wife were alive today she'd tell you about how she and I used to run and chase each other in the rain and in the snow sometimes and we had big fun, the Sexton said.

"Mr. Williams, by the way I want to thank you for asking me to volunteer at the church. It's been very rewarding. I've been able to get closer to God and I've been able to share it with my teammates. Certain scriptures of the Holy Bible have a great meaning for me and I've shared the scriptures with them too," Cobb said with great emotion in his voice.

I've also met Sadaya Ruby Day and we're dating. As a matter of fact, she's my girlfriend. "Oh yes. I know Sadaya. I like her a lot. She always has a nice kind word to say to me, the Sexton said. Of course as another man, I'd tell you to take your time. Taking on a wife is a big decision. When you have to sit down and look another person in the face every day, it can be very very challenging. Sometimes a man for instance, likes to be to himself and women don't understand that. They think you're cheating. That doesn't have to have anything to do with it. Me, I liked to fish so every Saturday I'd take my motorboat out on the lake and I'd fish. I've caught big fish, little fish, small fish. I'd be bringing home fish and she thought I got them in the butcher shop. I caught enough fish to populate the most famous restaurant chains, and she thought I was out with some woman. I told her I was going fishing but she acted like she didn't believe me. So one day she said, if you're going fishing then invite me to go fishing with you. At first I said no but then I started to feel sorry for her so I took her along with me. She was just as quiet as if it was her favorite hobby. She couldn't do enough for me after that. She loved me forever after that.

Cobb had gone to the rest room and he and Mr. Williams were talking. Cobb listened to him and took very seriously what he had to say about women. "Mr. Williams I appreciate what you've said to me today. I'm very serious about it because when I finally do get married, I don't want to be sitting down looking miserable. Right now at this stage of my life I'm financially capable of taking care of a wife and I'm wondering if Sadaya can handle me emotionally. For instance what I considered to be fabulous, I notice she considers 'yucky'. I hope and I pray as time moves ahead that were gonna get along. It's just that simple. It's a pleasure to speak to an experienced gentleman like yourself and I thank you," Cobb said. Mr. Williams suggested that Cobb Jackson speak to the pastor about the subject of marriage. Ask him to give a workshop on marriage and the single man, Mr. Williams suggested. Tell him I'd be interested in sponsoring the subject, Mr. Williams said. "I'm with you. I'd like to sponsor a pizza night that night for all of the attendees. Also if he wants to make up folders with information in it and little packet of products for men I'd be happy to pay for it. No problem," Cobb said.

And the journey continued with everyone who was anyone at the Black Memorial Baptist Church Picnic By the Sea. The weather was hot and humid. Everyone was perspiring and hot, hiding under their beach umbrellas. Their journey's purpose is unknown except to have a good time. There are fewer males than females there at the beach. Some single females glance at the single males and they see them playing basketball and then they look the other way, pretending not to notice. Sadaya and Cobb stood by the tree cheek to cheek, breast to breast and body to body. Hugging. Hug after hug after hug. Their only defense against the hot sun is to head to the water, which itself is hot as well. With great gentleness the water massages the skin. It refreshens the skin and cleanses it as well. After going into the water a certain healing feeling/sensation is felt. If you don't go into the water and you huddle underneath the umbrella you somehow feel warmer with the hot sun shining down on top of the umbrella and on top of you. New heat has formed along the shore and it causes everything to be hot. Sand, rocks, water, trees, fish and so much else. The food at the beach picnic is a nice distraction from the heat. The fish rise from the rise of the temperature beneath the surface.

Frankfurters, hamburgers, chicken, potato salad. Hmm. Body to body, breast to breast, cheek to cheek tenderness gentleness my temperature continues to rise.

Everyone was asked to bring one or two plates of food or 1 large aluminum pan of food, of their specialty. There were 2 busloads of people and many cars. The men set up the picnic tables and placed them in position next to each other so the food could be well-placed. Everyone was totally cooperative. The women helped by placing plastic tablecloths a top the tables with placing plastic and silk flowers on the tables as well. By the time they finished the tables and it didn't take long the food was quickly being put on top of the tables. There was everything you can imagine on the menu for the picnic dinner: turkey, frankfurters, hamburgers, meat patties, roasted and fried chicken, steaks, french fries, macaroni and cheese, mashed potatoes, potato salad, macaroni salad, collard greens, cold french bean salad, string beans, lasagna, corn on the cob, stewed onions, ritz crackers and a whole potpourri of breads crackers and cookies. Many people also made cakes, pies and fruitcakes and other desserts. Sadaya was ready before the first plate was put on the table. Oh my God my God my Holy Father I wonder how long it is going to take for me to eat. I know I have to wait on you Father, to arrange things, especially for human beings to make it happen Father. "I'll wait" was the prayer Sadaya said quietly to God. She was just needing to eat. The leadership of the church said 10 people at time should line up.

Some of the guest went into the pool house due to the cold. Some church members chose not to eat. They wanted to go swimming first. The children and young people were reassured their food would be saved for them. "Go go. Go for your swim," they were told. The pastor then stepped in and told everyone that each person should eat at the same time." Swim later," the pastor said. So most people ate and enjoyed themselves at the same time. Cobb and Sadaya sat next to each other at a picnic table but there was no food directly in front of them which gave them maximum space for their plates. Cobb enjoyed the food and went back for seconds. "My gosh the people in this church really know how to cook. I haven't tasted a food I'd didn't like yet," Cobb said smiling. There was also a 12 year old girl who was selling chocolate candy for her school, Cobb loved it. He gave her $100 bill for her candy sale. She said, "Oh my God" a $100 bill. Wow!" When she told her parents about it and gave them the $100 to hold for her, her father looked a Cobb and he recognized the Superstar Basketball Player. He introduced himself and was so grateful. Cobb said "tell your daughter to let me know if she needs another $100. Here's my card. Aye ai aye ai aye ai yes no problem," the girl's father said.

"All I want to do is go sit by the tree," Cobb said. Maybe later on we'll play volleyball games; he continued. The ocean beckoned the children to the sea. Un-alone and supervised they all took the plunge into the water. They yelled and screamed at the top of their lungs.

It was a wonderful outing that was had by all. The food was good, nobody drowned, everybody loved the waves of the beach. People loved games such as volleyball, basketball, handball and some of the young people brought electronic games on their telephones. Wow; I'm coming back next year. Next year. Why wait, when I came this year I wondered about next month, Cobb said, why not come back next month? Sadaya what do you think?' Cobb said. "I say let's go for it for next month. I wouldn't mind coming back in two weeks,' she said and agreed with Cobb. The problem with 2 weeks is not everyone would have enough time to come back. They'd have to arrange for the buses for transportation and I'm afraid it just wouldn't be enough time. It just wouldn't work. Maybe we can come by ourselves, in the limousine because it's a 2 ½ hour drive out here. If you really want to come back in 2 weeks, I can bring you back in 2 weeks, said Cobb. "I do I do I do want to. Please bring me back out here. I love it and I'm serious I do want to come back out here in 2 weeks," Sadaya said. Cobb looked at Sadaya's eyes and he started laughing. "You would have thought they were giving away one million dollars," he said. O.k. well be coming back here in 2 weeks. So Sadaya Ruby Day gets her desire and she'll be with me in 2 weeks. "Hallelujah," Sadaya said.

"Back to the Sports Organization which I registered you for. We have dinner reservations to eat inside of the hotel for 7:30 pm. Do you think we'll make it back on time?" Cobb asked. Sadaya said, "Of course well make it back on time; won't we? Yes, I think so or we can just leave early and take the limousine back. Oh Cobb, you're spoiling me baby and I love it," Sadaya said, while she gave Cobb a watery smack'n'kiss on his cheek. There are classes on Christian male / female relationships at 2 pm tomorrow. I'd like to go and see what that class is about. There's another fashion show for women only which I'd like to go to honey, Sadaya spoke and asked if it was about 6:30 pm or 7:00 pm. I forgot to tell you there's an article in SWAM Magazine about me and it said Sadaya Ruby Day might Marry Her Famous Boyfriend before the Year is Over, sources say. There's a picture of me on the grounds of the school I work in. I don't know how they got the picture, but they got it. Cobb laughed. Welcome to the limelight my darling. I'd like to see this article you're talking about. It's in my other bag in the hotel room. You can have it soon as we get back there, Sadaya said matter-of-factly.

What else does the Sports Org. offer as part of the convention? Cobb found a whole bevy of activities he would be interested in but he narrowed it down to two classes.

Wrestling: So you want to be wrestler

Sports Casting: So you want to be a sportscaster, huh?

"I won't worry about getting into the classes because I registered for you yours and mine when I registered early. Sadaya probably wouldn't be interested in wrestling and sports casting anyway," he thought. "Oh yeah; what am I worried about she got a fashion show for women only and some class on relationships. Good. Now we can both enjoy the convention. She almost feels like she's my wife. I feel like I want to give her money and spend money on her," Cobb thought. "I love her" Cobb thought. Sadaya came to love Cobb too. "We don't have to go to the same classes as long as we lock in the same lip" she said. Sadaya hugged Cobb and gave him a great big kiss kiss kiss. A man has to be made to feel wanted and loved. That's why I give Cobb my kiss kiss kiss, she said.

Hello there. I missed you. What time are we leaving? As soon as I see you jump into the ocean and swim, Cobb said. When you are in love it's the loveliest night and you want to make your heart beats fast with your love for her. Cobb said, Let's see your swim technique. She got up and pushed Cobb on his waist area: "I'll beat you there," running into the ocean shore. Cobb ended up beating Sadaya to the ocean shore. When Sadaya reached the shoreline, she almost fell because of the shells. There were all kinds of shells and some were broken pieces. She started straddling the shells broken pieces and all and ran into the deep water, thus having to rely on his "swimming technique." Sadaya and Cobb both proved to be expert swimmers. They swam next to each other in the deep water. They swam on the stomach, on the back and they floated about 15 minutes, too. What a swim what fun but we'd better go. We have dinner reservations Cobb said.

"The Holy Bible says, My people perish for lack of knowledge," let's go and get our share of knowledge. We've registered for 2 courses each through the University at the Sports Organization Office. The classes were taught by University Professors. The hotel was continually beautiful. The rooms were first class all day and night. Cobb was able to get an extra room for Sadaya with no problems whatsoever. The happiest couple got back to the hotel by 6:00 p.m. By 7:00 p.m. they were seated for dinner. Sadaya had the lobster and shrimp and Cobb had steak again. Before the dinner there was an update at 6:15 p.m. about the classes and who was going to teach the classes.

Dinner was very romantic with Sadaya ordering wine. The steak was carved into a heart. The lobster and shrimps were delicious Sadaya said. The dessert was also in the shape of a heart. Cobb touched Sadaya under the table with his leg near to her leg, romantically.

The next 4 days were filled with meeting and classes and one big luncheon. This included of course the $5,000 a plate dinner in the main Ballroom which attracted so many people, some of them were turned away at the door. "Gee," Sadaya thought: "They must have a dynamite publicity department. The main speaker for the $5,000 a plate dinner was the Vice President of the United States of America.

When Sadaya was thinking of her boyfriend Cobb, she was thinking it's a good thing I told him I'm not interested in sex that much until after marriage. "Although with all of that wine and the cocktails I had he could have talked my pantyhose off of me that night," she told him. He laughed a long time at that one. Do you know he acted like a gentlemen the whole convention? He didn't ask to come and to stay in my room or anything. One night Sadaya invited Cobb into her room to watch a movie on the 'In the room Movie Rental.' She asked him to get some popcorn which indirectly he did get. He had his chauffeur to get the popcorn. They had a ball sitting watching the movie and eating popcorn.

Cobb sat and thought about his experience at the convention with Sadaya. Had it been any other woman he knew, he could have had his own sexual way with her. Sadaya makes you feel the Christian inside of her. "I am dreadfully attracted to Sadaya Ruby Day, but I have not been able to tell her and to show her just how much in love with her I am. What's even laughable is I actually spend money on her more than I ever have any other woman," Cobb was thinking. "If she told me she wanted to buy a house today I'd buy it for her happily" what is wrong with me? he said. I must be in love because I can't go a day without talking to her on the telephone and asking her what she's doing. I must be in love. I've been in love longer than I thought, it feels like," Cobb thought.

"Knowing Sadaya has kept me humble and on my knees, I think I'm in love with her still true. I was speaking to the church secretary and she says she thinks I'm in love. I'm in touch with the Lord much more now," Cobb said. Cobb remembered in the Bible there were kings and the kings prayed to have certain women to become their wives. God gave the king the wife of his choosing. Can I have Sadaya is not the question but the answer. I want to make her my wife is what I'm trying to say. Sir Lord God. So far, Sadaya herself doesn't know I'd like to make her my wife. Also, being humble and on my knees before you Lord makes me get a natural high. Sadaya is a fine young lady who teaches your people in the 6th grade for a living. She can't match me monetarily or in athletics. She can match me in every other way. At the $5,000 diner she greeted people as if she'd known them for 20 years. She used her beautiful personality to bring them over to our table and to meet and/or say hello to me. I made 3 deals that night. I agreed to do 2 interviews on TV and one in Tribal Magazine. Sadaya really impressed me, Lord God and I'm worried about her being out there on her own without me. I travel a lot. I want her, Lord Sir although she lives with her parents. In the Name of Jesus Christ, Amen, Cobb prayed.

Taking her clothes off to bra and panty hasn't happened between Sadaya and Cobb. He wants this to happen although he's not desperate. He spoke to God about this sex issue too. He complained that he wakes up with sweats at night. Cobb did. His masculinity is so appealing to Sadaya. The man is supposed to be able to look at the woman. Sadaya feels that's why man was created. She fantasizes too that Cobb would wholly embrace her and hug her with manly hugs. Feeling his muscles turns Sadaya on. She wants to acquiesce to his manhood desires.

"Well, Lord Almighty God of the Universe, it is always a pleasure and a privilege to talk to you. I'm pleased to be able to talk to you about Cobb Jackson, my boyfriend. He has treated me with honor and respect. He has not tried to force me into a sexy physical relationship. We have kissed and he has put his hands around my waist. I spoke to the church secretary and she thinks I'm in love. Maybe she's right," said Sadaya.

Sometimes Sadaya thinks of Cobb in ways where she doodles his picture and she says I'll just make this cartoonist rendering and then indicate how many kisses I'll give him. Usually it's 5-7 per cartoonist rendering. She kisses the drawings too. A continuation of prayer: Well Lord God Almighty Cobb is still so physically appealing to me. His masculinity is so appealing. I know the man is supposed to look at the woman with admiring eyes but I have eyes too. In my opinion that's why man was created: for woman. I love Cobb so much that I fantasize about him. I see him wholly embracing me in nothing but his underwear and he hugs me with nothing but manly hugs. She sometimes feels his masculinity inside of her and she acquiesces to his manlihood. When he kisses Sadaya she reaches up and just feeling his muscles turns Sadaya on tremendously, she says. "I, Sadaya ask for inner strength to get through the physical temptation I feel when I'm with him. I fall asleep with my arms around my pillow pretending that it's Cobb. When he volunteers at the church I find myself sometimes looking around corners or going into the sanctuary just to get a glimpse of him. Oh boy Lord, I've really got it bad. Please help me lord to have more will power to stay away from him until he calls for me. I'm to have patience and wait on God, I feel. I wait for you Almighty God of the Universe. I love you Lord. I'll talk to you tomorrow. In the name of Jesus, Amen. Sadaya said.

The next day Sadaya planned to go to Bible Study. She thought her pastor was par excellence at Bible Study and she always looked forward to learning something interesting when studying the Bible with him, especially the lessons on Jonah and the whale, or as some people say the Big Fish. Jonah was swallowed up by that whale because he was running from God. Jonah is that Biblical character who found himself in the whale's belly for 3 days before being spat out. After 3 days he was finally safe. Jonah was asked by God to go to Nineveh and cry out against that great city because their wickedness came up before God. But Jonah got up to flee to Tarshish from the presence of the Lord. He went to get on a ship going to Tarshish. He paid it's fare to go to Tarshish running from the presence of the Lord. Jonah was upset that God did so much for the people of Nineveh. But the Lord had great mercy on Jonah and He forgave Jonah for running away from his call. As He did with Jonah sometimes the Lord will allow a real storm to overwhelm us for disobedience. He then has the option to forgive us and to pull us out of trouble. God wants us to forgive each other like he forgave Jonah and so many other people who needed it.

Cobb Jackson fell in love with Sadaya Ruby Day. He wanted to tell her but he couldn't find the courage to speak it. Sometimes when he was washing up in the mornings he'd practice in the bathroom mirror. It was the only place where he had privacy. "Well Sadaya, you know the day I met you is the day I took leave of my senses my dear Sadaya, you're the most fascinating woman I've ever met. Wait for me, darling. I have to go to the bathroom. Heh hehheh, Sadaya, you're the belle of the ball tonight. You look like a queen. Cobb would practice all of those lines and more in the mirror. He'd practice facial expression, hand movement and he'd say don't leave me. Wait for me. I love you, darling. He'd practice until he got it just right and then he'd go to get her and flub it by not speaking those words at all. "Scary" he'd say. All right, I have to give it a try. He had a romantic heart but not a romantic tongue for Sadaya. "Oh Lord, what am I going to say to Sadaya today?" he'd ask. He held the position as the most celebrated basketball star. He'd been in the limelight and he was making plenty of money; had given to a record number of charities yet he couldn't tell Sadaya how he felt about her. He'd get right to the point where he'd thought he would say sweet nothings but he'd flub every time. He could hold her in his arms and do romantic things but he'd flub again. It was downright painful. He did, to his credit, have some success at the church. Every day he would pursue his passions at the church he'd get three or four words out and then someone would come to him to call him for volunteer work at the church. He wondered if he should make an appointment to see a doctor to talk about this problem with his 'shyness' as he termed it. "Maybe I will but I can't right now. There's a little boy who was blind from birth, and he needs an operation." I'm going to pay for him to get the operation, Cobb was thinking "so he can see as good as me." He had negotiated and left out a certain amount of monies for him to give to charities and /or form his own charities. Millions of dollars were set aside for Cobb to do this. Cobb had hoped to take Sadaya to the press conference when they have it next month. She being a teacher would appreciate it, because the blind boy is only 4 years old. "She'd love this," he thought. She loves kids and she loves to be friends with the kids.

Somehow, Cobb would get over his shyness with Sadaya. "Actually, the Pastor of Black Memorial Baptist Church might be the answer. He's counseled many people. Maybe he could counsel me. When I get to the church I'll speak to his secretary and made an appointment," Cobb thought. I feel so much better just thinking about it. So here I am. Temperature is low. Snow is on the ground again and it's freezing cold. Cobb began to think about Sadaya and how he and she could be cuddled up under a big blanket by the fireplace at one of his houses. I can hear it now, coming from Sadaya. "I am not like other woman. I have a self-discipline they can't understand," Sadaya says all of the time. "If a woman doesn't want to have premarital sex, then she really doesn't want to have premarital sex, she seems to be telling me," Cobb observed. She was careful to tell Cobb that she loves him. "I give you big hugs and kisses to make you feel less alone, to make you feel loved because you are," she said to Cobb. She found peace and security with Cobb right there at the church. Love matters, the church matters. They'd sit at the church and Cobb would play the piano. He was such an accomplished pianist that the staff just let him play. He even tuned the piano. He knew what he was doing. His mother was a piano teacher.

Cobb Jackson was becoming the most celebrated basketball player ever. Many organizations both sports and otherwise were on their phones trying to get him to be Narrator, Master of Ceremonies, Guest Speaker and to do all kinds of activities for fundraising. One of the activities Cobb participated in was in Northern New Jersey at a University. Cobb was required to stand behind the cash register and to be a guest sales manager. The students were nice enough to let him sit down and so he sat on a stool while he was 'guesting,' as one student phrased it. Yippee, Cobb laughed out loud. He was taking everyone's money who had over $50.00. There were 2 lines about 200 people on each line. To the other guest, Cobb said he enjoyed watching Timmy Thornhill with the Baltimore Jolts Football Team (the guest.) Timmy Thornhill invited Cobb Jackson to dinner afterwards. Yeah, why not, Cobb thought. They said they'd go to The Iron Hand Restaurant after they finished at the University. The Iron Hand, Timmy said was known for their fish, and soul food. The University personnel said the two guest managers had to put in at least 2 more hours. Frankly, there were so many people the University had to extend the hours the bookstore was open. Sadaya had accompanied Cobb to this event. Where was she? On one of the lines? Cobb was looking for her but he couldn't see her. He kept ringing up the merchandise and finally he saw her. She had gotten on the wrong line. He walked over to her and he put her on the right line, which was his line. He was selling extremely well. No matter what he offered or volunteered people said, "I see. I'll take that. Yes, I'll take it. I'll take that too, or sold," people said. Sadaya came up to Cobb's register. He let one of the student interns handle Sadaya's merchandise. Sadaya estimated she had about $450 in merchandise but when the intern rang it up the bill said $7.99 plus tax. The amount was $8.23. Sadaya even had a testing kit in her group of items. Immediately, she asked the intern if there was some mistake because there was only $8.23 on the bill. "Oh don't worry about it," she said. The bill is right. "That's how much I'm charging you. Good luck and good-bye" the intern said and she started ringing up someone new. "You only charged me $7.99 plus tax. I'd rather you charge me the right amount. I don't know why you want to give me such a large discount but I don't want you to get in trouble doing this. Charge me the regular amount. I'm a Christian and I can't participate in this. This is stealing. I just can't," Sadaya said, shaking her head from left to right. Finally, the University intern took the bill and crumbled it up. She then started ringing up every piece of merchandise Sadaya had. The final bill of Sadaya's came up to $435.40. When the intern gave her the bill Sadaya said "Oh thank God. I feel so much better. My conscience wouldn't let me sleep at night." "Thanks to you and goodbye," she said. Sadaya went over to Cobb and told him what happened. Cobb laughed at Sadaya. "We'll talk about it later," Cobb said.

On the way home it was quiet in the limousine. Sadaya was going to be evaluated by her principal the next day. She had a paper in her pocketbook. It had definitions from educational textbooks and techniques for teaching sixth grade and elementary school-aged children. She asked Cobb to test her but he wouldn't. He was tired from the events of the day. He put his head back and closed his eyes. Sadaya slid over next to him and kiss him on his bottom lip, then his chin, and she then kissed him on his moustache. He continued to lay back but this time there was a smile on his face. Sadaya put her head to the nape of his neck. She lay her head there until she fell asleep and so did he. Cobb was the sleepy one but she was the one that fell asleep. He chuckled to himself. I guess we won't be talking about any cheap bill and what stealing means and all of that. Cobb looked at Sadaya's face while she slept only to be interrupted by his best friend Stanley Jensen on the telephone. Cobb answered cheerfully because he liked this guy Stanley. He told Stanley what happened over at the University of New Jersey. Stanley listened and he said he felt Sadaya was right. He said he once heard a story about a little boy who came upon a man shoveling pennies. When the boy asked the man what he was doing, the man told the boy to take what he wanted. The boy began stuffing pennies in his pockets until he saw the man shoveling quarters. Again the boy asked the man what he was doing and the man responded that the boy could help himself. The boy began to shove quarters into his pockets. Suddenly he noticed the man was shoveling gold coins into his pockets. When the boy asked what he was doing the man told him a third time to help himself. The boy looked down at his bulging pockets filled with less valuable coins; he had no room for the gold. Without hesitating he emptied his pockets of what he already had so he could fill them with something of greater worth.

"The point is if you want to be filled with God, you must be emptied of everything else. It is the first step in preparing for a move of the Holy Spirit in your life," Joy Strang, a Christian, said. Joy told him about a book The Bible and now Stanley shared it with Cobb. Sadaya was right. You either live for God or you don't. For Sadaya to have accepted the cheap bill would have been stealing and being disobedient to God. You cannot walk with God and run with mammon. Cobb heard Stanley loudly and clearly. Cobb then agreed with Sadaya and Cobb agreed with Stanley. "Since you put it that way, I do agree with you Stan," he said. Did I tell you the latest? "Oh." Sadaya said please let me out of the car. While Sadaya was away from the Limousine, Cobb shared something with Stan that Cobb wouldn't want her to hear. "The fact is that I'm madly in love with this woman Sadaya. Stan, I've thought about it over and over again. I am truly in love and I know true love because I can't sleep sometimes and sometimes I just get downright love sick. I had to pray and pray and pray so much that God finally lifted it off of me; the love sickness I mean. This woman Sadaya Ruby Day really means a lot to me Stan," Cobb said. Stan laughed uncontrollably. "Wow man. It's about time. You go through women like I go through changing my socks. I'm happy you finally found somebody who suits you. Does this mean you'll only stick to her?" Stanly said. "Let's not get drastic," Cobb said. "I'm still dating others every now and then. I got one problem though. I can't seem to tell her just how special she is to me. I'm talking about Sadaya. I always clam up every time I try. I get so shy and I don't know why," Cobb said. "I plan to see somebody about it maybe a counselor or psychiatrist or somebody about it," he said. Stanley had to hang up the telephone, he couldn't talk any longer. "We'll talk again soon," Stan said. Cobb was a little intense when he was talking about Sadaya but since Stan had to hang up, he though, "I'll be a lot more relaxed next time we talk." "I really have to get to the pastor soon, so I can tell Sadaya what I have to say to her and I'm sure I'll feel better," Cobb thought.

There was a thunder and lightning in the sky. Some people would say God was angry. "I always liked the rain beating down on my face though. Sometimes I went outside to be able to clean my face with rain water. Something inside of me said, don't wait. Let the rain water beat on your face. It was so refreshing and I couldn't wait to be able to run downstairs and to bathe in the rainwater. Thank you, God," said Cobb.

I hope he made it in ok out of the rain. "It was good talking to Stan. I'm glad I told him about Sadaya. I hope he doesn't think less of me because I'm still dating more than one woman, I mean, if I wanted to be with just one woman, I'd be married; wouldn't I? If other people knew, they'd probably call me a male chauvinist pig, he thought," when Sadaya came back to the car, she looked like a pretty professional model. She was dressed in an emerald green satin blouse and a cashmere sweater with a black midi length skirt. Those high high heels were green, with emerald green panty hose. She fully refreshed her makeup which was tastefully done. She repeated her Scripture, "I can do all things through Christ who strengthens me. I can walk in these high high heels SO help me God. Lord I'm never buying shoes this tall again. I can do all things through Christ who strengthens me," Sadaya said and repeated.

Cobb said, "My parents still think when you say it turns me on you're talking about turning on the television set." Ok I'll look that up in Hunk & Wagnalls. The term is turn on, of course. Cobb was trying to tell his Coach a joke. "Corny corny, corny, his Coach said, but a little funny." I try to get you to laugh at my jokes and you try to get me to exercise your bone-tingling exercises. "More like bone-breaking exercising," the Coach said. Well, Cobb I've had this on my mind. Matthew: 6:24 Kings James Version says No man can serve two masters. For either he will hate the one, and love the other, or else he will hold to the one, and despise the other. You cannot serve God and money. "You're the second person that has pointed that scripture out to me" Cobb said. There's one more I've got for you today: Matthew 7:15, Kings James Version Beware of false prophets who come to you in sheep's clothing, but inwardly they are ravenous wolves. You will know them by their fruit. Do men gather grapes of thorns, or figs of thistles? Even so, every good tree bears good fruit a corrupt tree bears evil fruit. A good tree cannot bear evil fruit, nor can a corrupt tree bring forth good fruit. Every tree that does not bear good fruit is cut down and thrown into the fire. Therefore by their fruits you will know them.

Cobb couldn't speak to Sadaya seriously about some things. When he was small he was diagnosed with cancer but this is something which he won't even talk to his own mother about. He'll only say well, don't deny the diagnosis; defy the verdict which is a popular Christian saying. At only 7 years old, he said he'd be a basketball player. He learned the term and everywhere he went he said "I'll be a style setter of basketball." His mother and father were mighty proud of him no matter what he did on teams. He was in Bittle League. All of his uniforms had clean, durable stitching. Well, son my advice to you every day was life is too risky with whiskey. Staying away from drugs and whiskey is the message. Cobb often says he would write a book about the lessons our parents taught us and jokes they made while trying to teach us. He said he believed it would be a bestseller. His mother told him he was worse than a snappin turtle – he'd bite at anything. Don't snap at just anything son, snap at the sure thing. When the Great Scorer comes He will not ask how many points you've scored but how you played the game. God heals. Exodus 15:26 Kings James Version says if you diligently listen to the vice of the Lord your God, and do what is right in His sight, and give ear to His commandments, and keep all this statutes. I will not afflict you with any of the diseases with which I have afflicted the Egyptians. For I am the Lord who heals you.

Who does the will of My Father who is in Heaven Matthew 7:21-23 Kings James Version is also great for you to read, the Coach looked at Cobb and he said. "Uh-huh, so how do you like them apples? I've been studying with my church too. I heard you were volunteering at the church down town. What's the name of the church? his Coach asked. "The Black Memorial Baptist Church. I'm really happy to hear you quote those scriptures; and you quoted them with such pride and happiness," Cobb said. "Oh yes. I am rediscovering my faith. Since I have been coaching, there was something missing, a kind of inner-strength and self-discipline that made me feel inwardly complete. I spoke to my pastor and then I started speaking to a Sunday School teacher and the Bible Study teacher. You know some people are just too busy for you but you know each and every one of them took time out and referred me to scriptures and gave me advice. The pastor now teaches Bible Study, was willing to meet with me one day a week but my schedule's too hectic for that. But how nice that he was willing to. It honestly made me love church. Now I'm going to church every

Sunday that I can, to show God that I love Him for blessing me and for giving me the career of basketball, and I love Him for so many other things too.

"You know you just gave me a great testimony?" said Cobb. I'm really impressed and happy too that God put me into basketball. "I knew since about the age of 7 that I was going to be in sports, basketball especially. I just hoped at first, then I knew. Also at the age of 17, I had a dream. By the way, I never consciously dream. But anyway I dreamt at age 17 that there was a big basketball about the size of a medium-sized airplane and it was in the airport hangar and I saw a seat in the middle of it; of the basketball. I was the only one sitting in the middle of the big basketball. I knew. I started talking to my mother and father right away. It's not too late. It's not too late. "I'm gonna play basketball," I told them, Cobb said. Cobb and his coach had more conversations about their basketball experiences and they ended up praying together and blessing each other that way too. Cobb promised his Coach that he was going to memorize those scriptures because he was so impressed by them. The Coach then told him, "o.k. man," it's time for some suicide drills and 3 man weaves for basketball. We've got the scriptures covered. Now it's time for basketball, the Coach said. This time practice was terrific and Cobb was smiling all over himself. "Now this is practice," Cobb thought to himself.

Cobb was telling some of his teammates about him maybe writing a book. In it the book would have a piece about his Uncle Biff who loved to play baseball. Biff was the type who liked to play ball, but one day, he had no hits at all. Strike one! Strike two! The umpire said – the bat hit Biff and knocked him in the head.

The book would also have a piece in it about his grandmother who loved to dance. Her name was Ruby. Ruby could dance but she could ride a horse too. She could ride a horse like a jockey. Ruby liked to dance and glide her feet. She could make up a dance to any beat. She danced to the east and danced to the west, she danced so much she almost danced out of her dress. Cobb already had ideas about what the book would say. Even though the book would have other sports in it too, the title would be Cobbie and the Basketball:

The Story of A Man Who Played the Game Straight and Won! "I remember my grandfather Cobbie is what I used to call him. He possessed so much God-given talent for basketball, a man who was determined to live his life above the muck and the mire of the ditch," he said. He inspired so many other young people to achieve their goals, a man who could still hold onto his own humility despite his accomplishments and popularity touched Cobb's soft side. He would be happy to write a book about Cobb Jackson, his grandfather.

Cobb went on to tell many of his teammates that Cobbie, his grandfather was the final cog in the wheel that helped roll his High School in to the winning spot to the Brooklyn High School Championship. He was seen as having tricky and shifty footwork, tricky ball handling and clever play making skills. "He was the 'idol' of his high school after he won the championships," Cobb said. He was pegged by the newspapers as the "New Boy-Wonder of Basketball," one of the Globe major newspapers said. With his medals and trophies won, he was successful and well- liked. His high school hadn't won a championship in 13 years and after winning, Cobbie became like Vesse Owens in basketball shoes. He was the key player in every game. Cobbie was also a good student. He graduated with honors in Spanish, Social Studies, English and Mathematics. He knew he had to continue to study and to do well in school in order to play good basketball because coaches like to check behind their players to see how they're doing academically.

Cobb Jackson was very very proud of his grandfather Cobbie Jackson. Of course being named after your grandfather helps. His grandfather, by the way helped Cobb to exercise many times: Cobb was told he had help from his grandfather that was meaningful.

Ask the computer system what these exercises look like. These exercises have made many a basketball superstar. Cobb helped him with warm-up exercises the side straddle hop Bend, the Stationary Run, the trunk rotation the Alternate tee touch the High Jumper and the Randolf Shuffle. Cobb's grandfather, he explained, that they did Standing Exercises such as the Reverse Stride Lunge, the Side Bender the Squat Bender, Plus, Pushups Leg Extension Sideward, Ground Exercises including the leg cross over, the hip raiser leg kick, two leg lift, the 4 count sit up, Leg lift with Spread, horizontal run leg lift with spread two man exercises back to back lift, back to back pull, leg push and rowing. Two man sit–up, two man chin, two main lift the grass drills and the Circle Exercises: the All-fours walk, the stoop walk, elbow knee walk, straddle Run the hopping, bouncing ball inverted all Fours Walk, Kick walk Bread Jump, Carry Walk, Toe Walk, Toe Walk spread, Side of Foot Walk. Cobb had to memorize all of those exercises the Coach said to.

Cobbie Jackson took courses in physical training and became an official army physical instructor. As an athlete he enjoyed all of the things that made demands on his athletic talents including jumping over ponds, leaping hurdles, running track, tumbling hiking and taking exercises. He also gave cadence counts . . . "hut, two, three, four, left oblique . . . left turn . . ." Cobb Jackson was described as a "bouncing rubber ball" who handles the basketball as though it was part of him. Many other players hoped to stop Cobbie's good moves, but of course they couldn't. There were many people that helped Cobbie to become a success in basketball: His own father and his own grandmother who loved basketball playing and who played herself for the Women's Union label team. She and Cobbie then years later Cobbie and Cobb practiced those exercises that would make for a great ball player. They also practiced by making 100 foul shots a day and other tips that keep a basketball player sharp. The other teammates on the Boxers Basketball Team loved to hear Cobb talk about his grandfather and what he had to do to become a great basketball player, because it reminded them of their own lives. It is intricately interwoven with their own lives. Sometimes you don't know what to do, who to trust, whose advice to take. It's not easy trying to be a success in life. There's always going to be somebody you think you can trust who will let you down. Do not trust man. Man will let you down.

There are two of Cobb's team mates who have ridiculous personality problems. Cobb was fantasizing about writing a book for them: "You think you're beautiful but you're really ugly and sad."

You're so ugly you look like you're mad. Cure hatred, a disease of the mind and the love of the greedy, learn to love all kinds of people and make it speedy.

On your back, you wear a colorful shirt but your mind is filled with negative dirt. Cobb Jackson, although a basketball player began to recite the following poem to bring home a point.

<u>Prejudice</u>

Some eyes that see are blind to me,
Some listening ears hear not my plea.
Hate rises madly within their chests,
Never given a moment's rest.
And then life's bruises seemed so safely hid –
Until memorable shadows raised the lid.
The creator made us all to treat each other right;
Some people he made dark and some he made light.
Look at life as a flowerbed,
Remembering the whole human race needs to be fed.
Now I am here to tell it all –
Unless we change, we will all fall.

© Adrienne Sealy

Poems Above Copyrighted by Adrienne Sealy.
Permission Received/Granted

"When the Great Scorer comes He will not ask how many points you've scored but how you played the game," Cobb remembered again.

Many times families have squabbled and quarreled. Did you remember to make up again? Did you remember to use the stay humble words like I'm sorry or to ask for forgiveness?

It matters to the Holy Father God how we treat each other, and how we end arguments. With Jo's wife there is the perfect example of what not to do. She brought negativity to an already devastating situation. It is important to be mindful of our words. In Proverbs we're told that death and life are in the power of the tongue [Proverbs 18:21 Kings James Version] By what we choose to say we can either bring life, hope and healing into the atmosphere of our homes and circumstances or we can bring bitterness strife and hopelessness, all things that lead to death. Make it your business to speak humble words, peace, joy positive words of joy, love and life. Ask forgiveness and be willing to forgive others, Cobb said.

Cobb recited scriptures showing that he has been listening to God and hiding His word in his heart that he might not sin against Him. He learned to get his heart right with others and with God. Cobb has became a more spiritually sensitive man and lover of God. God gave him basketball.

Are you kidding? I took leave of my senses the moment I saw you for the first time. The first time I saw you I knew you'd be mine. There were many times at the church when we'd catch each other's eyes and I almost couldn't take it. Oh my goodness, Sadaya said, the man is just so beautiful, so appealing to me, it's like when he's around nobody else is. I wanted to say can I go with you? I won't be any trouble to one of basketball greatest stars. He's so romantic. I want you significantly," she said. Like I said before, "I found peace and security with Cobb right there in church. "Now that I've heard it and I've heard about how he speaks of God, there's nothing else left for me.Okay. I'm totally finished with the situation. No more talk about it." Now that I see how nice and religious the man is, I'm ready to make him my husband, although I can't tell him," Sadaya said. I don't want to chase him away but I surely want to tell him I love him enough to marry him but I just can't because he'd run like Flo Jo on a mid summer's nights' eve," Sadaya reasoned. Meanwhile, Sadaya feels like she's climbing up a mountain of broken glass with her shoes off because she wouldn't dare talk about a wedding with him and she as the main couple. In the meantime unknown to Sadaya, Cobb can't talk to her about it either, because he really can't talk – clams up and everything. Actually, they have a real nice love affair going on. Mr. Austere knew that Cobb couldn't reveal his true feeling to Sadaya and he clams up. Wednesday, Cobb was at the church to volunteer and Mr. Austere the Choir Director said, "did you tell her how most she means to you? No I couldn't yet, Cobb said. The most celebrated Athlete of our time, Mr. Austere looked at him and shook his head. Go talk to our pastor. I beg you to" Mr. Austere said. He's helped me with my whisky problem and he'll help you, Cobb." Yes. I am" Cobb said.

He loves sports, God and Cobb not necessarily in that order the pastor does. One thing is for sure for eating better, for sleeping better and for loving better see the pastor. For some, the road to happiness is never easy but our love will be different and better once the pastor puts his sense into the situation. He's able to carry the news to a waiting nation on the radio every night and he's able to advise you and leave you feeling better after he talks to you and makes things right. Don't wait too long, said Mr. Austere. Mr. Austere said. "Oh yeah, did you ever find out who would be stupid enough to steal the $450,000 you had locked away in your desk? Mr. Austere asked. Cobb said, the police found a piece of fingerprint which matches the security guard that guards my house. Can you believe it? My own security guard, stealing from me. My lawyer is going to see if he can garnishee from the security guard's bank account and get every penny back for me. I'm still waiting to see what happens, "Cobb said. Mr. Austere, the Choir Director said, "God is not mocked. Whatsoever a man sows, that shall he also reap. You wait and see. That man is gonna fall on his knees someday and his conscience is gonna whip him silly, Austere said. For this reason I bow my knees to the Father of our Lord Jesus Christ, from whom the whole family in heaven and earth is named that He would give you, according to the riches of His glory, power to be strengthened by His Spirit in the inner man. That Christ may dwell in your inner hearts through faith that you being rooted and grounded in love . . . it's Ephesians 3:14–19 Kings James Version look it up. I can't remember it all," said Cobb; but any way I was thinking about God this morning and His principles. I was thinking about how sometimes brothers and sisters and families have squabbled and quarreled. Did you remember to make up again? Did you remember to use humble words like I'm sorry or to ask for forgiveness? Did you remember to ask God to fight your battles for you? Did you remember to thank Him for His Most Powerful Self and for His Omniscient Omnipotent, Omnipresent and Sovereign Self? I asked myself these questions this morning because I was away from the house too much and my mother argued with me about where I was. She threatened to hang up on me if I didn't tell her what was so important. I had to be away from home so much. She understands that I have to travel for a living but there are certain times she expected me home and I said I was going to be there, but I was not home. My fault and I know it's my fault so she ended up hanging up on me and not calling back. It bugs me because one of us usually calls back or says wait a minute or finds a way to stop the major chill that the phone call takes. This time the phone call stayed on chill and get this, Mr. Austere: Sadaya called while I was on the line with my mother and she acted like I was lying; like I wasn't really on the line with my mother. She sounded like she wanted to argue with me. I got her off the phone really fast and I told her I'd call her back later. After hearing her tone of her voice it'll be much later. As a matter of fact, it might not even be today that I call her back. It might be in the next two days to a week.

The natural talents and gifts that God gave us as humans are what we should be thanking Him for, each and every day. Cobb Jackson was gifted in the areas of sports, especially in basketball and baseball. Cobb often thought about going out for the baseball team called The Fets Baseball Team. If he had taken the chance he would have been great at it because he had been tested and his line ball drive was 90 miles per hour. It was clear that Cobb Jackson was born to win. He'd played on a few scrimmage teams and he played best as shortstop and second baseman and outfielder, but the basketball league refused to let him switch to baseball. They argued with Cobb and negotiated with him. In the end, the money they offered him was too good to turn down so he didn't. Rumor has it that there are a lot of professional baseball players who were thanking God and the basketball league that Cobb didn't switch over to baseball. Too much competition. Cobb's mother and father saw the wisdom in not switching over because the "money was too great," Cobb's father's view agreed with the money was too great. He encouraged him to quit while he was ahead. Take the money and run Cobb's father said.

Cobb called Sadaya back. "I hope her testiness has worn off by now. After all, we haven't spoken for 2 ½ days. She should be happy to hear from me," Cobb thought. "Hello," Sadaya said. "Hi," Cobb said shyly. Just thought I'd call and see how you are doing he said. "Cobb I can't talk long, hon. I'm meeting my friend Cynthia and we're going shopping. She'll be here in about 10 minutes and I have to jump into the shower, then get dressed put my makeup and get ready," she said. "Tell Cynthia I said hello," he said. She's the only one of your girlfriends that I really like. Also tell her I'll call her about the insurance packet I have from her. I've made up my mind about the insurance I'll purchase from her. As a matter of fact tell her to call me and we'll sit down at the stadium and discuss it," Cobb said. "O.K?" Cobb said. "O.K." Sadaya said.

Max Jack the Boxer, when asked why he didn't get up after he was hurt he said, "That 200 dollars the audience paid to see the fight. They paid to see a fight not a murder. That's what they would have seen if I had gotten up after being knocked down and hit like I was. You deserve to get ahead and to be somebody; not to be killed and then put to death by another boxer named Joey DiFama. After all, said Max Jack, I was 20 to 1 underdog." Maxine Jack won that fight to Sadaya's delight. There was a last minute knockout by Max Jack in this heavy weight bout event. Sadaya and Cobb couldn't believe their eyes when the fighter hit Max Jack hit Joey "DiFama and his legs gave out. Max Jack really won that fight and he should have," said Sadaya. I really enjoyed going to the fight with you, honey, Sadaya said to Cobb. Cobb told Sadaya she looked absolutely elegant. She wore a pearl necklace with a royal blue skirt set and she smelled of All for Us fragrance. Her handbag was matching her royal blue cocktail skirt set. Her royal blue skirt set was made of metallic sheen material and peau de soie material. She wore pearl earrings to match the pearl necklace her mother and father had given her. Her hair was long and straight. Cobb was careful to remind her that she looked stunning and she looked elegant next to him in her cocktail skirt suit. Cobb wore a black tuxedo. He looked very handsome according to Sadaya. Now that Max Jack won the fight Cobb looked at Sadaya and said "Come on, let's got to say hello." Before I knew it, he was climbing up into the ring for publicity photos to congratulations to him and all went well. He invited Cobb and Sadaya to go to the Post-Fight Celebration in the hotel where the fight took place. Max Jack told

Cobb and Sadaya not to go any where to eat because he ordered so much food they would even be able to take food home. "the food will be flowing." O.k. I'll be there and so will Sadaya . See you later man," Cobb said. Max Jack waved goodbye just as his 6 year old son gave him a hug. Max Jack stayed in the ring another 7 minutes and then he left to go to his room to freshen up for the after party. There at the after party There was food galore including lobster and shrimp, which Sadaya loved. Cobb enjoyed the prime rib and mashed potato and green string beans. The staff gave out the souvenirs which were chocolate boxing gloves. Cobb managed to get an extra pair for Sadaya's father. Cobb and Sadaya brought back a plate of food and a pair of chocolate boxing gloves. Sadaya's mother and father were happy. They received a midnight's snack plus a unique dessert.

Cobb was told by Sadaya that she had a spectacular time in the limousine. I love it when you take me places where I can dress up for you, to admire me, she said. Cobb took Sadaya's hand but he could not say anything to her to show her how much she means to him so he just held her hand and shook his head. She said, Cobb sometimes you're so shy. There's no need to be shy with me. You can talk to me without worrying about me repeating what you say. Please remember that.

Cobb thought about it: "I've got to remember to get counseling from the pastor at Black Memorial Baptist Church. I've got to hurry up and get that counseling. It's happened again. I want to tell her but I just can't. My mouth just clamps shut. This is just plain ridiculous." Cobb thought. Oh yeah. I got a phone call from my cousin Aretha and we're going out to dinner Saturday. Would you like to come along? Sadaya asked. What restaurant are you going to? Cobb asked. We're going to the Room Hotel Restaurant Bar and Grill. Great place. Millicent and Tom are going too Sadaya said. Who's Millicent and Tom? "I don't remember meeting them," Cobb said. "I do remember meeting them," Sadaya said. "Millicent and Tom are my mother and father," Sadaya said; smiling at Cobb.

You're so accustomed to calling them Mr. and Mrs. Day you forgotten their first names Cobb," Sadaya said, laughing. "Why if I didn't know any better I'd say she was laughing at me about something. I have no idea about what. Oh yeah, her parents first names. Why I'd laugh at myself with that issue. Millicent and Tom. Who could remember that one?

It just seems like Sadaya is a little grouchy lately. I asked her a couple of questions and she snapped back at me like I had just committed a cardinal sin. Oh yes, Sadaya said acting like she did not hear him. "Guess who I saw at the shopping mall the other day. Stanley Jensen," Sadaya said. "My Stanley Jensen?" Cobb asked. "Yes. Your best friend. He told me he was going to call you and tell you he saw me. I guess he didn't get a chance to," Sadaya said. "Well at any rate, he said he and another friend was looking to see if they could buy a new car. He told me he's looking for either a foreign car or American car. It doesn't make a difference because nowadays they mix both foreign and domestic parts so much you can't tell the difference between them. He said he was going to call you and talk to you about it soon, he also said he was going to ask you about going to the stadium to see The Boxer play. It's been quite a while since he has seen you play basketball. He wants to know if you have two tickets so he and his wife can go. He doesn't mind paying you. Yeah, he wants to definitely get them from you. Sadaya was quiet and so was Cobb. "What you thinking." Cobb asked. "I was thinking about the nice long conversation that Stanley and I had.

He was telling me about how these women that he knows on his job keep trying to seduce him. I told him to look up Proverb 7:12 Kings James Version: with her enticing speech, she caused him to yield. With the flattery of her lips she seduced him. He went after her straight way as an ox goes to the slaughter, or as a fool to the correction of the stocks, until a dart struck through his liver. As a bird hastens to the snare, he did not know it would cost him his life.

Actually, the chapter 7, the whole chapter, I told Stanley to try to memorize the whole thing. But gave him bits and pieces of the chapter 7. Verse 24 to 27: Kings James Version Listen to me now therefore o children and attend to the words of my mouth: do not let your heart turn aside to her ways, do not go astray in her paths, for she has cast down many wounded and many strong men have been slain by her. Her house is the way to Sheol, going down to the chambers of death. I pointed him to other chapters in the Bible that presents God's opinion about a woman who seduces and what the man should do about it before it gets out of hand. If a man loves God, I feel he should listen to God and obey him. He will see the benefits of listening and of obedience," Sadaya said. "Those scriptures are very interesting scriptures you gave to my best Friend Stanley Jensen. I'm sure he'll benefit from them. I'm benefiting from them just hearing about them myself," Cobb said. "Should I be telling him that you told me about the seductress Scriptures?" Cobb asked. After discussing this issue Cobb and Sadaya agreed that it might not be wise to tell Stanley they had been discussing his sex life or potential sex life. "My goodness is his wife going to love me," Sadaya said. Cobb let out a big howl of a laugh. "Yeah well, I kind of like you myself," he thought. "If only I could tell her. Oh well I'll just wait until I see the pastor," Cobb thought again. When he hung up with Sadaya the first number he called was the church to speak to the pastor but the pastor wasn't there. He left a voicemail message and he asked the pastor to please call him back as soon as possible. Cobb had to go back on the road in another 3 days. He worried about when the pastor would want to make the appointment for. Maybe he'll do an emergency appointment, Cobb thought about it again and picked up the telephone. He called the secretary to the pastor and she said she'd make sure the pastor understands the urgency of the phone call. Cobb was happy. Pastor's secretary would handle it. She's a very good secretary.

I've seen her in action before, he had told his parents.

The traveling Boxers Basketball Team will be making a special appearance. They will be at the St. Peter Claver Gymnasium to hand out foodstuffs and personal products such as soaps, colognes and lotions. That same day the Boxers are scheduled to compete against the Hawaii Jets. The Boxers unit consists of a few new additions, bigger and better than the past. They are well-managed by Cobb Jackson in most basketball clashes the Boxers win. We don't expect any different in the game against the Hawaii Jets. Go Boxers Go. GO Boxers Go! We want them to bring home a great record like they usually do against other teams. Cobb Jackson grew up in Brooklyn, New York. His nickname was Monk, which stood for Monkey-chaser and he was teased about his part West Indian background. Cobb worked odd jobs but his heart was into playing the game of basketball. Cobb, in the heat of the summer, in the cool of the winter, in the rain and in the snow loved to play the game, and play it well. Cobb Jackson has always loved basketball and he says, "I always will," basketball is a fast and exciting game. It is played and watched by more people than any other sport in the United States of America. Basketball rules have been translated into more than 40 languages. I'm proud of the game of basketball I respect myself more because of the game of basketball Cobb told many reporters gathered outside the locker rooms after The Boxers beat the Hawaii Jets. Cobb Jackson heads up the fastest and most talented group of young players assembled on a team around here in years. What competitive spirit those guys possessed. They have put up some fierce battles and show the greatest basketball savvy. All I have to say to The Boxers is go "lick-em," said Charlie Isles, Reporter for Confidentially Yours Newspaper; known for their sports coverage. He couldn't stop talking about "Cobb Jackson, the high point man for the League; He has turned in brilliant all around the court performances and it's a cathartic experience watching Cobb play ball," Charlie Isles complimented Cobb. Take your whole family to see the NY Boxers basketball team. The tickets are going to be on sale in 2 weeks for the home game. What a deal. See ya at the game.

† † †

"Phew, thought she was going to say no to my proposal of marriage because there was a long pause after I finished asking the fantasy question then I heard so many yeses repeatedly I started laughing Cobb said. "Of course she cannot imagine life without me, I reasoned." She was looking so beautiful that the only time I could imagine her prettier is in her bridal dress and veil. That will be the prettiest time ever. She has a nice personality too which will make her a radiant lass with a beauteous smile. She is not socially awkward. She is a friend to many and she has helped many people to get engaged and married. She has compassion for people and she doesn't like to hurt them. She's also a smart woman who assesses people's needs, strength and weaknesses; while at the same time not allowing them to go too far and to take advantage of her hospitability and goodness. "Gee, if I didn't know better, I'd say this was her talking about herself for the sake of good publicity, plus public relations." Cobb said.

I shall be forever grateful to God, the Chief Professor for my life and what it will be n the near future when Cobb and Sadaya, that's us and when we get it together as a married couple, we'll be two of the happiest people on earth. Are we really going to be that happy? Cobb asked. I'd say an unequivocal yes. "why?" Sadaya asked. I'm not foolish; I pray Sadaya said. Cobb was happy to know that Sadaya prayed for him to be her husband without knowing him first. She didn't have to know him. She knew his personality traits, that she wanted such as, not violent and peaceful, charming, frisky, sometimes comical, financier and rich Athlete, active in his profession. Sadaya saw his pictures in the newspaper and she fell for him Sadaya: of course Cobb told me he prayed too, Sadaya said. He said he prayed on his knees so much, it felt like he was in a professional basketball game workout. He said "everyday I sat back and I waited for people to leave my presence so that I could speak to the Almighty God of the Universe about who would be my future wife. I didn't know her name, her body size, her shoe size, nothing. I only knew I needed a wife in my near future. I knew what I'd like in a wife and I talked to God. I told God the desires of my heart. I asked God to give me the desires of my heart. I was so humble and oh my knew and I needed to write my own church love story and the Only One I could insist on being the One to coach me is our creator, our Almighty God of the Universe. I had grown anxious and lonely because I know some of the women who have approached me have been too loose even by some by some "loose" standard. I need a woman of peace who will represent me well in public as well as in private; Cobb was saying he feels this should be a general rule.

According to Cobb's parents, "whomever he marries should have enough social sense to know how to treat people with friends and influence friends and enemies of Cobb Jackson. She's got to be slick enough, graceful enough and merciful enough for both friends and enemies and to know how to work with people in social relationships, to make more friends not more enemies. "She's got to be one of God's respected Elite and do His work proudly." I was blindly praying about what I like in a woman and bam! There is such greatness in prayer. God answered my prayers even to the size of Sadaya's feet. I don't like a woman with tiny feet. God gave me a woman with a size 9 ½ - 10 feet. I can clearly say that God answers prayers. I thought I was in doomed situations but God works miracles.

"Oh yes, I also asked God to give me a woman who could cook for me and who cares enough to. God is so Awesomely Magnificent that I know I'll never turn my back on God. The Bible is awesome too. I believe in the Father, the Son and The Holy Spirit. God. He gave me my future wife Sadaya. I will forever be grateful to God for this and so much more." As I said before, "Prayer." I said, "Getting down on my knees respecting Him and humbling myself before Our Maker and Creator, bending my knees everyday made me seek God diligently. Before I knew it, the answers to my prayers started happening. I grew in a close relationship to God. I also went to a Christian Book Store and bought new translations of the King James Bible and other Christian literature. Reading the Bible everyday is important as well. It gave me the chance to memorize and among Christians and non-Christians to showboat the Word of God. I now have a major testimony about Sadaya and me, Cobb Jackson, that should influence a whole lot of people who need God" she said.

If there is to be hope of any kind we have to stay humble and stay on our knees. Staying on our knees and constantly talking to God everyday will cause God to answer our prayers much more frequently. That's the most important part of the Christian walk. Fantasy about marriage is over Cobb thought. It's time I turned the fantasy into reality and stopped playing games he chided himself. Staying humble and on our knees. Sadaya joined in with Cobb. She said the best thing she ever did was to make a decision to get to know more about Christianity and to get to know the Creator of the Universe better; the Almighty God of the Universe; our Father God, the Master and there have been so many names for God. Regardless of what He is called, He is still God. He blesses people everyday who have sins known and unknown. He blesses us everyday regardless of our sins. He loves people that much. Sadaya's requests to God were about getting a nice God-fearing husband that will not be violent prone or abusive. I'm tired of being lonely, not having a man. Right now working as a mathematics and social studies teacher pays the rent to her parents. Cobb Jackson has achieved more than he thought he'd achieve although he always thought he'd play basketball. He never thought he'd be a Superstar and the Captain of a Professional Basketball Team. He certainly never thought he'd be making so much money. He admires Sadaya and he'll be talking to her about important issues later that will affect his and her future. He seriously intends to speak to Sadaya in the near future, saying she is a great prospect for something he has in mind for his amazing future. It was amazing that Cobb Jackson was not dead. He made so much money that his relatives and his friends became concerned for his safety. He carried lots of money every day and it was well known that he made and carried money on him throughout the day; day after day. He made loans to many people and days on end, he was always seen in expensive jewelry and expensive cars.

When people know you have money or access to it they're more tempted to pull out a gun and commit crimes against well to do men and women. Some of them can't sleep for figuring out how they're going to get someone else's money or jewelry or other valuables. Some of them are drug addicted and alcohol addicted, and in desperation willing to perpetrate a crime against anyone they can find. But Cobb Jackson was working. He was putting his faith in action and trusting Almighty God to keep him safe and secure, to keep him making the right steps so he doesn't come into contact with the wrong people who would rob him or kill him. This is how much he was praying and so far he's been safe and secure from all alarm. He is trusting God. Someone stole money from inside his desk but he got it back.

Cobb Jackson believed strongly but he thought he was going to do curly flips when he was thinking about how Sadaya and he, the Captain of his pro basketball team met. He had to cry out for help and assistance in the church. Of course he was in the right place for sure. If he couldn't get help in the church, where could he get help? If not there, where?! God sent Mr. Williams, the Sexton to help and to assist and when some of the church members found out the nature of his problem with the car, they were glad to help. In the meantime, Cobb met Sadaya. The one woman Cobb was thinking "I could fall in love with her,' I'm certainly in the right place for that too. I'll do my best to make a good impression. My impression was good, because I got her phone number and her address.

"Sadaya Ruby Day, her name was impressive to me. Her parents could have named her anything and I would have fallen in love with her," Cobb thought.

Let's face it, Cobb "I'm in love with Sadaya Ruby Day. The state of denial doesn't work for me because I've already accepted this as a fact. I don't want to get my heart handed to me on a Chinese Dagger plate. This feeling of being in love has to be mutual. If not, it won't work. In my heart of hearts I believe God has given me a soul mate and a beautiful wife of the future and all I have to do is stand up and "claim it." All of those prayers I've prayed are being answered by God Himself because He loves me more than I'll ever be able to know. Prayer changes things for all of God's people who care to diligently seek Him and want to know about His power and His attributes and His promises to us His loved ones and His heirs.

God was letting Cobb Jackson know that all of his speed, his athletic edge, his running, jumping and skipping. His ballet abilities, his jumping jacks ability to do any kind of exercising at all and yes the ability to speak, to use speech and language skills and to communicate with other people. It all comes from God The Almighty God of the Universe. Just like God wakes up Cobb Jackson and tells him to go to the bathroom and to use the water that runs through the faucet. God is the Provider. The same Provider that when his car stopped Cobb got angry because of the inconvenience, caused Cobb to be introduced to Sadaya, his soon to be wife he hopes. All things work together for good for those who love the Lord. This was and is certainly true. Some people do not take the time to examine their specific situations and see what God has done and is doing in their lives. Be assured and reassured God is busy at work. He is working in your behalf making sure He remembers how you have come to Him in prayer,

On bended knee in a humble spirit and He remembers everything you have said and done and asked for. These words are some of the wisdom-filled words the pastor was touched by God to say. "Do you really love God?" was what the pastor asked. If you really love God then make Him your daily Friend. Promise Him and promise yourself that you're going to increase the amount of time you spend with God your Creator, your Friend and your Confidante. Have nothing but confidence in His ability to succeed with you. Have confidence in God. He's made certain promises to you and He means to keep these promises coming true. Ask God to help you with your areas of weakness.

Don't lose hope; don't lose your faith; don't lose your self-respect. Don't lose.

By the way, the pastor shared some other information with Cobb that was interesting. He said Sadaya's friend is dating now and everything was fine until Cynthia brought up the man's name. One of the friends that overheard the name said he knows that name and to please give him a few minutes while he goes outside to check something. He came back from the police wagon that he was driving and he showed the guy that Cynthia was dating rap sheet. He stood there and he told Sadaya to give it back to him for he didn't want to get in trouble with his superiors at the Police Department. He said he wouldn't recommend Cynthia let herself get to close to him because this one has a deep past as the rap sheet will show. To summarize, he's been through a divorce where he tried to scam his wife out of all her money. He spent 15 years in prison but the ink in the machine messed up where it said there was 15 years spent in prison for no one knows; machine broke in this area. Cobb told Sadaya maybe Cynthia could ask him why he was in prison for 15 years. Then they also mentioned some incidents that took place during junior high school involving him and another group of boys. It really read like a gang sheet. He was running with the gang. The police officer also asked that they treat Cynthia with tender loving care when breaking the news to her about him being in prison for 15 years. "I'll bet you he hasn't told Cynthia a thing and she believes this guy's every word and he's probably the nicest guy on earth to her huh?" the police officer told Cobb Jackson. Cobb nodded his head and he said "this is why the Bible tells us to watch and pray." Sadaya has opinions. I can't wait to hear her opinion about this situation and Cynthia.

There's also no telling what Cynthia's sister Aretha would say about Cynthia dating a known to the police department felon who has had many criminal flaws since childbirth almost.

What can you say? When something is true, something is true. Cobb thought he heard something familiar about that "no-good felon's" name. "When and if Cynthia Persons should ask for tickets for she and "boyfriend" to come along, what is Sadaya going to say? He can't go because he was in prison for 15 years. I can hear Sadaya now. I'm putting my voicemail on for the next 10 years. I can't share this with Cynthia; or can I? After all, she is my best friend. I'm supposing I'll have to think about this one. I need the best solution for this problematic situation. I think both Cynthia and Sadaya are going to be hurt by this situation. When Sadaya breaks the news, I'll be out of the country. I can hardly tell Sadaya how I feel about her and how much she means to me. How am I supposed to tell her about her own best friend's boyfriend? You see, its complicated already. I'll just leave it up to Sadaya. I'll tell her but I'll briefly skim the subject and reassure her a lot," Cobb said.

Sadaya is a nice sophisticated and refined young woman. She's no seen one seen 'em all; not just another pretty face woman. She truly loves God and would work for Him, nonstop, if she could. "I think our almighty God appreciates Sadaya Ruby Day very much and He protects her from struggles known and unknown. Cobb and Cynthia agree. I also think God protects Sadaya's best friend Cynthia Persons who works for God at a different church. They are two women who are just blessed. God has changed their life for the better and they love Him. Cobb Jackson has also had changes in His life to take place. He volunteers at the church regularly and he says he really enjoys volunteering and working for God when he can. He has carried the altar flower bouquets downstairs to the basement and returned them when Saturday comes, the day before the Sabbath. He helped to pick food and grocery items for 24 senior citizen individuals or families. He hand delivered each and every one of those grocery packages. He helped to wipe the dust off of the dining room tables. He brought in 600lbs of donated breads and bagels twice a week except for when he was on the road with NY Boxer Basketball Team. He joined the Mechanics Group with the Sexton Mr. Williams to fix up cars, trucks, SUVs. There are 3 mechanics that belong to the group as well. Cobb has learned to bless God no matter what happens. No matter how he feels, no matter what the weather is like, no matter how much money he has in his pockets, no matter whether he loses a game or wins the game, no matter whether he has a girlfriend or not bless God. Praise God and thank God as often as possible. He hears us. He hears every prayer. Cobb called Sadaya and he told her he had something to talk to her about and it's very important. It's about Cynthia Persons. Sadaya was on another line and couldn't talk long "honey, I'll call you back tonight or in the morning," she said. The class has a big test tomorrow. I'm giving out prizes to the highest scorers. Wish us luck. Good luck talk to ya. See' ya, she replied. He said "see ya. Good. This gives me time to think about how to tell her about Cynthia's boyfriend. Oh boy. This is where I could use the expertise and the experience of her mother and father. They've known Cynthia Persons since she was a little girl. They always know best, her parents do. After I tell them I can excuse myself and leave; go anywhere where I can get some fresh air and do tension reduction exercises and calm my mind; relax my mind, Cobb was thinking. There are also those breathing exercises which the pastor taught me to do when I'm feeling stressed and spazzed out," Cobb said. Cobb reached back into his mind. He reflected on the pastor's word which he had for Cobb in one of the pastoral counseling sessions. He told Cobb that Cobb was a great man who was born with a purpose and it is a mighty purpose. It's no mistake that God stopped his phone's battery from working at that split time he met Sadaya. Cobb had prayed for a beautiful wife to give him companionship and love and maybe children. Two children, maybe. Cobb told the pastor he "didn't want to rush things but he knew he didn't rule it out." Children should have both a mother and father home to be home to run the or lead the family. Cobb knew he travelled and he preferred to be home with his children if he would have any. Cobb liked being told by the pastor that he was a great man serving a purpose for God. He felt proud to be doing anything for God Himself. "I have often felt like God was planning my life and I'm satisfied with that," he said. God helps me to respect myself and to protect myself and my loved ones prayer fully.

Many times I have heard of major tragedies happening in people's lives and then they turn to God for comfort and companionship and relationship. It shouldn't have to be after bad and dangerous things happen that we reach out to God. It should be because He's been so good to us. Our loved ones are still alive. The sky, the sun, the moon is still hanging up in the sky. The car only smoked, it didn't blow up. The house didn't catch on fire. The burn was only about an inch wide; it could have burned my whole arm. The airplane had to land for safety it didn't crash or have to crash. The report was for the police to search and seize not to beat up the people in the apartment and they didn't. They were very professional in how they did their jobs. All of the things that God puts into our lives are really blessings in disguise and some of us don't have sense enough to see it, Cobb was thinking. I was having my comfort zone disturbed so that I could meet my future wife I think "Cobb thought.

"I couldn't see it happening ahead of time but God let me know after reading the Bible that everything that He does has a reason and has purpose. He also let me know this after praying to Him and diligently seeking Him," Cobb reasoned within his mind. Some of what I think about God, I wouldn't have a problem reading the Bible and looking for answers because that's what He tells us to do. If I want to know what God is doing about certain issues in my life all I have to do is to pray and read his Holy Scriptures and really discipline myself to making this a regular practice and to worship Him, in my life. All of a sudden things will become so clear and so succinct and He said to place all of our burdens at His Feet and to rest in His bosom. Sometimes I say, Father God, I rest in Your Bosom. I'm more than happy to rest in your Bosom and to rest my mind, my body and my soul with You, of course," Cobb was thinking.

"Even the fact that my time and my nerves were inconvenienced didn't matter much when my car was smoking although I paid all of that money for it. I still was able to meet Sadaya Ruby Day, I'm privately considering her my future wife. I'm in prayer about this," Cobb said. "I know within me that God will answer me with a Yes about her and my prayer concerns because He said he would give me so much in the Holy Scriptures. It's promises are true and I have learned to trust God for everything," Cobb Jackson thought and still thinks and he will always think. Make your life's puzzle abstract. Whatever type of art piece you choose, but make it pretty," Cobb was saying to some of his teammates when it came to how to play, make it pretty basketball. Put the pieces together and rock the opponent. Make the enemy shake and cringe with the greatness of your game. Cobb, as team Captain, told his teammates. "Make it pretty."

"Let nothing about you fail. Do your best to pass the tests that God gives to us sometimes. The more tested you get the more worry and fret you should give to God. Bow your head and bend your knees, with a humble attitude looking to God to calm you and to solve your problems according to His plan for your life. Don't be afraid to dream while you're going through," Cobb told Sadaya. "Don't let it stop your progress. Dream and Dream on. First you dream and then you make the dream come true," he said.

Cobb and Sadaya were successful people in their selected fields. He being a professional basketball star and she being a teacher of mathematics and Social Studies award-winning. They have both fallen in love with one another and they have fallen deeply. They both prayed to meet each other before meeting one another. God answers prayers and He's on-target. He is Omnipotent, Omniscient, Omnipresent, sovereign and so much more powerful than we as human beings will ever know. He promises us that he will work for us. He will guard us from dangers known and unknown.

Cobb Jackson was doing a photo shoot about 7-10 minutes drive from where Sadaya's school was. He called her and asked her to meet him for lunch. She said her lunch break was from 1:00 pm to 2:00 pm. He said he would buy all the food and have it ready for when they meet.

When Sadaya met Cobb outside for lunch, he was glad to see her. He pulled her close to him, chest to chest. He hugged her and then he kissed her tap kiss style. He seemed to be saying, "I am a man." The way he held her seemed to point out that which he was thinking: "a man is usually stronger than a woman. When I pulled her to me, I felt her power. I felt how a man is supposed to feel when he hugs a woman, the weaker vessel," Cobb thought. "I was being frisky. I was so frisky that Sadaya started calling me Mr. Frisky. That's my nickname for you from now oh," she said. He liked surprising Sadaya by slipping behind her and kissing her on the neck; by grabbing her hands and placing a necklace around her neck. It would be wonderful to do those things and to whisper sweet nothing in her ears. I also intend to surprise her in other ways; ways that will require me to overcome the problem I have with my lips clamping shut every time I try to tell her how much she means to me. There was a time a 4 months ago when Sadaya had a virus. Cobb had to pray for her to get better and she did. God heals.

Keeping Our Faith: A Prayer Poem for Women

May our hearts be resilient and never weary
in well-doing. May we understand
that God is for us with every step we take
and will never leave us or forsake us. .
May we speak to our mountains and truly
believe they can move and they do so.
May we fight with our faith.

© C. Jakes Coleman

Amen

When a man wants to look at a basketball game, he doesn't tune in to a Ballet sonnet programme. When a man wants a woman to help him to shape his spirituality he wants her to help him to shape his destiny too.

The man often for the woman's countenance to be soft bright and her lips to be loyal and moist. Her voice to be full like a basket full of beauty and cheer. Real beauty is about loving who you are as you are and I love my curly hair Little Miss California Cameron Davu said.

For truly I SAY TO YOU IF YOU HAVE FAITH THE SIZE OF A GRAIN OF A MUSTARD SEED AND YOU WILL SAY TO THE MOUNTAIN, MOVE FROM HERE TO

THERE AND IT WILL MOVE. And nothing will be impossible to you. But this kind does not go out except by prayer and fasting, The Modern English Version of the Holy Bible. Matthew 17: 19-21 Kings James Version.

Sadaya decided to share the above prayer and the above Holy Scriptures with her Bible Study class. She said anytime you need strengthening and obstacles moved out of your way, reconnect with God and there might be some hints and tips in the above that will help you. Good luck and God's Speed to you.

I want to be able to see more of you and to snuggle, wuggle and cuddle up I want you to feel me when I smile. Cobb had a unique way of saying the name Sadaya. The sound of my name on his lips was like listening to thunder and lightning strike, Sadaya thought meditatively. How does a teacher of 6th grade mathematics and Social Studies teach a world traveled Basketball Player how to be more loving? "I can't say that stuff to Cobb; he'll think I'm a loose woman," Sadaya said to her father on the telephone. Sadaya looked away from the newspaper which interfered with what basketball player she was drooling over in the Sports Section. "The pastor of the church said hello to you Sadaya," someone said. "Oh yeah, hi pastor, so nice to see you again. I'm here for Bible Study," Sadaya told the pastor. "Good I'll see you later," he said. Pastor teaches Bible Study. Cobb called Sadaya on her other line: "guess what. There's a special group of businesswomen here at the Stadium who blows me kisses all of the time and some of them dare me to take my shirt off and go shirt less. They're calling me sexy. They feel I'd look sexier if I took my shirt off. What do you think Sadaya? Cobb asked. "Cobb honey, I'm on the other line with my dad. I'll call you back. Please let me call you back. By the way there's an article about you in today's newspaper, the Sentinel 2. O.k. honey, I'll talk to you soon. Bye," Sadaya said apologetically.

Trainers and Publicity Agents are on Speed Dial. The New York Host Newspaper Sports of All Sorts Column Writer Host Hank Dezonie and Joan Arnow give any score at any time. They interviewed the famous Cobb Jackson on his way out of the locker room: we see you're doing well in your basketball career with 52 points won by you and you alone in your game against the Gleeful Giants today. How's your love life? "Joan asked, with Hank laughing." let not laugh and make my love life even worse. There are many women who look at me and communicate via the internet. They want me to take off my tee shirts and my uniforms and they want me to go shirtless. I would only go shirtless for about 10 women and their identities shall remain anonymous. Well, now you have my love life in a nutshell. I've been concentrating on building my life spiritually, honestly. The Bible has been translated in over 531 languages all over the world. It is an Amazing document and I've wanted to study the Bible more for the last few years. I'm making the right moves. I'm going to a church when I'm not traveling and I'm learning more; learning all that I can about our Creator the Amazing God of the Universe, said Cobb Jackson. "Well said," said Joan Arnow. There was inclement weather. It was a cold, rain, dark night. Cobb Jackson put his hood over his head and he ran to his car. His work was successfully done for the evening.

Cobb Jackson was grateful to be pulling into his driveway in such inclement weather. It was a pleasure to be home. Surprisingly, there weren't too many voice mail messages on the house telephone. There's a relationship Agency for God's People: God's people of the church.com Mr. Jackson, please call us back. We have the date for you, in case you're looking for a wife for yourself. Tastefully, of course.

Mr. Austere called and he as the Choir Director "would like to invite" Cobb to become a member of the choir. They meet every week on Wednesday, 7:30 p.m. Vivvie Jackson Cobb's first cousin is calling to see how're you feeling and can we meet and go to dinner or something. "Call me this week," Vivvie said. Also Mr. and Mrs. Cobb Jackson called: [Cobb's parents]

Son, we want you to take us to the movies. Can you come over tomorrow and take us? There's a new movie out, a love story your mother and I want to see it. Talk to you when you call us back. The weatherman said there might be snow and ice tomorrow. Better take your SUV. "No calls from Sadaya, Hmmm I wonder why. It's been almost 2 months since I've heard from her. As it turns out its good I have to travel for a living. I needed to get away to clear my mind. I'm glad I have a plan although my traveling schedule is hectic. Cobb sometimes travels with Victor McGrath who also plays with the NY Boxers team. He lives less than a mile from his teammate. They've become pretty good friends. Sometimes Cobb drives and sometimes Victor drives. A few years ago Victor and his wife Susan were going through a legal separation; a loud severe legal separation. My Dear God I bent my knees so much and got humble before the Lord so much, only God knows how much I did for that couple. He caused her so much misery. He tried to take the 3 kids away from her. He said she was sexually promiscuous; he threatened todisappeared away from everyone for 6 months.

They thought he was dead or close to it. The family, Susan in particular, was terrified. He had married 4 wives and all of them except for Susan were found dead by car accidents. He was always out of town, or out of touch. They never did find anything on him. The always accused his wife Susan of not being the best mother. There's nothing worse than a man who would take a mother's 3 kids away from her. He was a sadistic husband also sexually promiscuous and a possible murderer some people said. Cobb, when he rode with Victor, sometimes lightly broached the subject. Victor said the essence of who the person is inside makes the difference to me. It's like I heard you say, Cobb, "I'm a man who is determined to live my life above the muck and the mire of the ditch." The relationship took about 7 months to simmer down; but all of a sudden Victor and Susan were lovebirds. They said they made up with each other and it would last forever. So far, it has. At any given moment anyone can see Victor and Susan hugging and necking in the car before their kids get to the SUV or the Van; they have both types of vehicles. Victor now often jokes with Cobb about his suave way of dressing and Victor admires Cobb's style of dress. By the way, the last time Victor saw Cobb, Cobb was wearing a tailored silk suit with a white cotton linen shirt and a linen paisley tie. Victor said Cobb was a page in SQ and SI Magazines. "You look great. I've got to take my dress up lessons from you, Cobb. I'm learning, just looking at you," Victor said.

Every time I see Victor I honestly wonder about he and Susan and what really caused there to be success where there was once misery in their marriage. I think it was my prayers to God in their behalf. The cries to God of their brothers and sisters from their church caused miracles in their marriage too. Yes, the Bible says "prayer changes things." It certainly did change things for the McGrath's we pray forever.

Being motivated to present your best to the world matters. The advice from the Psychologist is don't be upset. You and your spouse are learning how to reevaluate our self-worth. Find solace in prayers, reading or taking a spa or gym fitness day. Try forgiveness, not anger. He who ceases from anger is from expecting the best and believing that miracles exist. "Although I am ultra feminine; yes, I am what is called a 'lonely only' on my job," said Sadaya. "This means I am the only African-American on my job. Sometimes this is a commodity," she and the Psychologist Dr. Washington say. It is that kind of thinking that caused Cobb Jackson to make so many 3- point shots. He looked very very much in shape because he kept his mind in tip top shape. He was grateful to his mother and father for their pep talks that warned him to stay away from drugs and alcohol every day. Those same pep talks told Cobb to practice every day. Shooting foul shots, practicing the 3 point shot, lay-ups and the set shots caused Cobb to become a disciplined basketball player. As captain of his team he talks to his team and he tells them what moves he going to make. Guard the lane, double team such and such a player are all a part of keeping them organized. Cobb's teammates trust him a lot more because of his self-discipline. When he turns a corner and he draws a foul, he's looking to his team to help to carry him to guard the lane so that he can either score or pass the ball. There's a lot of excitement in professional basketball, very little room for mistakes. The exercises given by his coaches to help him to accurately throw a pass and to accurately call plays were very helpful. They also helped Cobb to come up with more steals than anybody else in the league. Cobb is a smooth all handles ballplayer and he doesn't panic. His game is a progressive game. It gets better as time progresses. He is very fluid player and he has expectations for his team. He'll yell out double team I'm or he'll organize his team in a quick minute. It's reflex for him to talk to them and build their confidence while he's talking. When Cobb's team comes into the stadium and the lights are low with the loud music beat playing and they're calling out the names of the ball players, successful game. Cobb's in there helping with everything. He helps with rotations, organization of the ball players, scoring, getting looks, he helps the people off the bench and he's able to change gears while helping and assisting too. "He also accepts coaching too,: one fan said.

When you have a professional team and there are so many great and talented players, that's where Cobb Jackson is the most outstanding like the Jesse Owens in basketball shoes, he becomes so fast you can hardly see his moves. You look at him one minute and the next minute, you see him scoring. You can try to block the ball but that's about all you can try to do to stop a great ballplayer like Cobb Jackson. His last game Cobb scored 55 points and he's almost never in foul trouble. He's very capable Big expectations, big stage, big ball players like Cobb Jackson will outplay, out do and out compete and take on anybody and win. He's very rare Cobb is, he's always in the action, where the actions is, making things happen. Cobb will come along with the excellent move every time. Many people have looked forward to seeing him in the play offs for quite some time with both teams being highly competitive it ought to feel good to see the Boxers and whoever they play in the playoffs. You can bet Cobb Jackson will be brilliant. He's a true champion and a true winner.

Sadaya said, "You know I always heard he was good but man when you see him play in person you find yourself saying CobbCobbCobb, and making up a song about him almost. When Cobb has to sit down during game-play, then he comes back you can see the enthusiasm on the faces of the players of his team."

Cobb also knows how to ignite enthusiasm in the audience. He sees the openings while he's running plays and the guy is great. I can't give him enough credit. "He's worth every dollar they're paying him. This game is not easy at this level. I love watching Cobb Jackson play, because he makes it look like ice cream and cookies," said his teammate Victor McGrath.

Cobb's grandfather on his mother's side of the family reminded I'm of a different kind of sportsman. His grandfather Fitzie was a real great horse jockey. His favorite horse was the family horse Ted. The horse Ted had been driven and ridden by Cobb when he visited his grandparents. The family's horse Ted had grown old in age. What was once a strong and proud horse had became weak. Ted had often led the way through the sun and snow, up steep hills and across the mountains for the children to go to school. His once strong legs and knees now failed to stand. His life had come to a halt. "Now what are we going to do? How will we make it through?" asked the children. "Well, Ted is dead but this should not stop you from moving ahead. We will never forget that horse that led us across and over those steep hills.

In one way or another, we must die and leave each other. In life troubles may come sometimes but this is no excuse to stop the climb," said Cobb's grandmother. Many people years ago used to use the dandelion flower to makes salad, greens and tea. The dandelion was dried to make these things. They made their own soap to wash their clothes. They used baking soda to brush their teeth. They used it with water to heal athlete's foot and to kill odors that come from smelly cats. Baking soda was only used to clean clothes. Vinegar and water was used on babies for diaper rash. A paste made from aspirin in lemon water helped to make calluses on itchy, tired feet feel soft and smell good too. Some people used mayonnaise to relax their hair. Garlic is a wonderful spicy herb that grows in the ground. Years ago, people used onions and garlic to cure their colds. Children and adults still drink milk for their teeth to grow healthy and strong. Milk has calcium and vitamin D in it. We still exercise to keep our bodies strong and that's all Cobb used to do when he visited his grandfather and grandmother was use the above remedies exercise himself and the horse Ted. When Ted died, young Cobb Jackson didn't speak to anyone for about 2 weeks.

Cobb Jackson was put into the top bracket showmanship sphere. There were fans and collectors who were eager and enthusiastically greeted Cobb and his team. Cobb and his mother and father collected articles and souvenirs from around the world including Russia, China, Japan, Korea and France. The team was well-received for its 25th anniversary round-the-world tour. It was during this time that Cobb played it smart. He always stayed away from cigarettes of any kind. Basketball is a fast and exciting game. In order to be fast, Cobb didn't want to slow down his breathing and interfere with his breathing by doing any kind of drugs or cigarettes or both. Basketball is played and switched by more people than any sport in the United States of America.

Cobb also became friends with the top 5 referees of the World Series Referees. 10 Referees in all officiated the World Series of basketball. One of Cobb's friends, Matt Kennedy of New York. One of the best known referees was the chief of staff for the referees who were chosen. Each referee was cited as colorful dynamic, decisive and efficient. Cobb team, The Boxer's took the Championship this year!

Cobb has other situations occurring in his life. It seems to me that I told you quite some time ago that I do not cheat. I told you I do not sleep around I do not cheat and I do not lie," Sadaya said to Cobb. I am not accustomed to having men come to my job and accuse me of being unfaithful, she said. He needed to be alone for his peace of mind and for his sanity,' he said. He left Sadaya's job and he slammed the door harshly behind him. Sadaya yelled through the closed door: "somebody is trying to create a problem for us where there isn't one," Sadaya said. Sadaya was determined to follow the rules and keep her job. Approximately 2 years ago a student in the high school down the road was practicing for a diving match! He broke his back off the diving board and drowned in the water. His name was Desmond John. This year The Desmond John Memorial will be hosted by Sadaya and her school she intends to invite the press including her friend Cynthia from The Bear News Service. She also intends to have a smorgasbord of every kind of catered food a human being can think of. She made up her mind she wasn't going to let a fight with Cobb stand in her way. She's inviting the Superintendent of Schools, the Mayor and a long list of dignitaries.

"O Lord do not rebuke me in your anger, nor discipline me in the heat of your anger. Be gracious to me' Lord for I am week; O Lord heal me for my bones are terrified. My eyes wastes away from grief; it grows weak because of all those hostile to me. Depart from me, all you workers of iniquity; for the Lord has heard the voice of my weeping. The Lord has heard my supplication, the Lord accepts my prayer. May all my enemies be ashamed and greatly terrified; may they turn back and be suddenly ashamed.

Sadaya found out that her ex-boyfriend Thaddeus was married. Secretly, she was angry with him for getting married. "I've often thought of you. Let me take you out to dinner," Thaddeus her ex-boyfriend said. "I'd explained I am a Christian – I don't go with married men anywhere but to meet their wives. I am a real friend of wives," Sadaya said. Humbled and on her knees about unrequited sex, arguing with Cobb about getting couples therapy, Cynthia arguing in the church the Sexton was arguing with Jimmy someone nobody liked. The Sexton said in your future you might be wondering why your body and your teeth aren't in the same room. Sadaya has some sexual issues she wants to explore with a therapist; but first explore it in prayer with God. Remember the Bible says "prayer changes things." Give up the hate. Give yourselves time to learn to forgive. There was a fierce storm expected and the men of a village were expecting the storm. Everyone went inside under sturdy shelter except for 1 man. When he was asked why he didn't go inside the man said "I don't respect the storm. I tell the storm where to go. The next day the storm came and the man was killed. Well, the towns people said, "the storm didn't respect a fool." Nobody knows when their last day on earth will come, so stay humble and on your knees. Tomorrow's low temperatures may cause the team some issues because they have to fly on an airplane. This is their year, the Boxers Basketball Team. We've been seeing improvements all throughout the season, and we're very very happy! Have a great Championship Day Parade and may you Cobb and Sadaya have romance, plenty romance. The stadium was yelling "we are Cobb happy. We are we are Cobb happy. I'm Cobb Happy!" well-wishes yelled and laughed.

The pastor told Bible study class. "My mother and father have a good relationship I think. I'm interested in having a healthy, fulfilling relationship a relationship that is successful. I've decided to work for God wherever I am and I want to get God into whatever I do. God instructs man on how to be a great husband and how to love his wife. Women want to know that after God they and the children are next. That's all there is to it. If you come home and you've been home 60 minutes, and you've only said 20 words to your wife, something's wrong. Think productively about what you do with your wife and yours and her time. Put meat into the time you spend with your wife. Train her to spend the best quality time with you. Don't let your wife be the only one working on the relationship. Both the husband and the wife need to be working on the relationship to make the relationship work too many times we don't do that but we should. Create additional motivation for the husband and wife to work together. Sometimes review the advances made in the relationship. Add to the mutually shared experience of love and doing something special your relationship. Be she wife, girlfriend, boyfriend or husband. Let her see love shining through you. collaboratively impact the relationship. Don't let your love go without you saying more but not too much. Don't let your love go without you doing something special in the relationship. You've got the authority of the believer shining all over you. Some people have the anointing of God for the Ministry and some people are headed for leadership and familial success. Check larger ones. Maybe they'll have workshops and seminars with you," Cobb said. Make suggestions to theses churches. They're usually great about accepting suggestions. Good luck.

The Bible Study affected Sadaya in a positive way. Later, secretly, Sadaya was laying in her bed at home, thinking about what kind of home she and Cobb would have,; if he's still speaking she thought to me. I have to talk to him because I heard he was thinking of asking someone new to the Championship Day Parade. One thing is for sure: I didn't get asked," Sadaya thought. If we were able to get back together I'm not saying I have to have the biggest house in the state of New York; I'm saying the house should be roomy and modern. I prefer the white or ivory stucco beach house design. The décor should combine fresh, neutral, seasonal eye catching colors and new hues. I want to be able to color my world with mix and match bedding, with reversible comforters, reversible pillows and so much storage for our clothing that we'd be extremely satisfied with it. I'd like floral rugs to match the New Reversible water color Decorative Pillows. Versatile decorative pillows with stylish watercolor designs add splashes of bright color to décor. For the winter weather months, I want the studio down comforter; plush, cozy and comfortable plus the Paisley print sheet set, she said. "Of courseCobb and I will both have offices in the house of my dreams. I'd decorate the women's office with floral rugs and jute rugs too. I saw a chair for women. Wide seat in bonded leather with a matching piped back chrome accents, heavy duty casters and hydraulic eight adjustments. I want the jute rugs to have an over lapped geometric pattern. I also like hand tufted flower rugs. I also like the satin bedspread with ivory heart shaped designs on it for the guest rooms. I've got everything planned even when it comes down to the mats on the floors. They'll be called the hand-tufted um mats. Oh boy will they feel comfortable underfoot. Yes baby come home to mama" said Sadaya. "I love, decorating. I fantasize about it" she said.

"Come home to mama and help me in my new 2 oven gourmet sized and gourmet styled kitchen. What a beauty especially with middle island and all counter tops being deep grained marble.

Hotdog!" I love new kitchens. I like the marble fabulous. Sadaya grinned from ear to ear.

Sadaya laid still on her bed and closed and opened her eyes every time she thought something negative about Cobb." I opened and closed my eyes a lot," she thought.

"I don't' know why he's so angry with me. I believe in the power of God and I believe in the power of hugs. I hug Cobb Jackson every time we see each other to show him the power of the Magnificent Holy Spirit; to show him I love seeing him and being with him. I'm always excited to see Cobb," Sadaya said. This time though, he very belligerent and stubborn Thaddeus, my ex-boyfriend called me back and we talked. He said he wouldn't talk to me anymore if he couldn't [pick me up in an hour and take me to a restaurant. I instantly agreed and I was ready to meet him in an hour. I was happy to see Thaddeus after I thought about the fact that I could still have dinner with him, even if he was married. It's a fact I certainly would never sleep with him while he's married. I explained this to Thaddeus before and I think he understands my character. I told him seriously the next time we go to a restaurant I want him to take his wife and be full of smiles all night long.

And life goes on. . . Sadaya was invited by a friend of hers Judith Scoreo who works in the White House to a dinner at the White House. She turned the television up and she listened to what the President was saying:" . . . if we decline to invest in the children of immigrants, just because they don't look like us, we diminish the prospects of our own children – because these brown kids will represent a larger share of America's work force. Last year incomes rose for all races, age – groups for men and for women. Going forward, we must up hold laws against discrimination –in hiring, in housing in education and the criminal justice system. That's what our Constitution and highest ideals require. But laws alone won't be enough. Hearts must change," the President said.

Sadaya was trying to think of a way to ask her friend Judith if she could bring her class of 32 students; 6th grade students to the dinner, which would be the opportunity of a lifetime. How much is the extra fee for bringing the children with me? Sadaya sat up from her bed and she got up. "Well, no better time like the present. I'm going to write a letter to Judith and I'll see what she has to say about my request to be escorted by all of my 32 children. This ought to be fun. Of course, Sadaya got down on her knees and she asked God about if first. Then she wrote the letter to Judith Scorco. I gave the address to the school so that I can open the letter and read it to the children if Judith's answer is yes. I hope her answer is quick and happy for the children's sake, Sadaya thought.

In the meantime, while waiting to hear from Judith, Sadaya waited with great expectations. She heard from Judith in 4 days which was considered good time for the U.S. Postal Service. Judith's answer was a resounding "yes, no problem Sadaya wrote that she could charter the bus service. The school system has a standing contract with bus companies all over the United States of America. She also wrote that it would take approximately 5 hours to get there from New York but she didn't mind. The special experience makes it all worthwhile. People get pictures and special experiences with schoolchildren often for publicity. Especially those who are a nice class of children who knew how to act and have good manners.

The President and his staff love these types of children. Sadaya's school children screamed briefly. They were the happiest 6th grade class. They said they could hardly wait for this great dinner with the President of the U.S.A. to take place.

"You see there, if Cobb Jackson was still speaking to me, I'd invite him to have dinner with my class and myself and the President of the United States of America. The last time I called him was 7 days ago today. Maybe dinner. Yeah, that's the answer. I'll call him during my lunch break and find out if he's still speaking to me, Sadaya said. "If he's still talking to me he'll say something like 'hey there, hi there. You're my favorite chick. Where have you been for all of my life?" Cobb would surely say, Sadaya thought. At 5 past the hour 1:05 pm Sadaya used her cell phone and she called Cobb Jackson. She received his voicemail for about the 6th or 7th time since last week. I'm not sure you'll ever call me again Cobb. I still can't see where what I've done is so bad. Maybe with God's grace you'll call me back and explain it to me when you call me back. I have a special invitation for you to the White House to have dinner with the President of the United States of America. You know we said we will return to the beach just you and I but we didn't get a chance to return. Your schedule and my schedule were much too hectic. This dinner I'm talking about is 1 ½ months from now. Please call be before next week. ThanksSadaya Ruby Day. Oh yes, here's a quickie joke before I hand up. Nicky and I decided we'd been seeing too much of each other. So last night we turned out the lights. Ha Ha. Ha. Bye, I hope I hear from you soon.

For the rest of her lunch break Sadaya read the newspaper. One of the larger articles investigated Game shows. Sadaya was thinking about her mother's research and she copied one of the questions from the new Game Show: Name something a man should never say to a woman.

> You look bad/hideous
> You look ugly
> You look dumb
> You look pregnant
> You look different
> You look old
> You look tired
> You look hungry

What has 4 legs and flies? A man and 2 prs of pants? No silly 2 pairs of pants. Ha HaHa. Ha HaHa.

When Sadaya got home there was a voicemail message that sounded like Cobb's voice. He asked Sadaya to call him. He wanted to come over and to talk to Sadaya because he leaves town in two days. Sadaya was very happy to hear from him and to hear his voice. She called back and Cobb Jackson answered. Is this him? Is this really my Cobb Jackson? Oh, what a joy. I am overjoyed that I have heard from you, finally. Okay Cobb. When do you and I meet? Let me know now, Sadaya said. Cobb said "what about tonight. Let's meet tonight. I can be there in about 40 minutes. Sadaya, not wanting to take away the momentum said okay. I'll see you then. He said, "Let's go get something to eat at the new restaurant in the shopping mall. Okay honey, see you soon."

Sadaya had passions to pursue. She had to freshen up and change her clothing and refresh her makeup. Sadaya also wanted to have a conversation about the game show. "Guess what the name of the New Game Show is?" Sadaya asked. Her mother said, "I don't know maybe Spin? Drop? Snooty?" her mother said.

Sadaya laughed. "It's called, My Favorite Game Show." Sadaya's reaction was like her mother's. They both howled. They laughed and told jokes to each other for another 15 minutes.

The doorbell rang. It was Cobb about five minutes earlier than he said. He, of course, greeted Sadaya's parents with the utmost respect. He explained that he had come to pick up Sadaya and to take her out to eat. Sadaya's mother said she wanted fried shrimp. His father put in an order for a cheeseburger, salad and fries.

"Okay mom and dad. I'll see you and talk to you later. Call me if you need me sooner than when I'll bring you your food." Sadaya asked Cobb, "Am I riding with you or are you riding with me?" "Let's go limousine styling," said Cobb. "Okay, fine with me," Sadaya said. The night time weather was mild with wind basically blowing like a soft breeze through Sadaya's hair, making her look extremely attractive to Cobb. Sadaya suggested they take the food take out and then deliver it to her parents as soon as possible. That frees them up to talk about their relationship. So, after having dinner, Sadaya and Cobb left abruptly without mentioning their relationship plights. After delivering their food to her parents, Sadaya and Cobb decided to sit in the limousine and talk. Cobb told the driver to go back to the mall and to go get something to eat for about an hour. Cobb told the driver he would call on his cell phone and let him know when he's ready to leave.

Cobb and Sadaya were also very concerned about fans recognizing Cobb. Usually he gets someone else to get food for him because fans tend to be intense sometimes. Some fans don't know when to be on their best behavior. Sadaya and Cobb sat in the limousine and adored one another, although they hadn't spoken for over two months. There was a lot of laughter going on in the beginning. Sadaya decided to tell more of her corny jokes. They hurried and ate their food. They rushed to get the food back to Sadaya's parents.

Now that they're in the limousine they'll have privacy. Cobb told the limousine driver to disappear for about an hour and a half. Cobb said he'd call him on his cell phone when he's ready to go. The chauffer disappeared behind the wall of the shopping mall. Now that they're in the limousine and they have privacy, they slowly approach the subject. "Who is going to start this very difficult conversation? I will," said Cobb. I wasn't going to tell you that I knew something about you but the more I've thought about you the more I realize it's not good to keep secrets from one another. My mother and my father were out to dinner with me at Sheila's Restaurant. They and I myself laughed and had a very nice time until my father saw something. He got up from his dinner to go to the restroom. He looked into the other part of the restaurant. He wasn't' sure of where the restrooms were located. As he was about to ask the waiter for a clarification of directions, he saw you. He was going to speak to you and to say hello, but you were there with a gentleman friend. Your eyes caught his eye and when Sadaya recognized me she shouted; she was shocked, the way my father described it; honestly.

My father was just as shocked as Sadaya to see her in the restaurant with another man. "Excuse me, but this is how my father phrased this to me," said Cobb in exasperation after seeing Sadaya's twisted face. He also said the two of you looked intimate because he had one of his legs interlocked into one of your legs under the table, Cobb said. Sadaya stood up and said, "Mr. Jackson, meet my friend Thaddeus." Mr. Jackson did meet Thaddeus and he didn't stay long. He then told Thaddeus he had to go and then he left. He barely spoke to Sadaya upon leaving. When Cobb's father went back to his son's table at the restaurant he sat for 15 minutes without speaking. "Dad, what's going on; is everything okay?" Cobb asked. "You look like you've got a lot on your mind or seen a ghost," Cobb said. "Cobb, you're my son and you know that I love you. I have nothing but respect for you," Cobb's father told his son. Brace yourself because I don't want to be hurt if you get hurt so do I. Mr. Jackson told Cobb and Cobb's mother abut who was at the restaurant with Sadaya and about their legs under the table. Cobb asked his father where they were in the restaurant. He got up immediately to find Sadaya. His father yelled behind him, "We don't need negative publicity. Please don't start a fight.

That's why I got out of there as fast as I did. Think, son, think. We don't want the newspapers writing this up. Remember who you are, son," Mr. Jackson loudly whispered. Before Mr. Jackson could finish talking, Cobb disappeared through the alcove in the restaurant. He figured he would let Sadaya see him and not say anything; just a wave would do the trick. Just to let her know she was caught red-handed. When he went to the area where Sadaya and Thaddeus were seated, they were gone. Two and a half months went by. They're just speaking to each other for the first time since the restaurant sighting.

We don't want this to be common knowledge. Boy is my father right. That's all I need is bad publicity. I'm kind of glad I didn't see Sadaya today and here 'gentleman friend,' Cobb thought. Dad, they're gone. Nobody's there. "Good." Cobb's father was relieved. "Tell nobody. "We don't want any leaks to the press," Mr. Jackson said. "Ditto, Dad," Cobb said. Mrs. Jackson wanted Cobb to wait before he called Sadaya. Didn't want to give the impression that he's desperate for her. It was good that Sadaya called first and kept calling until she heard his voice because Cobb was about to empty his arsenal of black book names. Sadaya Ruby Day was the first one to be thrown out. He almost gave up on her. Cobb was upset. When he gets upset, Cobb is known to lash out at both the innocent and the guilty. Plus, in this town, Cobb was thinking, tongues wag like puppy dog tails. Sadaya explained that she too was upset. She stated she wanted to discuss this situation further. Cobb said he didn't know if he ever wanted to speak about this ever again. Are you serious about that guy Thaddeus? Why did you call him instead of me?

Is this the only time that you've been out with him? Does he want to be with you sexually? A whole list of questions came out of Cobb. With each question that was answered, Cobb got angrier and angrier. He never thought he'd be so jealous over Sadaya. Even Cobb's mother Millicent noticed how strongly Cobb responded when he heard that Sadaya was out with another man. E-mail photo album brain games – camera: Cobb kept thinking about the different functions and apps on his telephone to distract himself. He was very tempted to not speak any longer to Sadaya. Too angry. I need to tune her out of my mind. Too many negative emotions. "Sadaya, excuse me; I'll be back in a few minutes," Cobb said. With all the manners he could muster up as a gentleman, Cobb got out of the limousine and went into the shopping mall. He began to draw deep breaths which made him feel much better. He went into the men's room and he put cold water on his face several times, while drying his face soon thereafter with paper towels.

When in the men's room, Cobb's selfish side surfaced: "This was a shocking misuse of my time and resources. If I felt better, I'd pour oil on the troubled water and settle this situation for good," Cobb was thinking. There's just one problem: I have fallen in love with Sadaya, I think. I've been lovesick which doesn't feel so good. I've laid awake in my bed just thinking about Sadaya; how she dresses, how she talks, remembering what she says to me about her job, her parents, how she spends her time. I'm accustomed to handling and controlling situations and getting specific results. I never felt so out of control. I love her but I can't trust her yet. She didn't call me for so long and she did go out with another man. I'd better go back to the limousine and see what else she has to say, he thought to himself. He thought of one of the scriptures: Set me as a seal upon your arm; for love is as strong as death, passion fierce as the grave. It's fires of desire are as ardent flames, a most intense flame. Many waters cannot quench love, neither can floods drown it. If a man offered for love all the wealth of his house, it would be utterly condemned.

When Cobb returned to the limousine, Sadaya was on the telephone talking to the pastor about the church and the Freedom parish hall and the Sanctuary restoration completion. Sadaya sits on the fundraising committee. Sadaya hung up after five minutes or so. Cobb said, "it surely took you long enough." She said, 'oh hush up, it was only 5 or 10 minutes," Sadaya said, shooting words right back at Cobb. After those words, Cobb was quiet. Silent. The only thing he said was "were you cheating on me, Sadaya?" "For the record, I do not cheat and I do not sleep around. I DO NOT SLEEP AROUND!" Sadaya said emphatically. "It's best for you to tell me rather than someone else and it get back to me that way. Who is this guy Thaddeus to you anyway? Didn't you tell me he was your ex-boyfriend?" Cobb wondered. Sadaya screamed almost as loud as she could. You're hard headed. Try to follow the rhythm of my voice. I don't sleep around. I don't sleep around. Remember I told you this before. Cobb forced a smile. He then put his hands up and he clapped his hands for Sadaya. Excuse me Cobb, now it's time for me to get out of the car and go take a break. Sadaya got out of the limousine and went to the pizza parlor and ordered zeppolas with white sugar/powdered sugar on the zeppolas. She also ordered a large cup of Cola. Although she'd eaten not long ago, she hadn't anything sweet. Her emotions, the negative emotions were giving her a sweet tooth and making her more anxious. She took the zeppolas to the limousine and she offered them to Cobb. "No," he said glibly. She got back into the car with a don't care if you do, don't care if you don't attitude. "One of these days your little attitude is going to get you in a lot of trouble with me," Cobb said. The thing that Sadaya didn't know about Cobb is that he knows how to forgive but she didn't seem humble enough to him, for him to forgive. That's really what Cobb was looking for was humility. But Sadaya resented being seen at dinner with another man. Rather than to answer all of his questions, Sadaya simply said, "I'm not in love with him Cobb. I prefer you." Cobb was quiet again. If I wasn't so mad at Sadaya, I'd say, "how romantic" and I'd make some quick kissy moves on her and then she'd be on my arms before she realizes it. I'm never afraid to make a bold move. Go for a bold move and wake her up from her misery, Cobb thought. Sadaya said she was misery-ridden and confused about a few things but we'd have to talk about it at another time. She wasn't feeling good. She felt nauseous. Cobb had her to lay down in the limousine and he told her to go to sleep. He took his jacket off and he spread it over Sadaya, so she could rest during the 50-minute trip back home.

Sadaya fell asleep and didn't wake up until the limousine pulled up to her house. "oh my gosh; I feel like a brick hit me," Sadaya said. "Well, Cobb it's been a long night's journey into day. Call me. Right now, I'm still sick. I'm going into the house and lay down again" Sadaya said. "See ya, your moodiness," Cobb said and he walked her to her door. "Good night," Cobb said. "Call me this week," Sadaya said. Cobb never did say he would call Sadaya back, which did hurt Sadaya's feelings. She misses talking to him on the telephone and feeling close to him, but she did go out with someone else.

Sadaya was still feeling sick and weak. Her parents were anxious to hear what happened between she and Cobb. Sadaya apologized. She said she wanted to take a short nap because she didn't feel well. She said she'd wake up in about an hour and she'd tell her parents all about it. "Okay hone, go get your nap, we'll see you later."

While Sadaya was asleep in her bed, her mother and her father discussed her predicament. Above everything, they have defended their daughter Sadaya and they continually save her reputation. The fact of the matter is neither Sadaya nor Cobb are married. They can go out to dinner at any time with whomever they choose to go out with. Sadaya's father said to his wife, that hopefully Cobb and Sadaya's relationship will mature and they'll be as close as Sadaya's parents' relationship is. "Give it a few months and it will all blow over. This too shall pass. Also, it's not every day that you meet a Cobb Jackson. Lord knows, we certainly don't want to lose him. He's everything good for Sadaya and we want her to end up with him. He'd be the best provider, the romantic type he is and he would truly protect her. He'd also put up with her moods sometimes. I believe he'd make a magnificent father. If Sadaya plays her cards right, she'll win him as her prize; that would be a very generous gift. He'll also win her, out beautiful lovely daughter. I believe they both love each other," her father said.

Sadaya asked her parents, "What has four legs and flies? Two pairs of pants. Both parents began to giggle and to laugh. Ha, ha, ha. She also admitted to her parents that she has Cobb fantasies. He and I go on a game show and we win the game and he lets me have all of the money. It's called the Let's Win Some Money Game Show."

Sadaya also had a dream about Cobb. She was sitting in the Stadium and people were complimenting Cobb. Sadaya looked at a reporter and she said, "I know. They can't seem to score a point without him." The reporter said, "you know that's right." Sometimes I am taking a bath or a shower. I fantasize that we have two small children who are running up and down the staircases in the house. By the way, the children are the best-looking children I've ever seen. Both of them had curly, wavy hair, and clear skin; Olive complexioned skin. They were pretty children.

Sadaya was very pensive. At one point, she was contemplating whether or not she would tell Cobb that she has fantasies about him, and give him specifics and examples of those fantasies.

15 Minute Intermission – Go get a cup of coffee or tea.

Each character in Humble and On My Knees: A Church Love Story is drawn to God by the Almighty God. Some people do try to "runaway" because of their own likes and dislikes and fears. However, there is a royal and special connection between God and the main characters that happens royally; that happens scripturally; that happens spiritually; that happens mystically; and it's a miracle it happens at all, the way some people act. There is a mystical sparkle that God created in each person which spews love for God Himself. This book suggests that God has a place for our lives and all we have to do is re-establish our prayer connection to God each and every day. The mark you're looking for who is just right for you puts you in a specialized world; his world. God will straighten out the rough crooked edges and He will make them straight. You must believe God's Promises. Believe and keep talking to God. Later, He'll probably prove to You whom He is and what He's capable of doing in your life. You will see victories now and victories ahead for yourself. Keep talking to God and don't let go of God no matter what, regardless of how it feels. The Bible tells believers to lay your burdens at God's feet and now there are many Christians who are "just resting in his bosom waiting." Sooner or later many people come to God again and again. They rediscover the Solid Ground and they have been known to say my feet are planted on Solid Ground; and nothing; there's nothing that can turn me around. Yes, discover and re-discover the Almighty God for you. Cobb and Sadaya made rediscoveries and were rewarded. Keep talking to Him. He wants to reward you.

"When a man is interested in having a relationship with a lady, he's supposed to let her know and then render some kind of invitation to the lady such as would you like me to take you to the movies and to dinner afterwards."

"This Saturday I'm playing in a basketball game where they're honoring Dr. Martin Luther King, Jr. Would you like to come to see me play? I even have access to tickets to the Women's Games. Would you want to go with me to see the women play?" Cobb did not quickly seize the opportunity to ask Sadaya out to perfectly respectable places. As a matter of fact, Sadaya was initially worried, it took Cobb so long to ask her out. At first, I was happy as I could be and I was prancing around the house, singing, "He's fine and he's all mine!" As happy as I could be and then my father said, I don't know what you're so happy for. He hasn't asked you to go anywhere. What you smiling for? My father didn't know how badly he hurt my feelings but, as my relatives have always said, 'he's like the bull in the China closet. He never knows how to place his words wisely to keep from hurting people's feelings.' Well, I can't argue with you there but I'm sure he'll get around to it someday. Someday? Someday! You got that kind of time to waste? Mr. Day, Sadaya's father looked at the pain and disappointment and the look of discouragement in Sadaya's face. "Gee, Dad, next time don't spare my feelings so much Ha, ha, ha." Sadaya's facial expression frowned. Sadaya went into her room. Looking hurt and upset, she came downstairs and told her mother to please put her dinner in the microwave. Her mother looked at her and she immediately asked Sadaya what was wrong and why did she look like she wanted to cry?

Sadaya said she was tired and she had been singing earlier but her dad said something and he spoiled it. Anyway, she said I'm just taking a nap. Good night, see you later. Sadaya, do you want me to say something to him about it? Sadaya didn't know who she was more upset at; her father or Cobb who kept her waiting for so long. She wasn't pleased with either man at this point. It would prove to be a very ambitious undertaking. Sadaya, in an effort to settle herself and calm herself down, turned on the television. A car was torched around the corner; there were some determined demonstrators who had crowbars and batons and flashlights to protest United States issues. Their dreams and their success will be intermingled with the U.S.'s success sooner or later, they feel. The President told exit pollsters "nobody will be forgotten." So well- choreographed with so much prayer and so much emotion, our future is bright not dim. The going's on about politics and demonstrations took Sadaya mind off of her personal life and she fell asleep.

In Sadaya's sleep, she had a dream. She replied, "You couldn't look me in the eye." She hesitated and she wondered why she couldn't discern what the person in her sleep was saying. "Oh well, I knew what I was saying anyway. She said, "I don't know what you're saying but I can help you to be your best all day and I will do just that. Save what you crave and what God gave. Her? If you look in the dictionary you'll see the definition of fast woman. When Sadaya woke up in a pool of perspiration, she laid there in her bedroom trying to figure out what the dream meant. I believe a friends' recent mistakes, a female who was promiscuous was being judged by some of my colleagues and they called her bad names. Save what you have. Don't give it to her. Don't give what God gave you to her. In her subconscious mind she saw her father's words uttered earlier as a threat. She pledged herself as an ultimate personal goal to use all of the wisdom she could muster up, to save the woman in her dream and to let no harm come to her; if there would have been impending harm.

Sadaya remembered she had to go to Bible Study this night and she had to grade her 6th graders' test papers, and there would be no compromise. "I made up my mind to act worthy of myself. Bible Study helps me to be strong enough to do that. I love the way Pastor teaches Bible Study," Sadaya thought. When Sadaya got up, she went downstairs and she found her mother and father seated on the couch head to head, shoulder to shoulder, leaning on each other; asleep. The television was watching them instead of them watching the TV. Sadaya quietly laughed watching them and the TV, watching them too.

All of this we want to do. All of this we can do. All of this we will do, Sadaya was thinking about she and Cobb. Being his good-looking, handsome self, he didn't call her back. He didn't give up on Sadaya he was "just very busy," he said. "But I'm very glad that you called me, though; Sadaya I'm glad we both have such mutual respect for each other that we're no longer arguing nor are we showing each other indifference. Can I come over? Sadaya, don't you want some company? I can be there whatever time you suggest. What time do you want me to come?" "Come right now," Sadaya said. "I'll be there soon. Want some food? I'll bring it to you or do you want to go to the place and we'll get it ourselves?" Cobb asked. "Let's go get it ourselves. Okay?" Cobb asked. "Okay. I'll see you when you get here. Bye," Sadaya replied.

Cobb arrived in about 12 minutes. He spoke to Sadaya's parents and Sadaya then got into his car and left with him. They went to a neighborhood diner favorite restaurant of Sadaya's. "Cobb was very quiet tonight," Sadaya was thinking. Looks like I'm doing most of the talking about my 6th graders and how smart and wise my 6th graders are. I love them all the same. Each and every one of the 32 children in my class. It's self-evident to them and to their parents how much I love them. Sadaya gets turned on by the idea of equipping our children for the future. She has a downright fidelity when it comes to her loyalty to her children. They love being in Miss Sadaya Ruby Day's classroom. Cobb laughed when Sadaya told him four students already asked to be in her class again. They told her the Principal said she would 'mull it over' and think it over; not to ask her again until the end of the year. Cobb put his foot on the dashboard and listened as Sadaya told him how happy she was to see him. "There's something soft and alluring about Sadaya's voice. There's also a sense of authoritarianism about it," Cobb said. "If I ever did anything wrong, all she'd have to do is look at me and establish eye-contact. I'd straighten up and fly right, right away," said Cobb. "Let's get out of the car again and stretch. Well, let's go back to my house and you can stretch out on the couch," Sadaya said. "Cool," said Cobb. "By the way, I think my father has some questions to ask you about some basketball games you've played lately. He wants to ask you about some physical injuries he thinks he saw you received during the game. Talk to him if he's home today. Thank you in advance for doing this." Cobb said only if Sadaya kisses him quickly with three kisses all night long. This must be all night long, was Cobb's prerequisite. Sadaya felt something could be worked out and she promised all of those kisses for Cobb with a few extra hugs here and there. Well, don't want it to get too late. Let's go in and talk to your dad. Mr. Day was seated at the dining room table doing his tax papers. He did not hear Cobb and his daughter Sadaya when they came into the house. He was glad to see them and he said, "Oh yes, I have to talk to you Cobb. It's about your game against the Tigers last Saturday. That guy Hollings – was he bullying you?

Did I see him kick you in the leg near your lower thigh? I'm not going to have one moment of peace until I get told what happened by you; from your perspective." Cobb said, "I'm glad you asked because the referees didn't seem to notice a thing until near the end of the game; the last quarter. Our Coach started yelling at the referee and finally the ref's starting calling it. We won the game. Man, my leg is still hurting me on and off," said Cobb.

"We knew something was wrong. I thought I saw you limping on the court," Mr. Day said. "I didn't want Coach to take me out of the game so I tried not to limp, but it was hurting me too much. Luckily Coach didn't get too close to inspect my leg and my knee because my leg was really bleeding. The referee asked me if I needed a doctor and I said no" Cobb said. I'm going to visit the doctor in four days and see what he thinks. Sadaya left and came back in with a song on her mind: You are my love, the one I'm thinking of. Because you are the sunshine in my universe, you're also the ink in my pen baby. Love you madly. Sadaya sang the above song to Cobb and her father hollered. He laughed so hard at his daughter making romance with Cobb, in front of her own parents, no less. "Well, my son I'm sure that last game was tough on you but you made it through without your leg or hip being broken. I think if it was me, I would have had to deck him. Punch his lights out.

"I really wanted to, at first, but I thought from the Scriptures point of view, He who ceases from anger is blessed. It stopped me right away," Cobb said.

Sadaya went into the kitchen singing to Cobb and going back and forth, kissing him on his neck each time she saw Cobb. "Oh, yea baby," she whispered in his ears and then gave him kiss, kiss, kisses on his neck and his forehead. She teased him so much that Cobb himself began to smile and then he laughed. At times he even giggled. He giggled because Sadaya while teasing him; she tickled him. "Stop. Stop. If you don't stop I'm going to tickle you back," he said. "Ok, ok, ok," Sadaya said. "I was just playing with you, but if you play with me you'll mess up my clothes because they're a light color. Plus, I'm much more ticklish than you are. Besides that, you and my father probably aren't finished talking basketball yet. I'll be back later," Cobb and of course dad.

Sadaya went out get the mail out of her mailbox. Her parents didn't have much mail but she had magazines, catalogs, bills, and one letter. The letter was from the Professional Teachers' Association. After reading the letter, Sadaya was both flattered and happy. The letter congratulated Sadaya on being selected for The Teachers Success Citizenship Award. The award honors teachers who have inspired and motivated their students into success themselves. The Association was told by her students that they love being in Ms. Day's class and how she always has interesting lessons going on. They have been indoor skydiving, had ping pong tournaments for mathematics, had food feasts for International Day where everyone of various backgrounds, such as Spanish background and heritage would cook peas and rice or some other food dish, bring it to the school and share it with the students. This sowed the huge amounts of backgrounds among the school population and an appreciation for the heritage of the people. The Teachers Success came with an award of $1,500 and there were 10 tickets that Sadaya and the rest of the honorees were being asked to sell. The tickets were $100 each. Sadaya will be presented with a trophy at the Teachers Success event. Sadaya screamed when she saw the check for $1,500. "This money will come in handy for the rent I owe to my parents. They'll really appreciate this. I owe them $1,000 and I'll give that to them before the weekend is over. They're gonna love this," she smiled to herself. She began calling her brothers and sisters of the church and telling them about the tickets right away. After 20 minutes she went back into the kitchen and living room areas where she saw Cobb and her father watching the game on TV. It was a very exciting game. One basketball player went up to the hoop trying to make the basket and score but the biggest, tallest player of all of them threw him on the floor hard and twisted his arm while he was coming down from the hoop. It affected his shoulder, as well as his arm, and he fell hard on the floor crying from the pain. When the doctor came over to see what the problem was, he said his arm might be broken. He couldn't play the rest of this game and that was his shooting arm. Sadaya stood and watched the game for a while and when the commercials came on she made a quick announcement about her; her Teachers Success Award and she showed her parents and Cobb the $1,500 check that was sent to her, from the Association. Cobb got up immediately and hugged and kissed Sadaya and congratulated her. So, did Sadaya's parents. Her parents asked her if she wanted them to tell the principal and the people at the District Office about her award and how much the tickets are for the luncheon. Sadaya told her parents yes, she would like for them to make the announcement because if she were to talk about it a lot it feels like she's bragging. Her parents laughed long and hard but they promised that they would take care of everything that needed taken care of, including hiring a big 45-seater bus for transportation to and from the beautiful dinner The Association will have in Sadaya's and other awardees' honor.

Sadaya started writing down and taking notes and names about who would probably buy a ticket. She even had an antisocial and socialite list. The antisocial list included the ones that have troubles and have trouble getting along with people and those who act like they're angry at the world. If we figure out how to get along, things will work and then those who make it to every luncheon, dinner or dinner-dance banquet. Sadaya had an appropriate seating plan. This was one less thing for her parents to do, although they were comfortable helping out their "honoree" daughter. Her parents were glad to be expecting those who were difficult also because it prepared them for possible or potential problems. The previous year two people got into a fight. One woman picked up a plate of lasagna and dumped it into another woman's lap. All over the fact that one woman stood up and pushed her chair back too fast. She said, 'excuse me' but the other woman was already too angry. "She seemed like she had a fighting attitude anyway. She just wanted to fight someone," the head waitress mâtre'd said. Well, the Dinner-Dance won't be here for another two months so I'll have a lot of times to "get it together and to layout my fabulous and victorious wardrobe," Sadaya said. Sadaya had some clothing she had stored away in shopping bags that she hadn't even opened yet or worn. She had bought a color block sheath dress with three-quarter sleeves. It was made out of polyester and spandex, a beautiful Black/White Color block. There was impeccable tailoring on the color block jacket and she got it on sale. She was either going to pick from her closet or get the shopping bag in the future from D'Arcy's or Nack's 6th Avenue. She stopped at Janet's Beauty Nook and she freshened up her facial makeup too. What a cathartic and beautiful makeup experience as well. If it had not been for God and the Association and for Cobb, I wouldn't have been able to bless myself with such extravagant blessings this week. Thank you, for all of my blessings. Since the Bible says when we thank him it makes Him happy, I thank you a million times for the blessings you have given to me;

I believe you're very happy right now, Lord

Cobb came over to the table where Sadaya's parents were seated. He told them he would be back in about 10 minutes. He came back in 20 minutes and he handed Sadaya an envelope with a note in it and $1,500 in it. The note basically said he's happy for her award and he's giving her another $1,500 to match the Association's because he's proud of her and hed. like to escort Sadaya and her parents in the limousine to the Dinner-Dance in two months. "Oh honey, you're too good to be true. I'm looking at $1,500 more dollars now in cash. Hallelujah, thank you," Sadaya said; overjoyed.

"There's more money where that came from. You just let me Old Brother Cobb know if you need more money. You can count on me 'hon, you can count on me. I'll never charge you for the money I give to you, I promise you. Ok?" Cobb said. Sometimes it all adds up to one "S" word" silence. Sadaya was so filled up with emotion that she couldn't speak any further." His donation to her made her heart lighten up," she thought. A grey day and PM showers with breezy rain. Visibility reduced. As Sadaya was listening to the weather report, she had a thankful heart for her parents and for Cobb Jackson, the Superstar.

Sadaya was thinking that "sometimes the ones we love can get on our nerves the most; but Cobb is well-loved by me. I tolerate some of his strange ways because he's eight years younger than I am and yes, I admit it, I love him. The strangest thing about it is he never mentions our age difference. And never do I mention our age difference either. Heh, heh." Her hair and nails on all parts of her body; fingernails and toenails were all well done and Sadaya had a special facial treatment she put on her face every other night. She kept herself well-dressed for God and her man Cobb and he just gave her $1,500 more reason to. "I love Cobb. He doesn't order me around like some men have tried to do in my life or worse. Plus, he's pretty to me. I love those muscles in his shoulders. To me, he's cute and handsome all at the same time," Sadaya thought. "I love how it feels when he puts his hands on my waist and he pulls me close and then closer to him; then he holds me. I mean he really embraces me and he makes a feeling come onto me that makes me want to cry tears of joy and more joy," Sadaya thought further. The surprise with Cobb for Sadaya was that he took to the Black Memorial Baptist Church like a duck takes to water. And he's a superstar basketball player. Millions of people know him. He tries not to – really doesn't feed into the artificiality that fame brings with it. He enjoys the relationship with Sadaya. He listens well; especially to Sadaya. He's make a great husband; if she can catch him. Ha, ha, ha. Ha, ha, ha.

Cobb's father had been a staunch, strict disciplinarian. He was tough. It was tough being his son sometimes. But Cobb loved his father, even when his father would say things like, "you mind your mouth boy or I'll be putting my fist in it." Cobb respected his father tremendously and he would usually say, "Ok Dad," and/or he'd stopped talking. Cobb said he could remember a day when his father was driving through inclement, windy, gusty weather and 10 years old at the time Cobb said, "Daddy, I'm scared I don't want to die." His father said, "Cobb, I'm struggling to see. Here, take this cloth and wipe the window over there." After that, his father was quiet and so was Cobb. My only time to get tough with Cobb was when he was talking too much and he needed discipline. "It wasn't always each word; sometimes all he had to do was just breathe and I would just shut up." It wasn't always easy being his son," Cobb said.

"Sometimes he had a certain toughness about him that I wasn't about to fight," Cobb said. Now that Cobb Jackson is a household name, his father laughs about how he doesn't have to put the fear of God into his son Cobb any longer. His father, loves his son Cobb and he defends Cobb to this day with everything, especially since now he is much more involved in the Black Memorial Church. I don't find that toughness in dad any longer. I guess because I'm a grown up human man now. Like when I told that joke before: What has four legs and flies? Answer: two pairs of pants. My dad didn't laugh. "Everybody else found it funny but my dad just sat there and he didn't crack a smile," Cobb said. "Your team the Boxers, they find it hard to score a point without you. I'm so proud of my son Cobb," Mr. Jackson said. Cobb always says his father doesn't impress that easily and he's flattered that his father is still impressed with him. Besides, telling Cobb that he would be wondering why his teeth and his body would be in two separate rooms, "my dad was cool," Cobb said.

Well, well, well. How are you, Cobb? Long time no see. How ya been buddy? Cobb turned around and he was surprised to see an old friend Bob Johnson. "Bob," Cobb said as the two men embraced. "Wow, it's been a long time." Cobb inquired about what Bob's been up to since they saw each other last. Cobb explained he might know of a job that Bob could apply for, at his team's stadium. Cobb, I've been honestly looking for employment, so this is good timing you and I should see each other after about 10 years. I thank God. The two gentlemen exchanged verbal notes about how Cobb had been more involved and more active in church lately, how Bob has skills that the future employers might be looking for and where each of the men live neighborhood wise. Cobb was extremely glad to see his long-lost friend. They exchanged phone numbers and Cobb said he'd call Bob the middle of next week and Cobb said he'd speak to some friends of his in the front office of the stadium about employment for Bob. After Bob left, Sadaya was called by Cobb. "Wow, I'm so glad to be able to help Bob," Cobb told Sadaya. "I hope that job I heard about is still open. I'll call and find out. I don't even remember the job title but they said it pays more than $100,000 a year. It could be assistant to the General Manager. It might be an assistant to the Assistant Manager's job, but when I heard them discussing it, I thought it had good terms. I just called the office and I left a message on the voicemail. Hopefully, they'll get back to me before the week is over."

<u>Hold To God's Unchanging Hand</u>

Time is filled with swift transition,
Naught of earth unmoved can stand,
Build your hopes on things eternal,
Hold to God's unchanging hand.
Trust in Him who will not leave you,
Whatsoever years may bring,
If by earthly friends forsaken
Still more closely to Him cling.

© Jennie Wilson

Sadaya shared this song with the world. The idea is hold to God's Unchanging Hand. God is working it out in our natural everyday life. Sadaya wanted to remind everyone to keep holding on. This song was handed out in choir practice and in Bible Study.

Barkie the dog started to bark. Sadaya was thinking about a few months ago when Cobb said, "Don't tell him he's a dog. He thinks he's an Emperor of the whole African continent, the way he has me waiting on him hand and foot." "Thanks for the housekeeper who had helped me with Barkie. I love that doggie, though," Cobb said smiling. "I have always loved animals; I'm usually too busy to spend a long, long time with them but I've always loved animals, especially dogs. If I buy a lot of animals, I would have to assign them to the housekeeper, though," Cobb said. The animals I like and love are so even-tempered and trusting. The more trusting they are the more treats you want to give to them; massages you want to give the animal you love too. Barkie often sits around waiting for his real master Cobb to come home and to do various activities together. Cobb always brags about how he and Barkie go for long walks on the grounds of his property playing with the frisbee, and Cobb feeds him water while he plays with the baseball and catches it. "You can tell this is an Athlete's dog because he's so agile all of the time. Barkie catches the ball and catches the frisbee as well as me," Cobb said laughing. I treat my dog with tender loving care. It's always best to treat your dogs similar to how you would treat your children: very loving and very well.

Sadaya called Cobb at 11:00 p.m. His voicemail was on. The message she left was meaningful and sweet: "Hello babe. Just calling to ask if you're going to be at the church tomorrow. I'll be there for Bible Study. Stop by. Pastor is really great when he teaches that class. I heard your team lost the last game. Remember, no matter what the scoreboard says, we're still winners. Call me. Bye. Sadaya."

Oh well, that's what I get for dating Cobb; being the Superstar Athlete that he is. Always busy and always doing something. Sadaya sat down on her chair. She closed her eyes and she saw an image of Cobb. What's his hands feel like? He was a man who had a gentleman's hands. Were they rough, soft, engulfing or is there a voidance in his hands? The reporter from WNNG Network of News Galore put her microphone in front of Sadaya's mouth: "Cobb Jackson's hands were medium rough and engulfing, welcoming. Warm hands he has," Sadaya said. "By the way, I've also felt those same hands around my waist. I like his hands no matter where they are," Sadaya said.

Sadaya and her 6th grade class have been complimented on how they all get along in school. They manage to get a lot of schoolwork and they manage to use words such as peace-time, being clam, my brother, peace and love and many other words that bring them closer together. "I'm very proud of my 6th grade," Sadaya said. They're a very good class. Their intelligence is far beyond their chronological years. When it comes to test taking, they're top notch. They know not to waste the precious gift of time.

But Sadaya had something else preoccupying her mind. Sadaya has just learned that Cobb is seeing someone else. She found out from the media on Cable-TV. She told Cobb off and hung up on him. Click. She told him to never call her again. "You've got spunk . . . I hate spunk," Cobb said. Her best friend Cynthia said, "Fight, girl. Fight for your love and for your future family. Fight as creatively as you can, but fight. Turn something bad and turn it into good. I always remember what Dr. Mallard says, "If you're going through it, keep going!" "I needed to be able to look up at the sky. No man or woman could put the sky and the stars up there. Yes, we are covered by God. We are covered under the warmth of the sky, when the sun shines and when the rain comes too. I needed to look up at the sky and remember to be humble and on my knees," Sadaya said. "Perhaps I didn't pray to God enough.

I will now and I will consider the fact that Good is the One Who controls. If He wants me to have a husband from church then that's what will happen. So, what if he's a future billionaire now multi-millionaire basketball player. Truly, only God can give me Cobb for my husband although Cobb is not ready to get married now. I have to talk with God more about this situation. "The Bible says God wants good things for us," Sadaya said. "I thank God for being able to fight on my knees," Sadaya said.

When Sadaya and Cobb first met, they were both so attracted to each other. He liked how her clothes looked on her and he liked her pretty eyes. He said her hairdo was nice too. She also liked the way he was dressed. He was well-dressed with a white shirt, French collar and cuff links. His hair was neatly cut and she was thinking "now that is a fine-looking man. He's fine and famous too." Sadaya said, "The man was so beautiful to me; he became my instant temptation. I wonder how my friend Sheila is. Let me look her up and see if we can go to the movies or something. She was at the church when I first met Cobb. Maybe she has some ideas and good advice for me. She's the one who's always saying she knows how to get a man and how to keep a man. I have to talk to her. I have to see if I'm doing the right things or if I'm doing something to chase the man away. I'll have to surely contact Sheila and also find out if she ever got a chance to meet Larry J. Johnson, the host of the sports show was Not Injured. I told her to try meeting him on her own and if not, then I would introduce her to him. I wonder how she made out with that project," Sadaya said. "After all, Larry J. Johnson is a good catch. He's not a ballplayer, he's a Sportscaster. Oh, you should see the ladies swooning all over Larry J." Sadaya called Sheila and the voicemail was on. She left a message telling Sheila she needed to speak to her as soon as possible and to please call her. Somebody needed a good cry; it was going to be Sadaya's turn soon. "Soon I'll be crying and on my knees to God," Sadaya said. "I can't wait to get home. My parents are going to the play tonight. Good, I'll have the house all to myself. I can hardly wait. I'll be crying up a storm soon," Sadaya thought.

When Sadaya got home, her parents had left her a note:

> Hello to Our Darling Daughter. We decided to have dinner downtown. We're going to have steak and lobster before the play. We'll see you later honey. Don't forget to get your beauty rest. We love you.
>
> Mom and Dad.

"Ok mom and dad have yourselves a great and fabulous time," Sadaya mumbled to herself. "It's kind of tough when nobody's home and you've got troubles and struggles. Of course, the obvious answer, the obvious Best Friend is the Almighty God, the Creator of the Universe. Whatever problems you have, according to the Bible, God encourages us to place our burdens at His feet. He also says we can rest in His bosom and let go and let God. The more you fall in love the more your heart can break in two. Where there's big love there can just as easily be an explosion of heartache.

"Well let me get comfortable and I'll crawl in bed and sulk," she said. "I'd better make myself a cup of tea." Sadaya sat and she waited patiently for the water to boil. She carried her tea into her bedroom. She only had one phone message and that was from her sister who is away at college. One day this week I'll call her back. I'll be in better spirits by then, she promised herself. Sipping on her hot tea Sadaya sat in her bedroom chair and she relaxed, closed her eyes and put her head against the back of her chair. The tea flavor made the room smell like a fresh breeze at the beach. Sadaya breathed in 10 times and she fell asleep in her bedroom chair for two whole hours. "That's what happens when you're working eight hours a day. Grace, talent, beauty, had inner strength and love in her heart is how I, Sadaya want to be remembered and most importantly, tried to obey God and love Him, to the best of my ability. These are my thoughts while I enjoy another cup of tea; this time peppermint tea; not lemon tea." "My ex- boyfriend used to call me Wonder Woman. I've slowed down since then. Well, Lord God, I come to You in the name of Jesus Christ. I am so happy to be one of Yours, Father God. The main issue on my mind has to do with a potential mistake that I might have made. I went to dinner with Thaddeus, my ex-boyfriend. Someone saw us eating and enjoying each other's company and told Cobb. He took it hard. You'd think I was sleeping with the guy or something: Which of course, I am not. As a matter of fact, I am not sleeping with either guy or anyone at this time. There's no reason for Cobb to be paranoid and get upset with me just because I'm enjoying my dinner! And of course, this had to happen when I am fantasy-active," Sadaya said. "Fantasies which are supposed to be warm and full of heart-shaped wishes are quite enjoyable; it's facing the reality afterwards that can offer the reality-sting."

Cobb was so upset with Sadaya that he kept calling her both on her cellular telephone and on her land phone at her mother's and father's house. Every time he'd think of her having dinner with Thaddeus her ex-boyfriend, he'd pick up the phone and leave a message on her voicemail. "Well I guess you're busy. I hear you have a more active social life so I guess you don't need me as you used to. I'm calling you so much because I want to talk to you. I know you're busy and you have a beautiful dinner coming up with The Association in about 1 ½ to 2 months. I want us to talk now because I don't think you should be going out with other men and I don't think you should be looking like y'all cozying up.

It was clear to Sadaya. It was time for a break in she and Cobb's relationship. "Maybe we should take a six-month break," she thought. In her fantasy life, Sadaya said that's never supposed to happen. Fantasies are supposed to be warm and full of heart-shaped wishes. While they will probably not come true, they can be entertaining. Whether it's a chilly winter morning or a warm spring night Sadaya felt lush and cheery. "I don't really want a separation but Cobb has too many women," Sadaya said. She was in the mood to write her columns for The Experts Newspaper. Sadaya preferred not to think about her love life. It's so unpredictable. Plus, Sadaya got the sense that Cobb really cares about her but he's fickle, changeable and moody. Thaddeus, she can't allow, but so much love and caring to be shown. Why?

There's a very simple truthful answer: He's a married man.

She hadn't heard from him in two whole years and now that he's married, all of a sudden, he's available. "Ha, ha, ha. What kind of fool do you think I am? My Dear Wonderful man! Is life ironic. Maybe I'll write a novel about my fantasies and his realities someday. Maybe I'll present it to the public with all of the honesty I can muster up," Sadaya thought. My novel, my keepsake, my life story all packaged up into a life-storybook. Would I mention Cobb Jackson or maybe I'd be married to him by then? Who am I kidding? Hades, with my luck be married with six children ourselves by then my pastor said. Sometimes life throws the curve balls and they're looking for speed. So, the curveballs are flying 90 mph speed and I don't know whether to catch the ball or to hit the ball or how to tame the ball from going awry. I want to leave a message on your voicemail:

You're making me purr like a kitten with all of this under the table action. Not long after making the kitten statement, the M.C. called for Cobb to be introduced. While Cobb was speaking to the audience, Sadaya though, "Oh Lord, soon this man is going to want to make love to me." Meanwhile Cobb gave a powerful performance when he spoke to the audience. He came back to the table and the people gave him a standing ovation. What rousing applause he received for his comments. His comments were attention-getting and compassionate. The governor of our state was the last speaker. It was a beautiful dinner Sadaya told Cobb as they drove back. They drove two hours back to Sadaya's house. By then, there was a drowsy Sadaya sitting in the limousine. "Tired from the drive," she said.

> We found that staying true to who you are is all that matters. Please forgive me I can't stop loving you. Please forgive me. Our hearts together ring true. Never say good bye. Never say good bye. Holding on to never saying good bye. I can feel your body swaying to my amateur composer's songs. You've touched my heart. In my silence I adore you.
>
> Love 'ya much, Cobb

A message sang into Sadaya's voicemail.

"I want the ball to play my game, not the other way around. So, if I feel like I don't know what I'm doing, I'll take a break and refresh my skills and get sharper at it. Then I'll come back at it and try it again. But I certainly won't give up!"

Cobb hadn't stopped calling Sadaya and leaving voicemail messages on her phone numbers: Sometimes Cobb was replying to Sadaya's messages and sometimes he was adding his own wisdom. Sometimes he'd say "Do make sure you don't get too close because your dinner partner I hear has a past: A past that includes the works. He's been through a divorce, he's spent 15 years in prison but I couldn't for the life of me get it out of me why he was in prison in the first place. Cobb saluted as if he was giving upon Sadaya. When he saluted and put his hand to his forehead Cobb said he's going to stick with Sadaya but she doesn't know he's made this decision. "We have some issues which have to be cleared up first he told his best friend on the phone."

† † †

There is no blood pressure to take no hippocampus to measure for brain activity, no medication to take at home or anywhere else. There was no more taking of blood. All gone. Everything having to do with life in his body was gone. The breath is gone from the body and that is what has happened at the pool where there was a swimming accident. Desmond. Desmond Johns was an expert at swimming. I truly believe in my heart of hearts that he should not have died. However, it was permitted by God and I know God has His purposes and His reasons. I defer to God. He always knows best. He always has the best solutions and the best reasons. There were no more MRI nor CT scans which could have been given to Desmond. He, Desmond's Doctor was very sure that if Desmond had survived the fall from the Diving Board that he would have been in a vegetative state. He would have no idea of who anyone was; especially himself. I can see myself going to the hospital and Desmond wouldn't have even known me, his own mother, as tears welled up in her eyes. "I miss him so much," she said sadly. Desmond's mother's smiles have vanished as if she had never smiled in her lifetime. She was a lost cause in this area. Where most people could smile and laugh, Desmond's mother completely lost her smile and her laughter. Desmond was her only son and now he has gone.

Saturday night Cobb planned to surprise Sadaya Ruby Day and he was planning to go to church. For a long time, he has not been seen during the Sunday morning service. Cobb loves God and he loves his parents and Sadaya after that he was thinking. He thought he'd take her to one of the places on the Avenue if they weren't serving delicious food at the church. "We'll see," he thought.

It's Sunday. Cobb Jackson doesn't get too much opportunity to go to church on Sundays. He was anxious to go to church this morning, though. He got up at 5:45 a. and he took a bath plus a shower to relax his nerves. "Aah," he said in the privacy of his washroom. If only I had a masseuse in here. Cobb sat and leaned his back all the way back to the wall. "Aah, how great this feels," he quietly whispered to himself." Well I guess I'll see Sadaya today, while thinking, let me put my hands on one of those new suits I bought a few weeks ago. I want to be suited for success with Sadaya today. I'm just going to take the initiative and sit her down and give her a good talking to, he thought, remaining pensive. Cobb had all of his dress shirts, shoes and ties all laid out. His new suits were ready to be worn for Sunday attire as is appropriate. Sadaya and Cobb were both thinking of one another this Sunday morning; though technically neither of them have spoken to the other since Sadaya went out to dinner with her ex-boyfriend, Thaddeus. This is going to be a very interesting.

Sunday for sure," Cobb muttered to himself. Sadaya is not going to be expecting to see me because I'm not in church on Sundays usually since I travel with the Boxers Basketball Team," Cobb was thinking. He smiled to himself. "Heh, heh, heh, uh-huh. I've got her this time," Cobb laughed gently. Finally, Cobb was dressed and ready to go. He looked debonair, dashing and he looks suave with it. He is the kind of man that any woman would be attracted to because he's rich and self-sustaining; any woman could attract him or be attracted by him. He looked in the mirror at his home for the wrinkles in his suit: none. The seams were perfectly pressed and his Picasso's designed tie was worth every penny. "I paid for it," he was thinking. Let me call my driver and get him ready to face the day. I don't feel like driving today. It'll only take him about 20 minutes to prepare himself. He, the chauffeur, doesn't know it but I as his boss watch him very closely. Ever since I saw him in my limousine with two women and a man and he couldn't look me in the eyes, I've been keeping him extra busy picking up people that I know and picking up people that I don't know for business purposes. Like I told him, I don't want any orgies in my limousine. Cobb had done a self-appraisal of his chauffeur and he checks out well. He's professional, he uses professional language, he opens and closes the doors when appropriate, he stocks the car with sodas and Champagne and other snacks. He's always polite and he usually establishes adequate eye contract. "Now that I've given him extra work he can work it and not shirk it. I haven't had any trouble since piling up the work on him so I guess that was the answer to the problem," Cobb was telling his parents on the telephone. He asked them if they wanted to go to church with him. They told him they'd call him back in 10 minutes. After 10 minutes they called and said they'd go with him. His father didn't feel like driving. The schedule planned, Cobb intended to be in church about 45 minutes early so he could catch up with Sadaya and talk. I want to be there for Sadaya. I want her to feel safe and nurturant with me. I almost told her like a bad rash if she goes out with him again I'll be over her. Something stopped me from talking so harshly. Ok she was bored, Cobb thought to himself. That's why she went out with him. "I find Sadaya to be compassionate, intelligent and spiritual and I really do want her to feel safe above all else with me, he told his parents as they drove to the church. I've done an observation-based assessment. I've tracked her progress and I honestly believe the reason she went out with her ex- boyfriend was boredom. She doesn't see enough of me. She needs me. Mom, Dad, did you hear what I just said? I said she needs me," Cobb said, not cracking a smile on his face. I'm maintaining my love for Sadaya mom and dad because I love her spirit and I love her personality, Cobb said being honest with his parents. If there's one thing I want Sadaya to learn It's this. if you're a couple, whether you're in love or not, yes, you're going to have problems every now and then. Yes, you're going to have fights and doubt might creep in sometimes. You might wonder why you're still in this relationship but in the end, you're still in love. This is what I see in the relationship between the two of you, mom and dad, Cobb said. The two of you can be arguing and be fussing with each other. You might have been at it for about 20 minutes of fussing. The both of you decide that the arguing and fighting session is over. Five minutes later mom says, "Tommy baby, you want a sandwich? I got turkey and bologna. He'd say, "Right on, honey. Bring it on. I'm ready." Life goes on like they never ever argued a day in their lives. They'll be celebrating their 53rd wedding anniversary soon. "That's the kind of relationship I'd like to have with Sadaya; mom and dad. I don't want to take the arguing; mad with you side of our relationship too seriously. I want to be able to turn the anger on and to turn the anger off and then function like a normal and harmonious relationship again. This way both of us have the chance to think about what's been said and decide if we're going to agree finally without fighting like cats and dogs. It is a good way to function in a relationship," his father said, and his mother agreed.

"Yes, son. I think you're right to want to have a harmonious relationship. It gives me a certain amount of security in our relationship to know that your father is not going to storm out of the house and leave me just because we have a few words in disagreement. In addition, sometimes it is a Christian woman's role to take a back seat and to observe and to see what her husband is going to do as the leader of his family. Sometimes it is a Christian woman's job to plant seeds also so that her husband has the chance to savor the flavor of the disagreement and of her logic. I'd rather have peace in our relationship and be able to talk things over at a nice even keeled decibel level, Cobb's mother said. His father put his arm around his wife and he hugged her with a long embrace and everyone laughed happily; celebratedly. Cobb's father went on to encourage Cobb. Don't let her give up on herself either, Cobb. Encourage her, compliment her and check on her self-esteem, make sure she feels good about herself. Make sure she's confident about herself and that she knows what she wants in her life. Make sure you're supporting her every step of the way and that she knows it. And above all, son regardless of what she's saying to you or not saying to you, don't be afraid to humble yourself before God; get down on your knees and pray. The Holy Scriptures say, "Watch and pray; also "God is able to do exceedingly abundantly above all we can ever ask or think according to the power that works in us." If there's something you see in Sadaya that you don't like to tell the Master; God, the Almighty God of the Universe. Ask him to change her and you know that God will do that for you? God will give you inner strength and power and a love for your wife whenever you get one, that will make you feel invincible and unstoppable.

Cobb, I don't know who you're going to marry, but I know whoever you'll marry will love you deeply because that's how I'm praying as your dad. Remember, Watch and pray, son; Watch and pray, Cobb's father said beseechingly. "Also, forgiveness is key," he said.

The limousine pulled up to the church about 40 minutes early. Oh, thank you, we can get decent seats before the crowd gets here. Cobb's family always likes to sit in the middle of the church audience so they can hear everything and see everything because there's a nice loud speaker there where they sit. "Oh, thank you I got to sit in my favorite seat. Even this is a product of answered prayers. The Bible says prayer changes things. I had been praying for two weeks that the next time I come to Cobb's church, the Black Memorial Baptist Church that I would get to sit in my favorite seats and here I am sitting in my favorite seats. Ask and it shall be given seek and ye shall find, knock and the door shall be opened unto you. "Wow, I'm on a natural high for Jesus Christ," his mother whom Cobb calls mom said. Very few people had sat in their seats yet. The inside of the church looked good. The banisters were well oiled; they were made of cherry wood. The walls were lily-white semi-gloss paint. Everything smelled fresh and new. Cobb was saying similar to what Sadaya was saying. He likes larger churches because you can see where your money's going. If you give them money for a building fund, then that's where the money is to go into the building; nowhere else, unless they have an emergency meeting explaining that they need to transfer or switch funds around and the reasons why. Then they should wait for approval. Black Memorial Baptist Church had bouquets up and down the altar and at the main podium. Anyone would want to attend this church with all the beauty spread around the sanctuary.

Cobb told his parents he was going to look for Sadaya. "If you see her before I get back tell her to wait," he told his parents. She always gets here early. Cobb went to the church's eating hall, the Freedom Hall and he looked there: no Sadaya. He went into the choir room and he looked there: no Sadaya. He went to the Sunday school rooms: no Sadaya. He decided to return to where his parents were left sitting. As he walked back into the Sanctuary his parents were beckoning him over. They told him Sadaya was there but that she had to find another parking space because she was double-parked. She'll be right back over after she moves the car" she said. "Oh, good that gives me time to go to the men's room," Cobb said. When Cobb came back there was Sadaya sitting with his parents, laughing about something. When he came back the laughter was slowed to a minimum. Well, my job was to keep you company until your son got back so I guess I'd better go," Sadaya said. "Our son has something to say to you," Mr. Jackson his father said. Sadaya, I need you to sit over there and to talk with me for about 10 minutes, before church starts. Ok, see you later Mr. and Mrs. Jackson. I'm going with Cobb now. "Don't be too hard on yourselves," Mr. Jackson shouted, smiling. "How have you been? Every time I call you these days I keep getting your voicemail. Sometimes I don't even want to leave a voicemail message. I'd rather talk directly to you. Oh Cobb, look. What an adorable child; with the curliest hair I've ever seen. She put her little cute hands on my knees to help her to stand up. She looks to be about a year and a half; two years old at the most. I wonder where her parents are," said Sadaya. At that time a boy looking to be about 10 or 11 years old said excuse me, that's my sister. "Oh, we were wondering who that cutie belonged to. Bye, bye sweetie. Ok cutie," Sadaya and Cobb said. The little girl blew kisses to both Cobb and Sadaya, and she waved good-bye. "Children are such a blessing," Sadaya said. Soon they're going to start church. The people have started to sit down and find their hymnals. Also, their Bibles. You want to meet after church? My parents won't mind. Sadaya wanted to know what Cobb wants to talk about. He said, "something very important to me and hopefully important to you." "We could drop your parents off to their home and then talk at a restaurant or right there in the limousine," Sadaya said. "What do you think?" Sadaya asked. "Ok, let's give it a try," Cobb said. "I'll tell the chauffeur to take us to a restaurant right away because I'm going to be very hungry after service. We'll all eat and then I'll take you to my parents' home and then you and I can talk. I can't let my parents starve," Cobb said. "Whichever way you want," Sadaya said and replied. The church started filling up and Sadaya said, "My place is with the choir. Let me know how you like our singing this morning. "Bye," Sadaya said. Cobb deep down inside of his heart of hearts was hurt. He really wanted to speak to Sadaya and to get it over with, so he could erase the negativity that had occurred between them, but because of circumstances, it didn't work out the way he wanted it to. We'll see what happens this afternoon after church, he thought to himself. He went over into the pews and he sat with his parents. Two young boys asked for his autograph along with their father. He gave them the autograph. The organ music played along with other instruments and church began. The Black Memorial Baptist Church Ensemble sounded like it was on fire for Jesus Christ that morning, as it does every Sunday morning but this was a special Sunday morning. Cobb Jackson was in church and Cobb believed that God was happy and singing too. Hallelujah.

The restaurant was Italian. It was too crowded. Too many fans there to overtake Cobb. Sadaya noticed it and suggested they go somewhere else or get his dinner take-out. They all opted for take-out dinners. Cobb had to go and sit in the limousine while Sadaya waited for the take-out dinners. They had Sadaya to leave her car in the church parking lot while she rode with them in the limousine. "We could all go back to my house and eat," Sadaya suggested. "That wouldn't be such a bad idea," Cobb's mother said. Cobb told the chauffeur to go to Sadaya's home address and that they all would eat there. She called home and alerted her parents to what was happening. They said ok come one, come all. Everybody's welcome. Sadaya was smart. She had bought take-out food for her parents too. As usual, Cobb footed the bill; thank you for him. He likes going solo and footing the bill for someone other than himself. What a blessed man he is. He is so well-dressed that Sadaya said, "Everything you look for in a man I've got it in you. You really know how to dress too and you look so handsome; shaped up with seams and with stitches in all of the right places. You look extraordinarily handsome today; like a D'ebonié model for males. Your face is so smooth shaven; you have a timeless sense of warmth and style. You've really got the essentials on today; and you shaved oh so closely and so carefully. Phew, I have to take your picture with my phone. I think this is the 'prettiest' I've seen you in a long time. What's the occasion? There must be some special occasion going on for you to dress so impeccably," she said. "No, I just dressed like this because I know God see all and He sees me putting on my best for Him. All of my wardrobe, especially the suits and special ties and shoes and boots are a tribute and salute to God." "Oh, come on, you can tell me. These threads are new, right? I'll bet you bought them this past week," she said. "Actually, you're right. I bought them less than two weeks ago. But now before we start our serious talk about our love, might I add that I love that laced velvet dress you look nice in?" A big smile on her face, Sadaya grinned from ear to ear.

This is my tribute to God too. Along with the velvet dress, Sadaya had on a spring leather jacket, Sunglasses. The luxurious look of colorful leather was pretty the color called rose quartz: packable, mixable and comfortable, yet nice enough to war it to the Lord's House and to fit right in.

You know, Sadaya you'd make a good sales executive," Cobb replied. "Alright enough of this MAS mutual admiration society staff. What else did I want us to talk about?" Cobb asked. "I suppose it's like you said earlier, 'our love' you wanted to talk about," Sadaya said. "Smart girl. I can blame you for that. You hit the nail on the head," Cobb replied again.

"Ok let's find some place to sit and talk. Let's go into the limousine," he said. "Ok. I'm coming but I must go to the restroom first," Sadaya said. Too many people around for me to be exposed like this. My fame won't let me stay out here. I'd be mobbed. I'd better go to the limousine like Sadaya and I agreed. Fifteen minutes later, Sadaya came out of the restroom after freshening up her makeup. Together, they seemed like the consummate power couple; the kind who would help anyone. It would be unlikely that they would undermine each other. Greed, power and lust didn't seem to have any place with them. Cobb had it all so there really wasn't much more to get. They made many dear friends at church. Nobody ever heard them argue or say one bad word against each other. They were not only a nice couple but they were a nice looking handsome couple. Cobb never liked her ex-boyfriend Thaddeus. He was out to ruin their relationship and to break them up was Cobb's opinion. Before Thaddeus came into her life again, Sadaya was an outgoing loving and carefree friend to most people, especially at church and at work. Cobb, being a man also, figured out the darker side of Thaddeus and what his motivations were. If he were a piece of merchandise, Sadaya would have returned him credited at the discounted price. May not be redeemed for cash or combined with other offers. Sadaya laughed and joked with her parents about it earlier that week. "He sure ain't worth much to you, Sadaya, that Thaddeus; he's quite a character ain't he? You can do better; do that. Do a lot better, honey," her father said. "A lot better," her father said again. When discussing the Thaddeus situation, Sadaya wanted to hear what Cobb had to say first. Cobb told her what he thought and he briefly gave her the explanation on the page before this one. The gist of it is that Thaddeus is out to destroy the Cobb-Sadaya hook-up. Cobb was and is determined not to let that happen. Sadaya explained to Cobb in the limousine that he had nothing to worry about. "Do not worry, do not fret," she said, "because I believe that God's got our back; He's supporting us as a couple." "Cobb, I must admit I've been lovesick over you. I've been lovesick over you in this treacherous world of sports," Sadaya said. She also said she'd been miserable since the two of them argued about Thaddeus. Cobb was trying to get Sadaya to say that she would not go to with Thad again; but she did not. "Has he asked you out again Sadaya?" Cobb honestly asked. "Well, he calls me a lot and I believe he will if I give him the chance to ask me out again. Cobb, I'm being totally candid with you. Thaddeus is married. I wouldn't let him do anything with me but go to dinner once in about six months and say by the way, bring your wife," she said. Cobb reached over and touched Sadaya's hands, gently. "Thank you; I feel better," he said. Come here Sadaya. I want a tight hug. Sit next to me. Sadaya did what she was told by Cobb and the rest of the time was filled with the two of them cuddling and holding each other while the chauffeur drove them back to her car still sitting in the church parking lot. "You want some company, honey? I can park my car at my house. Let's do something; let's go somewhere," she said. "Yeah, how about if we go somewhere else to eat. I'm still very hungry," Cobb said. You know something, I never thought I'd say it but I'm hungry too. Let's go eat some real food at The Blue Lobster Tail Diner. Mmmm Mmmm sounds delicious. These new plans for dinner made Cobb hug Sadaya with much more passion and compassion. Sadaya had a wide grin on her face. Did you ever buy the beard that looks something like someone else? The beard that nobody can recognize you when you put it on? Don't you have it in the trunk of your limousine? I seem to remember it being hidden in the trunk, Sadaya said. Cobb mentioned this to the chauffeur and he stopped the car almost immediately. He knocked on the back window and when Cobb opened the window he received the large beard. "Well, here's my disguise soon to be on my face. Are you ready Sadaya? Here we go," Cobb said. Two minutes later Cobb had put the beard on. He looked like the President of Cuba, not Cobb that's for sure. Now this helped the Superstar Cobb Jackson to be incognito; to get around without adoring fans crushing him. They don't realize how much the fans crowd can crush a celebrity; because they all want to hug him, they all want to kiss him, they all want to take a picture with him and ask him questions. Thank God for beards that look like the President of Cuba.

Cobb and Sadaya did exactly as planned. They ate twice. The second time was at the Blue Lobster Tail Diner. Cobb looked at Sadaya and he said, "I've got the feeling that someday you're going to need to disguise yourself too." Sadaya says "no thanks, especially after I see what you have to go through to get away from people so they don't mob you half to death. My life is suiting me just fine, thank you very much. I like it when you talk to me and tell me what your fans ask for you to do like take off your uniform and go shirtless and show your pretty body.

"I don't know if you know it or not but that stuff really turns me on. This stuff is exciting. Just thought I'd let you know what I've been thinking," Sadaya said. "I've got some things I want you to do too." "Like what?" he said almost begging. "Oh no, oh no. I'll tell you at a more opportune time. I'm not ready to tell you now; not yet," Sadaya said. "I will give you a hint though. It's a very good hint. The hint is: I want you Cobb to go somewhere out of town with me," Sadaya said. "There's something I want you to buy there. Ok too much hint. So much for that. I'll let you know in about six months." "I've got some things I want you Sadaya to do," Cobb said. "But I can't tell you for another six months anyway so I'm sorry I mentioned it. The mystery of it'll kill you almost," Sadaya said. "If I didn't' know what I wanted I'd be really quiet, but I'm going to have a delicious laugh out of this. See you in six months with this one, Cobb," she said.

"Are you serious? I've got to wait six whole months to find out your plans for me; pardon me for 'us.' You're right, you shouldn't have brought it up, dagnabbit. I'm going to be all guessed out and I know it, by the time six months rolls around." "Dag, I hate to wait. I HATE to wait!" Sadaya said. Cobb sat in the chair and a fresh smile came upon his face. "Oh, come on, tell me now Cobb." "You have a secret for me and so do I, for you," Cobb said. "I'll do anything almost if you tell me now," said Sadaya. "I can't but it'll be worth it by the time the six months rolls around," Cobb said. Cobb looked at Sadaya's facial expression and he planted a kiss on her ruby red lipstick lips. He placed his arm around her shoulders. He placed another kiss on her forehead. Cobb thinks this might be true love. The pastor thinks only time will tell, if it's true love or not between Cobb and Sadaya. With love, it's always time will tell. We've had our skirmishes but right now we're loving each other in peace. We are a love-strong couple. Sadaya didn't tell Cobb about the time when her stomach ached because of all the changes she saw and she went through. Her nervous stomach was weak and she had to sit down to have a cup of tea to settle her stomach. The place was a horrible mess but she sat down at the insistence of her friend. The man Sadaya was nervous and upset about name was Cobb Jackson. No one else will be able to compare to Cobb in Sadaya's mind. Of course, Cobb doesn't understand this yet. While Cobb was entertaining and allowing himself to talk off the clothes of other women, Cobb being as bold as he was had no idea that Sadaya would start to see someone else. She bought embellished skirts, leather dresses, cashmere sweaters and coats, Afrocentric and African prints, Red hot thigh high

Boots and skirt suits that had other men fascinated with Sadaya, but she always turned them down. Except for one who technically she turned down the first time but she wanted to hear his story about his marriage and why he didn't marry her, Sadaya instead; She told him yes the second time he asked her to go out. She said, "The next time we go out after this, I'd like to meet your wife. I'd love to meet her. Maybe she'd like to go out shopping with me," Sadaya said.

Ask her and let me know what's going to happen," Sadaya said to Thaddeus or Thad which she used to call him. Cobb's parents say it's up to Cobb. He ought to know whether he's in love or not. His parents who have been married 57 years said, "If it stands the test of time then it's love sweet love." Sadaya's parents obviously think that Cobb Jackson is the winner in their book of decision making." "We think if Sadaya doesn't choose him then she wasn't in love with him or he wasn't in love with her in the first place. As long as he treats her with true love and tenderness, then I think she should choose him and he's to choose her. He's such a catch and I've seen how the ladies circle him like a barracuda circles its prey. He has so many women after him it's sickening and I bet he could be a real player planner if he wants to. I bet he could fool around and have about three women per day if he wanted to, then blame sports travel for the times he wants to stand 'em up," Mrs. Day, Sadaya's mother said. "My daughter should have her head examined if she doesn't choose him," she said.

As meaningful as the relationship is between Cobb and Sadaya, I know Sadaya ceases from anger. She's not the type to depress a man by fussing with him all of the time. She's not the combative type of woman. If you ask her a question, she's going to do her best to answer you with as much respect, intelligence and loyalty as she can. She's the type to go out of her way to help someone. She wanted to make herself to look more youthful. She went to D'acy's Dept. Store. She bought skin softening cleanser, day creme, Serum, eye crème moisturizing creme. She bought a whole replenishment program. Why? So she could be a looker, someone who looks younger for her boyfriend Cobb Jackson. "That man has so many women I bet he probably didn't even notice her new youthful looking skin. I like him for who he is in the world of sports but I don't trust him," I said to my wife. "I believe he has other women. I'm glad my daughter went out with someone else. The other guy she went to dinner with ain't fooling me. He's slick too. I'm going to sit down and talk to Sadaya very soon," her father said.

"You know people will take advantage of you if you let them. DON'T LET THEM! I taught that principle too often maybe. I myself had to learn the principle called Let go and Let God. Sadaya is not my baby girl any longer. She's all grown up now. There are certain decisions she must make for herself and on her own. The times have changed but also have only been slightly rearranged. I'm still Sadaya's father, this I'm happy to be. When she was a little girl, Sadaya would smile and she'd call me 'Dad, Dad' you've made me proud of you. Of course, this is what I used to say to her. Hone, Sadaya you got 100 on your mathematics test and this is the 3rd one: I'm so proud of you," he said. So now I've been told by my wife that our youngest daughter Sadaya bought up a lot of beauty products for her face to impress Cobb. Yes, I am still her father. I've seen lots of faces on my Sadaya. I've seen a hopeful face; I've seen a wounded face; I've seen the grieving face; and I've seen the reward me face and the role model face. Every face means something special in her life, her mother's life and in my life. The hopeful face on Sadaya was important when she was trying to win 1st place in the Spelling Bee. She won. Her wounded face showed up when someone broke our car window outside when she was in the Spelling Bee. We never found out who broke the car window. The grieving face was for when her grandmother passed away in a car accident. The reward me and the role model faces are similar for my Sadaya. It reveals her as someone who is competent and able to get things done and who deserves to be rewarded hopefully in her paycheck so she can inspire and be the role model for her mathematics and Social Studies 6th graders. They love her dearly along with the rest of the Staff at the elementary school where she was chosen to work. "I know the many faces of my daughter Sadaya. My question is does she know Cobb's faces? Will he have more faces than Sadaya? The many faces of Cobb, is it? Or is it the many faces of Cobb's cobwebs? Will he be just hanging around like those cobwebs so weak and so flimsy? Or will he be able to do the Reward me face and the Role Model face with distinction and show himself as every bit the gentleman that he is, I'm sure in front of the public." These are questions and answers that Sadaya will be able to find out over time.

During this phase of her life she is still thinking about taking a break from Cobb but Cobb might think it premature. He thinks Sadaya is in his near and longtime future. Cobb said she should be secure in God and in herself. She is determined not to be defined by who she is dating. Sadaya loves to share with children and to be friends with children. We must appreciate those we have in our lives rather than just the things we have in our lives. Will Sadaya and Cobb take a break in their relationship? Only Sadaya can tell because she is the only one thinking of a break in the relationship. Only a confused woman would let Thaddeus, a now married man break up her relationship with a new billionaire, who treats her well. "So there," Sadaya said. "I wouldn't have to be in a relationship with him anymore." After hearing what Sadaya was thinking, her parents felt they should have special family time again even though Sadaya is a fully-grown adult. At the end of the week on Sundays, the family has agreed to sit down and talk for one hour. This means Sadaya, her mother and her father but not her sister because she is away at college. Family time for The Day Family is to be at 4:00 p.m. unless church is held over too long. Then it is up to the family's discretion as to what time they will meet. Sadaya didn't think to meet with the pastor during the week and it's a good thing. Cobb plans to meet with the pastor during the week. He'll be meeting about not being able to communicate his love to Sadaya. Cobb is very happy to be able to meet with the pastor who, by the way, drives a motorcycle. This tidbit Cobb intends to exchange notes with pastor about because Cobb has four motorcycles himself. "Men who drive motorcycles are more confident," the salesman said.

When Monday came, Cobb called and spoke to the pastor of the Black Memorial Baptist Church. He arranged to come in the next day with his secretary, Camille. Cobb felt so excited. This guy must be really great; he's got me waiting with such anticipation already. Well, we'll see how great he is tomorrow at 1:00 p.m. Camille, to Cobb, sounded like someone he knew in his younger life. "Waiting with baited breath, I am," Cobb thought. Fantastic, phenomenal and fabulous, that's how I feel as I am waiting to speak to the pastor. I think the pastor must have said some special prayers over this first session we're going to have. Cobb said he'd ask the pastor tomorrow. Cobb was in a rush to get to the Boxers' Basketball Team Gymnasium for practice. He had been exercising alone at his house. That night, the gym was crowded but Cobb was glad to be there. He went home early after practice, wanting to relax at home. He fell asleep. When he awakened it was morning. Cobb found himself wondering at what time in his lifetime would he have someone to look at every day, to wake up next to each and every morning and to go to sleep next to each and every night. He, for the first time in a long time, was not only thinking of himself. "I wouldn't mind having a woman to lay next to and a little girl or a little boy running into the bedroom and waking us up in the morning time. One day, Cobb spent the night over to his Godson's parents' house. When he woke up in the morning, his Godson was rolling a toy truck up and down his leg, scaring Cobb to death, almost. Cobb wasn't accustomed to someone small waking him up. He got to the point where he stopped himself from thinking about it. After all, today's the day I get to speak to the pastor of my church.

I'd better hurry if I'm going to make it there on time. The day was bright, cool and sunny. It was a beautiful day. He wanted to eat out today. He put on casual clothes and left his house at 12:00 p.m. noon. He was lucky because the beard he was wearing allowed him to go Drive-Thru without people mobbing him, for he was a basketball star. That's important to a number of celebrities. Cobb said that they're able to go about their everyday lives without being interrupted, disrupted or being detained. It's at this point that life smells sweet.

Cobb pulled into the church driveway at 12:45 p.m. He felt refreshed and ready to talk to the pastor about anything. Cobb always liked being punctual; on time, and freshly showered; ready for the occasion to happen, the situation to happen. Camille was well-groomed and she seemed to be in a happier mood than most. Camille is the pastor's secretary. Good job as usual. The pastor was there, waiting for Cobb, the legend that he was. Cobb had heard good things about the pastor and he was anxious to get started again. Cobb didn't ask whether there was a fee or not for this session. Cobb sat in the office waiting. He was called in by the pastor at 1:15 p.m. because the pastor received a phone call.

Well, hello Mr. Cobb Jackson, how's things? "Fine," Cobb said. I want you to sit down and when it's comfortable for you, I want to hear about your situation from your perspective. Let's sit down and explore your life. The people tell me I have a 98% Satisfaction Rate. I'm happy to know this. I have some strawberry-banana yogurts in side of the refrigerator. Would you like some? Well, I just had some food, but my answer's yes; I'll have one. The yogurt was delicious. Cobb and the pastor made small talk while enjoying the strawberry-banana yogurt. "When you're ready," the pastor said. Cobb was ready six minutes later and he explained where the two of them, Cobb and Sadaya met, which was there at the church. "There are many times that I am volunteering here at the church in the church secretary's office, and she would wink her eye at me, or she would accidentally on purpose rub up against me, flirting with me. Sometimes I'd schedule my lunch breaks on Saturdays so she and I could eat together and we had lots of fun. I began to realize there was nothing we were doing that was wrong and it felt good. I didn't have sex with her but we did kiss each other many times and laugh and joke and enjoy each other's company. I began to realize there was more to life than just sex and as my mother used to say, 'being loose,'" Cobb said.

Sadaya was fun to talk to; she was a good listener and she rarely interrupted Cobb when he spoke. He never got the sense that she judged him. She tried to tell jokes, but they were corny and the corniness was funnier than the joke usually. These attributes caused Cobb and Sadaya to grow closer. He started to ask her out places and then he began to take her to high-brow $5,000 a plate dinner, $1,000 a plate dinners, to luncheons and bruncheons and dinner-dance banquets. They also went to the movies. Sadaya explained to Cobb that she would be slow with the sex because God didn't want them to do that yet. Cobb continued to explain that he and Sadaya had gotten closer but had never had sex or made love to one another. Cobb was ok with this arrangement. He thought it a compliment to her. He also admitted that he occasionally saw other women on the side usually only going out to dinner or to the movies; usually friendships. Maxine was still trying to come back to Cobb and sometimes he let her. But Cobb Jackson was undistracted by anyone else when it came to which woman he was in love with. It was "truly" Sadaya. "I have never felt about anyone the way I felt about her. She was the sunshine in his universe," he said. He was always careful not to step over the boundary line when it came to sex. "Very considerate of you, Cobb," the pastor said. The pastor asked Cobb how he felt about going under hypnosis. Cobb indicated he didn't have a problem with a nice light form of hypnosis. He suggested not many more sessions would be needed, the pastor did. Cobb explained that he's having a big problem expressing his love to Sadaya, telling her that he's in love with her and that he wants an exclusive kind of relationship. He told the pastor that he gets the distinct impression that Sadaya would say if she wanted an exclusive type of relationship, she'd have married herself a husband.

The pastor was smooth. He welcomed Cobb back to sit down and to talk to Sadaya at any time but she's first to speak to the pastor. Next, we'll come up with strategies to use for Cobb you to speak to Sadaya with. We'll talk about tone of voice and verbal flogging and when to end the conversation after getting what you want and achieving influence. Cobb wore his beard into the office because he didn't want people to know he's been getting pastoral counseling. "The first session was excellent," Cobb thought. "I really feel comfortable with the pastor." He's not far from Cobb in chronological age.

He relates well to both young and to the elderly; senior citizens. He wields a lot of power because as the pastor he gains the confidence of the people and he hears their deepest secrets and has their deepest confidences. Cobb also liked the fact that the pastor told him that he Cobbcould pay any amount up to $100,000 for pastoral counseling. Cobb gave the pastor $25,000 to pay for the entire amount of sessions which the pastor said would be most likely 3-6 sessions. Cobb's 3- 6 sessions were not covered by his insurance. He had the money, he's a billionaire so he was able to settle his account immediately. Cobb also promised to give the church more money if they should have more sessions added on between the pastor and Cobb. "Since we only accept donations, the pastor accepted Cobb's money," he said. Cobb was also told that easing his pain would be fairly easy for the pastor to do.

Cobb got the impression that the pastor knows what he's doing. Like he told the pastor, maybe to someone else it wouldn't be such a big deal. But to Cobb, as an adult, it's important to communicate with your girl and to tell her what you feel about important issues, and emotional issues. This is not just an ordinary relationship. This is not just you and me saying hello and just waving her hand and I'm waving my hand to simply acknowledge each other's presence. This is someone as close as a girlfriend. A girlfriend is potentially the person you might find yourself laying with every night if you marry. That's a very important relationship. A girlfriend is an exclusive relationship. You keep things confidential in her behalf. When you worry at night you worry about her as if she's a member of your family. A girlfriend relationship is a very important exclusive type of relationship. You pray for her like you bend your knees for your twin brother. After all, Cobb is a man who offers hope to many people each and every day. He is also a man of inspiration. He started a business where every month he sends a poem along with chocolate hearts one month, the next month, bagels, the next month, a poem with oranges, the next month, cookies and each month there was a new surprise. When he remembered he had started this type of business, Cobb thought he would get Sadaya involved and he would marry her. She'd be good with the poetry, Cobb thought. He hadn't even shared this with his pastor yet. She had not given him any idea that she thinks the relationship needs a break. They're on two; both sides of a coin that are two opposite sides. Cobb wants to express more of his love to her. That's one side of the coin. Sadaya doesn't see this relationship lasting because she wants a break. The pastor doesn't see Cobb wanting a break.

He has suggested that Cobb keep seeing her. She wants a break which means a temporary separation. They're going to have to talk at some point, Cynthia, Sadaya's best friend said. "I can't believe you're talking about separating from such a handsome billionaire," Cynthia said. "Well, it's just that I've been reading where he goes out with other women so it means I'm nothing special to him," Sadaya said. Cynthia told Sadaya that love is often a mystery. When it comes to the heart, you just don't know in which direction his love will go. Sadaya ended the phone call with her friend Cynthia because she had to go to choir practice. She ran into the kitchen, kissed her mother and father good bye and she ran outside. She got into her car and drove very fast to the church. I think I'm going to give the choir a delicious chicken party. "All members of the choir will get three selections of chicken with Rice crackers and delicious cake as a celebration of the fact that the choir exists and sings every week. The choir is a gift from God and we thank Him. There are about 40 members of the choir so I can do everything. I can ask my mother and father to come to the church with me next week. They'll help me to carry everything. I think I'll bring some Mr. Goodie yogurts to the little celebration too," Sadaya thought. There. I'm glad I have everything, well-organized in my mind. It's just a matter of doing it, she said when she was talking to the Choir Director Mr. Austere. "Oh, what a beautiful thing to do. You have food and you have culture. How sweet of you Sadaya. I'm sure the 40 members of the choir will remember this for a long time. You say next week? I'll be ready like Freddie. I'll be waiting dear," he said. Oh yes, Sadaya wanted to know if Cobb was still going to the radio station WNYO in upper New York. "Has anyone seen Cobb Jackson today?" she asked. "Mr. Austere have you seen him?" No, Sadaya, I haven't. By the way, a friend is coming to New York in two weeks from Virginia. Do you think he can get us some tickets to the game? Oh wow. What a beauty. I love your outfit. What color is your outfit. It's not burgundy, is it? It's boysenberry cashmere. The whole skirt-set is made out of it. Cashmere. "Phew. Nice," Mr. Austere said. "You know I bought African mud-cloth last week. They had other Afrocentric prints there at the boutique too. I put some on and I figure those suits follow my curves very comfortably. I'm determined to wear the high-quality fashions I so richly deserve. I saw these red-hot thigh-highs Bedazzle boots too. I think I'm going back and buy those boots," Sadaya said.

"Sooner or later I'll see Cobb around here and I can ask him a question for you and a question for me. See you guys later. Ok. Choir rehearsal starts in 10 minutes," Sadaya said. "Oh hello Mr. Williams. You're looking extra attractive this evening. Thank you. Did you see Cobb around?" Yes, he's in the parking lot. "Thanks,"

Sadaya said. She walked outdoors into the parking lot and she saw the door open to the car. Cobb was rearranging his trunk. He had luggage in the trunk. Sadaya was standing behind him. "Aha," she said darting left to right and right to left. "Ha, ha, ha," she said. He said, "I was just thinking about you, Sadaya. Would you go to dinner with me tonight after choir rehearsal? "Yes, but I have to be to work early tomorrow," Sadaya said. "Are you going to join the choir?" she asked. I'm thinking about it. My time is limited as it is but I'm going to sit in and see how things are run, since two people asked me about joining it already. "Are you going to sit with me?" she said. "Yes. I'd be happy to sit next to you," Cobb said.

"Phew. I thought he was going to tell me our relationship is Kaputs; finished, gone; Sadaya thought. He asked me to dinner; something he's done often. I'm kind of hungry so going is the right move anyway. Hee, hee, hee . . . ha, ha, ha . . . ha, ha, ha. I'm lucky I'm adorned with the Holy Spirit. "I'm believing that everyone notices I'm adorned with the Holy Spirit," she thought. Choir rehearsal started on time. Mr. Austere the Choir Director is usually punctual and extremely musical. He was extraordinarily gifted this evening. Cobb gave him a whole slew of compliments. He told him he used to play when Cobb was a little boy but Mr. Austere was so great that he wanted to know if Mr. Austere gives lessons on the piano himself. He said yes, Mr. Austere said yes and he offered to give Cobb piano lessons. The whole choir started laughing. I guess you just had to be there to see the humor. Before it's over with, Cobb will be so busy he'll do nothing but sleep, play basketball and church.

Cobb will be so busy he won't have time to sniff his shoes. Sadaya looked beautiful and she complimented Cobb's style of dress. Tonight, he too wore a cashmere sweater. He also wore a 22K gold chain with a cross on it and a Steffy pair of jeans. Everything you look for in a man's neat wardrobe Cobb had. That's how much, like Sadaya, he loves clothes. When he buys clothes, he buys maybe five sweaters, 10 suits at a time; 20 shirts at a time. There's no such thing as a crappy look about Cobb Jackson. He likes to dress and to be ready for any occasion.

Cobb and Sadaya, both early for choir rehearsal went into the choir room. He sat next to the aisle and Sadaya next to the Cobb that she's come to love, although she didn't tell him because she has fears that he'll quit her. She wants to keep him on the chase, "chase her" so that the relationship is interesting. Sadaya lacks an accurate understanding of where Cobb is emotionally because he isn't able to tell her. He isn't able to tell her that he's in love with her so both of them are just guessing when it comes to where the relationship is at this point. This is whyCobb sought the pastor's perspective on the situation. He'll meet with him in another five days. In the meantime, both Cobb and Sadaya are enjoying each other's company at church, the best place.

Sadaya was sharing some of her corniest jokes and Cobb was laughing so hard he was almost under the chair he was sitting on. Sadaya put her Sunglasses on her face. Cobb laughed again. "What are you doing Sadaya?" he asked. I put my sunglasses on because I'm embarrassed. You've laughed at my corny jokes and me. I didn't expect for you to find me so funny," Sadaya said, with her head lowered and no smile on her face. She felt like going for a short walk before choir rehearsal. Sadaya excused herself and she went to the car parking lot. It was now dark outside and the sky was incredible and magnificent at the same time. "I love how God arranged the sky; the firmaments. He really knew what He was doing . . . Well Lord, here I am waiting again for yet another choir rehearsal. Pretty looking weather today, though chilly. Sadaya breathed in and breathed out. Breathed in and she breathed out again a total of 10 times and then she ran back into the church. To her surprise, there was a very pretty woman seated in Sadaya's seat laughing and talking to Cobb and he seemed to be loving it. Sadaya saw him give the pretty woman his card and she gave him a card. Ah, the old exchanging phone numbers before the girlfriend gets back trick, 'eh?! "I can't believe I'm so jealous over Cobb,"

Sadaya said. It's probably just business anyway, she thought. But Sadaya was pretty herself and this seemed to be something she didn't understand. Any type of attractiveness that anyone else had, she had too. Cobb's heart was with Sadaya whether he went out with someone else or not. She was a beautiful in his book and she was refined but not in hers.

In her book, she was "ok. Attractive, not ugly," is how she saw herself. She certainly didn't see herself as Miss America material. She was wrong. She was Miss America material except for the fact that she was overweight. This problem she had mentally planned to work out, by going to the health spa at least twice a week. She also wanted to get "Trim Faster," to supplement her foods; her solid foods. This would give her a Younger, youthful look and maybe she'd see herself as more attractive. At any rate, the other pretty woman was seated in her seat. "What are you going to do about it?" she asked herself. "I'm going right over there and get my seat back," she thought, but peacefully like a Christian woman should, she thought. Cobb didn't put his disguise on tonight so they know who he is. Mr. Austere is the only one and the pastor who knows about the disguise for Cobb. Pastor told Cobb not to come in church disguised as a woman to which Cynthia howled when I told her. "I didn't think it was so funny, though," Sadaya said to her best friend Cynthia.

Cobb was still seated in the aisle seat and Sadaya's seat next to it was occupied. Sadaya walked down the aisle and put her knee in to the leg of Cobb's and smiling, she looked at the pretty woman and she said, "That's my seat you're in, still smiling. Sadaya then motioned for her to move from the seat with her hand," smiling even wider. The woman stood up, displeased by the moved, to the back of the choir room. She was there as a guest of Mr. Austere's to do duet masterpieces with him as a demonstration for a possible performance on Sunday mornings. "Thank You Sadaya was able to be assertive and get her seat back," she thought. Cobb's eyes looked like they were noticing a little too much about how her clothes were fitting her, Sadaya noticed. "Thank you, were going to dinner after this," she thought. I don't even know where these thoughts are coming from," she thought. "After all, he doesn't have to say good bye to me and to drop me. This Sunday we're all going to be in Church and it is going to be massive in terms of the quality of the performances and the amount of people who will be there, she thought. "It's going to be fabulous, this Sunday. This is how I should be thinking. I feel better; Sadaya found herself thinking clearly. The Black Memorial Baptist Church has invited 10 other choirs from other churches to come and to have a bite with us after church ends. We'll have dinner and we'll be growing the economy of the church as well as increasing the cultural atmosphere of the church. Thank God for music and food and culture. Cobb and Sadaya sat nicely and peacefully through the choir rehearsal. Cobb secretly admired Sadaya's singing voice which was a surprise to him. They met for one hour and seven minutes.

The pretty woman's name was Clarita Acostre and she said she was from Cuba. Her father was American and her mother was from Cuba. The whole choir welcomed her with open arms. At one point during the choir rehearsal, Sadaya looked at Cobb and she smiled. He smiled back at her, while she was singing from the music sheets that were handed out from Mr. Austere, the Choir Director. When the choir rehearsal was over, Cobb was very impressed. He leaned over and he told Sadaya to hurry up because he was starving. "Ok, honey, I'll meet you at the restaurant. Don't forget to put your disguise back on. I'll see you there. Bye," Sadaya said. "No limousine this time I'm noticing," Sadaya was thinking to herself. "Oh, let me stop. Cobb probably wants a change of transportation, that's all. I don't know what's making me so negative-thinking about him. I'm going to have to really humble myself, bend my knees and talk to The Master. He is someone who won't abandon me and who will give me a truthful perspective. Life is not perfect but The Master, The Almighty God of The Universe is. I want to and I will talk to Him soon. He has all of the answers, all of the knowledge and all of the wisdom and so much more. I'm going to meet Cobb and I'm not going to sleep before I have a Big Talk with The Big God Upstairs," Sadaya thought to herself.

Ok, so I'm here but Cobb didn't' get here yet. Anyway, I can reserve a table for two. After Sadaya sat at the table for two she called Cobb on her cell phone. He answered and he said he was stuck in traffic but there was a voice in the background that caused Sadaya to put her ear closer to the phone. It sounded like the woman she just met at the choir rehearsal Clarita Acostre, from Cuba. "That's ridiculous. I just saw him get into the car in the parking lot at the church. I'd better stop being so suspicious, she mused; calming her nerves.

The problem is simple. I took Sadaya out for pizza because she said she wanted some. I was a gentleman during all times with her. We're leaving the shopping mall where the pizza place is and I see this attractive young lady stepping through the swinging door. I held the door for her and she and I smiled at each other. She said, "I know you. You're Cobb Jackson." "Yes, I am," I said. Sadaya flew mad. She didn't say anything but you could see the anger and low tolerance for me in her eyes. She folded her arms and she started patting her feet, as if to say, 'hurry the hades up.' Cobb went to open the door for Sadaya and Sadaya went through another door on the other side of the shopping mall to keep Cobb from opening the door for her. Cobb went to the other side of the shopping mall too. He asked her, "What is wrong with you. Why are you acting like this?" Sadaya didn't like Cobb "flirting with other women," she said. They exchanged about eight sentences and argued among themselves quietly until they go to the car outside. "The argument was silly," Cobb said. It did get louder inside of the car. "I wasn't really looking at that girl in the mall," Cobb said. Sadaya really misunderstood.

After 45 minutes, Cobb walked into the restaurant. He apologized and he then over- apologized. He said he would take her somewhere or do something special with her to make up for it. Sadaya asked him why was it such a big problem when she saw him get into his car in the parking lot? He said, "You sped off and left fast. Just after that Clarita Acostre came out of the church and she flagged me down. She asked for a lift to the "better place for getting a taxicab." She said she didn't want me to take her all the way home. Just a lift. Cobb sat quietly after that. "Is that all?" Sadaya wanted to know. The Superstar basketball player spoke to the award winning teach and made a sign of the cross on his chest. "That's all that happened. Sadaya please listen to me. That's all that's happened," he said. "Ok Cobb. I, Sadaya realize that you only had about 20 minutes to get to the restaurant and the time factor is not that bad a problem.

"We sat in the car and we talked a while but no big thing," he said. "Well, Cobb, sex is not something that all women choose. Some are smart enough to see that there are many men that have sex with them and then abandon them. Flirting and hurting. Flirting and hurting. Flirting and hurting. She hides it well. Hides what well? The way she flirts well, I think," Sadaya said about Clarita Acostre. But flirt doesn't always mean sex. It's time some men learn this," Sadaya said. "I learned that if you smile the same way you smile to get people to like you, you'll be liked by him anyway. Spending time getting to know him doesn't have to mean sex. Quite frankly, women have a lot more at stake should they get pregnant and have the baby than men have. And then for some of the less mature boys or men, the flirt yes hurt rule does apply. Usually the hurt part of the scenario involves abandonment.

Then the young lady, girl or woman feels all alone; like the trouble will never end. Sooner or later, they will see that motherhood has its rewards. Many rewards. Thus, the same for fatherhood. It comes with much maturation, appreciation, lessons, respect and positive experiences. These rewards occur for both mothers and fathers in the majority of the cases. So, the nice couple, Cobb Jackson and Sadaya Ruby Day sat and they conversed about male and female relationships. It was during this conversation that Sadaya realized that Cobb was not going to drop her or abandon her. "Boy oh boy, was I paranoid," Sadaya thought to herself. She asked Cobb to tell her where he sees their relationship going. No way in the world he could tell her he's been thinking of marriage for him and her. It would take more sessions with the pastor for him to answer that question. "I don't know. What do you think?" he said. Sadaya said, "I have a very good feeling about us. I believe we'll make it through and we'll make it through to the next level. Cobb only smiled and he drank his soda drink. Sadaya smiled too and she let him get away with just smiling. After all, this is the same man that she thought would dump her moments earlier. Luckily, he left most of the language up to Sadaya and he heard good positive advice come from her. He is proud of Sadaya. He knows she's not rich like him. She dresses well and he likes her results he noted in the school students she's responsible for. He's very satisfied with the job she does. A+, Pride and Satisfaction. That's a nice combination. A nice report card for Sadaya Ruby Day from Cobb Jackson. A+. I'll bet Sadaya will never find this report card information out if she has to find it out from Cobb," Cobb's parents said. They called while Cobb and Sadaya were at dinner. Sadaya spoke to them on the telephone. She privately asked them if she asked him the right question when she said she wanted to know how far this relationship would go.

By then, Cobb had taken a walk to the men's room. Sadaya explained this fact to his parents on the telephone. His mother explained that sometimes Cobb has a difficult time expressing himself to pretty women. She told Sadaya to look for it. She also gave Sadaya more tips about how to bring the strategies out on Cobb to fight his shyness. Sadaya told his mother she hadn't noticed he was that shy with her. The mother Mrs. Jackson and her husband Mr. Jackson told Sadaya to test it out. If she knows what to look for, she'll see it, both parents agreed. We tested our theories on our toughest critic: Cobb and we found it was best when he didn't know he was being tested or when he didn't know he was the sample. The last thing Sadaya could hear from his mother is that she believes that he is in love with Sadaya and he can't say it" she said. Yes, Cobb's mother spilled the beans. "Don't tell him I told you about this. He would be very angry and upset with me, said his mother. He'd probably stop speaking to me, she said; not invite me to your wedding if this should every happen or never let me see your child once you have one. Who knows what else he could do to make my life miserable," Mrs. Jackson supposed. "He holds grudges sometimes, you know," his mother gave Sadaya insight. "Please pray for him and pray hard for him. Ask God to give you the gift of prayer," she said. Over time, you will find a great relationship between God and you. You will find that after a certain amount of time, your prayers will be answered and that God reveals Himself to those who diligently seek Him. Do that. Diligently seek Him each and every day. You'd be pleasantly surprised at how God will answer you," Mrs. Jackson said making small talk. "Oh yes, I will. Cobb's back from the men's room now. Here, talk to him. Cobb took his phone back from Sadaya. "Hey mom, how 'ya doing," Cobb said. "Fine, son, I'm just fine. We were keeping Sadaya company while you were in the restroom. Thanks for her lovely conversation. We'll talk to you later, son." "See 'ya," his mom and dad said. As Cobb hung up it struck him funny that his mother said, "See 'ya." That's what he said most of his life to them. "See 'ya." Everywhere. I went every day, I said, "See 'ya" to my parents. I guess I was conditioning them without knowing it. After hanging up with his parents, Cobb started telling Sadaya about them then he asked her how did they treat her?!" Very well was always the answer, when it came to Cobb's parents. They kept it secret to everyone, but they privately loved Sadaya and they were asking God if she could be their daughter-in-law. "She just fits in, I think. She's a God-Fearing professional woman with a beautiful personality and a beautiful face. We hope Cobb recognizes this and that he sees things like the potential we see in her," dad said.

We love her very much were the exact words that were used describing how they feel about Sadaya. His parents told Cobb, "maybe she'll be your new wife someday before your father and I leave this earth. Just dropping a real hint," his mother said.

Sadaya felt cold with the cold chilly winter wind blowing at her back. She shivered and began to look at her coat. She wondered if she should get up and pull her coat off of the rack and spread it across her shoulders. "I guess I'll try to hang on." She smiled to herself. "I guess I can hang on and hang in there." "Maybe Cobb would like to hang on to me because I'm shivering cold," Sadaya said. When she asked him if he wanted to cuddle, he said he was too hot to cuddle "tonight," then he burst open his pants laughing at Sadaya's facial expressions. He was in a jovial mood. "Go ahead so you can laugh. You know I need you and that I have thin skin," Sadaya told Cobb. "Hold me, honey," she said. He laughed again at Sadaya while telling her he's too friggin' hot to be bothered. Sadaya was really cold then and she stood up and began walking down the aisle to get to the coats hanging on the rack. Her cold hands felt like they were craving for the gloves in the coat to warm the blood in the body of Sadaya. I surely am cold. When Sadaya went to pick up her coat off of the rack, she felt Cobb's hands playfully around her neck. With that maneuver he scared the living daylights out of her, and she said, "No No, No, that's ok." He said, "Now you want to cuddle and huddle, huh?" Sadaya never got the chance to pull the coat off of the rack. "He" had it. Everyone knows that being a Star Athlete, he was a member of the Elite basketball crowd and his reflexes were better than Sadaya's and everyone else's because he had to rely on those reflexes every day of his God-given life to win. He beat her twice getting to the coat, grabbing it and putting it right back on the rack. Cobb was teasing and he was happy to be teasing. By the coat rack, he placed his lips on hers for a tap kiss. It was love, love, love; instant love Cobb felt.

He felt that spiritual connection that a man chooses in the woman that the is in love with and getting ready to marry. He and she stood by the coat racks and they hugged each other. For Sadaya, this was a warm beautiful display of her love to Cobb. It served a purpose too – it warmed up Sadaya's cold parts. As she explained to her parents after she got home, "it was an awesome pleasure to dine with Cobb this evening, especially now that I'd been allowed to get warm," Sadaya said. This made me think of a woman I used to go to school with. She and her man met. For 5 ½ months they dated. They'll be getting married in three more months. Wow. The fact that these two responsible adults would get married after only 8 ½ months of knowing each other is miraculous. "I'm sure God must have had a hand in putting this one together. I thank God, this couple decided to marry instead of to burn. Don't ask me, as God. He said it's better to marry than to burn; in the Holy Scriptures," Sadaya said to Cobb.

Cobb liked to joke with the people he loved even though he possessed tremendous physical strength. His mother, grandmother and his friends all knew that he was like a kitten with a ball of yarn, when it came to those who he was close to. Sadaya, in the restaurant, was being "played with" because Cobb loves Sadaya, purely and simply. As time goes on, it is believed that Cobb Jackson will loom as one of the greatest basketball players ever to have played the game. If Sadaya was alone in a private place, the competitor in Cobb would say, "just go inside with the women and let them tell you what to do."

1 Corinthians 7:9 Kings James Version It is better to marry than to burn. If Cobb remembers correctly. Sadaya was intelligent, could get along and socialize with anyone, was sophisticated and she had a profound belief in The Almighty God of The Universe/

Cobb took Sadaya's hand and he began to rub the top and rub the sides and inside of Sadaya's hand.

Sadaya first jerked her hand away reflexively. Cobb turned his head. He made that final turn of his head and he saw her for the beauty that she is, for the first time. She was adorned with the Holy Spirit, she said. God decided to let her adorn herself. As Cobb made that last walk around the corner, he saw her and he stopped walking. Thinking of Clarita Acostre, she was nice, but she wasn't Sadaya. In spite of all of that, a burden was dropped on her shoulders that couldn't be removed at all; it felt like that anyway. Sometimes, though, fame and fortune ignites betrayal. This could have been a heartbreaking, emotional story but the rejoicing would have given us all sessions of tears. This will be a triumph of love, of friendship and of second chances; wherever it's appropriate. I'm hoping this will be a can't put it down page turner book. Cobb says if they ever write my life story; it's be a hit. I would write it with Sadaya Ruby Day. She's competent at it.

There's something in the writer's work that readers would come to love. There is a way she descriptively explains things to you that keeps you updated and clinging to her for more information to learn by. She delivers.

A movie critic said Sadaya began to think about her home which she shares with her mother and father and her sisters away at school. She had just bought a funky floral 6-piece Comforter Set. There was a solid flange on the comforter and the shams and Sadaya thought she'd better remind Cobb that she had to leave in order to prepare for her job early tomorrow. She chose "funky floral" 6-piece Comforter; color was Seafoam, Multi. "Oh boy. I'm starting to see my bed before my very eyes almost," Sadaya said. Cobb said he'd like to join Sadaya and see what her Seafoam comforter feels like. His face was so serious, it almost looked like he was to cry. He really looks serious. Sadaya answered Cobb with "My goal is your complete and total satisfaction. I want to delight you, whether under a funky comforter or not. Cobb and Sadaya looked at each other and he said, "you're just pulling my leg and patronizing me and I know it. You aren't going to let me come upstairs to your room with your parents' room there, on the same floor. Some things just make sense and some things don't make sense," he said. "Yes, we're adults, but I am not ready to break my parents' trust and the respect they have for me. First and foremost, I'm not ready to lose God's respect and admiration either," she said. Cobb grabbed Sadaya by her sweater. He said, "you know I think your cashmere sweater is softer than mine. Give me a big hug and I'll be ok. Someday we'll make love all day and night and I won't know how to act. Enough said," he said. "Ok, enough said" said Sadaya. "Ok well I was glad to see to it that you've eaten because sometimes you don't eat and I sense you're losing weight the wrong way, Sadaya. Remember, nothing beats broccoli, string beans, peas, asparagus, carrots, plus a small portion of bread, which is a starch or baked potato. Healthy food got me to where I am on the N.Y. Boxers' Basketball Team. I really do feel great when I'm on the basketball courts wherever they are. My heart feels great and so do my arms and legs," Cobb told Sadaya. "Alright. I feel I have more understanding about yours and my situation than you give me credit for. But that's ok. I'm patient and God gave me a peace that surpasses all human understanding. Sometimes I talk to God when I'm playing on the basketball court. I ask Him to please give me some moves to use on my opponents and to keep me winning and to continue to help my shooting. "Help my swishes, Lord I ask you. I almost said I beg you but the Bible says you don't have to beg," he said. Ask and it shall be given, seek and ye shall find, knock and the door shall be opened. We are God's children. We ask but we must have patience. The patience to wait for our prayers to be answered. Ask Him and He will give it. He must have time to arrange things, and to give you lessons in patience or whatever He's working on within your life. For everyone who asks receives and he who seeks finds.

What man is there among you who, if his son asks for bread will give him a stone? Or if he asks for a fish will he give him a snake? If you then being evil, know how to give good gifts to your children how much more will your Father who is in Heaven give good things to those who ask Him! Therefore, everything you will like men to do to you do also to them, for this is the Law and The Prophets.

"The longer I live, the better I feel. What made me feel so much better was reading the Holy Bible, and memorizing some of them. The Holy Scriptures Mom and dad said: Did you know that we were the first ones among my family and friends of ours to jump the broom? There was also a ritual of waving the broom over the wedding couple. These customs the jumping the broom and the waving the broom over the couple were customs believed to have been brought over from West Africa. It was also very inspiring during the civil rights movement when people such as Coretta and Martin Luther King, and Malcom X and Betty Shabazz served as role model couples, as role models symbols or the beauty of love. They helped America to showcase the beauty of love and the beauty of black love. While fighting for our and their civil rights, these two power couples believed strongly in their concepts of God. The Office of the President of the USA was enhanced by Michelle and Barack Obama's loyalty to their marriage. They were reminding us to keep relationships a priority simply by just being there and being a together couple. Thank you, God for all of the people who were able to hang in there for the good of love. Being a role model for a healthy couple in marriage gives us a chance to pick and choose and influence ourselves," Sadaya's parents rested their case.

"Don't worry about how high you go; just fly. If you're going through hades, keep going." I'll remember that; I'll always remember that," they said. After that, then onward to a blessed stage of their lives; having children which are a blessing that runs deep. My on-line TV pastor always said never allow anyone to get you HALT: too hungry, too angry, too lonely or too tired. HALT; that's when you know it's time for you to take over and correct your body status. Don't let the body count rise again with you in it. Your body count means whenever there are healthy people you should only be counted in among the healthy. Cobb hardly even had anybody who wanted to use and abuse him because he was so obviously tall. Sadaya was a different story because her current height she reasoned was about 5-5-5'56" and she wore those impossible heels; the 10 Charles Stanley ones that made her speak the Holy Scriptures: "I can do all things through Christ who strengthens me," the Holy Bible says. My mother and father taught me to touch when appropriate when it comes to sex. Explaining about hormones was very important along with discussions about sex. Whatever a young person decides to do about their sex life is their decision. Sometimes this may be an awkward decision but it's not anyone's decision but their own. Cobb agreed with Sadaya and they both saluted to a wine toast. Arm in arm they drank, toasted to the wine and they said, "we know we're right." Be empowered and be informed. Cobb seemed more amorous tonight. He went to the men's room and he came back quickly closing his lips over her lops and smiling. She was so beautiful she would have made a great Miss America or Miss USA or Mrs. America, Cobb thought. He kissed Sadaya again, this time deeply and with much more energy and passion and verve. Sadaya was really being tempted this time. She wanted him and she wanted him naked and in bed but if she ever got pregnant, her mother and father would die and kill her all at the same time, plus God doesn't' want us to do it like that. He wants us to wait until we're married. But still, she wanted to be touched and hugged and felt like she was his only and best lover. She smiled at him and she put his hand into her mouth. Kissing her mouth is what he was after but his hand got in the way. The feelings between those two were oh so sensual and true love sometimes gives a euphoria that just won't end. File this experience here's one for the fantasy books under the title sex fantasies coming true if I don't hurry up and stop them from coming.

It certainly was fun while it lasted. But then not everything that's fun is good for you, Sadaya was thinking. What opened up her eyes good and wide was that Sadaya didn't want her parents to lose respect for her or to have a baby she didn't want nor had the time for. She and Cobb would begin their sexuality someday but not now. She gently shoved his hands away from her blouse and they both smiled while looking and gazing into each other's eyes. Cobb took Sadaya's hand and walked back into the eating seating section of the restaurant. He was accustomed to being gently shoved to the side for God. He had no resentment or jealousy in him. Live well, laugh much and love often; this was what wisdom Sadaya was trying to impart onto both she and Cobb. "I'd day I lived it about ¾ of the way and I'm working on the last 1/4. My dear, you're so beautiful that you add elegance to a room just by being there. In the peacock lounge you're the peacock. Peacock Sadaya you effortlessly grace the room with charm, poise and savvy. The peacock had a majestic style about it and so did Sadaya. She depicted all of the right actions for joy, prosperity, longevity and happiness. Sadaya set off an elegant ambiance. She was so exquisite. She had a touch of class that was unlike many women of her day, of her class and of her age. She was of this personality type and Cobb found himself taken in by her so much that he kept wondering if he had fallen in love with her or not. He asked himself if he had truly fallen in love with her and he kept coming up with what he knew to be the answer: Yes, He kept wanting her in his bed. If he didn't see her he missed her fiercely. If he didn't see her at the Church he was sad. He actually later grew lovesick and depressed. Then there were those fantasies Cobb was having about Sadaya. He had fantasies surrounding the bedroom that would make a grown man shy. Every piece of evidence and feelings inside of him told Cobb he was in love with Sadaya. If she and Cobb were to marry and she becomes Mrs. Jackson, she deserves the title and the love and the lifestyle. As Sadaya sat back down in the dining room of the restaurant, Cobb told her he'd be back soon. Cobb needed to go for a walk or a drive or something. He moved to the glass window doors. He put his gloved hands on the steering wheel and he drove for 10 minutes. He got into his car and he pulled in a deep breath. He drove for about 10 minutes. He then, after drawing another deep breath, returned to the dinner restaurant. It took him about 12 minutes. He felt like a new man, refreshed and rejuvenated. He turned into a parking spot in the parking lot. He walked back into the restaurant with a smile, a wide smile on his face.

"How do you do? I'm glad to see you," he said to Sadaya. "Did you eat any food yet? Did they bring it out from the kitchen yet?" he said. "Ah, here they are." They came with the food just as Cobb came back from his 10-minute excursion. In Cobb's mind, even the food tasted better. He was thinking that he would call the pastor of The Black Memorial Baptist Church and see if he could get an emergency appointment visit or meeting with him for tomorrow or the next day. The rest of the evening with Sadaya was terrific. He ate some of her food and she ate some of his and they spoke about everything from here and to under the sun. Cobb was so happy with Sadaya, he glowed, she believed. No artificial heart valves here. This was all real thought they haven't been making love all the way in bed or outside of it. "What an unagitated state I'm in. Boy do I feel good in this unagitated state," Cobb said. "We'll have to do this more often," he said. Only next time, I want you to cook for me, baby. Just you, me and us. I want to taste your cooking again. I must tell you that I keep seeing you with him. What do you mean him? Who's "him?" "I still think of Thaddeus my ex-boyfriend sometimes, I admit it," she said. "I knew it wouldn't last. My unagitated state," Cobb said. "I like to think that men are the champagne of the male/female genders," Cobb thought. "I just knew she'd do something to spoil my mood. It's a good thing I love her because if not, I'd strangle her," he thought. She had to bring him up. I thought she wasn't going to see him, anymore, since he was "married," Cobb thought to himself. The only reason Sadaya said she thinks of him is because they were close to each other like brother and sister, would have done anything to help each other. They even talked about going into business with each other, buying a house together. "We talked about some pretty intimate things. After a four-year relationship he just dropped out of sight. He stopped calling me. He stopped coming by, he stopped seeing me and I never was told why he just dropped me, stopped communication of all kinds. Then two years after not hearing from him or his mother and father, I started thinking about Thad again. So, I called him. This time he answered the call. He said he missed me and yet he couldn't have called me because he was getting married and he couldn't tell me. He didn't have the courage to let me know he was getting married," she said. "What a bum," Sadaya said. He "just couldn't" is the way he phrased qit. "I just couldn't face you," he said. "The no-good goat," Sadaya thought. Sadaya looked at Cobb. She asked him to trust her. Cobb thought about the Holy Scriptures and how the Scriptures say Trust God not Man. Man will let you down. His mother says that all of the time. "If more people would take God and His Word more seriously, they might learn something and they might get blessed a thousand-fold," he thought. Thaddeus was criticized and he was ridiculed for keeping his marriage a secret from Sadaya. Many nice people would have said that Sadaya should have kept her mouth shut and not told Cobb that she went to dinner with Thad because this would be interpreted as her going out with not only a married man but another man. This is exactly what Cobb's reaction was. He's hated Thaddeus ever since, although he's never seen him in person. Never had any conversation with him. A woman's wish is God's wish says an old African proverb. God will bless Sadaya for not breaking the marriage vows of Thaddeus. God bless Sadaya; That's no small thing to God, the Holy Scriptures say. Sadaya's

Christian training was the answer. He who ceases from anger is blessed She was slow to anger although she was shocked at the news of his marriage to someone else. "I don't know how to handle the pain from this type of situation, Lord God. I really loved Thad. Now that Cobb has heard I went out with someone else, I don't know what's going to happen to my relationship with him," Sadaya said in her prayers, humble and on her knees. "I don't want to lose Cobb. I love him now. My love for Thaddeus is mostly in the past. I've got to work harder on the relationship with Cobb. He's paying me a lot of attention lately. The problem is we only see each other once in two weeks because he travels so much. Lord please help me to come up with the best solutions for my problems," Sadaya tearfully asked these things of God. She prayed for a long time; approximately two hours and 20 minutes. The Holy Spirit adorned her well. She was a visible role model and God was pleased. He will raise up a favorable portion for Sadaya, who is adorned with the Holy Spirit every.

Praying every day, her amount of praying time averages about 1 ½ to 2 ½ hours each day. When a person prays, they are communing and making a relationship with God which will last a lifetime. God loves it when we form a relationship with Him. Many people don't know it but there are promises that God has made to His people and his Word, His Holy Scriptures never fail, they never return void. God is a giving God. If He says He is going to give you something, wait on God and expect it to happen for you. It will happen. Believe in your mind that it's going to happen and say, there's no doubt in my mind that it will happen. God waited on him and he actively waited on God. He went about his daily business while waiting for God to do what he asked him to. God guarantees it and He promises it. If your parents told you they were going to give you something you'd most likely believe it. You'd have patience and wait for them to produce it. Believe God. He said victory is something we should focus on because He is God and he can make things happen. "Keep repeating to yourself,

Victory is mine. Victory today is mine," Sadaya kept whispering to herself. I see what's happened. This is the philosophy Cobb used to become a superstar basketball player winner. Sadaya had asked God to send a rich sports type, tall and handsome and someone who respects Him with a capital R. "So, in walks this beautiful basketball player who caught my eyes the very first time I saw him," she said. I privately asked myself is this him? Could this be my man, my Prince Charming that God sent me? The way he looked at me, it would have been easy to think so; to think that he was my very own. I've got to let Cobb teach some basketball ology to the church team for a long time. There's a method to his madness. Cobb and Sadaya's pastor was in attendance. He was their spiritual guide and he approved of Cobb's basketball ology for the youth. "He's the one I love," Sadaya thought.

"God's Scriptures tells us do not worry, do not fret; be anxious for nothing, because the 'victory is mine,' meaning the victory belongs to God's people," Sadaya explained. Trust me, one of my grandfathers was a preacher pastor. The pastor of Black Memorial Baptist Church chimed in: "there is a God and he knows everything there is to know, especially when you talk to Him of Jesus Christ, He blesses you and if He wants to, he gives you ultra-mega blessings. Keep talking to Him even if it doesn't feel like anything is happening that will help your situation and you will see an improvement. Soon your problem will be over but hopefully not your conversations with God. The Bible says God only wishes good things for His favored ones like you and me the pastor said. One of the most beautiful things to happen is that Cobb Jackson himself has formed a relationship with God; the Almighty God of the Universe Himself," he said. I have seen Cobb and heard Cobb praying and I believe God has His hands onCobb's life. What an honor. The Most Powerful Force in the Universe is God and many are called but few are Chosen. I believe He has a chosen Cobb for something great. Basketball too," the pastor said. "I'm just excited that I've been able to hold his interest, for so long, not to have had sex with him. I'm thanking God that he hasn't gotten rid of me because I think he's [Cobb] is used to a wilder lifestyle. I'm a homebody," Sadaya said. "When I was growing up, I always thought that I would make a great news anchor broadcaster for network television news. It wasn't until after I grew up and became an adult that I actually put together a demonstration tape and tried out for a television station show. I was able to do substitute work and was on TV regularly; on different channels. Then the TV gig dried up for me and that's when I went to the School of Education route which was what I was trained in during college," she said. "Be nice to people. That's how I've lived my life and that's how I'm sure I'll die," Sadaya said.

Cobb Jackson was feeling frantic emotionally. He wanted to speak to the pastor and to be counseled. He called the Black Memorial Baptist Church and put in an emergency phone request to the pastor's secretary. She said, "Sorry, but the pastor is out of town. He'll be back in town in two days. I'll tell him you called the next time I call him which will be tonight, about 8:00 p.m. – 9:00 p.m. Sorry to wait so long, but he told me to wait until 8:00 or 9:00 pm because it is when his day winds down and he can focus and concentrate on what I'm saying to him. Such topics do arise: who called for emergency phone calls and who came into the office to see him today and other things. He's one of the speakers at The National Association of African-American History and Culture in Washington, D.C." the pastor's secretary said.

Cobb Jackson told the secretary how much he enjoyed the choir rehearsal and how he might join the choir. She said she thought they were the greatest thing since sliced bread. She said, "you know I'm already a member of the choir, and God really spoke to me for the first time that I know of when I was working closely with the choir. It's better with the choir, believe me. The secretary went on to tell Cobb but her husband loves the ground he walks on and she wants her husband to meet Cobb Jackson as well as her two children. She then said she'd see what she can do when it comes to making arrangements with the pastor. The pastor loves you too. You have a lot of fans, Cobb. But I'm sure you must know that," she said. "Yeah, they have ways of surprising me, telling me I should take my uniform off, telling me I should take my uniform off, telling me I should wear a wig, do more commercials and find somebody to marry. My fans send me food and cakes and nut loaves, fruit cakes all kinds of things. They never cease to amaze me. There are so many of them I have a whole team to organize any gift that's sent to me and to organize and read/respond to mail. Mr. Cobb Jackson, can we have a "Meet the Members" Cocktail Sip Cocktail will be sparkling apple cider of course. A cocktail sip would really encourage people to get to know people like you and other members of clubs here at the church. Do you want me to talk to the pastor about it? Yes? Good," the secretary said. Cobb first smiled then he burst his shirt open almost with laughter. I guess she really wants that Cocktail Sip to happen, so I'd better jump on the band wagon, Cobb thought. "Ok so I'll see you Sunday. By then I will have spoken to our illustrious pastor," she said. "Ok," said Cobb. Cobb offered the secretary's husband some tickets for when he plays in two weeks in New York. She screamed into the telephone and she said, "Can we all go?" Cobb said "yes, that's what I meant, you, your husband and all of your kids, which would make it a pleasure for me. See to it that your children see me after the game. This is Meet the Players Day in two weeks' time. Tell them to bring a bag because the players will be giving out souvenirs and autographs," Cobb said. They'll also be selling jerseys and hoodies for $10.00. These are genuine players jackets and hoodies for only $10.00. This is like a 90% off sale for young people. I hope I see you in church this Sunday so I can give the tickets to you. Thank you, Jesus. Thank you, Jesus, thank you Jesus!" the secretary said. "I'll see you before or after service this

Sunday. Ok, have a blessed week," the secretary said. "Good bye," Cobb said. "It will most likely be after service that I'll find you. That's fine. See you then," he said. When Cobb Jackson was free to go home; free from sports traveling, he visited the Black Baptist Church (Black Memorial Baptist Church). He did volunteer work at the church. He helped to bring in free food donations to senior citizens, he helped with the After- School Tutorial Center and he had a basketball clinic for children aged 9-14 years old; every two-weeks, Cobb did this.

Sadaya Ruby Day liked sports too. Sometimes she'd sit in the gymnasium when the boys were playing and "socializing" together. One thing that impressed Sadaya was the personalities of the children. They loved playing for Cobb. They didn't mind winning for him; he was impressed too. When the games were over, Sadaya stayed and brought lunch for Cobb. He was most appreciative after exerting himself. As life would have it, Sadaya always seemed to find Cobb first. She blew kisses at him wherever he and she went. When they bumped into each other in the Narthex, in the gymnasium or in the choir room, Sadaya always showed him an Adorned quality of the Holy Spirit, as best she could. She always related well to him as his future wife though she was careful to never say this is what she wanted. Cobb would gently and quietly take her hand in his hands and he'd kiss it.

Sadaya was in the choir room helping to make copies of a program for a concert forthcoming. The tickets will be $15. The $15 includes a fee for a snack box dinner. She came out to take a break. She decided to sit in the Sanctuary and she prayed. Ten minutes of sitting in the Sanctuary and who sticks his head in? Cobb, of course. "Hey there, it's my favorite individual," he said. He sat right next to her and they both looked at each other, smiling. "I was hoping you'd be here today," she said. He said,

"Boy do you look better than a two-mile long school of long finned tuna, to a starving man. You're like my Air Sea Rescue Team. You always show up on time," Cobb said. Cobb sat next to Sadaya on the cushions on the church's bench seats. Sadaya put her arm under Cobb's arm and she laid her head on his shoulder, next to his neck. She said, "you don't mind if I rest my eyes, do you?" "Of course not, girl." He then kissed her on her forehead, lovingly, playfully and he embraced her right there in the sanctuary. This is a beautiful place to sit in and pull your mind into normalcy. The stained-glass windows are so enjoyable. You can open and close them and enlighten yourself about God and what He wants for His church. There are Holy Scriptures on every window and boy are they expensive, those stained-glass windows. Meanwhile, Cobb and Sadaya were able to sit in the empty sanctuary uninterrupted. "I feel so comfortable with you Cobb, especially here in church," Sadaya said. Are you going to the Women's Day program next month?" Sadaya said. "She might go with Cobb but she's not 100% sure; if she'd go at all. The atmosphere in the sanctuary was refreshing because one window was open and another window was open and there was a cross breeze of fresh air which both Cobb and Sadaya could feel. As Cobb put it, "Oh yea, this feels so good. Now this is relaxation and tension reduction. I like this love we're showing to each other too. "Come here, girl," he said. Cobb loved the sanctuary. It was carpeted, the seats were cushioned and there were bouquets at the altar with sweet fragrances. Holding Sadaya was lovely. Her eyes were so beautiful they reminded Cobb of the sweet scent emanating from the flowers at the altar. Well, we've both had our break so now it's time to work, not shirk. Cobb was sad to let go of Sadaya. He loosened his grip from around her waist and he stood up, waiting to see if she was leaving or not. Sadaya said "well we've got work to do. Let's see how much we can get done, then my darling, I want you to do me a favor, won't you?" "Anything," Cobb said. Sadaya looked at Cobb and she touched his hand lovingly. I want to be taken to the movies and enjoy some popcorn, and pretzels dipped in delicious milk chocolate. Please take you and me to the movies," Sadaya asked. Let me think about it. Five minutes later, Cobb found himself saying "ok, I'll take you out to the movies." "Where else do you want to go? To have dinner in a nice fancy restaurant or to do the fast food route and eat take-out in the car? Cheeseburgers and French fries or filet mignon?" Cobb asked. "I want to have filet mignon today, Mr. Handsome. When are you leaving to go out of town?" Sadaya said. "The day after tomorrow," Cobb said. Remind me to give you my spa-like massage before you leave, she said. "You'd give me a massage?" Cobb asked. "Yes. You're one of my favorite men," she said humorously. "Of course, I'd give you one. I'd meet you," she said. "Call me and let me know where to meet you. I am serious about this massage. I hear you sell braces for the body. For the back and for the knees. I have braces for every part of the body almost that's sprained. I hear you sell braces for the back and for the knees, so do I, Sadaya said. "I have knee braces, leg braces, wrist braces, ankle braces. You name it and I've got them," Sadaya said.

"What kind would you like to have?" Sadaya asked. Cobb said, "I want to be able to run faster so I'll take the knee brace." "How much do I owe you?" Cobb wondered. "Not one red cent," Sadaya said. Cobb wanted to know if Sadaya was selling the braces, especially back and knee braces because he had customers for them already among his teammates.

Comment? "I have a career in education, not sales, Sadaya said. I just have a lot of braces because salesmen have come to my classroom and given free samples to me. You're welcome to any or all of them," she said. "I'll just stick to the knee braces for now," Cobb said. "Thank you," he said. Sadaya said she'd bring the knee brace when they "meet tomorrow." You would think he wasn't even my boyfriend; asking me how much. "How much do I owe you? I'm insulted," she said. Sadaya also had toy hoola hoops she was trying to give away. She knew they were invented in 1957, and she offered to give his whole team a hoola hoop. One to each of them.

I'd ask around and see how the fellas feel about hoola hoops," Cobb said. "You might be very surprised. They might have a little more woman in them than you think," Cobb said.

"Some athletes do," Sadaya said.

Cobb and Sadaya began to speak more consistently on the telephone landline or their cell phone. Cobb began to see Sadaya the first chance he got. He loved her deeply. One of the things he was aware of because she told him was that she hated to be embarrassed. She was thinking of how Maxine, his former girlfriend was embarrassed and put to shame after he lost interest in her and he started dating everything that walked with two legs.

Sadaya told Cobb she didn't want to be put to shame like that. She told Cobb that if he ever felt that he was tired of her that she would rather he tell her and told her and the two of them would probably agree to take a break from each other. No newspaper or magazine or radio or television interviews like what happened with Maxine, his ex-girlfriend. A number of people opened the newspapers and Cobb and Maxine's business was in the papers. Sadaya felt that when the news and newspapers and various magazines want to find out some things about a celebrity; especially the large news corporations because they would pay. It's just that simple. Sadaya told Cobb it would kill her almost if she had negative press. As it stands now, believe it or not, the press does not know who Cobb Jackson is dating on a serious basis because he is seen with so many people. He's always seen with the members of the teams or someone else because he knows many team captains and their relatives. They don't even know who he's seriously thinking about marrying. He has been very careful about Sadaya. Careful to grant every wish that he can to make her happy. Happiness is a gift from God.

It was an extra dark night. The skies were cloudy. It looked like it was going to rain. Cobb and Sadaya were eating Niecey's chicken and laughing about how he practically ate his opponents the Bears for dinner in the last ball game they just played the night before last. Sadaya confided in Cobb and she asked him to keep it a secret. It had to do with a car she's buying for her parents. She liked the car with the peace sign on the front and back of it. The name of it is the Methods Mobile. It's in 2 versions, V6 and V8. Leather seats come standard. "All of the wonderful features you could ever want in a car, this one has," Cobb said to Sadaya. Sadaya wanted her parents to have a safer car than the one they have now. Her parents were stuck twice last week and her parents had to sit outside in the cold waiting for the mechanic to come not once but twice. Her father is talking about sticking with the mechanic. Sadaya unequivocally wants a new car for her parents. She doesn't want them exposed to a possible Criminal element. Twice for one week is just too much, Sadaya confided in Cobb. They should get a new car. But Sadaya's parents don't want to get into any new debt. Sadaya called her sister at school and the sister said she wanted nothing to do with new debt either. "What. Are you kidding me? No, I can't help you," her sister said. I suppose I'll just have to foot the bill myself, Sadaya told Cobb. I don't pay rent to my parents so this is an opportunity for me to pay them back. I'll buy them a car. The one I saw is a beige; a tawny beige sedan with regular tires on it but I think I'll order the best tires and the best battery for the car. Cobb basically agreed but he wondered why get another battery when the car comes with a new batter anyway? Oh well, so much for logic.

While Sadaya was looking for the car in the Showroom the next day, a new saleswoman came to her and asked could she help her. Sadaya said yes. Sadaya ordered the car without Cobb. She felt the car had all of the right features that she would want for her parents, so they wouldn't have to be stuck outside in 20 or 30-degree weather. Hallelujah. Thank Him for daughters like

Sadaya. Cobb wondered privately if her own parents would feel that way. "I know one thing, they'll like the satchel brown leather seats," Sadaya was thinking. "Oh boy are they going to love me after this," Sadaya was thinking. "I feel safe now just knowing my parents will be," she thought. "Safe and secure from all alarm," she thought. "I'm supposed to pick up the car in three days and I'm going to see the biggest brightest smiles on their faces. Bigger than I've ever seen before. My parents aren't fools, they know a nice car when they see it. They'll love it," she was saying to Cobb. He was sure they'd love it too, agreeing with Sadaya. Cobb asked Sadaya why she didn't want anyone to know. She said, "She didn't want it to get back to them and then they would turn the car down. I'm picking up the car in three days. Try to keep a lid on this, will you please?" she asked Cobb. "Oh, no doubt," Cobb said. "I won't tell a soul." Sadaya breathed a sigh of relief. Thank you for making the choice not to tell anyone. Every choice has a consequence. "I'm a pro basketball player not a swami philosopher, Sadaya," I said I wouldn't tell so that's it. I won't. Plus, I've only got three days before you get the car. What a cinch, Cobb said. "Easy as pie," he said.

"Easy as Dutch Apple Pie, with cheese on top. Hmm Good. I can wait until you get the car. I'll take you to the car dealership to get it. As a matter of fact, I'll take you to the four corners of the earth to get this car. Where are we going? Tomorrow we're going to 1495 Juniper Road, in Towson, Maryland. I've got the phone numbers," she said. The name of the Dealership is "Cars for Less," she said. "I'm so happy to be able to do this for my parents. I'm a little nervous about it but that's natural I guess" Sadaya said. I want my parents to love the car madly. Sometimes they are so unpredictable. I want the car to be unstoppable and positive. I want to say a little prayer to God for me being able to afford the car. As Sadaya hung her head down, humbling herself. Cobb watched. She was so humble that her whole body became limp. She had to get down on her knees and thank God for her job and her life situations that have caused her to be able to surprise her parents with a brand new car. How wonderful to be able to do such a thing. After praying out loud, Sadaya felt much stronger and so did Cobb. It was now 7:40 pm and tomorrow's the big day when I oh, excuse me Cobb, we go to pick the car up and then bring it to my parents. What time do you want to pick it up?" she said. I'll come to get you at 9:30 am. Will you be ready? Yes sir, no doubt about it. Cobb and Sadaya tap kissed and then she waved good-bye to him. See you tomorrow, as he sped off and disappeared into the hills. "Get some sleep," Cobb yelled out of the window; "and don't be late tomorrow," he said.

Nine blocks down the road, there were three new structures, two motels and one new hotel. Cobb didn't let anyone know what he was doing. He pulled into the parking lot of the new hotel and he asked the guard if there was a men's shop anywhere near the hotel. Yes sir, about 3 miles down the road, there's a shopping mall. Just keep driving straight. Cobb got back into the car and drove to the mall with his disguise on. Nobody will recognize him except for his household staff and Sadaya. He liked the shopping mall. He bought many new shirts of all kinds. Dress shirts, polo shirts long sleeves and short. He bought 9 new suits and 3 pairs of shoes. For him this was light stuff. He opened up his wallet and he looked at his money and he still had a lot of money left. He looked up to the sky and he whispered, "Thank you, Lord Sir. I like how you have planned my life. Whatever you want me to do, I promise I will obey you. I promise I will obey you as best I can. I am still practicing praying to You for longer periods of time and the way I see it, I could pray about an hour a day. Please let me know what you think of my goal of one hour a day. Your servant, Cobb Jackson, Amen. Cobb got back into his car after praying that short prayer and he drove to the hotel. He checked in with no problems whatsoever. He brought his new clothes in with him. He laughed to himself. He ordered room service, and chocolate layer cake. He was in the hotel room all day by himself with nobody to bother him and that included teammates, trying to eat up his food and chocolate cake. He ate and then took a shower and got into bed and he watched 2 movies for the evening. He then snored.

Sadaya wouldn't have called Cobb again until the next day.

She was in bed by 11:30 p.m. She watched the nightly news and she turned the TV down low. It was prayer time for Sadaya. She said, "Lord if I don't keep talking to You I feel like I'm going to miss something. She then shared her feelings about her parents, about the new car, about her sister being away at school, about how her sister didn't want to buy any car for her parents and about Cobb and whether he's husband material or not. She fell asleep by 12:45 a.m. forgetting to set her alarm to wake her up earlier to be ready to walk out of the door by 9:30 a.m. to meet Cobb. "Boy, I can hardly wait to see that handsome face tomorrow," she told God. Sleepy time 12:45 a.m. finally. She had 10 voicemail messages on the landline phone. She listened to them while rolling her hair and watching television. Everything gets done with Sadaya. She is a great role model for her students and colleague teachers. She is a strong testimony for the finish of what you start school of thinking and thought Sadaya is very thorough at whatever she does and Cobb is very thorough at what he does. This was one of the many reasons they were so strongly attracted to each other. Good looks didn't hurt each of them. Talent was great. Both of them were talented in Music and the Arts and Sports. Their sense of self-esteem was at least high average. They'd be stupid not to pursue each other now. They've all the right equipment inside and out. Cobb was just reminding himself that tomorrow he has a session with the pastor of Black Memorial Baptist Church.

It's all about Sadaya and she doesn't know it is. She doesn't know that Cobb has gotten to know the whole front office at the church. Soon the whole front office will be attending his basketball games; home games, at that. That is a blessed office.

"Well, my sister basically abandoned me. I think I'll put her up for a fast adoption. She was disgusted and her stomach was all knotted up. She said because she didn't have enough money to live, much less to go to school and to buy her own parents a car. If I could identify with anyone, I'd identify with the one who says she had knots in her stomach. My knots came for an opposite reason, though my knots in my stomach came from the fact that I knew my parents needed a newer car. It didn't have to be a brand new car but I'm buying a brand new one anyway for my parents. There's nothing too good for them. I'll give them a kiss of endless bliss and they won't have any more car problems," Sadaya said.

Sadaya's sister called to say she couldn't meet her and that she was sorry. Although Sadaya identified with her sister she didn't like the fact that her sister didn't show up to help to buy the new car for their parents.

I don't have to deal with my sister and her old fuddy duddy ways anyway. My sister seems to be nutty toward the beginning of the week.

Now, I only call her sometimes. I've trained myself to think of the nice, lovely, true things in life. It felt better to think of things with more of a positive theme. Please forgive me for not telling Sadaya how I feel, Lord God but we, meaning my God and me know that at that time, I couldn't have. Sadaya was thinking about Cobb. She had been praying about him for months.

Sadaya was thinking about Cobb: I want him to say, "Sadaya I love you baby and I will always feel my deepest affection for you," she thought and prayed and she fantasized about Cobb. She didn't take time to think much about her sister. Cobb was all she could think of.

She said, "If that man Cobb called me baby on a regular basis, I'd say, surely baby I'm yours." This had been a fantasy of Sadaya's and Cobb's. After hearing him say he loves her, Sadaya imagined she would go limp in his arms as he pulls her lovingly, yet strongly to himself and they make wild passionate love all night long. Neither person of the couple can say this has happened but it might and could for the sake of love and peace in the relationship and long-lasting togetherness and marriage. Cobb had finally found someone that he wanted more than anyone, more than anyone ever in his life. He smiled with all of the love he had in his heart for her and life began again, it seemed. When either of this couple smiled at the other person in the couple, it felt like both of them were breathing the same breath.

Today when Sadaya had on sweat pants that showed the word LOVE running up and down the side of each leg, Sadaya, who referred to herself as pleasingly plump, was comfortable with her curves in this gym apparel. She felt confident. "Nice touch," Cobb was thinking. Even when she's dressed in jogging apparel, she's all dressed up, he thought. I'd rather have a woman that looks dressed up in everything.

It presents a formal, sophisticated side to her that many people haven't seen before. What was Sadaya thinking? Wherever I go, my man goes with me in my presence in my heart and too in my mind. He's here even now. Cobb looked at his friends and his relatives. He was tempted to call. He called Vivvie Jackson. He called her and her voicemail was on. "I'll leave a message," he thought. After all, she was his cousin and she always had good advice for him, her cousin. They were always Cobbie and Vivvie, two close cousins and they were like friends.

I'll bet Vivvie calls us a 'love strong' couple. She and her urges usually intensified urges about life and love in Cobb's life. Her advice was always good. "I'll speak to her later," he thought.

Cobb picked Sadaya up at 9:30 sharp. Sadaya was ready for it too. "I'll speak to her later," he thought. Cobb got out of the car and he opened the passenger door for her to slide over into the seat and then fasten the seat belt to herself. Cobb froze for a few minutes. He had held her hand to help her into the car but now he found himself and his hands separating from her hands and his hands separating from her waist. Her hands were dropped and his eyes moved from her hands to her waist and then to her eyes. His eyes approached her eyes. There was no way he wanted to rush this time. Just to be on the safe side of the situation, he asked Sadaya would she like to get some coffee or a cappuccino before they go to pick up the car for her parents. Sadaya was really appreciating this experience with Cobb. When they were riding together, they usually rode in the limousine which was so nice, but in the same in a private car. In a private car there was only the two of them in the front seats talking and of course communicating. "I didn't want to rush you so much this morning," Cobb said. "I want you to enjoy giving this big gift away to two people that deserve it," Cobb said to Sadaya. Cobb kissed Sadaya. "It feels so good to feel your hands again and your lips on me," Sadaya said coyly. Like I said before, it feels so good to feel, to hold you, to touch you. I have this lace blouse on again just in a different color; an alluring so you'd want to rip it off of me but I'd only play the tease and keep you from it. She looked at him and smiled at him. Don't give up. Don't give up the fight. You fight whatever you can that needs fighting and aah yes, fight for love. She was finally able to live again, talk again and love again. Aah yes, to breathe again. Be tough. Be the winner that competes. Oh yes, I love that kind of man; the competitor. But of course, still happiness calls, Sadaya thought. "Our eyes locked with each other's and Cobb said I am like the vibration in her universe and the sunshine too." This is a wise person's notebook, she wrote in her journal, something to be proud of. It touches all generations. Cobb breathed in air from the cold outside weather. I want you in my life, Sadaya. Haven't you ever thought about it for us to be more than just friends forever? For us to laugh together is forever. What else goes together with this line of thought Sadaya wanted to know.

Cobb decided he would tell Sadaya a little later. He felt that pastor healing him. He felt less struggle with trying to talk to Sadaya about their possible future together. Where'd that come from? Gee, that pastor was even better than I thought. There have been tears of regret in this relationship and tears of fear, but there have been massive tears of joy as well. There have been times when

I had a heart hangover and the misery didn't leave until I got up off of my duff and shook myself and ended my misery myself. I let myself get involved in so many activities at my job and work at my parents' house and activities at church. The misery didn't leave until I started fighting it with prayer, and with activities. The heart hangover didn't leave right away, but it left over a short amount of time. The short amount of time was equal to a week or less. God has all kinds of ways of moving and removing those negative emotions from our systems. "Bowing our heads and knees helps to get faster feedback I believe," Cobb said to Sadaya. Cobb leaned his head near to Sadaya's for a tap kiss. A tap kiss he surely received from Sadaya. It was feelings of love, instant love that the two of them felt for each other. Perhaps they were frightened, afraid of close and true intimacy. It couldn't he avoided because every time he placed his lips on hers for a tap kiss, there's something. The pastor says only time will tell. Time always tells with love.

When Cobb and Sadaya arrived, the car dealership was closed. "Lord please don't tell me we came all this way for nothing," she thought. Cobb asked for the phone number to the car dealership. I thought this was Columbus Day or a holiday and they were going to be closed. When she called to the number someone answered and said they open at 11:30 a.m. It was not 11:00 a.m. Cobb and Sadaya decided to go for breakfast with coffee, tea or latte or cappuccino. Some of the people on the street made recommendations were to eat breakfast. It was only a five- minute drive from the car dealership. Cobb and Sadaya sat and ate to their heart's content. The breakfast was excellent. Sadaya was laughing at them. Hmm, they cook almost as well as I do. She smiled and then handed the check to Cobb.

"Well, Cobb I hope and I pray all goes well with this car for my parents," Sadaya said. "I'm ready. Are you ready Sadaya?" Cobb asked. "Yes, but I'm still a little nervous," she said. I'm going to rely on my faith and that will bring relief and solace in the name of the Father, Son and The Holy Spirit. Well, let's go, Cobb said.

They drove back to the car dealership. Plenty people were standing in front of the dealership waiting to get in. Cobb and Sadaya went inside of the dealership. There were new and newer cars that had been added to the car collection. Sadaya had the salesman to show Cobb the car she bought for her parents. Cobb liked the car the first time he saw it. He said he felt the car Sadaya picked was the pick of the litter. Sadaya couldn't wait to pay for the car and drive it to her parents' house. She gave a money order to the dear salesman and a nice big smile came on his face. "Cash. We like cash and money orders," the dealer said happily. Sadaya made sure the extra's she ordered which included the compact disc audio system was installed; checked the air lock brakes, brake system and other things that needed attention. She remembered what her father once taught her. "Crisis reveals character," he said. Funny, but when Cobb was at the Stadium about 1 ½ weeks ago, he was working, smiling and waving. He had gotten a job for Bob and he was grateful to Cobb. He now has a way to pay his bills. It was like rain to a farmer. "Call me when you're ready to not argue," Cobb said. "Because I said it was like rain to a farmer?" Sadaya asked with hurt in her voice. "Nothing. I'm just going to spend time with Bob today," he said. "I don't mean anything by it; I'm just saying," Cobb said. He did such a turnaround when it came to the parents' car she thought that maybe Cobb was jealous of her parents and the fact that they're receiving such a nice car as a gift from their daughter. It can't be that, Sadaya was thinking. This man Cobb is a billionaire. He can't be jealous of my gift to them. Maybe he's jealous of our close relationship my parents and I have. Right now, we're closer than ever because my sister is away at school.

Crisis. What kind of crisis is he talking about? Sadaya asked him to explain what he meant about crisis. She didn't see any crises. Things were running smoothly in her opinion. "Oh nothing," said Cobb. Cobb had nothing but a great big smile for Sadaya and he left it that way. She did too. Sadaya continued to do business with the car dealer and Cobb waited. Cobb was anxious to see the looks on her parents' faces when she told them to come outside. After the long drive back to Sadaya's parents' house, Sadaya told Cobb to stand by the car while she goes in to get her parents.

The car dealership gave Sadaya a nice big red bow to put across the window and the roof of the car. Sadaya's parents came outside and they saw the car. What did you do, buy by yourself a new car? Wow this is a nice one. Her father put himself in the driver's seat. He said, "geez, I love this car. It is really an SUV because it sits up high. It has a leather steering wheel, antilock braking system, a compact disc, OSE music system and so much more." Sadaya's father said "Well, you darling enjoy it and don't spend too much although like I said, you deserve it." Sadaya looked at her mother and she said, "I agree with my father. I feel you deserve it." "I know you deserve it," Sadaya said to her parents." "It's yours, with my love, she said. Please, don't argue with me or anything. Just take the keys and have a nice time in your new car. With all my love and with all my heart," Sadaya said. Sadaya's mother screamed and her father howled with happiness. Both of her parents got in the car and they said they were just going for a drive around the corner. Twenty-five minutes later, they hadn't returned.

Sadaya and Cobb laughed from inside of the house. They've got that new car and they're probably visiting all their friends from church, from the retirement senior center and everybody they can find to brag about their daughter and the great gift she's given to them. "That does me more good to know that my parents are happy and safe, she said. Gee, time flies. It's time to eat again.

You want some of my cooking Cobb?" Sadaya asked. "You'd enjoy it. I guarantee you. I made lasagna last night for my parents and I intend to enjoy it. I wouldn't want you to think that I eat in restaurants only. I can cook she said. "Oh, ok. I'll try some of your homemade lasagna and whatever cake you have too," Cobb surprised Sadaya and Sadaya said, "Gee, I never see you eat dessert. What came over you?" she said. "I'm helping your parents to celebrate," he said. "Heh, heh, heh," he laughed. So did Sadaya.

Sadaya decided that while Cobb was laughing she would remind him about one of her fantasies. She's still fantasizing about Cobb. He and I go on a Game Show and we win the game and he lets me have all of the money. "It was called 'The Let's Win Some Money Game Show'," Sadaya said. I could probably make most of your fantasies come true with that money. That's mula, she said. I've had other fantasy sex-life types of fantasies. Sex is emotion in motion the Hollywood Actress Mae West said many years ago. You should hear my fantasies.

"I'm going through h because you won't have sex with me" he said. Sadaya changed the subject.

I forgot. There's a brand new cell phone for you two in the glove compartment. Let dad fiddle around with that and see what he can figure out about the phone. "Well, Sadaya, it can't be too complicated. I'll take a look at it and see how it works. Bye darling daughter," her father said. "See you later. Bye, mom and dad. See 'ya," Sadaya said. "We'll be back in about an hour to bring you guys something to eat too. Love 'ya, bye," said Sadaya's father Tom. "Well, Cobb I'm glad to know all is well," Sadaya said. "When did they say they were coming back?" Cobb said. "In about one hour," Sadaya said. "They're bringing food back for us, they said," Sadaya said. "I know they're still in shock. Leather seats all of those special features like heated mirrors, OSE stereo premium, also heating system, CD-DVD music system, special air conditioner system and so much more. It happens to be a very nice looking SUV too. The color of it makes it stand out. It's light so you can really see it well at night," Sadaya said. No sooner than she got the last word out of her mouth, Sadaya felt Cobb's arms surrounding her waist. She felt his whole chest up and down in the area of her behind, her legs and near her knees, the back of her knees. He hugged her from behind. The two of them hugged each from behind for a long time. Cobb said nothing but his hug said I want you, baby! He kissed the back of her neck and the side of her neck and he kept hugging as if it was for life. As was the case earlier, Cobb said nothing but his hug said everything!

Cobb and Sadaya really have found true love but up until now Cobbwas unable to express his love verbally. He has an appointment for tomorrow, the day after his pastor has come back into town. When Cobb sees his pastor, he'll have a lot to talk about, no doubt about it, Cobb agrees with that point because he asked for an emergency appointment day. If Cobb hadn't asked for an appointment he'd probably see Cobb a month from today. In that case, thank you for emergency appointments with Cobb. Sadaya felt relaxed. She wanted to be like the sunshine in Cobb's universe. She told Cobb she felt good when he gave her a foot massage with skin rejuvenation and foot leg massage to make her sleep and to massage her dried cracked feet. Sadaya wanted a foot leg massage to make her sleep better and to reduce pain. "I wanted a healthy massage," she said. "Something I could feel." Cobb laughed and he kept holding her from behind, rubbing her back from behind. A healthy massage is something to be proud of according to Sadaya.

Massages touch all generations. It feels quite great, especially when the person giving it is special to you. She was finally able to live – again to talk again, and to love again. Aah yes, to breathe again, a story unto itself. There was the intensification of the urge for Cobb and Sadaya. The kitchen was almost like the bedroom as Cobb leaned Sadaya against the island countertop in the middle of the kitchen room. He massaged her, but her hands kept blocking his. She was thinking he was trying to move her onward towards sex. He was really trying to massage her, like she asked, while he was kissing her. "Did his hands feel great," Sadaya thought.

"Should I let him go on or should I stop him from having such a good time with my impending sex," Sadaya asked herself. "If he massages me which I now feel him starting to do, maybe this won't lead to sex, especially here in my mother's and father's space-age kitchen. Plus, my mother and father are probably on their way home. They said they were bringing chicken.

"How nice to feel his strong and hard muscle-bound arms. They feel so good," she thought. Cobb whispered to Sadaya. "I wish I had those machines that you use to massage different parts of the body. Sorry, kiddo, nothing doing right at this moment when it comes down to massage machines," Sadaya wasn't thinking sex either. She was the type who had dreams that reached her consciousness. "I've had dreams that this would happen between us right here in the kitchen. It can't go any further right now, because my parents are on their way back home, Cobb honey," Sadaya said. Cobb, being the gentleman with the gentleman's hands said to himself, "if that's not love, I don't know what is. I have a hades of an urge," Cobb was thinking. "I'm in the wrong place at the wrong time to get release for my sexual urges," Cobb kept thinking. Massage. Massage. Ok the lady will get what she asked for. A massage. Her back, her right and left arms, her thighs. "I promise you God this is as far as I go if I can help myself. Phew," Cobb said.

The weather network announced the weather each hour. Today, it snowed. Overnight it had snowed. The meteorologists were overusing the word cloudy in their accu-weather forecasts. There had been a winter storm warning in effect until 9:00 p.m. 3-day radar had been extended. Today had been what meteorologists said: cloudy with a touch of rain and snow; areas of fog. At night mostly cloudy with a little rain in the evening turning breezy late, precipitation 61%. Thanks to the AccuWeather.com network, many meteorologists are as accurate as they can be. Snow accumulations 10 to 14 inches. This will be the blowing type, the hazard type snow and storming type. Impacts: Hazardous travel due to snow covered roads and poor visibilities. One quarter mile or less at times. Temperatures low to mid 20's. This weather report makes an excellent homework assignment for Sadaya's 6th grade children.

The children liked researching the weather. They were to answer one question: "Were the meteorologists right or wrong about the weather predictions they made re: the New York areas? Make this answer one page long."

Ms. Day

By the way, Ms. Day was true to form. She was fabulous from hips to lips and beneath that. She wore a pair of shearling boots with coyote. The coyote ran from the heel of her boots to the top of her knees. This was the thickets plushest type of fur. She looked stunning. Although this was not the first time she'd worn her cashmere, it still looked new and different. She wore a black cashmere sweater and a black cashmere skirt with a cashmere colored short sleeved under- sweater, which matched her beautiful boots. Everything matched something. She had on an onyx black-colored ring and she wore a cashmere top coat with a fox fur collar and a fabulous name brand leather bag. She bought the bag from D'Arcy's.

"I look good," Sadaya Ruby Day said. When she was a little girl, the Cardinal told her to always look in the mirror and openly admire herself. Sadaya never ever forgot that. She looks in the mirror at least twice a day and she admires God's handiwork, because she was lucky to meet a Cardinal and he told her what to do as a 10-year old. As an adult, now Sadaya dresses from her hips to her lips and everywhere else. She always out-dresses everyone as if she were in a fashion show competition. If the Cardinal's intention was to boost Sadaya's self-esteem and self- adequacy needs, the Cardinal met his goals with Sadaya Ruby Day. Her self-esteem was boosted for the rest of her life. The Cardinal told her she was beautiful when she was 10-years old. These days as an adult, she looks in the mirrors in her house or at her uncle's house or at her neighbor's house or at the mirror in the restroom at the church; at her job and they all have the same greeting: "Hello there you beautiful woman, you," Sadaya says to herself.

Sadaya encourages her 6th graders to wash, take showers and use lots of soap. She tells them to save their allowance money and to tell their parents they want to go to the store and buy body wash and perfume and colognes to make them smell better. She tells her students if they should smell someone under their arms and it doesn't smell good, not to laugh or make fun of them. That could happen to anyone. Anyone can have a bad hair day, a bad underarms day or just an overall bad smell day. That's why people say there but for the grace of God go I. He blesses who He blesses. God loves us all, and He rewards us all, in different ways. Ms. Day's students always see her in fresh clothes and she wears fresh perfume, lotion, body wash and of course, soap. She also keeps her breath mints with her so that her breath doesn't smell. Sadaya Day keeps her students well informed and well-equipped. She has classroom game shows and she gives away bottles of lotion, gargle rinse, breath mints, body wash and many prizes to inspire and to motivate these 6th grader children. Her class loves her and so does her boss, the principal. The principal has complimented her several times. She's gotten complimented about her wardrobe, about the incentives she's offered to the children about the in-classroom guests she's had to come to speak to the children and to work with the children. Sadaya had made quite a name for herself and many people were guessing that the Office of Education would offer her an Assistant Principalship or a Principalship, somewhere within their educational system.

Sadaya hasn't heard any promotion promises yet. Cobb Jackson, her boyfriend has always felt he wouldn't want his wife to work anyway. The only people that know that are his mother and father and maybe an aunt and uncle. He kept all of that in the family. He usually says he's not ready to discuss it because he's not ready to get married yet. Sadaya loves Cobb and she is confused. She doesn't have a problem discussing it but she hasn't been asked to marry someone yet. She figures she won't be discussing it anytime soon. "We'll see," her father says. "Our Lord and Father God Almighty has many ways of surprising His people. We'll see." Speaking of surprises, Sadaya's mother wanted to speak to her in private. He father had fallen asleep. This was the prime opportunity to speak, for the two ladies mother and daughter to speak to each other. Ok mom, what do you want to talk about? I wonder what's happened to your best friend, Cynthia Persons. Nobody can seem to hear from her anymore. Have you heard from her? Mom, I can't say that I have heard from lately. "You remember the last time we had to look for Cynthia, we found her in a liquor saloon across the street from her hotel room. She was as drunk as a skunk, Sadaya. I have a feeling that this is not going to be the same type of situation this time, Sadaya," her mother said. She might have just gone off to hibernate and to think awhile. Still, as her best friend, I think you should call her and make it your business to find out what's happening with her" her mom said. Sadaya said, "Ok mom. I'll do that within the next hour, or less. I know that sometimes she just likes to be alone, so she can figure things out about her life, her boyfriend the deceased one and anything else she might want to think about," Sadaya said.

Sadaya thought about it and she said she'd Let go and let God. After an hour was up, Sadaya stopped grading her students' papers and she picked up the receiver to her telephone. She called Cynthia Persons, her best friend. The phone rang 5 times and then the voicemail message came on. This is your friend Cynthia Persons. I'm busy doing something important but not so important that I can't call you back. Please leave your name and number or else I'll be talking to the wind. Sadaya left 2 long messages. "Cynthia, don't you keep yourself a stranger from me. My whole family is wondering where you are and if you're ok. Call me Cynthia. You're my best friend. Let me know where you are. Let's go shopping which both of us love.

Call me as soon as you get this message. Love, Sadaya. One of these days, by the way, we're gonnahave to find a husband for you and a husband for me. That and first and foremost God is the answer to all of our problems. Love you, kiddo. I'm remembering what you said to me, "Don't give up the fight. Never ever give up the fight," Sadaya said. Sadaya loves Cynthia so much. She called back a second time and she said, "It's me again Cynthia. I just had to check on you and make sure things are swell with you. Stay humble and Cynthia I know you. You're on your knees somewhere, crying out to God. It takes a lot of emotional expunging to stay on your knees with God. You've been crying and on your knees.

God loves you Cynthia. He loves it when you're happy too, though. Stay humble and on your knees but let God see you happy and humble too. Find something to be happy about all of the time. The last time we talked you told me you met a man who said he loves you. Be happy about that. Aah yes, love! It's time to Let go and Let God, Cynthia. How wonderful that you can tell yourself, "Aah yes. Now I can love again. I can finally live again. Aah yes, I can breathe again. Thank you for saving me, God. Every day the sun rises at 7:00 a.m. and it sets at 5:15 p.m. You're rising and setting with it, Cynthia, which I am so very happy about. He's given me my best friend to shop with, to drive with, to eat with, to talk with and so much more. Spiritually you've had another knockdown drag out fight. Be time-sensitive. Only let the enemy have a small amount of your time, if you can. It's time to invest your time to inspire and to motivate your friends, me, your family and yourself. It's time to have a family meeting and decide on how each of you can pursue happiness, with your family. Reset the family clock and decide to make each and every one of you outstanding. Life has choices and dreams. Choose to dream and choose to make your dreams into reality. Discuss this with your family so you can all participate. How? Have the family meetings and discuss it. Not long ago there was a car. The car flies off of the Pittsburgh Roadway Exit. The car was demolished but the driver gets up and walks away. That driver was your brother, Cynthia. When is the last time you spoke to him? Help each other. A healthy massage would make you sleep better and reduce pain. Do that for each other as an example. This way, you don't have to worry about who to trust and you can visit each other's houses and each week or 2 weeks or each month you can chip in for chicken or cheeseburgers or whatever your preference is.

Sadaya told Cynthia Cobb massaged her. "With him, I could get massaged every day," she said. Her fingers, her hands and her back, was his specialty. Sadaya felt so good, she was wilting like a state flower. He felt good making her feel good, he told her. If she's asked for a massage, I certainly am going to give her what she asked for, Cobb was thinking. "I'm certainly not going to force the sex issue; especially here in a kitchen. As it is now, I'm pushing my luck. This kitchen floor is so glossy and shiny, I could fall and break my neck, or my leg or my arm, really easily," Cobb was thinking. Thank you, God for me having self-discipline to be able to stop "almost" having sex with Your Sadaya and mine. She seemed like she was holding back when she and I were necking. Thank you for giving me the strategies to help me and to train me to stop, before Sadaya became too uncomfortable. In Cobb's opinion, no two women are the same. Each woman has unique needs and experiences. This woman wants a foot/leg massage. Hmmm, I wonder if she'll return the favor, Cobb thought to himself. I just never seem to be in the right place at the right time with her. She's either picking up a car or going to catch up on broadcasting classes or she's on the phone with her best friend Cynthia. Sadaya was always busy doing something. I did catch up with Sadaya to take her to dinner on numerous occasions and to the movies. Those were her favorite spots. Cobb was saying he shouldn't complain because at least she liked him enough to go out with him. Cobb went home to get some rest and looked forward to meeting with the pastor tomorrow morning. The peace that Cobb felt really felt like a peace that surpasses all human understanding. Cobb felt calm when he thought of being with the pastor and talking to him. He should get to the office early tomorrow.

The secretary said he's anxious to talk too. It's expected to be damp tomorrow. Cobb decided to let his chauffeur drive him to church. He left Sadaya's house and he kissed her before he left. "Good-bye hon," she said. "I'll call you tomorrow, ok?" "Yes, call me and we'll talk about what I was told about the Association Dinner coming up in another month. Good-bye. Drive safely, Cobb" Sadaya said. Aha, Got you to the point where you worry about me but don't forget God is my Shield and He's my protector. Of whom and what shall I worry about? Nothing, Cobb said. Do not worry. Do not fret. Be anxious for nothing. Those were the words from the Bible that were inspiring to both Cobb and Sadaya when they studied and learned during church services at the Black Memorial Baptist Church. Cobb went home, sat down and fixed a hot drink to keep him calm, listened to music and he prayed before he went to bed for 27 minutes. He prayed that he would overcome his shyness when it comes to Sadaya. She's so beautiful and so easy to get along with. Thank You God Almighty. Cobb sought a relationship with God as best he could. He reveals Himself to those who diligently seek Him. Cobb has started to see the world differently. He tries to obey God as much as possible and it has paid off. God's Word works. He has taken control of his religious training and life has gotten much better with God's Word and prayers. Cobb was determined to make a difference.

The next day, he was up bright and early, ready to go to the church for pastoral counseling.

Cobb could hardly wait for his appointment to finally come.

His appointment was sorely needed. "Come in Mr. Cobb Jackson. You felt this was an emergency case," the pastor said. "Pastor, I broke out in cold sweats and I have been suffering from lovesickness, I think," Cobb said. Along with the sweats I get this fear that I'm going to lose Sadaya to somebody else. Furthermore, I feel I'm getting better when it comes to verbally expressing my love to her, but I still have lovesickness for her. Sometimes I get the impression that she might be going through something similar; if I'm lucky.

Lovesickness: I am lovesick for her. Cobb looked up the meaning of the word lovesickness. He read it to the pastor. An informal affliction that describes negative feelings associated with rejection, unrequited love or the absence of a loved one. There can be physical as well as mental symptoms. A yearning for someone you love until it hurts. Person is unable to act, produce normally. Pastor, I don't want to go through lovesickness alone. The pastor seemed to scoff at the notion of Cobb wanting someone to suffer with. He's so excellent at everything else, the pastor was surprised he wanted Sadaya to suffer with him. This session was an excellent session. The pastor was able to convince Cobb that Sadaya does love him but that he has to speak to her s if she were his wife. Call her honey, darling, puddin' face and names of endearment. Write the words I Love You on a piece of paper. Take a rubber-band and wrap the words I Love You around his wrist. "Whenever he gets in the mood to say I love you but he can't, look at the wrist paper and simply red it out loud and glance at Sadaya when you say and read I Love You from your wrist paper. Place the paper anywhere from your wrist to the middle of your forearm," pastor said. The pastor also gave additional information about lovesickness. Cobb was grateful for such a knowledgeable man. Cobb came away from this session feeling like it was a cathartic experience. He felt refreshed. He told the pastor he felt like the fish that was out of the deep-sea water being thrown back in. "I felt better," Cobb said. The pastor gave many coping strategies for Cobb to use to talk to Sadaya. He only gets to see Sadaya every 2 weeks and he gets sad after that.

Cobb came out of the pastor's office smiling. "I feel so much better," he said to the pastor's secretary. "I want him to know he did an excellent job," he told the secretary. The best thing for me to do is what he said, Cobb reasoned, Sadaya is my love interest and I hope I don't say anything to put our relationship in jeopardy, Cobb thought to himself. I feel better, so much better. I have a woman who loves me, I think. She's so good at everything and she's an excellent teacher. I'm convinced that Sadaya is the woman. The one woman I'm in love with, Cobb thought. He further expounded, "I feel compelled. I feel very compelled to tell her. I can't fight this feeling anymore. Cobb thought to himself. I feel better, so much better. I have a woman who loves me, I think. She's so good at everything and she's an excellent teacher. I'm convinced that Sadaya is the woman. The one woman I'm in love with. I feel compelled. I feel very compelled to tell her. I can't fight this feeling anymore. I'm going to make sure I treat myself well during this process though," he told himself. Cobb told his chauffeur to take him to one of the most marvelous restaurants in town. Sometimes I wonder what my life would have been like if I hadn't met Sadaya. I really enjoy the way she teaches school and how she controls her 6th grade classes. She's a genius at it. After she teaches them and tells them she loves them, she gives all of them hugs each and every day before she sends them home.

"She's perfect for the classroom and she's perfect for business. The man who gets Sadaya Day gets a real gem," Cobb's father told Cobb. "I believe my father was right. I'll have to tell Sadaya how she was complimented by my father. His father also liked the fact that Sadaya was and is a churchwoman and that she's in prayer many times through the day. She's also a woman of patience and she has a giving spirit. She'd also make a good mother and she doesn't strike me as over-emotional," Cobb's father said. So, if someone in the relationship should mess up, you wouldn't get a knife wound in the back. Truth if I ever told it because that happened to me. The woman I'd been seeing for 8 years went berserk. She told me she hated me and she wanted to see me dead. She took a penknife out and she stabbed me in my right arm. Sadaya cringed. Cobb's father said, "You don't want that kind of woman." "I could show you the wound but we'll have to wait for warm weather when I can take my shirt off and show you. Sadaya doesn't depress a man by fussing at him and by henpecking him all of the time. Some men need prodding and picking but you're not that type. You're the kind of woman a man can rely on and depend on. Some women will hurt you if they feel they can't depend on you or they are being cheated on. You're taking your life in your hands with some of these women, son. Some of them are nothing but wild. I know you know the deal, son. I know you know how to conduct yourself with a woman. I'm reminding you. If you love Sadaya, be kind. Have eyes for her, Cobb's father then winked and smiled.

Cobb seemed to have a lot on his mind. He was thinking, "Every time I think of Sadaya, I get weak and I bow to God. I bow my heart and my head and I get humble on my knees. I feel that happiness is calling us and I want to marry Sadaya. I think I'd like to honeymoon in Hawaii. Soon and very soon I know I'll ask her to marry me. I'd say something like Sadaya I want you in my life. Every time I think of Sadaya, I get weak and I bow to God. I fall on my knees and I humble myself before Him, as much as I can. God is the only one who can bring me through lovesickness and other struggles of life.

Cobb's father exhorted, "You might want to marry Sadaya someday soon. Nobody is getting any younger. We; your mother and I want grandchildren." Cobb's dad went on to explain that Cobb and Sadaya could have 5 or 6 children if they want to. Make us happy grandparents. To me, that would be something to brag about besides his career. "Since you travel a lot, I suggest you propose the other half you've been looking for, Sadaya. Good luck and Godspeed to you son," Cobb's father said. When the pastor spoke to Cobb, his words and of course God's words from the Bible lifted the burden off of my shoulders. My father has that gift too. I received a double whammy of it today which I felt I needed;

Cobb left a message on the pastor's voicemail thanking him and telling him he might pop that most special question to someone.

I had prayed to God for a woman like you. He gave me my wish and He answered my prayers but I will still be praying to God and being on my knees, regardless of what God give me, I'll be humble and on my knees to Him; humble and on my knees loving Him.

Yes, God, the Almighty God of the Universe has answered Cobb's wife's requests and He stands by to answer so many more requests coming from Cobb Jackson's heart. Cobb Jackson cared enough to bend his knees and humble himself before God. He also cared enough to volunteer at the Black Memorial Baptist Church and to make use of his physical as well as his intellectual capacities. "God has blessed Cobb and He will continue to," the pastor of Black Memorial Baptist Church said.

For the first time in his life Cobb went to Sadaya's house unannounced. It was Valentine's Day. He didn't tell her parents he'd asked her some special question today. He figured he'd let them observe today. He breathed in air from the cold outside weather. Cobb was so excited. He bought her a bouquet and a ring on the same day. He visited and her parents said she'd be back in about 15 minutes. She was moving one of the cars for them. Will you think about this? One side of me asked the previous question. The other side of me said I've thought already. When Sadaya came back into the house, Cobb was there. At first look, a look of surprise on her face and then a big hug was waiting for Cobb which she gave to him. Cobb engaged in small talk with Sadaya. "I want you in my life, Sadaya," he said all of a sudden. For us to laugh together, sleep together, win together, dress together, eat together, never lose together unless its poundage and weight loss together. "Whoops," Cobb thought. "Where'd that come from?"

Sadaya interrupted Cobb. "Come in for a few minutes. Would you like some coffee and muffins?" Sadaya said. "Yes," Cobb said. "But first, where's my proverbial tour of the house while your parents are gone?" Cobb asked. Ok. Here you are, this is my room. This is your bed; huh? Cobb said. Both Cobb and Sadaya lay on the bed fully clothed.

You don't know how badly I want to make love to you, Sadaya. I have too much respect for your faith and your love for God. I must admit I have not been the most faithful to anyone but time has taught me marriage is too important. I will be faithful once I am married. Now that I am single, it is hard to be faithful. You don't know how badly I want you. I am virile; I could make love to you all night and still have energy left to eat. I admit the man inside of me wants the woman inside of you to bend and submit. I'm so shocked to see myself on this bed with you that I can't get over it. "Your shoulders look so strong. Your whole body looks strong and masculine. What a tremendous turn-on, Sadaya replied. So, they, Cobb and Sadaya, both laying on the bed fully clothed are watching and looking at each other. No one has reached for the other. This is a change from the usual. If this was any other person, Cobb would have grabbed them and had sex.

Cobb looked at Sadaya and he shook his head. You know, I have faith in God too. We now have a MAS Mutual Admiration Society and we love each other but we love God more, Cobb said.

"Well, Sadaya, I respect you completely. Yes, and I'm a gentleman around you. You have brought out my respect for God and I have learned from you, Sadaya," Cobb said. You ignite my love and rekindle my desires. I love how you love to laugh and it puts a smile on my heart. I'll tell you what else I was thinking on this very day. I cherish you, Cobb said. "Wow that pastor is good. I am actually telling Sadaya my feelings," Cobb thought. The pastor Gee, he was even better than I thought, and I thought he was great to begin with. A little bit of hypnotism and it was good news from there. Cobb pulled Sadaya close to him: "I love you so much it's scary and I want you in my life, Sadaya I want you to be my wife, Sadaya. Won't you think about marrying me and being the main one in my life forever? Marry me, Sadaya, he said.

She couldn't help but feel herself smile, until Cobb whipped out the ring; the 7.05 carat clear diamond engagement ring. Sadaya screamed when she saw the engagement ring Cobb had for her. She said, "Happiness is calling." I can hear the bells ringing now. Just in case you're wondering what my answer is yes yes yes yes yesyes! The couple's eyes met and locked on each other. Cobb told Sadaya she is the sunshine in his universe, the mildest vibration on his earth. "No more crest fallen feelings of sadness. Happiness is calling," Cobb said, while they hugged. Happiness is calling us. We've been humble and on our knees and God has rewarded us. Cobb embraced Sadaya tightly. "I love you baby," he said. I told you that you ignite my love and rekindle my desires. We'll spend the rest of our lives together and happy we will be.

I hope I have satisfied god and you with this story.
So long and farewell. Look for my next novel and
God Bless you.

Adrienne Sealy

Special Notes Section

I offer my indebtedness to personalities for their sincere cooperation and valuable guidance. About the Artist

Unita Rayford drew the book cover for "Humble And On My Knees". It was designed by Adrienne Sealy.

Unita is currently living in Brooklyn, New York where she is pursuing her career in graphic arts.

Thanks to Cora Jakes Coleman for The Prayer Poem for Women. The name of one of her books is Poems for Women. The name of one of her books is Keeping Our Faith: A Prayer for Woman; also Faithing It: A Prayer Guide, Destiny Image Publishers, July, 2016.

Humorist, entrepreneur and writer Samuel Clemens was known by his pen name Mark Twain. He was also known as a book publisher. His books were and continue to be inspirational. Mark Twain was featured in the movie "It's a Wonderful Life". He was quoted in the movie in the 1946 version (December 20, 1946) produced by Frank Capra, based on the book "The Greatest Gift" by Philip Van Doren Stern.

About The Author

Adrienne Sealy is a writer and psychologist in the City of New York. She is a poet, author and public speaker. She has received close to 300 awards and citations for literary and humanitarian achievements. She has appeared as narrator, critic, mistress of ceremonies and storyteller. Her first book 'And Even A Child Shall Lead Them' was written between the tender ages of 11 and 13. She is noted for traveling abroad and in the U.S.A. motivating and inspiring young people to succeed despite negative odds. She has made special appearances as guest speaker, narrator and consultant.

Adrienne Sealy's main purpose for writing is to help to spread the Word of God so that He can get the credit for the great things He has done. In Adrienne's first book she expresses the view that people are like big balloons, they can burst at any time. She believes that man cannot hang one star in the sky or make the sun shine- there is Someone greater than all who controls. She has received her BA, M.S. and PhD. Degrees.

Adrienne Sealy has written other books besides her first one, The Decaying See: A Youth Speaks No Hill Is To High; Mama Watch Out I'm Growing Up; The Color Your Way Into Black History Book; Hang On: Poetry for Millions to read; Tommy and The Basketball The Story of the Man Who Played the Game Straight and Won. As a poet, author and public speaker she hosted her own CATV television show. Some of her poems are hanging in the United Nations Building and Adrienne received the Jefferson Award from WNEW TV Channel 5 Broadcasting station and many other places. There is a library named in her honor.

Besides public speaking and traveling the author has appeared on many radio and television shows. The Daily News, the Amsterdam News, Ebony Magazine, American Girl, South Africa's Drum Magazine and other periodicals have featured Adrienne Sealy. She has been guest speaker at graduation ceremonies, churches, youth centers, libraries, schools, plus many other places.

Anyone who wishes to may contact the author at the following phone numbers:

(347) 972-5428
(929) 434-9871
(929) 234-3319

Other Books by Adrienne Sealy

And Even a Child Shall Lead Them Decaying Seed: A Youth Speaks!

No Hill Is Too High
The Bilingual Reader
Tommy and the Basketball
The Skin I'm In
Hang On: Poetry for Millions to Read
Mama Watch Out I'm Growing Up
The Color Your Way Into Black History Book

The following posters have also been written by the author:

Growing No Hill Is Too High I Promise
A Message to the Students Teach Me
A Great Somebody Garden of Success
The Decaying Seed

To Inquire about books and posters please call

(347) 972 – 5428
(929) 234 – 3319
(929) 434 – 9871

I offer my indebtedness to personalities DNC Barack Obama we are the change we seek the speeches of Barack Obama edited by EJ Dionne and Joy Ann Reid September 20th 2017.

Scriptures quoted in "Humble And On My Knees":

Romans 8:28 Kings James Version "And we know that all things work together for good to them that love God and them who are the called according to his purpose. Work together for good for those who love the Lord to them who are called to his purpose."

Philippians 4:13 Kings James Version "I can do all things through Christ which strengthens me."

1 Corinthians 7:9 Kings James Version "But if they cannot contain (exercise self control) let them marry. For it is better to marry than to burn with passion. It is better to marry than to burn."

Matthew 7:7-8 Kings James Version "Ask and it shall be given Seek and ye shall find. Knock and the door shall be opened unto you."

Psalms 150:6 New International Version "Let everything that has breath praise the Lord." New International Version

Songs of Solomon 7:1-13 Kings James Version (See for more detailed version.)

Songs of Soloman "And your mouth is like the best wine. May the wine go straight to my beloved. I want to get drunken off your lips like wine. The wine honey flowing gently over lips and teeth your kisses be."

Matthew 6: 28-33 Kings James Version

"And why take ye thought for raiment? Consider the lilies of the field, how they grow. They toil not neither do they spin: And Yet I say unto you, that even Solomon in all his glory was not arrayed like one of these."

"Wherefore if God so clothe the grass of the field, which today is, and tomorrow is cast into the oven, shall he not much more clothe you? O ye of little faith?"

"Therefore take no thought, saying, What shall we eat? Or, what shall we drink? Or, where withal shall we be clothed?"

"(For all these things the Gentiles seek:) for your heavenly Father knoweth that we have of all these things".

"But seek ye first the Kingdom of God and his righteousness; and all these things shall be added unto you." King James Version

George Waters "The Guest" Rochester, Minnesota 1994 The Poem The guest.

Therefore take no thought saying What shall we eat? Or What shall we drink or Where withal shall we be clothed? For your Heavenly Father Knoweth that ye have need of all of these, things. But seek ye first the Kingdom of God and His righteousness and all of these things shall be added unto you.

Psalms 34:1-10 Kings James Version

"I will bless the Lord at all times. His praise shall continually be in my mouth. My soul shall make her boast in the Lord: the humble shall hear thereof and be glad. O magnify the Lord with me, and let us exalt his name together. I sought the Lord and He heard me and delivered me from all my fears. They looked unto Him and were lightened and their faces were not ashamed. This poor man cried and the Lord heard him and saved him out of all of his troubles. The angel of the Lord encampeth round about them that fear him, and delivereth them. O taste and see that the Lord is good: blessed is the man that trusteth in him. O fear the Lord, ye his saints: for there is no want to them that fear him. The young lions do lack, and suffer hunger: but they that seek the Lord shall not want any good thing."

King James Version

Church. A building used for public Christian worship. House of God. House of worship. A joy of my life: They came to church with me.

Noun: The church. Both people were churched and are still. A Biblical word for assembly. It can mean all Christians living and dead. The church is interesting and vital. There's food on my table and shoes on my feet. It teaches us to love each other including our enemies, no matter what.

Church: One of the most loved places in the world.

It was also a gathering place for two people in love: Cobb Jackson and Sadaya Ruby Day. The Church is not just a bureaucracy but a love story with its arms wide open.

The Regency Bible from Thomas Nelson
Publisher. This is a King James Bible 1990
Special thanks to the New York State
Department of Medicine.

Also special thanks to Michelle Howard for typing this book and
helping to organize it.

Hold to God's Unchanging Hand
© Jennie Wilson 1904
91st Printing 2015 Triad Publishing
All scriptures are King James Version Zondervan, 1984, Dallas
Texas Brown Books, 2004

DNC Barack Obama We Are The Change We Seek: the Speeches
of Barack Obama Edited by EJ Dionne and Joy – Ann Reid CNN
September 20, 2017.

The World's Greatest Collection of Church Jokes Compiled and
Edited by Paul Miller, Ziondervan Publishers © 2013